KGB agent Igor Tchevsky isn't sure how deeply involved Adrian Dumas is in the CIA, or how much Dumas knows about the Watson Mines plan. But Tchevsky knows how to make him talk...

"First things first, Adrian. I want to tell you the rules of this game. I'm going to ask questions. If I'm not pleased with the answers, Adrian, I'm going to gag you tightly and hurt you. Feel at liberty to scream behind the gag. Nothing but a hum or bearable growl will come out. Now, when I think you can talk without screaming, Adrian, I'll remove the gag and you can tell me what I want to hear. If you try to call out instead of talk, Adrian, I'll knock you unconscious, gag you, revive you. And hurt you so much, so long. Understand?"

Adrian doesn't understand. He doesn't know about the plan, he doesn't know about the CIA, and he doesn't know why Tchevsky assumes he does. But he is soon to find out...

Novels by Michael Bradley

Imprint
The Mantouche Factor

Published by
WARNER BOOKS

ATTENTION: SCHOOLS AND CORPORATIONS

WARNER books are available at quantity discounts with bulk purchase for educational, business, or sales promotional use. For information, please write to: SPECIAL SALES DEPARTMENT, WARNER BOOKS, 75 ROCKEFELLER PLAZA, NEW YORK, NY 10019

**ARE THERE WARNER BOOKS
YOU WANT BUT CANNOT FIND IN YOUR LOCAL STORES?**

You can get any WARNER BOOKS title in print. Simply send title and retail price, plus 50¢ per order and 20¢ per copy to cover mailing and handling costs for each book desired. New York State and California residents add applicable sales tax. Enclose check or money order only, no cash please, to: WARNER BOOKS, P O BOX 690, NEW YORK, N.Y 10019

The Mantouche Factor

A Taut Thriller of Nuclear Power Politics

by Michael Bradley

WARNER BOOKS

A Warner Communications Company

All the characters in this book are fictitious, and any resemblance to actual persons living or dead is purely coincidental.

WARNER BOOKS EDITION

Copyright © 1979 by Michael Bradley
All rights reserved.

This Warner Books Edition is published by arrangement with Dorset Publishing, Inc., 355 Markham Street, Toronto, Ontario, Canada

Warner Books, Inc., 75 Rockefeller Plaza, New York, N.Y. 10019

 A Warner Communications Company

Printed in the United States of America

First printing: January, 1981

10 9 8 7 6 5 4 3 2 1

For Wendy and Jason

The Mantouche Factor

Respect

- TEO LEI
15th Century

信
敬

...respect for the kind of
   intelligence that enables
grass seed to grow grass;
the cherry-stone
to make cherries.'

Prologue

Igor Tchevsky's shadow blotted out a heavy, black square on the glittering pavement. It seemed to mock him. Tchevsky noted that his head was merely a fat rounded knob disfiguring the stolid shadow.

He glanced out over the sea of grass for the third time in as many minutes. The speeding black dot that was the distant Moskva had, perhaps, grown a bit larger. The car looked to him like a tiny black beetle laboring over an expanse of huge green carpet. Sometimes it disappeared into the gentle undulations of the steppes that made men and their works insect-size. But it always worked closer.

Tchevsky flipped his cigarette into his shadow and saw the thin cardboard bounce accurately on his thick neck. There was a flash of sparks and the butt rolled out of the shadow, spiralling on the hot cement.

He had grown to hate his shadow. Its shape had never bothered him in Moscow. He'd never even thought about it there. And he'd only noticed it once or twice in East Berlin among the taller Germans. But at least the East Berliners were always carefully subservient.

"Think of it, Colonel," the beaming General had said, "no more damned North European fog. No more clammy rain. You're a lucky man."

Tchevsky recalled it wryly, the congratulations from comrades and colleagues on the occasion of his special, and completely unexpected, transfer to sunny Tashkent. It was all true. No fog. No clammy rain. Blinding bright summers and equally sparkling winters. And always the shadows. Was he really so squat? Tchevsky decided that he preferred the leaden Baltic skies of East Berlin.

At first, Tchevsky had chosen to pretend that his shadow among the others always just happened to be particularly distorted by the sun's angle whenever he happened to notice. As time went on he proved unable to conceal the truth from himself. It was the students, of course. Afghans, Arabs, Berbers—all so tall. But the blacks were the worst.

Towering, slim, ebony—seemingly polished in the sun. In Tashkent they were all around him. In his classroom, and in the mess halls. Walking beside him back and forth to classes along sun-bathed walkways. Tchevsky had taken to keeping his eyes lowered, as if he were head-bent deep in professorial thought. But even then he could not avoid the shadows. One day not long ago, while walking with his students across the shimmering quadrangle it had flashed into his mind that his shadow among the others seemed like something plump and sacrificial, surrounded by hostile spears.

No, Tchevsky admitted to himself that he felt more empathy with his Latin American and East Asian pupils. The little Burmese were nice.

He suddenly realized with a faint twinge of guilt that because of the striking height which they all seemed to share, the Africans looked very much alike to him. He hadn't mentally adjusted to the individuality of black faces, or even to bronzed ones from the sub-Sahara of Afghanistan. Tchevsky recognized his failure as some sort of latent colonialist attitude that could, no doubt, be cured by appropriate re-education. But what was it that Russian circus trainers always said? "The old bear is stubborn." Or what was that American phrase? "One can't teach an old dog new tricks . . . ?" Yes. That was it.

No, Tchevsky admitted to himself that he had not accepted the reality and individuality of Afghans, Arabs, Berbers and blacks. And he knew he never would. Yet he also knew that his outward behavior could not be faulted. He was methodical. He had studied. He could boast that he knew the histories of these new peoples better than they themselves, knew the geography and the flora and fauna of their countries. Such knowledge was essential for successful guerrilla warfare leading to liberation. Even though tactics and strategy were not Tchevsky's field of special expertise, he'd made it his business to learn all he could about these new people and their unfamiliar, irrelevant world. It had been an act of will.

The distant Moskva had grown perceptibly larger. It was no longer a black beetle adorned with occasional senseless reflections. It boasted tiny windows, bright jewels of shining hubcaps.

Tchevsky turned his head and looked into the south where, some hundred-odd miles away, the jagged peaks of the Elburz floated pink and snow-capped above the nothingness of an invisible steppe horizon. He grinned remembering the time one of his Iranian students was telling tall tales about a narrow escape from a tiger in those mountains.

The Iranian had been a smuggler before coming to the University to learn the arts of terrorism and guerrilla war. This incident with the tiger had allegedly happened during the Iranian's smuggling days in the jumbled border area between Iran and the U.S.S.R. near the Caspian. A group of Turks, Burmese and Africans had listened politely to the smuggler's tale, but with the obvious disbelief. Tchevsky imagined that the story itself had probably been false, but he had been able to break in and support the Iranian's assertion that there were, indeed, tigers living in the Elburz. For the benefit of the open-mouthed Turks, Tchevsky had gone on to tell them about the snow leopards of the Caucasus, on the very border of Europe. And, in passing, he'd mentioned the delicious flavor of the Erevan melons. That was study. That was methodology.

By a conscious effort Tchevsky had been able to discern some mark or feature on the faces of each of his students and to associate it with his catalogue of facts concerning the student's country of origin and special characteristics of the terrain affecting the war of liberation, present or future, to be waged there.

He knew which of his students were from Angola, which were from Zimbabwe and who had been sent from S.W.A.P.O. As an interrogator, memory was Igor Tchevsky's strong suit. With absolute honesty he could recall that he'd never made a mistake, even in casual conversation, with one of his students.

Still, Tchevsky felt a certain relief that his job as an interrogation instructor in Tashkent was neither his career nor his primary assignment. It was more in the nature of a cover. One that would be shed soon. He doubted that he'd be able to make a successful career of teaching the methods of revolution to eager Third Worlders. Accepting another latent colonialist or, worse, racist tendency in himself, Tchevsky concluded as he lit another cigarette that there was some lack of commitment among most of these people. No, they were definitely not motivated by sound ideology alone.

Flinging a match into the stocky vastness of his shadow, Tchevsky gazed pensively in the direction of the Elburz, permitting his eyes to search into distant folded strata and snow crevices as if seeking some secret in the geology that eluded the firm grasp of modern psychology. What, for instance, had happened to the Iranian smuggler?

A coalition with reactionary Islamic forces had been a temporary necessity to get the Shah toppled. Everyone had accepted that. But now? The erstwhile smuggler, who had been carefully trained at extravagant Soviet expense, was—so the agents reported—sitting in the dust somewhere near Isfahan listening intently to the lessons allegedly revealed by Mullah Nasruddin jokes, as told by a filthy, smiling Dervish. And the progressive Marxist counter-revolution which was to have toppled the Islamic Republic in its turn? A few shots, a few riots, a few mobs of students. A lot of signs and placards in downtown Teheran taken very seriously by the Western press with warning cartoons showing Ayatollah Khoumeni sitting on a Soviet sickle as he assumed the seat of power. All very encouraging—except for the fact that a not inconsiderable number of would-be Marxist revolutionaries were, at this minute, in mosques discussing the descendant of Ali and Fatima, their expensive, Soviet-made combat boots lined up neatly by the door.

Yes, some of their ancient traditions and religious opiates obviously retained considerable potency, Tchevsky told himself. Just today, while he was sitting in on an infiltration class, the instructor was discussing the latest social fads in the decadent West and the usefulness of trends and mass-movement as cover. Of course, a fad or a movement must be studied carefully so that the infiltrator who would use it as a cover became intimately familiar with the norms, values and tenets of the craze. The instructor's point was that religious cults, environmental groups and militant anti-nuclear movements could be very valuable to the *agent provocateur* whose goal was social disruption and the sabotage of power and communication facilities.

Everyone had taken careful notes and seemed to be concentrating on what the instructor was saying, but Tchevsky had also noted a few sidelong glances between countrymen. He was prepared to swear that in some unfocused way many of these Third Worlders shared mutual concern about matters other than class struggle and the uses of power. For them, he suspected, history was not materialist inevitability. In the halls of Tashkent he'd heard almost as many muted conversations about deforestation in Bolivia caused by metal refinery gases and Zambesi water pollution as appropriate discussion of guerrilla tactics. He'd only overheard references to Western, colonialist developments. But he was no fool. There were Soviet developments, too.

Sometimes, when the tall Afghans, Arabs, Berbers and blacks walked along beside him, looking down on him, Tchevsky got the distinct impression that, to them, both the Russians and the Americans looked alike. They didn't see the vast philosophical differences between the Soviets and the West. Just as he had difficulty in telling the Third Worlders apart.

No, he, Tchevsky, could not endure a career of teaching these new people at Tashkent. Sooner or later he'd begin to react to the veiled ideological hypocrisy all around. He required allies—and enemies—who wanted the same kind of world, and for whom the conflict was merely a matter of who dominated it. His superiors must have understood that about him. Tchevsky realized thankfully, and with any luck he'd be leaving Tashkent soon. He'd helped to forge a powerful new weapon against the West, he understood. Soon, it would be the time to use this weapon. And he could leave the Third World students to their own vague irrelevant designs, whatever they were. He wondered briefly whether his opposite numbers in the CIA shared the same misgivings about their own Third World allies.

Tchevsky flicked an impatient glance toward the north. The black Moskva was considerably closer. He could barely make out the indistinct shapes inside the car, the driver in front and the masses in the passenger seat which would be Koffler and his luggage. Far away behind the car the tiny cluster of modernistic buildings wriggled in the heat waves. The airport was much further away than it looked, the flatness of the steppe and its clarity of air had always proven deceptive. Again, Tchevsky had underestimated the time it would take. Thinking carefully, he estimated that it would be another ten minutes before Koffler reached the University. In spite of the fact that he could clearly see the Moskva making good time over the airport highway.

He considered going back inside out of the heat to wait for Koffler, but then noted that his squat shadow had lengthened and his sticky shirt cooled suddenly in a breeze blowing down from the faraway snowy Elburz.

All things considered, it had gone very well. They'd be leaving Tashkent very soon now. If Koffler's surgery was suitable. No, it would be the best.

While he would not regret leaving Tashkent, he had to admit that it had been the best possible location for the project. Not only were the physical facilities superb at the University, but the security was almost foolproof. Tashkent was hard to infiltrate. The Western Powers had few Central Asians on their payrolls. About the only way of cracking the security at Tashkent was to try to infiltrate a student, an agent, into a group of pupils coming from one of the Third World countries. This was possible, barely. It had happened once or twice, but the agents never lasted long. The groups of students were generally too cohesive.

The Americans tried with their own blacks posing as nationals of Liberia, Nigeria or Zimbabwe. The French had employed a couple of agents from Tchad. The British utilized mostly East Asians, Burmese or mixed orientals from Hong Kong. None had survived long. Some had served as object lessons in Tchevsky's lectures on interrogation techniques. The lucky ones had assisted in the demonstration of sophisticated narcotics techniques. Others had endured more primitive methods. One agent had caused some embarrassment. Tchevsky grimaced slightly in the remembrance of his only lapse while at Tashkent. If he closed his eyes, Tchevsky could conjure up the ebony sheen and could still become fascinated with the glowing contortions of the stomach. The undulations of the muscles captivated him: the flow stimulated in the long black body. He'd simply stopped listening to the screams and the eager rush of sobbing words. He'd just kept pressing the button which made the torso move in waves beginning down at the pubis where the wires snaked away and flowing up rhythmically to the expanding up-thrusting chest that heaved, jiggled to produce the shrieks. She'd died before they learned she'd been born in Baltimore. He'd gone too fast. But it had been those lovely muscles. Tchevsky remembered that when it was all over and he was wiping the sweat from his face. Some of his students had been looking at him oddly.

Yes. Tashkent had excellent security. Much better than Europe. The whole of Europe was one large playground for spies. As much as he would have preferred to work there, Tchevsky had to admit that the project could have been easily compromised in such an atmosphere. Out here in Central Asia, though, insulation from Western eyes was almost total. He and Koffler would take Ottawa and Washington by surprise, with complete cover.

The black Moskva whirred to a stop in front of the building. Tchevsky tossed his second cigarette aside and jogged heavily down the steps to the car. Why must Moskvas sound like cheap sewing machines? The poor Americans believed that the Moskva was only a copy of a late 50's Ford, but they were wrong. Moskvas are much worse.

Tchevsky opened the rear door of the sedan and stepped back. Koffler, for that must be his name from now on, climbed out and gazed levelly at Tchevsky.

Tchevsky examined the man carefully: the prominent nose, the sunken eyes and high cheekbones. Even the scholarly grey pointed beard was perfect. Tchevsky shook his head in amazement.

"Excellent likeness, is it not, Colonel?"

"Unbelievable likeness," agreed Tchevsky. "You have the orders?"

Tchevsky accepted the thick envelope from Koffler's hand and started to open it. Then he hesitated. "Time enough for that later, Koffler. First, let's go see what your namesake thinks of you."

Koffler grinned and the two men walked up the steps to the building.

"Anything else come out after I left?" asked Koffler. "I have been away so long that I have been out of touch with my real self. I have become Koffler."

"That's how it must be. No, nothing else came that was of importance. We'd already wrung him dry, as our American friends say, before you left."

"Then I am complete, Comrade Colonel?"

"Most assuredly, Koffler. And he is but a husk. You have everything."

Koffler and Tchevsky walked along the blue-tiled corridor, past classroom doors, until they came to a bank of elevators. The two men went down several floors, well below ground level. When they emerged from the elevator, white corridors with steel doorways stretched before them. Air conditioning hissed and the sharpness of antiseptic assailed their noses. They walked a long way, their footsteps echoing hollowly. At length, as they neared the end of the corridor, they began to hear screams coming, muffled, from behind one of the doors.

They both soared happily at crazy angles above the village. Looking down, they beheld the dark and rich warm brown of the logs of the cabins, and the fertile black earth of Poland stretched far away to all sides. For it was after harvest time and the earth lay fallow. Bela was a splash of color as she looked down, laughing, at the villagers who looked up at them, smiling. Koffler soared, too, but was dressed more somberly. Far below, he could see the Rabbi's face glancing up with twinkling, friendly eyes and fringed by a fuzzy brown beard that matched the flat fuzzy fur hat on his head. Down below, Koffler could see that even a goat was looking upward at the spectacle of himself and Bela flying in the air. The goat, too, seemed to be smiling and its pointed beard seemed to twitch in merriment. For once, its brown-yellow eyes were filled with contentment, not mischief. It was his goat, seemingly, and Koffler knew its ways well. Such was the happiness of their wedding day that even that goat's malevolence was quelled. Koffler's mind took in the bells that all Polish villages possess in great profusion even when they possess little else. These particular bells had been roughly and brightly depicted by Marc Chagall with bold cakes of brilliant color. But if the painting belonged to Chagall, created in memory of his own wedding and in memory of his own beautiful Bela, Koffler owned the vision of the painting in his mind. The village was his, he'd borrowed Chagall's Rabbi because his own had not been so friendly-looking, and the goat very much resembled his own. Chagall could not complain about the bells, because they belonged equally to everyone. Koffler's mind grasped the bells and he could almost feel the texture of the caked paint applied by Chagall. His mind revelled in the richness of the bells' metal. Thick brass. Age-worn iron. A few small ones in precious silver. Seeing them so closely, Koffler perceived that all of them began slowly to rock back and forth and in his mind he heard their pealing. Across the space of the painting, his Bela's soft brown eyes glowed and her dress arched in the sky like a spangled comet of lace and silk. As the bells pealed, Bela smiled downward. Koffler knew that somewhere in the painting, on the other side from Bela, he was smiling downward also. The bells pealed rhythmically and the carillon became louder. Koffler smiled at this completed vision of sight and sound. It was his last possession. No one had taken this from him. He sank into it as he had done many times before, lulled by the voices of the bells in the painting.

But, after a while, it happened as it had always happened before. Gradually, Koffler realized that the bells and their rhythm were echoes of footsteps. He soon knew that they were coming for him again.

And he began to scream.

By the time "Koffler" and Tchevsky reached the door, Koffler's screams from inside had subsided into a resigned sobbing. As Tchevsky turned the last number of the lock's combination, Koffler managed a last, despairing shriek and then fell to sobbing again as the door rasped open.

Tchevsky and his companion looked into the cell.

Koffler was as he always was. Naked in the far back corner of the cell, hunched on the metal bench with his knees drawn up and his eyes tightly shut. Tears ran down his gaunt face and he covered his eyes with his hands. On the backs of Koffler's wrists, Tchevsky could see the old tattooed numbers. On the bony forearms, he could see the new wounds of many, many needle punctures. Between Koffler's sharp shins and angular ankles, Tchevsky's eyes took in the useless and withered genitals which cascaded down in wrinkles of skin, misshapen swellings of flesh. This, too, was pock-marked with recent punctures from electrode, not hypodermic, needles.

"Koffler." Tchevsky said it softly, with tiredness.

The head began to shake slowly and the hands squeezed the eyes shut more tightly. Koffler took in a deeper breath so that he could begin to scream again, for the sound of his own screaming always shut out the pain a little. Koffler gathered himself, but the shriek came out of the raw throat like a croak a crushed frog might make.

"Koffler . . . It's over now." Tchevsky said it gently.

Slowly, the head came up out of the despair of the cupped hands. Koffler raised his eyes. They were large and a soft brown. Once they had been animated with flashes of light and excitement, as when soaring with Bela on that long-ago wedding day. Or deep with concentration, feeding information to the hungry brain that once dwelt behind them, as in study and work in Warsaw and Prague. Or vacant with fear and bruised and bloodshot with agony, as at Auschwitz when Bela had been taken from him. And now.

"Yes, Koffler. It is all over. I promise. No more."

To Tchevsky, the eyes appeared familiar. He had seen them that way on many occasions. With Koffler. And others. They pleaded silently for it to be the truth, but, down in the depths, could not believe.

"It is the truth, Koffler, I promise you. We're through with you." Tchevsky motioned to the man beside him. The man moved slightly into the cell so that Koffler could see him more clearly. Koffler's eyes struggled to focus on the man. At length,

19

Tchevsky could see that Koffler recognized himself. Koffler closed his eyes and small tears were squeezed from between the lids. He nodded almost imperceptibly.

"So, you see, Koffler. It is the truth. We have no more need of you."

Koffler nodded.

"The question now, Koffler, is what to do with you. I am authorized to tell you that the U.S.S.R. will try to rehabilitate you, if you wish. If you recover, you'll be resettled somewhere in Siberia, I imagine. Or in the Urals. Somewhere. Perhaps, Koffler, someday you might be able to . . . function again. There may yet be a measure of happiness for you."

Koffler looked up slowly and opened his eyes. He managed to focus on Tchevsky and then looked at the man beside him. Then, closing his eyes wearily, he remembered the bells in the Chagall painting. Koffler smiled, opened his eyes briefly and glanced up at Tchevsky. Then he glanced down at himself, seeing distantly the ruin of his own body as if it were someone else's and noticing vaguely the futureless shapes between his thighs. He closed his eyes and saw Bela soaring as she had done long ago in the dazzling colors of Chagall. But the children's faces had already been dim for many years. He could not remember how they looked before Auschwitz. Only Bela remained. Soaring in the painting.

Koffler softly shook his head.

Tchevsky understood the negation. "I think it is best," he said, taking a case from his breast pocket and opening it. It did not take him long to assemble the vial and the hypodermic. Tchevsky held it up and pushed the plunger so that the air was expelled from the needle and a drop of liquid grew upward from the point, quivered, then collapsed and ran down the gleaming steel.

"Are you quite certain?"

Tchevsky watched Koffler nod his head slowly. Tchevsky walked across the cell to Koffler and unfolded one of the skeletal arms across the tops of Koffler's knees. "There will be no pain," said Tchevsky. "Only sleep."

Koffler nodded again. Quickly and gently Tchevsky found a vein in Koffler's forearm and buried the needle in it. He pressed the plunger slowly and firmly.

Koffler's body relaxed and he molded gently into the corner of the cell, his knees splaying apart and his arms falling to his side. Tchevsky stepped back, took a look at the smile forming on Koffler's lips. He turned away and walked from the cell, followed by the man who was now Koffler.

The warm village lay below and the black earth stretched away. The villagers smiled upward. The Rabbi's friendly eyes twinkled. Koffler and Bela soared in happiness while the bells pealed.

And this time they never ceased.

1

1

Radagast's fat apple bows looked like the puffed cheeks of a cheerful Bavarian oom-pah reveller adorned with a mustache and unwiped beer-head foam. From his perch on the galleon's beak overhanging the bows, Adrian Dumas could look straight down to where *Radagast's* blunt and heavy cutwater divided the blue of Lake Ontario to either side of the hull. It could not be said that *Radagast* rode the lake's modest billows gracefully. The little ship rammed the waves, plowing doggedly through them, throwing spray in front of the blunt bows with every confrontation with the chop. Occasionally, when *Radagast* challenged a particularly high crest of swell, bright necklaces of water were thrown upward far enough to splash through the perforated floor of the beak. On such occasions it was Dumas' wont to give a yip or a mild curse as he shook the crystal beads from a startled ankle. Offshore, the water temperature was Lake Ontario's customary forty-two degrees.

Looking speculatively at the extent of the mustache of foam rolling away from either side of the cutwater, Dumas estimated that they were making about six knots over the bottom. Resting his hand on the quivering aluminum bowsprit that jutted well out into the air over the bows and beak, Dumas looked directly into the square expanse of straining Dacron that wrenched its yard, and the bowsprit, in the gusts. The spritsail swelled outward like a budding, unexpected breast beneath a surprised girlish camesole. At times, with the catpaws of wind striking out of the otherwise steady breeze, the bulging fabric tugged at the yard and the bowsprit and set both throbbing. The restraining ropes at each corner of the sail imparted to the Dacron a shifting pattern of urgent clefts and furrows. Moving to the rhytmn of *Radagast's* shouldering through the swell, these reminded Dumas of changing centerseam tensions in well-filled feminine jeans promenading Yonge Street. Or the swaying distortion of Quebec flats silk-screened to the front of stretched, piquant Rue St. Catherine tee-shirts.

Out and above, at the corner of the sail, a brass grommet winked in the sun. Dumas smiled and turned to look astern. Forty feet away, across the open space between the little galleon's castles, Rachael stood behind the wooden wheel on the sloping poop, feet planted solidly on the teak deck. Her auburn hair streamed out over her orange windbreaker at an angle toward Dumas. She held *Radagast* on a broad reach, extracting the most sensation of speed, and the little ship headed toward the blue horizon and the center of Lake Ontario. Dumas knelt down and peeked forward under the edge of the straining spritsail. At a surprisingly large angle to his right he could make out the needle of the CN Tower far away and, barely, a delicate green spray above the blue that might have been the tops of trees on Toronto Island.

Dumas scrambled out of the beak and crawled onto the ten-foot-deep and semi-circular roof of the forecastle where he gratefully entered for a moment the sliver of shadow from the bulging mainsail above. As *Radagast* heeled in a catspaw, he gingerly crawled the length of the forecastle roof and grabbed onto a handful of thick halyards alongside the waist-sized aluminum mainmast. Thus secured against *Radagast's* heel, he swung his legs around and let them dangle over the after-edge of the forecastle. He sat there for a moment feeling the heat of the sun out of the wind and looking down at Pia's long body below on the main deck. The thick magenta towel under her was darkened with perspiration for almost her whole length, from her feet, which were surprisingly slim considering her size, to the soft-looking mounds of flesh that squeezed out between the towel and her gently breathing rib-cage. A dampened mop of tangled blonde hair obscured all of her head except for the tip of one disconcertingly red ear-lobe and the barest suggestion of the normally pink bow of her lips. Noticing the flung-aside straps at the top of her bikini, Dumas judged from the lobster-scarlet back that confronted him that Pia would certainly suffer no strapmarks on her sun tans for some time to come.

Dumas shoved himself off the edge of the forecastle and landed three and a half feet lower on the deck. He padded gingerly across the hot wood and knelt beside Pia. An exploratory finger, poked gently into the flesh of her shoulder, resulted in a pale round mark into which the redness seeped immediately. Dumas grimaced and looked up accusingly into the mid-July sun.

"Pia . . . Pia!"

The tangled blonde head moved petulantly. "Hmmm. Vat do you vant . . . ? Lemme shleep." A hand came up and brushed clinging strands from the nape of her neck. Pia sighed and worked herself more deeply into the soft pile of the towel.

"Pia. Wake up." Dumas winced and shook the shoulder gently. "Wake up."

Dumas caught the fluttering motion as her eyes opened somewhere beneath the blonde hair. "Adrian? Yes. I am avake. Vat's wrong . . . ?"

"Nothing," Dumas said. "Except that you've gone from an attractive pinkish medium rare to well done. Verging on very well done."

Pia squirmed over onto her right side and clawed the hair from before her eyes. She blinked like a great, surprised owl and then she squinted, looking around. She followed Dumas' gaze and looked down at the long curve of her flexed left thigh. A neat line bisected the flesh, bright red on the back, Pia's normal Danish paleness on the front. "My God!" she wailed. "That bashtard, Edvard! He vas supposed to keep me oiled . . ."

"I haven't seen him," said Dumas. "He must've gone below a couple of hours ago."

"But it didn't seem that hot up on the back . . . there . . ." Pia waved vaguely up at the poop. "Rachael and I were cold."

"It's the wind up there," Dumas shrugged. "Down here on deck you're sheltered from it." He smiled comfortingly, glancing involuntarily at her heavy breasts, which strained down from her ribs. Magenta reflections from the towel bathed her in an artificial burgundy glow that rendered the shell pink of her nipples all but invisible. Dumas stood up again thinking how ridiculous it was for Pia to bother with the tiny triangle of bikini bottom that matched her towel. He walked down the slight incline of the deck and bent to pick up the plastic lotion bottle that had rolled down the lee rail. When he turned back to her she was busy with both hands behind her back, re-tying the bikini top. When she finished he tossed the bottle to her. "You'd better get below and find Edward. You're going to need a gallon of this stuff."

"Then I must come back up," said Pia.

"Don't you think you've had enough sun for one day?"

"My God, Adrian. I can't valk around like this. Vithout both halves matching."

Dumas watched Pia's scarlet back disappear down the companionway set into the center of the poop deck's forward wall. Somewhere below a sleeping or reading Edward could catch hell shortly. Dumas climbed up the four steps to the poop deck and walked carefully over the slanting teak toward Rachael. She was grasping the spokes of the large wheel firmly, her eyes were shining and she smiled as he approached, although it was obvious to him that she was tired. The cool east wind whipped slant-wise the length of the deck and Dumas felt immediately how different it was from the sultry sheltered main deck between the castles. The orange nylon of Rachael's windbreaker crackled and he saw that her cheeks were wind-burned pink, her eyes becoming slightly red-rimmed. Her tanned legs bore goose-bumps from the braced tendons in the hallows of her thighs where they emerged from the unseen bikini bottoms and the over-hanging windbreaker down to the brown tops of her bare feet. Here, near the stern, Rachael at the wheel remained in the partial shade of the mizzen squaresail behind her. For a moment, Dumas watched the smooth play of the long muscles in her legs as she trimmed the wheel continuously, glancing down into the binnacle, in response to the demands of the unseen compass card. Dumas came up beside her and the wind pushed out tendrils of her hair in order to stroke his face.

"Oh, Adrian! This is fun! How'm I doing?"

Dumas glanced astern and took in the flat, marbled blue-and-white wake stretching out straight behind them. "Just great. Straight as an arrow, love."

"Your wakes *are* like pretzels," Rachael agreed.

"I wouldn't go *that* far. Let's just say they're not completely straight."

Rachael grinned and Dumas enjoyed the sparkle in her grey-green eyes. The corners of her mouth dimpled slyly. "Okay. Not completely straight. The secret is," she said, pointing down into the binnacle, "you have to choose a course and keep your eye on the needle. That way the boat goes straight."

"What's your course?"

"Southwest by south."

"What . . . ?"

"Southwest by south," she repeated and cocked a challenging eyebrow. "Can't you box the compass? . . . I can."

"Box the compass? It's already in . . . in that thing." Dumas waved vaguely at the binnacle.

"Binnacle," said Rachael.

"Alright. Binnacle." He paused. "I thought they grew on hulls under water?"

"Southwest by south. About two hundred and twelve of your un-nautical degrees."

Dumas peered into the glass of the binnacle and, sure enough, saw the lubber line hovering around two hundred and twelve degrees. "There's only one thing wrong with your course, Miz Master Mariner."

"What's that . . . ?"

"Well, it's taking us to Buffalo, that's what."

"Oh, I know, Adrian. But she's going so fast!"

"We're gonna have to turn arou—"

"Jibe."

"Alright. Jibe. We have to. We have to get to work in the morning."

"I know."

"I'll take over. We'll stagger in the general direction of Toronto. Maybe, if we're lucky, we'll get in before sundown. This sow is a bitch to park."

"Berth."

Dumas grinned. He had been afraid that she'd have trouble adapting to life aboard *Radagast*. Now, Rachael had become almost unbearably nautical. Dumas trusted that it would wear off soon.

"Pia fell asleep down there," said Dumas, "and Edward forgot to baste her. She's going to need more than her suntan oil. Why don't you go below and break out the Solarcaine?"

"Oh, I warned her. With her complexion. How long . . . ?"

Dumas shrugged. "A couple of hours, I guess."

"I'd better get down there . . . Was . . . Did she have a blueish tinge?"

"Not that bad. Just bright red. Like one of your Maritime lobsters."

"Thank goodness." Rachael handed the wheel over to Dumas and headed forward to the steps, leaning against the pitch of the deck.

"And darling," Dumas called, "you might as well send Edward up. I need him and Pia probably doesn't about now."

Rachael nodded as she stooped to go down the steps to the center deck, her arms outstretched for support to the rails on either side. As she bent over, Dumas caught a quick glimpse of the slight semi circular ridge in the bikini bottom against the thin fabric. Mini-pad. *Radagast* had certainly helped her. Hard-

29

ly any cramps and very little tension. Dumas fondly recalled the healthy play of Rachael's leg muscles at the wheel. Maybe a slight extra-pedantry with the nautical terms, but only after a tiring two-hour trick at the helm. And coming off the deck with flushed cheeks and bright eyes. With her straight-arrow course calculated for maximum speed. So different from the house in Don Mills, with one or two days of monthly dullness in her eyes.

Presently, Edward's red head appeared above the edge of the poop deck as he unfolded his more than six-foot bulk out of the companionway. Edward looked a bit hurt, Dumas decided, as he swung his red-bearded face around to look up questioningly at Dumas at the wheel.

"We gotta turn this thing," Dumas called. "We have to trim the sails."

Edward nodded.

Very slowly, Dumas put the wheel down and saw *Radagast's* bow tracking northward across the horizon. Edward ambled to the starboard rail and lazily gathered four ropes into his massive right hand. With his equally massive left hand, he began plucking belaying pins from the rail. Dumas shuddered, but as *Radagast's* bow pointed first to the west and then northwest toward Toronto, Edward gradually let all four ropes pull through his hand, controlling the strain of two sails with apparently effortless contractions of his fingers.

Dumas stooped at the wheel to peer between the lower edge of the mainsail and the upper edge of the spritsail further forward. Through the clear slit in the expanses of uniformly white Dacron, Dumas could see the blunt tip of the bowsprit poised above the green spray of trees on the horizon. He shrugged. Good enough.

"Okay, Ed. Belay the starboard sheets."

"Ay, ay, Sir. Captain sir." Edward flung a withering glance up at Dumas and then bent to the business of securing the ropes to the rail.

Dumas shook his head sadly. "And Ed, you'll have to trim the port sheets for our new course."

Edward nodded and walked the width of the deck to the port rail. Gathering the ropes in his hand, he looked aloft, watching the flags on the masthead which indicated the new wind direction, and hauled in the sheets until the two sails were pulling true. He looked up at Dumas. "What about that one?" He pointed to the untrimmed mizzen above Dumas.

"Come up and take the wheel and I'll do it," Dumas called down.

Once the spokes of the wheel had safely disappeared into Edward's hands, Dumas walked back to the stern railing and trimmed the mizzen at the same angle as the other sails. Dumas looked back over the rail when he had finished and saw the definite right-angle turn in *Radagast's* wake now several hundred yards behind. Distance made the sharpness of the turn deceptive. What appeared to be a sudden dogleg in the wake was actually a curve some hundreds of yards long. Dumas leaned his back against the stern rail. From there, high up on the poop at the very back of the little ship, Dumas could see all of *Radagast* stretching out in front of him. His dream for many years. His insurance against a world becoming crazier every day. Dumas had long ago come to the conclusion that a few hundreds yards of water was the best possible insurance against social chaos on land. And what with continuing energy crises, spiralling inflation, and threats of Armageddon in Iran, Indo-China, Rhodesia and too many other places where small political bush fires could easily plunge the major powers into a giant conflagration, Dumas took out insurance.

Not a nimble sailer, perhaps, and difficult to handle, but Dumas' miniature galleon replica had several advantages. He had designed it himself, and had chosen the galleon template because of its immense roominess on a modest length of just over forty feet. Ample room for living. Ample space for supplies and equipment. If it should come down to survival. And if it didn't? Well, there were somewhat inaccessible parts of the world that Dumas had always wanted to see. Some matters that needed investigating, having to do with certain alleged lost cities on the Xingu River in the Mato Grosso, and some gigantic sunken walls off Andros Island.

Dumas had designed *Radagast* with those projects in the back of his mind, and others, but primarily for survival in a seemingly disintegrating Western World. *Radagast's* chubby hull was decidedly over-built of one-eighth-inch steel plate over frequent ribs and beams, also steel, of surprisingly large dimensions. Dumas figured that, at a pinch, he could leave *Radagast* in the water all winter if the necessity arose and if he were willing to do some energetic chopping around the waterline if the ice grew too thick.

Radagast had evolved with agonizing slowness in a welding shop in Port Hope. All the money that Dumas and Rachael could spare had gone steadily into *Radagast,* but for years, seemingly, the craft had assumed a recognizable form at a snail's pace.

The Steinberg commission had changed all that and *Radagast* grew apace. Dumas' unexpected, but not unearned, windfall saw *Radagast* quickly launched and, in a measure, fitted out, although there was much yet to be done.

Thinking of Steinberg made Dumas think of Edward. Dumas saw his broad back at the wheel and the tip of his jutting red beard. A Viking-looking personage, but conning the wrong type of ship. Edward still exhibited occasional testiness, like just now on the deck, and Dumas reflected; his failure to oil Pia together with subsequent repercussions was not the whole explanation. For all his Viking looks, Edward's outlook was rather staid and domestic. He was unused to spending several nights in jail. Dumas suspected that questions posed by certain police officers might not have been in the most polite manner.

Dumas walked forward to the wheel beside Edward and clapped him jovially on the back. "Has the weekend helped to make up for it, Ed?"

"I'll credit your tab, Adrian."

"Christ, Edward. It wasn't even my fault. Hell. I wasn't even *there*. It was just a screw-up. Wrong place at the wrong time."

"I've been thinking about that, Adrian."

"That's good of you."

"You're as innocent as hell, Dumas. But that photograph I was taking must have had something to do with something."

Not too long ago, Edward had had the bad fortune to have been on assignment taking advertising photographs for one of Dumas' clients. Simultaneous events, including a still-unexplained explosion which took the life of a hawkish American presidential hopeful, had cast a measure of unfounded suspicion upon Edward and his photographic rig. The equipment had been supplied by Dumas. Dumas had learned of these events while chatting in a bar with Steinberg, although they had not come altogether as a surprise.

Dumas shrugged. "Hell, Ed, I'm as much in the dark as you are."

Edward grunted.

"Pia is a bear for punishment," Dumas noted. They looked down to see two heads, one blonde and one auburn, bobbing up out of the companionway below. Pia's back glistened and in places its redness was muted by swirls of liberally-applied goo of a whiteish color. The women looked up at the sails and then down at the deck where odd shapes of brilliant sun splashed between the moving shadows. With Rachael's assistance, Pia lowered herself into one of the islands of light. By curving her body she could barely get all of herself into it. She leaned back on the magenta towel very carefully. Dumas saw her wince. As Pia settled huge round sunglasses over her nose and placed her arms carefully beside her for tanning, Rachael began to apply oil to such areas of jiggling white flesh as were not restrained by the magenta whisps of Pia's string bikini. Dumas watched these thin, taut strings hopefully, especially when Rachael's exertions with the lotion began to result in a heavy side-to-side swaying of Pia's chest, but nothing untoward occurred. Dumas sighed and looked shoreward to the north. Small angular shapes had climbed above the horizon. These must be new apartment developments in Whitby or Ajax.

"Ever strike you that it might be too much of a good thing?" said Edward, gazing down at Pia.

"I'm not sure I know what you mean, Ed," Dumas said cautiously.

"Fashion. She always wants to wear the latest thing. Whatever it is. Now it's string bikinis," Edward sighed.

"So . . . ?"

"Do you really think they were intended for girls with . . . so much?"

Dumas managed to regard objectively the tiny triangles that inadequately stretched over the various mounds of Pia.

"I mean," said Edward, "speaking esthetically, as a photographer, those scraps and strings look dumb on a girl Pia's size. I mean, there's just no reason for them. Know what I mean?"

"I think so."

"Esthetically, again, Pia needs something a lot larger or nothing at all. I think I'd rather see her in a one-piece." Edward paused and turned his gaze toward Rachael. "Now Rachael can get away with those string things because she's smaller. A crisper line."

"Hmmm."

"Edvard! You vatch me this time good, please. If I fall ashleep, please oil me like Rachael."

"Hell," said Dumas, "don't worry, Ed. I'll look after her for you. You can go below if you want."

"Thanks anyway, Dumas." Edward handed the wheel back to Dumas and made his way forward down the steps to the

33

center deck. As soon as Edward was clear of the narrow steps and their railing to both sides, Rachael came up beside the binnacle.

"I think it looked worse than it is," she said.

They looked down at Edward, now assiduously applying goo to Pia's arm.

"Are you happy, husband?" Rachael asked.

Dumas nodded. "You . . . ?"

"Yes, Adrian. I'm still getting used to it. It happened so fast, really."

"But it's comfortable enough? There's still a bit of finishing to do . . ."

"There's only one thing I really miss."

"What's that?"

"My gardening . . . But there's so much to compensate. I feel really free. I'm having trouble getting used to it. Adrian . . . ?"

"Hmmm?"

"Do you mind if I don't quit the library just now?"

"You want to keep working?"

"I'm used to it. I like it. To live on a boat in a yacht club . . . well . . . I sort of feel useless and . . . well . . . scandalous."

Dumas laughed. He had suspected that Rachael's staunchly Protestant upbringing among United Empire Loyalist's forebears might have this result. Idle hands. Devil's workshop. Dumas was glad that his own hazy Louisiana French ancestors had bequeathed him no similarly noble compunctions. Given sufficient money, Dumas had little difficulty imagining a heartily satisfactory life of leisure. "Sure, honey. If that's what you want."

"Then I don't think I'll give my notice," Rachael said.

"Feel better? Now that that's off your chest?" Dumas grinned.

Rachael nodded and smiled, hooking her arm through his, leaning against Dumas' solidness and feeling comforted by it. Adrian had done something. Something to do with Steinberg. Something connected with the explosion in Niagara Falls. She was sure of it. Something that made *Radagast* come more quickly than either of them had dreamed possible. Something that still made Edward and Pia a bit brittle, not that she could blame them after what Edward had gone through. In profile, Rachael felt reassured by the slightly crooked line of Dumas' jaw, where long ago, it had once been broken. Not strong like a movie leading actor's but enduring and sometimes implacable. Stubborn. She'd long ago decided that that jawline completely suited the Taurus he was. Brown eyes were supposed to be easier to read than grey-green ones like her own, but she had come to accept that the very openness of Dumas' eyes could be the best concealment. She snuggled closer against him in the breeze and felt no tension in the sturdy body that braced her. She reached out and brushed aside the shock of dark hair that the wind played with on Dumas' forehead.

Dumas smiled, feeling the pressure of her cool breast against his thick elbow. "You must be getting goose-bumps again. Where's the windbreaker?"

"Took it off. Didn't want lotion all over it."

"You feel better? Now that you've stuck up for your job?"

"You really don't mind, Adrian?"

"Rachael, I only wanted to give you the opportunity to be useless and scandalous. I never said you had to take it." Dumas' eyes travelled around the decks, measuring and considering the railings that safely enclosed them all. "You know," he said, "maybe we could do something about gardening."

Rachael looked up. "On a boat?"

Dumas shrugged. "Why not? Look there," he pointed around the railings. ". . . I don't see why we couldn't have some window box type things hanging over the side. That way, the rain and your watering would just wash the dirt overboard."

"Wouldn't they get in the way of the ropes?"

"We wouldn't have to put them everywhere, dear. We could have a couple right there on the poop rail beside the steps. Maybe a couple more on the center deck down there. And one or two hanging over the stern."

Rachael looked around. "If it wouldn't spoil the boaty appearance . . ."

"Who cares? You could grow flowers. Maybe even some tomatoes . . . if the boxes were large enough. We stay berthed most of the time. Even under sail I don't think they'd get in the way. Might lose a few tomatoes from time to time . . ."

Rachael looked at the sturdy rail speculatively. Yes, it could be done. "Adrian? What's that? Is there a fire on shore?" Rachael was pointing over the starboard rail toward the now distinct artificial skyline of Toronto's eastern satellite towns.

Dumas squinted and saw a plume of white smoke or steam climb into the air suddenly, become torn by the wind and drift rapidly to the west in ragged streamers. "I'd've said it was a smokestack in Oshawa," said Dumas doubtfully, "but we're already past." He fumbled at the binnacle for the cheap Eatonia binoculars in their plastic case. He handed them to Rachael. "See if you can make it out."

Rachael braced her back against Dumas and twirled the focus wheel between the binocular's twin barrels. "It's coming from a funny dome thing on the shore. Here. Look."

A quick glance through the lenses showed Dumas the egglike dome of the Pickering nuclear reactor at the mouth of Frenchman's Bay. The steam roiled upwards from stacks flanking the reactor dome. He handed the glasses back to Rachael. "It's the Pickering power station."

"The nuclear one . . . ?"

"Uh huh."

"Oh, Adrian. There's so much smoke. Do you think it's going to blow up?"

"I sincerely hope not. It's probably just blowing off steam." And how many deadly particles did those streamers carry with them? None. Not one, came the solemn assurances. None, pledged the experts of Provincial Hydro. It was a safe source of energy, so safe, in fact, that Provincial Hydro planned a score more nuclear power stations. The next one to be constructed would be at Darlington, now thirty miles astern of *Radagast*, next to a Provincial Park. And Darlington Station was being ramrodded through with no environmental enquiry and a deaf ear to the objections of people living nearby.

Dumas recalled the safety of the Enrico Fermi A-plant on Lake Erie just south of Detroit. The reator dome was permanently sealed off because of a fuel melt-down in the mid-sixties. With luck the dome would remain sealed for the next 20,000 years, at which point some of the radioactivity may have decayed to supposedly safe levels. An earthquake, plane crash or just cracks from shoddy workmanship, and you could say goodbye to large chunks of Lake Erie, the states of Michigan, Indiana and Ohio, and the province of Ontario. Then, one could always reflect on the safety of the Harrisburg A-plant. After the leak at Three Mile Island, the nuclear experts euphemistically called the radioactivity levels a "glow" and some enterprising person had produced tee-shirts with the grim message "Hell, no. I don't glow!" for residents to wear. Or what about the safety of the reactors at Chalk River which had twice contaminated the environment? Provincial Hydro's nuclear station at Douglas Point in Georgian Bay continually leaked its poison into the waters, adding yet another danger to the threat of acid rain.

Thinking about all this safety made Dumas wonder exactly how much radioactivity clung to the mustache bow wave beneath *Radagast's* beak.

He had pondered this many times before. And the more he

thought about it, the more thoroughly he came to realize that *Radagast* was pitifully inadequate insurance in this crazy world. So you managed to survive the chaos of a disintegrating culture? What then? Poisons already seeping would get you. Or, one might starve through reliance upon fishless lakes of acid rain.

"Adrian . . . There's an awful lot puffing out. Do you think it's safe?" Rachael lowered the glasses carefully, concentrating for a moment on disentangling strands of her hair from the binoculars. She shook her head, letting her hair be carried to one side by the wind.

"I have no idea," said Dumas. "I'm not sure I want to find out." Feeling the coolness of her back braced against him, Dumas slipped his arm around her waist and pulled her closer. His hand molded to the gentle swelling of her belly, his finger brushing the cloth-covered string of her bikini, feeling the goose-bumps.

2

If anyone noticed, no one commented on the way Cyrus Watson pushed out through one of the back doors so soon after dinner. He'd walked out with that too-casual stride that masks tension. He'd run thin and yellow-stained fingers through his sparse silver hair. His eyes held a certain vacant aspect. As if, while eating brussel sprouts, he'd expected messages to materialize on the pseudo-Tudor walls, or as if he suspected that the cool east wind in the tops of the Caledon Hills' trees was murmuring secrets.

If anyone noticed, no one commented because everyone was used to Cyrus Watson's ways. Except when rare guests dictated the pace, Watson's meals seemed to lack the savor to promote lingering. He never fingered his crusted silver napkin rings, nor gazed fondly upon his crested villeneuve tablewear. The beams of artificially-blackened oak, though genuinely cut from England's famed Sherwood Forest, might as well not have supported his plastered walls and ceilings for all he seemed to notice them. Cyrus Watson was not awed by the gaping abyss of his slate fireplace in which a spitted ox would enjoy considerable elbow-room. Even though his knives, forks and spoons bore heraldry, Watson evinced little regard for the hollow suits of full French armor that flanked his fireplace. Had they only been allowed, and had Watson been inclined to listen, these crustacean husks of chivalry could have whispered tradition, romance and breeding, however spurious, and the gaping slate square of the fireplace would gladly have echoed them authoritatively. But Cyrus Watson was a man who passed by mirrors quickly, too conscious of his own transparency to heft the medieval solidity his wealth had bought.

In the view of his staff, Watson appeared to be a simple man.

They alone knew that his own private room was spartan. And they well knew that his only source of pleasure lay not in baronial play-acting, though surely sufficient props were readily to hand, but in solitary walks in the garden. Even in the severest winter blizzards, when he was not away on business, Watson's soul sought surcease in nature. And the Madonna.

Watson had walked some distance from the low rambling house, and its windows were by now small and cozy squares of muted yellow. But he did not turn back to see them beckoning. Nor did he look up to take in the blaze of the stars hanging over the tree-fuzzed hills. Watson's ears did not really hear the eager and lascivious sawing of the crickets. Although gladiolus, tiger-lilies and snap-dragons crowded the path, Watson did not stop to admire their colorful offerings in the flattering light of the burnished moon.

But his nose finally told him that he was near. The heavy perfume of peonies and American Beauty roses reached him suddenly. He hurried around a corner of the shimmering path and then he saw her. He stopped for a moment and then proceeded more slowly. She was a luminous cross in the moonlight, with her stiff draped figure and her arms outstretched to either side. Watson knew that her yearning marble fingers caressed the sorrow of invisible purple-and-pink bleeding heart bushes on either side. The bushes obscured her fingertips. Her fingers, being marble like the rest of her, couldn't feel. She could only accept. That was her saving grace. She always dipped into sorrow and accepted.

Approaching closely, Watson fell to his knees before her. He felt the fragments of crushed stone bruise his knees through the thin summer seersucker.

He ground his knees into the stone.

Looking directly into the closed and heavy-lidded eyes of the Madonna, Watson was assured that she had not revealed him. Weighed down by so much suffering, Watson knew that her eyes would not have flicked open for his guilt alone. She waited.

My God ... Mother of God ... I saw him ...

And she waited.

It was him. And he looked at me. He knew too.

And the moonlight illuminated the compassionate marble lips.

He was waiting for me. As I came out of church today. Across the street. But I saw him and he was waiting. I thought he was dead ... I thought she ...

A breath of the dying east wind gushed out of valleys in the

Caledon Hills. It set the world murmuring. Bleeding hearts surged against the Madonna's fingers. Tell it.

But how many times must I tell it? Over and over to you . . . ? Until the end of time? You know that I was born Cyril Watçek . . .

Shadows, perhaps of gladiolus, tiger-lilies and snap-dragons, danced across the marble face and the Madonna shook her head.

But you already know . . . you must . . . for you know everything.

And she waited.

She looked much like you . . . I think . . . Sarah? Large soft brown eyes . . . Are your eyes soft? . . . I hope so, but I've never seen them . . .

Watson whimpered and worked the stone into his knees.

I was only a guard. A Pole. Even after three years the Germans never really trusted us. But they'd gotten used to us. Sometimes they would humor us. We could laugh. Joke. We could swing little deals . . . sometimes . . .

Going to pick up the new workers was always a festive occasion. A holiday. A chance to get out of the city and out into the countryside. Somehow, they always managed to keep the old Skoda running. They were lucky to have it and the Germans turned a blind eye to it, or maybe it was just too old to bother commandeering. Also, Watçek suspected, the Germans let them keep the truck because it saved them the trouble of transporting workers to such a small factory. Maybe the fact that Ruzycky was so big and blonde helped a lot. They weren't stopped often and when they were the combination of Ruzycky's Nordic looks and the proper requisition forms in Watçek's pocket soon sent them on their way. Somehow, wheezing and rusted as it was, the Skoda never failed them. He and Ruzycky were young and energetic, car crazy like all young men their age, and they became avid mechanics. If they couldn't scrounge proper parts, they always managed to make some sort of substitute from scraps in the factory and a bit of machining. Together, he and Ruzycky kept the Skoda running. It was useful enough for the factory's odd jobs that fat old Wilenczyk, the foreman, grudged them the time to keep it in repair.

The cab leaked from a rusted dent in the roof and the windshield wiper on the driver's side skipped over cracks in the glass. Ruzycky always had to crouch down to look under the cracks when it rained. Even so, the Skoda slipped almost sideways in the muddy ruts. Ruzycky always drove too fast, but the Skoda's knobby tires pulled them faithfully along the ruts and clawed them out of the ditches. They had mended the tarp over the truck's bed so many times that Watçek had just about given up. The fabric was brittle and grey with age and weathering. Long ridges of rust discolored the canvas where it was stretched, distorted, over the tube supports that arched over the bed of the truck. Looking back through the cab's small oval window, Watçek could see rivulets of warm spring rain pouring through holes in the tarp onto the rusted sheet and finally swirling the length of the bed to cascade from the tailgate.

Watçek remembered the rain of that trip because it had been the time that he, Ruzycky and the manager, Wilenczyk, had finally taken the risk of changing the requisition form. Old Wilenczyk had even supplied the bottle of schnapps, the bribe, but Ruzycky and he had to take the major risk of offering it. If anything went wrong, there was nothing to lead back to Wilenczyk. Maybe, if anything went wrong, he and Ruzycky could plead youthful high spirits. The Germans might let them off with a snarl and a cuff. Or, they might wind up inside the camp instead of being factory guards. During the drive to the camp, Watçek had talked to Ruzycky about forgetting the whole caper. But Ruzycky only grinned and would have none of it and Watçek had been thankful.

The conquest had affected various towns in various ways. Watçek had heard that some excitement could be found, underground, in Warsaw if one knew the right people. But a smaller plate like Radom remained careful, watchful and all but dead. No chance of a respite from fear and frustration. Everyone, and especially the women, stayed off the streets as much as possible and certainly after dark. Ruzycky and Watçek had grown tired of talking, thinking and imagining. It had been Watçek's idea originally and he'd finally spoken of it to Ruzycky. Then, sometime later, they had gone to old Wilenczyk. They had watched his small eyes narrow in thought, seen him tug at a thick lip with the tip of an oil-stained finger, and witnessed the growth of a slow, sly smile. Yes, it might work out. Watçek knew that Wilenczyk's mountainous wife and cabbage-sour flat were powerful incentives. If they could share. Now that it was spring, the coal room for the boiler could be cleaned out and roughly swept. Wilenczyk had found a steel bed frame and a fly-spotted mattress. Watçek and Ruzycky had carried it in the back of the Skoda. Old Wilenczyk had wheezed and sweated it into place. They fashioned a lock for the metal fire-door of the coal-room.

It had been surprisingly easy, after all. For all that Ruzycky drove too quickly, the rich black fields crawled past slowly.

Watçek occupied himself watching the horses plod in front of their plows in the rain-muted distance, counted workers in the new rows bending over planting beets and potatoes. Watcek enjoyed the damp and musky perfume of the earth after the oil-and-hot-metal smell of the factory in Radom.

But inevitably they pulled up to the gate. Watçek stayed in the Skoda as Ruzycky climbed out with an assured grin. Watçek saw Ruzycky walk up to the guard house and present the requisition to the guard as usual. Watçek saw the guard nod as he read the paper. Ruzycky stood around in the drizzle as he had done on other occasions, with his hands crammed into his pockets. Finally the guard nodded and picked up a telephone, waving to Ruzycky to drive on in. Ruzcyky jogged, hunched and sodden, back to the Skoda and climbed quickly in. Ruzycky started the engine and the truck lurched and whined through the gate and between the tall fences. Up ahead, Watçek could barely see through the water-dappled windshield armed guards shoving two gaunt figures from the line of men, sending them stumbling toward their approaching truck.

Ruzycky brought the Skoda to a bucking stop and told Watçek to stay inside. Clumsy in their leg chains, the two gaunt men were prodded past the cab and around to the back of the truck. The tailgate screeched and fell down with a clang. Watçek heard the rattle of chains on the truck's sheet metal and the heavier clinking of Ruzycky locking the chains around the tubes and ring-bolts.

Beside the line of men, but separated from them by a high wire fence, Watçek saw a similar line, but of women in brown sack-like shifts. The guards were walking down the line, looking and barking questions.

Ruzycky slammed, dripping, into the Skoda beside Watçek and crouched to look anxiously through the windshield under the cracks.

"They know we need someone who can type and operate an adding machine," said Ruzycky. "Maybe we'll get a decent one."

Watçek thought that the chances were poor. The legs protruding from beneath the shifts were mostly gaunt. Watçek noticed that the line of men on the other side of the wire watched the selection silently.

Finally, one of the guards pulled a woman out of the line by her arm, looked her up and down, and shoved her toward the truck. Guards swung open the gate and Ruzycky hunched out of the Skoda. Through the rain-spotted windshield Watçek noticed a disturbance in the line of men. Because the window was rolled up tightly against the rain, Watçek could hear only indistinct sounds, but he could see a thin man screaming and struggling between guards. Watçek noted the trim dark beard and high, strong cheekbones. The Skoda jiggled and Watçek realized that the woman was grasping the fender of the truck, clawing, sobbing.

"Sarah!" the man shrieked. "Bela! . . . Bela! . . . Don't go away . . ."

A guard slammed the man in the pit of the stomach with a rifle butt. The man doubled up and fell down in a flurry of kicks.

Ruzycky unhooked the woman's fingers from the fender, grimacing at the guard who pulled at the woman's waist. Watçek saw a confusion of tangled brown, grey and Ruzycky's soiled khaki work clothes as they hustled the woman past the driver's window toward the back of the truck. Again, there came the rattle and the clinking and the heavy clumping of Ruzycky's work boots. The Skoda swayed. Watçek noticed that the woman's sobbing was quieter.

Ruzycky's boots squished and sucked in the mud as he came back to the cab. He climbed in beside Watçek, flinging wet strings of blonde hair from his forehead. He glanced over at Watçek and grinned, and picked up the brown-wrapped bottle from the seat between them.

"Here," said Ruzycky, "take this. When he comes out of the guard house, just hand it through the window."

Ruzycky started the engine and craned his head around to peer through the small oval rear window of the cab. Slowly he backed up, weaving slightly, between the two barbed wire fences flanking the road. The Skoda slipped in the ruts, but soon the guard house appeared by the side window. Ruzycky ground the truck out of gear and pumped the brakes to a stop. The fenders vibrated with the rough idle, making water dance on the metal. Watçek quickly rolled down the window. For a moment, under the dripping helmet, a fleshy face smiled and winked at Watçek. Then a pink hand came up and whisked the bottle from Watçek's grasp.

Ruzycky put the Skoda in a shuddering turn and, spinning the wheels in the mud, drove away from the gate and the guard house. Watçek looked back through the small rear window of the cab and saw the sprawl of fences and buildings filling his small horizon in the distance. Ruzycky had told him that the main entrance was much more imposing with its sign:

Arbeit Macht Frei. But also more carefully watched. Hundreds of service vehicles came and went to smaller gates every day. With small gifts, one could get on the better side of some guards. With so many inside, and so many deaths every day, one or two unaccounted bodies made little difference. Also, Ruzycky had said, with the rumor of defeats on the Eastern Front administration had become more frantic and less efficient.

Ruzycky flicked on the lights of the truck against the overcast sky of early evening. The lights bobbed loosely on the fender-tops and their beams jounced along the road. They should be able to cover the thirty kilometers from Ostroweic to Radom before dark—and the curfew—fell.

Workers in the fields became indistinct shapes of drab colors to Watçek as the overcast lowered and darkened and the Skoda's windows started to fog. Squirming around in his seat he peered through the small window and let his eyes adjust to the gloom under the tarp. Her brown shift and hair melted into the weather-beaten grey-brown of the canvas, and it was a moment before he could make out that she was hunched on the metal bench with knees and arms drawn up. As far as the chains would allow her, she bent away from rivulets of grey water that splashed on her shoulder from a hole above her. Without warning, she lifted her head, and Watçek found himself looking into large brown eyes. He looked away.

"That fellow in the compound called out 'Sarah' and 'Bela'," Watçek said to Ruzycky. "I wonder which it is?"

"What does it matter, eh, Watçek? Call her what you like. Me, I don't need to know." Ruzycky turned to grin at him. "Why are you interested?"

Watçek shrugged. "Just wondered."

"You have this soft spot in you, Watçek. Having second thoughts?"

Watçek felt Ruzycky's mocking smile on him and he shook his head. "Not at all." It didn't sound certain, even to Watçek.

"Well, I have none of your problems, my friend," said Ruzycky. "And do you know the reason why?"

"Tell me, Ruzycky."

"It's like this, Cyril, my tender friend. Whatever we do with her, or even what fat old Wilenczyk does with her—whatever we do will be better than what they'd do." Ruzycky jerked a thumb over his shoulder back toward the sprawl of buildings and fences many kilometers behind the Skoda. "After they starve 'em, and work 'em, then they melt 'em down for the little fat on their skinny bones. Me, I don't intend to starve her, Watçek. I like soft women." Ruzycky's teeth flashed, grinning.

"Perhaps . . . after . . ." Watçek said slowly, trying not to stumble over his words, "Perhaps . . . after . . . we can somehow let her go so they won't find her."

"I don't care what you do with her, Wattçek," Ruzycky said. "Do that if it'll make you feel better. But just remember, she's better off with us than back there."

Watçek kept this thought in his mind during the next weeks. Even by the time the Skoda whined up beside the darkened factory in Radom, Watçek felt that they'd be doing her a kindness—in a brutal way, but then the world was cruel. There was at least no doubt, from what Ruzycky had said, that they'd saved her life. Watçek decided that he'd insist on getting her safely away after they were through with her. He knew some kind people in the country, living up in the wooded hills above the Nerew River. Not far. He would drive her there. As they waited for the factory workers to be prodded from the factory, chains dragging on the short plod to the labor-barracks, Watçek assured himself that she would be thankful in the end. In saving her life he'd earned her.

Watçek waited in the dripping cab while Ruzycky went around in back and hailed the guards prodding the queue of hunched men. The line was halted and Ruzycky jumped into the truck bed and Watçek heard the metallic clanking and clinking as Ruzycky jerked their chains from the truck.

"Two more for you," Ruzycky called out to the guard.

"Just in time for their warm-supper and beds," the guard laughed back.

Watçek glanced through the side window to the back and saw Ruzycky shove the two men into the back of the line of gaunt shadows that stretched past the rusted frame of the window. The guard looked incuriously at them while Ruzycky and another guard attached them to the long chains that connected right hands and right feet. The waiting guard yawned and looked toward the truck idly, but Watçek knew that he couldn't see in under the tarp from his angle. Ruzycky stepped away and clapped the guard on the arm.

"*Schnell, jetzt! Machen auf, Juden,*" the guard called. He prodded the last figure in the line. Stumbling, the queue moved off down the street. Ruzycky stood staring after them until the last glint of the guards' guns disappeared into the darkness. He walked over to the side of the cab. "Coming?" Ruzycky grinned through the window.

Watçek hesitated inside the cab, listening to the scuff of Ruzycky's boots as he walked to the back of the truck and then feeling the Skoda lurch as Ruzycky vaulted into it. Watçek heard only the occasional tinkle of chain for a few minutes. Then Ruzycky swore and Watçek heard the loud rattle of the links pulling through ringbolts and around the tube supports of the bench. At last there came the heavy sound of Ruzycky jumping from the truck to the pavement and the soft brush of the girl's bare feet. Ruzycky must have lifted and swung her down. Watçek heard the screech of the tailgate being lifted and then Ruzycky slammed it shut.

Watçek sensed the small brown figure come up beside him and turned to look across the top of the bowed chestnut hair into Ruzycky's rueful smile. Ruzycky shook his head.

"She bite you?" Watçek asked. "You swore."

"Her? No, Watçek, there's no fight in her. I just remembered our deal with Wilenczyk. Come on."

Ruzycky shoved the girl in front of him across the concrete of the loading dock, and Watçek heard the clumsy slapping of her bare feet on the cement, but caught no more than a flash of white behind Ruzycky's bulk. Ruzycky held up the leg chains so that there was no scraping of metal. Watçek left the shadows beside the truck and crossed the lighted expanse of the dock quickly. He came up beside Ruzycky and the girl at the huge rolling loading door. Ruzycky rapped softly on the peeling metal. The light hanging over the door dimmed out and they found themselves in comforting shadow. Watçek glanced around quickly to see if a policeman or soldiers had come into the street. Patrols started at curfew and curfew was any time now.

"Wilenczyk. Open." Ruzycky rapped again.

Watçek stood behind the girl to shield the sight of her from any curious eyes that might be trained on the loading area. He saw that the flash of white must have been a leg. The sodden shift clung to her buttocks in a small semi-circle and the wet fabric was bunched and wrinkled around her waist, plastered and hanging to the flare of her hips.

Without warning, Wilenczyk's face appeared ghostlike in the small square of wired glass set into the peeling green expanse of the loading door. Slowly the door crept upward with a rolling sound. It stopped. Watçek breathed a sigh of relief—the sound of the door's bearing broke the curfew quiet.

"Higher, Wilenczyk," Ruzycky whispered harshly.

"No, Ruzycky," Watçek said softly. "He's right. The door makes too much noise. Quickly, now. Roll under."

Ruzycky glanced up at Watçek from where he crouched beside the door, nodded, and quickly dropped full length in front of the door and rolled under the lip into the absolute darkness of the factory.

Watçek pushed down on the girl's shoulders, forcing her to her knees. Just as he was about to help her lie down to roll under, Ruzycky pulled the leg chains suddenly and her feet were pulled from under her. She managed to throw a bracing hand out before her head cracked on the cement. She rolled on her side, facing Watçek and he saw the soft shadow in the triangle of her thighs. Chains tinkled and the thighs straightened out. She was pulled under the lip of the door, the brown shift peeling up over her ribs. The soft halo of chestnut hair left a track in the dust.

Watçek hesitated long enough to cast one glance around and then himself dropped full-length and rolled under. He stood up slowly in the dark, completely blind for a moment. The door rolled slowly with its hollow noise and met the cement with a dull sound of thick wood. Watçek began to be able to make out shadows. There, by the side of the door, was the huge darkness of Wilenczyk holding the soft slack of the rope's length against the cement column beside the door. Up above, a pulley gave a final settling creak.

The tiniest beam of careful light stabbed from Wilenczyk's shadow. Watçek saw the red glow of cupped fingers around the light. The light wandered around the cement floor. It caught Ruzycky's startled eyes in its beam, a squint and then a nod and a smile. Watçek saw his own boot caught briefly in the searching light and then a girl's knee. The yellow circle travelled down the thigh and took in the roundness of one buttock slightly flattened on the concrete. Water trickled down the thigh and gathered in a small pool with dust particles swirling in it and throwing tiny pinpoints of light. The light moved on to partly disappear in the slim dark crescent at the small of her back. Watçek looked down, seeing seemingly far away in the small pool of light the bright hook of an illuminated hip bone, a grey shadow curving away beyond and an island of white swelling up with the surprising round small void of the navel. The island fluttered. The navel slid into darkness and suddenly Watçek saw again the soft, curling puff of brown sparkling with tiny crystal droplets.

Wilenczyk chuckled and Watçek heard the careful scuffle of his boots dragging in the dust as he crossed the darkness. The beam stayed on the brown tangle, but grew smaller and more intense as Wilenczyk came closer. Watçek thought he could make out some hint of shape beneath the wet brown spirals. A sharp shadow in the flesh beneath disappearing into the deeper darkness between the clamped thighs.

The light travelled slowly up the fluttering swelling of stomach and the navel again came into view, but this time Watçek could see into the gentle funnel and note the filigree of delicate swirls of skin within. The blob of light was disfigured into a limp oval as it crossed the bottom of the ribs and Watçek could see the ribs separating slightly and rapidly as she breathed.

"He earned your schnapps, Wilenczyk," Ruzycky said as the light slid and bumped over the ribs. A white mound suddenly quivered, startled in the beam. "She must've been a new arrival, see, because they're not scrawny."

Watçek looked down on the strange thing centered in the light. A dark small circle with an upstanding tiny fingertip of pink-tinged tan. The oval circle itself seemed to breathe, lengthening and filling as the creamy stuff it floated on surged quickly beneath it. It took some moments for Watçek to realize that he was looking at her nipple and breast moving in response to the concertina breathing of her chest.

Intruding into the light, Watçek saw the cracked and oil-ringed nail on Wilenczyk's forefinger. It sank gently into the cream and pushed back and forth. Watçek saw the brown oval swirl in the light and the fingertip pinkness bob and bow.

There was a rasping expulsion of breath that caused the creamy mound with its small oval island to swirl heavily and come to a shuddering stop, bulging for a moment over the downward curving of her ribs. Then the mound flowed back up to its domed shape. It did not move for some moments, but then it slowly began quivering as the girl started her rapid, shallow breathing again.

Watçek began to hear another sound. It was the moist breathing of Wilenczyk. The finger reached out slowy into the light and pushed into the mound again, teasing it gently into waves. Wilencyzk raised the finger and placed it over the center of the swaying dome and let the little pink fingertip flip back and forth under it as the brown oval gradually ceased spiralling.

Watçek watched spellbound. He'd never before seen the strange soft thing in the pool of light, never known that nakedness and swirling the puffed full thing with a blunt finger could cause skin between the ribs to bunch and stretch so quickly. Never known that merely to play light upon a bare belly and the triangular springy forest below it could cause a girl's stomach to flutter and the navel to dance. Thighs to clamp together in straight, dark shadow. For the first time, Watçek knew the answer to something he'd noticed but never questioned until now. Why they did it. What was under the black dresses and black stockings. Why they wore things that kept it from moving. Why no one talked about it. For if everyone knew, and peeled the black cloth away, why the world might burst. It was not like the preoccupied and quarrelsome fluttering of chickens. Nor was it like the vague thrusting of a bull atop a complacent cow. Both kept chewing. Watçek had avidly noticed this behavior. And he had wondered about people, assuming vaguely that it must be something similar. So ordinary that the black dresses and stockings were natural, so ordinary that the priest's indifference to the subject was unstudied. So ordinary ... but the world might burst. And that was the answer.

It was only then that he heard Ruzycky's laughter. It came from far away and he saw only blackness where he'd been looking. Could he have passed out? No, he was still standing. He felt the pins and needles in his feet, encased and distant in the heaviness of his boots. He looked down and saw the worn flannel of his trousers pyramiding out from the swollen pleats. He saw the stretched gaps as harsh shadows between the buttons. Wilenczyk's light centered on the rounded peak of the cloth and the thin fiery rainbow ring around the edge of the light threatened to burn through the flannel like acid and expose him. Ruzycky's laughter came through to him clearly and the pounding in Watçek's chest told him he'd been holding his breath. The world might burst.

"Ah. He's breathing again, Wilenczyk. He'll live," laughed Ruzycky. "I was wondering whether his eyes would pop out first or something else."

Wilenczyk grunted, and shifted the circle of light up Watçek until he rested on his shirt below the point of his chin.

"Never seen one before," said Ruzycky. "I thought not."

Watçek took a deep breath. "What?"

Ruzycky chuckled. "A tit."

"Sure I have ..." Watçek began. Then, defiantly. "No."

How could he have? Thirteen in 1939. Soon after Confirmation. Then three years of fear, in his own eyes and in the downcast ones of girls hurrying through the streets to put the thickness of a door between themselves and the hostile evening streets. The freedom of the rusted, wheezing Skoda, working on it and making it run with Ruzycky, had erased the fear. Slightly. The trips from the factory.

"No," Watçek repeated.

But the curiosity of his own nimble brain, and his longing once the Skoda had begun to run, had conceived the plan. Even if blonde-assured Ruzycky had had to face the guards. Even if it depended upon fat old Wilenczyk.

"What about it, Wilenczyk?" he heard Ruzycky say in the darkness. "Give the kid a break."

"We agreed," Wilenczyk's heavy voice. "We agreed."

"Sure. I know," said Ruzycky's voice. "But that was only because of the long shot we'd get a virgin. It's the blood, Wilenczyk, after all these years."

"She might be . . . unmarried . . ." Watçek realized that the word 'virgin' had too many meanings. Wilenczyk's voice rolled wetly into the darkness.

"There are other ways to find out." It was Ruzycky.

"All right." The circle of light shifted on Watçek's shirt and he knew that both Ruzycky and Wilenczyk were looking up at him. "But I don't trust you, Ruzycky."

"Then you do it."

The beam jiggled away, burying Watçek gratefully in the darkness. He saw the circle of light snake away across the cement floor and climb over a flaring, flattened flank in its pool of water. And disappear. Suddenly, the faces of Wilenczyk and Ruzycky glowed wierdly. A darkness rose between Watçek and the bare beam, and it seemed to him that the darkness rocked from side to side, sometimes making Ruzycky's face glow more, sometimes Wilenczyk's. Watçek then heard the slap of a hand on wet flesh. Again. And again

Suddenly, the darkness between Watçek and the light cleaved deeply and he briefly glimpsed a swaying, wet thigh in the spill of light before the shadows snapped shut, erasing the quiver of white. Wilenczyk's glowing face leered downward and his shoulder bunched rhythmically. Straining to make sense of the patterns of light and darkness, Watçek finally realized that the rising mound of darkness had been the girl's legs being drawn up defensively, that they had spread surrendering to the slaps and had closed again. Wilenczyk's fat shoulder undulated in the glow and Ruzycky looked down wistfully, quickly flicking his tongue over his lower lip. Presently, Watçek heard a wet, sucking sound.

51

Watçek looked between white, hanging thighs where Wilenczyk's hand scuttled like a burrowing crab. Between the ribs and the grasping fingers of Wilenczyk and Ruzycky that held her down, thick cream oozed and bulged as Wilenzyk's other delving hand produced plopping sounds somewhere within the droplet-sparkled soft shadow between the hanging thighs. Watçek's eyes strained to see, fascinated, looking into the shadow where Wilenczyk's hand worked. His middle-finger had seemingly disappeared somewhere into the shadows. It made the slurps. Wilenczyk's forefinger crooked nearby and the tip of it searched in her crevices like a hopeful stubby worm.

"My God, Wilenczyk, your hand will come out her throat," said Ruzycky, after a moment.

Wilenczyk grunted.

"Are you quite satisfied?"

"Just a little ridge. Not enough for . . . for . . ."

"Blood?" asked Ruzycky.

"No."

Watçek saw Wilenczyk jerk his hand out from between the thighs. Ruzycky held the light higher and Watçek saw the girl's knees draw up again. They closed. And began to rock back and forth slowly. Wilenczyk examined his hand. It glistened.

"No," he repeated.

"Well, then?" asked Ruzycky, "What about it . . . ?"

"Alright," said Wilenczyk. "He can go first . . ."

"Hear that, Cyril? Good old Wilenczyk."

Watçek felt himself nodding.

"The boy's useless," Watçek heard Ruzycky saying. "Let's take her into the room, Wilenczyk."

Watçek then saw bobbings of light in the darkness and heard the metallic clinking of chains in cement, receding from him, and the stumbling slaps of her feet on the floor.

A few minutes later they came back to him. Wilenczyk remembered to flick on the light outside, searching for the switch with blinding zig-zags of the flashlight. A pattern of diamonds materialized on the floor and Watçek realized that it was the wires in the glass panes of the loading door. Dimly, Watçek could see machine shapes marching away into the darkness.

Wilenczyk pushed the flashlight into Watçek's hands. "Don't take all night."

Watçek stumbled off into the darkness, bracing himself cautiously against hard steel shapes which rose up in front of him suddenly. At last he made out the tall black rectangle of the coal room doorway and the shadow of the open door beside it. He closed the door behind him and it shut with a scrape and a dull boom.

In order to save the batteries of the flashlight, Watçek walked quickly to the corner of the small room, striking a match to light the candle they had placed on the floor. The yellow glow flickered and seeped throughout the room.

Her shift had fallen down when Ruzycky and Wilenczyk had walked her here. The shadows of the leg chains drooped down the wall and angled out onto the floor. The spotted mattress on the ruined bed dipped toward the floor. She lay on her back with her head turned to the wall. Watçek wished that they had left her as she had been on the cement near the loading door, with her shift pulled up above her breasts.

It took Watçek several minutes to take hold of the cloth where it hung damply in the valley of clamped thighs. He tried to work it upwards, but her weight on the springs and mattress held it down. He pulled and heard cloth tearing, and the brown ripping revealed a growing triangle of white. The cloth parted at the neck and Watçek flung the two halves of it aside. Slowly, she drew one thigh up over the other and the chains clinked against the metal frame of the bed. Watçek looked down and saw her arms slowly crossing across her chest. The mounds squeezed from clutched fingers. Watçek unpeeled them and raised them above her head, shoving her hands between the metal frame of the bed and the mattress.

Watçek saw that she left them there and merely buried her head toward the wall into the molded mattress. As Wilenczyk had done, Watçek poked a forefinger into a mound. He waggled his finger in the surrounding softness. Then he let the nipple brush against his finger, just as Wilenczyk had done. The softness was a marvel. Climbing onto the bed and sprawling across her, Watçek poked with both hands at once, alternately and then together. The ovals whirled before his eyes and their little fingertips flipped and bobbed on the waves of cream.

Watçek experimented. He began the poking over and over again. But sometimes he would intercept the little spiralling fingertips and roll them between his thumb and forefinger as his sudden pulling made the mounds shudder to a halt . . .

Presently, Watçek began to wonder how Wilenczyk had managed to make the sucking sounds in her. It had something to do with the springy brown shadow clamped between the thighs.

His fingers clawed downward, but the crossed thighs allowed him no more than a fingertip dip into the moist furrow. Watçek remembered what had been done on the cement floor.

He hardly heard the slaps because he was watching the flesh whipped into crests with the little ovals and fingertips always flinging upwards and never submerged in the waves. He felt urgent pressure against him.

Her knee almost shoved Watçek from the bed. He looked down and was reminded of the pale underside of a frog he'd seen in a roadway. The legs had been opened in the same wide diamond, feet together. Knees wide. The same tendons pulling from the groin. But there had been no rocking triangle of soft hair. His fingertips entered the fuzz of the springy forest and plowed into it. Watçek wiggled his fingers. Some encountered only tendrils of hair, but his longest finger fell into the furrow. The furrow became deeper and moister as he slithered his finger downward. Until it sank inside. Surprised, Watçek jerked out and there came a soft sort of plop. Then he ran the finger in deeper and felt the warmth surround it. He straightened his finger suddenly, flinging it out, and it made the wet, sucking sound that Wilenczyk had made. The lips surrounded his finger again. He pushed in further.

"My god, Wilenczyk, your hand will come out her throat!"

Just a little ridge. Not enough for . . . for . . .

It must have been the thing that made virgins virgins, Watçek thought. That made them bleed. But didn't all women bleed? From time to time? Watçek thought so. He felt the ridge that Wilenczyk must have talked about. That made the jokes? The sweating desire? It was just left-over skin, Watçek realized, that made this ridge. From what Wilenczyk had said, Watçek imagined that somehow this skin had once partly sealed her. Wilenczyk had wanted to rip it, but someone had already done so.

The man who had struggled in the compound . . . ?

"Sarah? Bela?" Watçek whispered.

Then he saw the girl's mouth open and close, gulping air, and the throat swallowing to keep any sound of sobs from escaping. Her head flung from side to side with the effort and Watçek saw tears skittering over the cheeks.

"Sarah . . . ? Bela . . . ?"

With the sound of the names, she rocked her hips and tried to wriggle higher up on the bed to outrun Watçek's finger and hand between her legs, but the motion served only to slip them deeper. Watçek felt a sudden seeping of warmth and moisture. Her movements made the heavy white breasts sway and the nipples swirled on their own. Watçek knew suddenly where the swelling in the flannel fitted. He'd never been able to tell amid the fluttering of the chickens, but it was obvious enough with the bulls and the cows. Except that people could do it this way, the way they were lying. Facing each other. Watçek had always wondered.

He fumbled at a button in the flannel and helped it to find its way out. His other hand, already knowing the way, opened the lips of her cleft. Warmth surged past the spreading fingers. When the head of it touched into the opening, Watçek shoved. It hit the ridge and her hips tried to stutter away. Watçek shoved harder and it squeezed past the ridge.

When that happened her elbows flashed down for an instant over the breasts and her legs drew up involuntarily. Her elbows rose away from the mounds and pointed upward into the air on either side of the flinging head. Watçek saw that her hands were grasping the angle-iron of the bed frame which pressed into the bulging mattress. Her fingers squeezed under the frame, burrowing into the mattress. As the hands gripped there, Watçek wondered if she would at last try to fight. But the hands merely gripped white as her hips continued to stutter and squirm and he decided that she needed the clutching to help her get through what he was doing.

And anyway, with her elbows pointed high like that and the arms locked, somehow her breasts had become softer. The cream flowed more freely over the ribs as her hips worked. Watçek gripped the mattress on either side of her with his hands, cradled on her with the quivering pressure of her raised thighs against his hips. Watçek mouthed the nipples as they moved beneath his lips. He closed his eyes, resting his head on the flowing pillows of white. Gripping the mattress, he shoved further. Relaxed. And shoved again.

Her hips rose from the mattress and he felt the muscles and tendons in the thighs that clamped his hips. But she could go nowhere and the movement only made him sink deeper.

"Sarah . . . Sarah. Bela . . . Bela . . ."

Presently, Watçek knew that the world was going to burst. He shoved.

"Sarah . . . Sarah. Bela . . . Bela . . ."

Watçek felt her legs give one strong push down into the mattress, the hips held him up and her breast surged beneath his cheek. It was hot and stretched. Watçek felt it spew then and he spilled into her. He dimly heard a crack as her chest rose beneath him. Then, as it was still pumping, Watçek's cradle collapsed.

It took a few moments for Watçek to realize that there was no throbbing in the chest beneath him. No squeezing in the warmth and wetness around it still pulsing. There was no pressure from her thighs.

Watçek's eyes fluttered open. He looked up and saw the underside of her chin beyond the bed frame, the thin edge of the angle-iron crushing into the throat with the bulging mattress pressing the neck up from below. Then he remembered that her back had arched at an impossible angle just before he'd spewed. And collapsed limply.

The truth stabbed into Watçek's stomach and he felt it shrivel, sneaking backward from the warmth and wetness.

Rolling off the bed and standing to fumble it back into the flannel, Watçek looked down. The thighs spread slackly and the creamy mounds swelled over the ribs. But there was no quiver anywhere. Nothing.

Watson ground his knees into the stone. Round and round. Back and forth.

How many more? How many more? The wind sighed it.

None! None! I swear it!

3

Koffler leaned back in the cloth-upholstered chair, swung his legs up onto the edge of the bed and wiggled his toes. The toes had hardly ever felt more comfortable and Koffler was inclined to attribute this to the quality of his hand-sewn Gucci loafers. Settled, he reached again for the tumbler of ice and crystal-clear liquid on the motel desk nearby. The tumbler left a ring in the cheap veneer and Koffler, being a meticulous man, always replaced it in the same place after each sip. He lifted the tumbler carefully upward, so as not to enlarge the ring.

He took a deep appreciative sip, and another, and replaced the tumbler on its wet ring. He held the vodka on the back of his tongue, and let it slowly trickle down his throat. Its fumes wafted up through his nose, clearing his sinuses.

"Not bad. Not bad." He said.

Igor Tchevsky regarded Koffler sadly. "My friend, with all the vodka available in this decadent capitalistic world," he asked, "why is it that you must buy the cheapest sort from Alberta?"

Koffler shrugged. "It isn't bad at all, Tchevsky. Perhaps no worse than your Prince Igor. Personally, I'm inclined to think that you merely enjoy a reactionary fantasy based upon a coincidental similarity with the names."

Tchevsky smiled. "Irving, you are not the first to have noted that. The military attaché in Washington on my first North American assignment, he teased me about it too. Long ago." Tchevsky swirled the tumbler in his hand and the ice tinkled in a friendly manner as he gazed down fondly at the decanter-like bottle on the dresser. The label glowed with luxurious reds and golds and raised intaglios of precious metal. A whisper of Tzardom, a hint of crusted Fabergé treasures. And not only that, but the colorless contents too, for less than ten bucks Canadian.

"Yes," Tchevsky admitted with a friendly smile at Koffler, "it was the name, I suppose, that started me buying it whenever I came to the West. Later, I noticed the ads in magazines. They confirmed the habit." Tchevsky's imagination had been captivated by the tall, dark prince. The slashing ribbons and the gaudy decorations and the rich furnishings in the background of the photograph. There had been the aristocratic wisp of the woman in the champagne silk, too, lounging against the grand piano.

Madame Tchevsky also played, and well, but she sat on the bench like a huge dumpling. Igor sighed, conjuring up the image of the monocle in the Prince's eye, and deciding that the advertising agency had probably gone too far there. But Tchevsky appreciated their problem. Tradition was foreign to Americans, if longed-for, and the more foreign-looking the better. Nothing looked more foreign in a land of soft contacts and lineless bifocals than the ridiculous uncompromising harshness of one orphan lens.

Koffler wriggled his toes.

"I thought he'd run yelling and tearing his hair," Tchevsky said.

"Yes," Koffler said, "At first I thought he hadn't seen me at all. With all the people coming down the steps I assumed he was distracted. But just before he got into the car. Then he looked up at me. I knew he knew . . . and remembered."

Koffler saw the silver-topped head, and its distorted reflection, staring across the glossy black roof of the gently rocking Lincoln. Koffler had simply stood, and stared. Watson's eyes had widened and he flicked the fingers through the hair before his head had disappeared below the obsidian metal. As the long car moved off, Koffler had remained standing, waiting for the inevitable nervous glance to be flung back through the tinted rear window. Koffler, and Tchevsky, had not been disappointed.

The face framed in the window had completed the small pieces. Tchevsky and Koffler had been assured of it before, of course, but the confirmation in Watson's widened eyes was a natural relief. Snatches of refugee stories, brief scrawled notes in Polish Resistance files, no more than hints and some names among the thousands of yearning secrets in Weisenthal's ill-guarded Vienna filing cabinets and boxes . . . Koffler's own long tragedy . . . they were all tiny bits of an intricate puzzle that came together in Watson's eyes, complete.

Koffler shook his head in admiration for those painstaking experts who had pieced it together. "It is truly amazing, Tchevsky. Such a small story."

Igor Tchevsky smiled. Koffler was a junior who'd been chosen because of his physical resemblance, mannerisms. Tchevsky could understand Koffler's awe. It was truly fascinating to watch the work of those dull little clerk analysts.

Tchevsky nodded. "I've always thought it was the chess, myself," said Tchevsky. "They're most always chess experts, for some reason. Very dull in other ways. But their heads are always full of patterns and combinations. You'd be surprised how often they can come up with something."

Koffler nodded. "But such a small story. You'd think it would have been buried."

It had been. In the crawling back alleys of a few minds. Tchevsky had opened some of the minds, and had slithered along the crooked roadways of memory to where some secrets lurked in dark doorways. A few of Wilenczyk's doors opened onto rooms so dank and fly-spotted that Tchevsky had been happy to hear him die. And Ruzycky. Tchevsky wondered briefly how many other horrors lingered coiled in Central European brains and undulated beneath Poland's rolling countryside. Small stories, contained silently in tiny stifling rooms moldy with eternities of fearful sweat where echoes of unheard pleadings and struggles and screams still clung to damp walls.

"It is a big story, now. It grew," Tchevsky sighed wearily.

"Tomorrow's the meeting in that hotel?"

"The Royal York," said Tchevsky.

"We'll need to get there early, again, just in case. I'll turn in." Koffler wriggled his toes, thankful for the Gucci's. He'd be doing a lot of standing around during the next few days, waiting for Watson to pass. The east wind today had been cool, in spite of the hot sun, and standing in the wind so long waiting in front of the church had made Koffler's sinuses act up. Without the comfortable Gucci's his legs would have ached, too. Koffler drained the last of the vodka and carefully replaced the tumbler.

Tchevsky winced, imagining the liquor going down, and grasped the voluptuous bottle of Prince Igor, leaving the empty tumbler on Koffler's dresser. Tchevsky walked to the door.

"Yes, you're right. We've got some full days. Good night, Koffler."

Koffler nodded as the door clicked shut. He looked across the bed and the room to where strobe lights carved the sky in paths through the thin curtains. He swung his legs down, wearily raised himself, and walked sock-feet to the door. He locked it and flicked off the light.

In the darkness of his room he could see the bright white patterns more clearly through the curtains. He walked over to the expanse of glass and looked down onto the crawling headlights on the expressways below. Some headlights outpaced other visibly and Koffler reflected that Canadians were even more reckless drivers than Russians. Where were the police on the highways? What was this toothless threat of radar-enforced speed limits?

Koffler glanced up and out, seeing the sparkling white cake of Toronto Airport's terminal buildings and counting the winking, circling strobe lights in the air. The distant howl of a jet came to him, muted, through the double-paned glass. He searched around the terminal buildings, but could not make out the aircraft that was catapulting toward the end of some runway. Finally he saw flashing white and red lights lifting impossibly slowly from the blackness he assumed was the ground. They drifted up and then Koffler saw the tiny silhouette, like a far-away hawk soaring into the afterglow of the sunset. Heading west. But its spread tail-feathers winked red, and wing-tips blinked white, like no natural bird. From its size, Koffler imagined it to be a big 747 on a long-distance flight. Perhaps an Air Canada to Vancouver, or maybe heading even further into the West until it became East.

4

Walking up the hill, Dumas glanced over his shoulder in a dutiful attempt to read the O'Keefe Centre's marquee to his right. But it angled toward him and the letters blurred. He side-stepped a few paces east on Front Street in order to get a better view.

Augustyn and Kain. La Fille Mal Gardée. Rachael would like to see that. She'd watched the ballet recently on *Radagast's* small portable television and Dumas had perceived that the scale of the presentation had dulled her enjoyment. He peered through the glass doors into the lobby, taking a few tentative steps, but saw no figures at the box office. Too early. Maybe he could pick up tickets at lunch.

Dumas walked back to the corner of Yonge and Front and waited for the light to change, idly watching the passage of multi-colored traffic. A block away to his left, the Royal Bank Tower blared its rich gold bulk high into the blue sky where its angular serrated facade ended in a saw-toothed silhouette threatening puffy passing clouds. Dumas' eyes slid up and down the ridges of gold-tinted glass. Somehow the early sun made all its edges gleam more brightly on Monday mornings. Perhaps the resumption of commerce awakened it, twinged its appetite, after the brief famine of weekends. Dumas noticed the stream of workers and businessmen trickling toward the building to feed it.

To the south lay the harbour—no longer a work-day waterfront. With the downtown building spree, even the wharfs had gone trendy. The Hilton's Harbour Castle Inn squatted over the once-functional docks and its carpeted bulk prevented impatient ferry toots from intruding into the maturing city. The tall luxury towers of Harbour Square housed beautiful people where, once, rusty freighters had surrendered their burdens to sweating stevedores and oil-streaked forklifts. Presiding over the city's new look was yet another tower almost at water's edge with an address that claimed the very essence of Toronto. One Yonge Street. Home of the Toronto Star, whose eager reporters filled the newspaper's pages with chronicles of increasing crime, soaring inflation, rising unemployment, heights of governmental corruption and crescendos of environmental tragedy. Toronto had come of age.

Radagast, Dumas decided, had become a two-edged sword. Needing to work in the city, but wanting *Radagast* for a home, he had managed to wheedle a berth in one of the yacht clubs on Toronto Island. The logo he had created for the marina, plus the brochure and imaginative booth he'd designed for the Canadian National Exhibition Boat Show had all contributed to the magical discovery of space for *Radagast* amid a forest of other masts, within the costly montage of pastel glass, polished brass and winking chrome. Dumas had contrived paradise as he had imagined it for years. Boat living in a city he still needed.

Paradise extracted costs and complications.

Rachael's job meant day-care for Becky. That meant that Rachael took the car. That meant sheltered parking near the ferry docks within the bowels of Harbour Square, for the Abarth's highly strung engine seemed reluctant to start at the best of times and Rachael required a heated garage to coax it to life in the winter. Rachael's taking the car meant that Dumas walked from the garage, where he kissed Rachael and Becky good-bye every morning, up Yonge Street to his office.

And that, in turn, gave Dumas ample opportunity to dwell upon the growing city and to peer curiously at the doughnut on the spire of the CN Tower, the tinted glass of the office towers' facades.

There seemed to be a secret he could not fathom within the revolving restaurant and beyond the tiers of windows. With all the unemployment and economic problems, who could afford the expensive suites? Who worked upon their deep carpeting? With luxury apartments claiming the docks, where could real wealth be loaded? Unloaded? With everyone striving to be an executive and to work within those stylish towers, live within them, where were the producers of all those things that must be accounted, contracted for and promoted? Where were the fishermen? Loggers? Miners?

Maybe, Dumas decided, there was no secret. Maybe the gold, silver and black-tinted glazing of the skyscrapers amounted to no more than the ultimate form of castle-building. Huge ethereal clouds floated past in the reflections from the glass, moving from the west now that yesterday's wind had backed to its normal quarter, heading in the general direction of Ottawa where a plummeting dollar poked holes in cotton candy economic policy and the national debt swelled by millions every day.

In his daily walk from the foot of Yonge Street, Dumas pondered this. His enforced stop beside the O'Keefe Centre gave him his only respite, reading names on the marquee, thankful that people like Kain and Augustyn still offered grace to a world of gaudy reflections and harsh shadows.

Generally, by the time Dumas reached his small office building on Yonge north of Wellington he was in no good humor. He pulled open the brass door and walked gloomily along the worn red carpet.

"Good morning, Mister Dumas." Gladys pronounced the final "s." "Isn't it just a perfect day?"

She was waiting beside her elevator with its old-fashioned sliding grille, a youthful sixty, Dumas guessed, with pert red pageboy hair framing a gamin face. She wasn't often waiting. Usually, Dumas had to ring the buzzer and wait. Sometimes he gave up and used the spiralling stairs because the elevator was slow and if Gladys was having tea it didn't come at all.

"I guess it is at that, Glad. You're good for the soul."

"And don't you look tanned and fit? My, my."

Dumas grinned. Gladys made him feel like the self-indulgent brat he was quickly becoming. The heavy grille slid across the doorway under the pressure of Gladys' slim arm, its brass bars changing to diamonds. "Gladys? How old are you?"

"Oh, Mister Dumas . . . I'll never tell." Bright brown eyes twinkled back at him over an elfin shoulder.

"Sorry," Dumas said sincerely. "It's just that you're so young you make me feel like ninety."

"Nonsense, Mister Dumas. How's that pretty Rachael? Is Becky going to school next year?"

"Year after. Rachael's just fine."

The elevator jerked to a stop on the fourth and highest floor. Gladys was sometimes casual with her driving. "Watch your step, Mister Dumas," she said. Dumas nodded and stepped up the six-inch difference between the elevator's floor and the fourth.

"Thanks, Gladys," Dumas said as he said every morning.

"You know what you need, Mister Dumas?"

Dumas hesitated and turned back. Gladys leaned thoughtfully against her grille, keeping it open. "What's that, Glad?"

She looked him up and down with the judgement of a long-experienced eye. "Too much routine, Mister Dumas. It makes some men start to feel old. You're getting fidgety and cranky, like an old bored woman."

Dumas laughed.

"I mean it, Mister Dumas. Remember—I've seen you come and go with quick step and hardly any time to spare a 'hello' to an old woman like me. That's when you're yourself."

"Maybe you're right, Glad."

"Sure I am. You need something exciting." Gladys nodded emphatically, as if sharing a secret with him. She stepped back and the grille slid across. Dumas heard the old elevator clank into gear and saw the cage lurch downward.

There had been some hurried comings and goings during the Steinberg business. On the other hand, exciting things could sometimes prove dangerous. Still, Dumas recalled that he'd had no time to feel stale.

Walking a few steps from the elevator, Dumas grasped a polished brass knob set into a walnut door. The latch clicked with the well-oiled snick of metal and the door opened. Such was the solidity of the door and the depth of carpeting inside that only then did the irregular tapping of Debbie's typewriter reach him.

Because of Gladys' gentle lecture, perhaps, Dumas felt himself smiling as he'd once done every time he entered the office. At the small but profound sea of royal blue carpet that extended to all baseboards of their modest suite of rooms. At the geometric inlays of Debbie's massive desk. At the Hogarth prints on the walls. At the low fruitwood cabinets with matching geometric inlays. At the fact that except for the unavoidable modern necessities of typewriter and telephone, not one technological office contrivance could be seen. A square photocopier squatted efficiently in the suite near Debbie, but it did its reproducing behind the stolid modesty of an oiled walnut partition. One intruder from the present century betrayed its presence by cheerful tinkling and humming, although actual sight of it was hidden by a discreet billowing blue curtain in a corner window. Debbie's persistence had triumphed, thankfully, and coolness enveloped Dumas. He sighed happily—the radio during breakfast had mentioned a high of almost thirty Celsius. The air-conditioner actually defeated hot sticky summers while for years Peter's window fan had deluded itself by merely roaring defiance at them.

Dumas clicked the door shut. Debbie's tapping ceased as he ambled over to her desk.

"Good morning, Mister Dumas. You look 'orribly, 'orribly fit. Where to this weekend?"

"Just down to Kingston. You're the second woman to tell me how fit I look this morning."

"I shouldn't wonder, Adrian. All bronzed and weathered."

Dumas grinned. "Keep it up . . . Any messages, luv?"

Debbie shook her head. "Nil," she said with emphasis, drawing the word out with a pink tongue arched attractively up to sparkling teeth.

"Pete in yet?" Dumas swivelled around to peer into his partner's office through a walnut-rimmed doorway. He saw the empty leather chair pushed hard into the edge of Peter Tompkins' too-clear desk.

"Mister Tompkins had that early meeting. Remember? At the Royal York?"

"Yeah, Debbie. Thanks. I forgot."

"All is quiet, Bronzed Sir . . . for a change," she added.

"What's this thing at the Royal York? Pete tell you . . . ?"

"A great bloody client was wot he said," said Debbie. "Peter seemed veddy happy about it." She paused. "He needed the lift, Adrian. After all your stuff coming in," she said seriously.

Dumas nodded.

"Took me arm in arm, he did, up to Harvey Wallbanger's and plied me with gins and tonic until Marc rescued me. Then I rescued Marc. I haven't seen Mister Tompkins so happy in weeks."

"Speaking of Marc . . ."

"Oh, yes, Adrian. We're coming."

"Great." Dumas began to turn away, then stopped. "And, Debbie, luv. Please, please try to convince Marc not to wear white ducks and a blue blazer . . . I'd never live it down. Jeans will do nicely."

"My Marc *can* appear a bit snooty, cahn't he?"

"I didn't say that," said Dumas. "Let's just say he can be—well—awfully, awfully proper in public."

"Thank Gawd he isn't in private, eh?" Debbie's brief dimpling smile was erased by the purring of the phone.

"Hmmm." Dumas jangled keys from his pocket and walked to confront the solid door of his office. Peter left his door always frankly, innocently, hopefully ajar, but Dumas never did. This had posed problems with the air-conditioner. Greedy for coolness, yet unwilling to yield privacy, Dumas had opted for the removal of his particular panes of pebbled glass, which topped all the suite's partitions between the inevitable walnut and the ceiling. Dumas had done this on a weekend, with some stealth but only a twinge of remorse, presenting Peter with a *fait accompli* the following Monday. Peter had accepted the destruction of the suite's symmetry with an upper lip that remained stiffer than usual for a few days.

> *Promoter: of persons, products, establishments and concepts. Well-versed in the arts of communication, marketing, design and sales. Resume, references available on request. Contracts confidential.*

There was a phone number, an undistinguished address considering the newly-risen towers soaring all around, and the cable-code "Hardradha."

It was the reverse of one of his business cards in a brass frame on the door at eye-level and Dumas read it with satisfaction as he turned the key in the lock. The front of his cards read simply "Dumas" in heavy Bodoni bold on a simulated beaten-gold metallic foil paper. Dumas enjoyed the pretension of his cards and the slight antagonism they sometimes produced.

"Mister Dumas?"

Dumas turned in the open doorway to see Debbie holding the phone away from her ear and punching a call onto hold. "It's Mister Tompkins on one."

"Okay," said Dumas. "I'll take it in here."

He closed the door and picked up the receiver, stretching the springy cord as he edged around his desk. "Morning, Pete. What's up?" he said, dropping into his old leather chair.

Dumas cradled his head in its accustomed place against the fat spine of the massive green lexicon and let his eyes wander vaguely over voluptuous reflections on the brass samovar across the room. "Yeah, that's what Debbie said just now. A big one. Congratulations."

He extended his hand to pull the curtain ropes and thought better of it, not relishing the sight of the bare rusted fire escape outside his window. "Hell, Pete, sure. If you want it. Be glad to talk about it."

He looked up on the wall beside his desk and grimaced at

the neat cardboard chart—a flow chart, Rachael had termed it—illustrating the creative march toward completion of various projects. More crap: Dove mufflers for McClintock and Premier Parts. Another marina flyer and some ads. Surprisingly, more radio commercials Steinberg had ordered for the cleaners. Must be doing well. . . .

"Lunch? Sure, Pete. Give us time to chat."

Cigarette billboards to be tested on the goddamn machine . . . why had he invented it? Graphics and research for the television show . . . what was it this month? Dinosaurs and birds . . . right. And the point-of-purchase stuff, Lovable's ivory collection.

"Dick Turpin's sounds fine by me," said Dumas. "Twelve-thirty? One?" Another test . . . some ads for a gritty soap for teen-age girls. "Great, Pete. I'll be there."

Dumas replaced the receiver, still regarding the chart ruefully. Good solid bread and butter stuff, all of it. No problems. No challenge. After three or four years he was doing McClintock's ads in his sleep. The ads for the ivory would be a problem . . . for the client. Why did they all like short copy for point-of-purchase? Ivory was romance. Hatshepset sailing for Punt, Senmut sailing for Punt, Hiram and Jehosaphat sailing for Ophir. Ivory . . . so exotic and desired that intrepid Senmut sailed for three years to get some and bring it back to his Queen and probably lover, the beautiful Hatshepset. Deep into the heart of Africa at the dawn of time to Punt where ivory was. Senmut had it fashioned into delicate brassieres to caress and support the bosom of Egypt's mightiest Queen . . . and the most beautiful, save for incomparable Nefertiti. Tell *that* story and any woman who read it at a jewellery counter couldn't leave without one of Lovable's cheap floral trinkets. He could substitute Nefertiti's famous head for Hatshepset's in the photograph. Hell, who would know the difference?

The machine had added a new dimension. Perception Approximation Analog, Dumas called it. Maybe he should think up something snappier . . . Environment Reproduction Analog? ERA. No, people could confuse the anagram with Equal Rights Amendment. Probably would.

Dumas had toyed with his machine for a number of years. People got in the box, wore a helmet attached to a long pointer at the back. They looked at a screen. When they turned their heads to focus on what they saw on the screen, the pointer waggled around and a little motor-driven pencil on the end of the pointer made dots on a piece of paper. By studying this paper appropriately, it was possible to discover what they'd looked at most carefully, looked at longer. Or rather, what they focused on, directly in front of their noses, with the image of the screen falling precisely into the *fovea centralis* of each retina simultaneously. With color acuity concentrated in the *fovea*, and with vision cells crowded together there . . . well, the pointer should indicate what they'd see best and remember longest. This had application for advertising. It might be nice to know what people actually looked at in an advertisement. Did men remember the busy girl, but not the car or the brand-name of the booze? Did women remember the girl's hair-do, but not the panty-hose or the brand of television dinner?

Lately, Dumas had been thinking about adding something to the machine. Why not a lie-detector galvanic-skin response thing? To tell what people got excited about when they saw an ad? Or a brain-wave monitor? Then, instead of a little reciprocating pencil making dots . . . why not have a flashing light on the end of the pointer? The light could fall onto photocells . . . 2N5777 photo-sensitive diodes should do nicely . . . and when the light stimulated the photocells little counters would activate. Save the time of counting dots. No vibration. Not so primitive as the little pencil making dots. But no better. Still, in the advertising business, appearance, not reality, was very nearly the only consideration. Whether it was any better or not, well, the flashing lights and the automatic counters would *seem* more scientific. And if it had a sexy console? With maybe a uniformed girl to operate it? Or what about lab coats? Better yet.

Dumas opened an untidy bottom drawer of the desk and rooted around for catalogs. He chuckled. 2N5777 transistors went for seventy-seven cents each. Now counters. 6VDC counters for twenty-five bucks apiece. Six volts? He could run the whole machine off batteries. And make it portable. Dumas had brief, wealthy visions of a van parked in shopping center parking lots. Testing ads with a better profit margin. Crowds of ordinary customers willing to be tested for free, because it was fun, because it was something new in the plaza.

He rummaged for a pencil in the center drawer and came up with a sharp one and a pad of paper, drew circuit schematics for a few minutes, tabulated costs. He sat back grinning.

Not that the Perception Approximation Analog didn't make money now. There was a steady, growing trickle of customers. But Dumas had never thought about making it commercial in the strictly exploitative sense. It had, after all, once lurked in the basement of the Don Mills house along with rat mazes and aquaria, used only for Dumas' personal investigations into rather esoteric aspects of behavioral psychology.

But with the completion of *Radagast,* much in the basement had had to be jettisoned. The rats, their mazes and the fish and their aquaria had been accepted by a university psychology department. The machine had posed more difficult disposal problems. An advertising acquaintance, Sam Jones, visiting for dinner one night, awakened Dumas to the commercial potential of the machine. Together, he and Dumas had found a home for Perception Approximation Analog in a small warehouse. Together, they had hammered out a contract covering its use. Dumas had created a brochure describing the machine and its functions. Its advantages for effective advertising creativity. Jones, thus armed with brochure and usage of the machine, had begun to solicit business. The results had been surprising.

Dumas' contractual responsibilities included designing the tests and doing the statistical analysis of the data produced inexorably by the little dot-making pointer. Well, not quite inexorably. Dumas had not built Perception Approximation Analog with commercial volume in mind. And certainly not the type of volume that the acquaintance was selling. Another of Dumas' contractual obligations entailed keeping the machine in working order. This was proving to be a chore. With one test following another with increasing frequency, Dumas found himself repairing Perception Approximation Analog more often than he liked.

He examined the flow chart balefully. He would have to improve the machine in self-defense. Yes. It could be made almost completely automatic. The wheels and shafts of the dot-making pencil could be replaced by a flashing light. Even Sam Jones could change a light bulb and read the totals on simple counters, and therefore could "analyse" the data himself.

Dumas double-checked the circuit schematic. He shrugged. There didn't seem to be anything wrong with it. It should work. Why not? He would do it this week. Dumas made a few quick phone calls to check on the availability of components. Cursed moderately from time to time. Checked in catalogs from time to time to read the specifications of substitutes, made more calls and finally sat back about mid-morning with a smile.

Before he glanced up at the flow chart again, he phoned out to Debbie. "What's the chance of getting a cup of coffee?" he asked. Informed that the odds were favorable and that the mail had come in, Dumas summoned the courage to look up at the chart. He brightened. Ivory.

Dumas rose, stretched the small of his back, and turned to the bookcase behind him. He pushed the back of the chair away from the Lexicon so that he could peer closely into the shelves. They ranged from floor to ceiling and the width of the wall. The top rows roughly categorized into psychology, biology and zoology. Lower down came sailing, sea stories and aspects of piloting and navigation. Then well-thumbed erotica and history. On the bottom shelves was an assortment of books on driving technique and mostly unopened tomes on advertising and marketing. Dumas looked at these sadly and considered putting them somewhere where clients could see them.

As with the flow chart, Rachael had offered to catalog Dumas' shelves, to organize him, in much the same manner as she administered the volumes in the university library. Dumas had declined politely since he not only remembered all the books, but also most of the words in them. Occasionally, a paragraph or two grew dim in the memory and required another scan, but not often. Dumas searched one such hazy paragraph now and grasped Paul Hermann's *Conquest By Man*.

Had Senmut been Hatshepset's chancellor and lover, or admiral and lover?

Dumas' door clicked open. "Here you are, Mister Dumas."

"Hmmm." Turning to lower himself into the chair, Dumas watched Debbie carefully balancing a mug of coffee in one hand and squeezing a sheaf of envelopes in the other. "Any cheques?" he asked, always hopeful.

Sipping coffee, he thumbed through the envelopes. A few. And a few bills. He slit the envelopes and extracted the cheques. He'd deposit them in the gold-glazed tower on the way to Dick Turpin's. From one highwayman to another. Dumas' brain flashed briefly across the unfortunate role the chartered banks had played in Canada's development, the profits hoarded with little risk in a country requiring investment, the parliamentary calls for investigation. He shook his head slightly. He doubted that his modest contribution would add materially to the golden lustre.

Being unused to handwritten letters coming to the office, Dumas' eyes took a few moments to adjust to the envelope. It was addressed to him. The return address in the upper left corner said merely "The Mantouche Society, Cape Croker."

Dumas shrugged and slit the envelope.

Dear Mr. Adrian Dumas,
  By the time you get this I will be in Toronto. I know about the ideas you presented to the Native Peoples' Federation of Canada. Perhaps you would help us with something else. Please call me if you'd be willing to help us.
    Mike Red Sky

Dumas made a note of the name and the phone number at the bottom of the letter. He recalled that he hadn't been able to help the Native Peoples' Federation at all. No one had seemed keen on his ideas regarding community development, and least of all the tall and bearded, soft-spoken and bespectacled white—what was he called?—"animator," who was acting as an advisor of some sort on a government payroll. Dumas had suggested some ideas for getting wells dug among the Micmacs of the Gaspé Peninsula. Wells that the Indians could not afford, especially given the prices charged by the owner of the only drilling company nearby who also happened to be a member of the Quebec National Assembly. Dumas' ideas involved glossy photos of a little girl, say about six years old, stumbling under a heavy yoke and buckets as she fetched water from the stream in which typhoid was reputed to lurk. You know, thin knobby knees, short dress and just a hint of undies beneath the dirty hem. The kind of photo no newspaper could resist printing as a human interest filler, with a brief but explicit little caption outlining the problem, the cost—and the owner.

Dumas figured that the wells would get drilled very shortly after the member of Quebec's parliament read about himself in L'Action Catholique or Le Journal de Montreal.

He had had other ideas about how to get English-Wabagoon pollution cleaned up and, after consulting with a lawyer, conceived some very dramatic charges that could be laid against certain Ontario government officials respecting the mercury content of fish eaten at Grassy Narrows.

The animator had seemed more nervous the more Dumas talked, although Dumas noticed speculative looks between some of the Indians. The animator had thanked him, but had pointed out that the major problems had to do with cultural alienation and the importance of revising their traditions. Dumas had shrugged and had left, vaguely assuming that the animator would counsel some sort of report and increased emphasis on handicrafts.

Mike Red Sky . . .

Dumas rolled paper into his typewriter and after consulting Hermann about the status of Senmut completed the copy for the Lovable point-of-purchase posters by noon. Then he picked up the phone, dialled, and reached a sleepy Pia. At twelve? What did they do all night?

"You should be ashamed of yourself, shleepyhead," Dumas mimicked, "abed at this hour."

"To hell with you, Adrian, and your damned boat. I vas in agonies all night."

So, that was it.

"How do you feel?"

"Vorse."

"Ed there?"

"He left early. He said the bed vas getting too sticky. Ve ran out of lotion and I shtarted on the olive oil about two."

Dumas grimaced. "Tell him to call me at the office. There's a job for him," said Dumas.

"I'm not sure he's interested, Adrian. Not after the lasht von."

Dumas sighed. "Just some pictures from books, Pia. And maybe at the museum. Nothing exciting."

"Okay, Adrian. I tell him. Maybe he'll call."

"Okay. I hope you feel better."

"Sho do I."

Dumas hung up and glanced at his watch. Time for Peter and the bank.

5

"Adrian, old sod, it's the biggest thing that's ever happened for us." Peter's trim mustache quivered and his eyes twinkled. Dumas noticed that Peter's cheeks were more flushed than usual under the impact of an extra Bloody Mary.

"That's all very nice, Pete, and you've been saying it over and over for the last half-hour . . . but couldn't you just tell me something about it?" Dumas looked up questioningly from shovelling chopped sirloin into his mouth.

"That's the devil of it, Dumas. That's what I'm trying to tell you. I can't say anything about it, Adrian. That's why we got the account. Discretion."

"Oh." Dumas paused and swirled a piece of baked potato into some sour cream. "Ah, Pete? Just how'm I supposed to help you if you can't tell me anything about it? You want me to play twenty questions? You'll tell me when I get warm?"

"Alright, Adrian. I can tell you that it is in the resources industry field. Very big. Highly technological. International sales and marketing."

"I write in French? German? Spanish?"

Peter considered this carefully with a sideways, faraway look. "English for now, I would imagine. Later we can have it translated."

"Fair enough," nodded Dumas. "Now, what do I write?"

"Watson Mines needs an entire series—"

"Watson Mines?" Dumas stopped chewing in genuine amazement. "Peter, you just said Watson Mines."

"Damn. So I did." Peter shrugged. And smiled. "Had to come out sooner or later, old man." Having made the *faux pas* he'd been waiting for, Peter turned serious attention to his shrimp-filled crêpe.

73

Whenever Peter said "damn," Dumas thought "damme," as in some previous century featuring snuff, ruffled shirts and scandalous bodices. Dick Turpin's was the right place. Wrong time. Peter affected the air of an English country gentleman, a certain stylish vagueness, like a fugitive from the more glamorous pages of *Tom Jones* or a bemused refugee from *Vanity Fair*. Just beginning to grow out of colonialism—and not very quickly in English Canada, either—Canadians still tended to respond respectfully to the mere existence of a British accent. Because of its currency, many young Englishmen after the war took a brutal look at Britain's post-war prospects and sailed for the colonies with little else to recommend them. The accent, and an affected languid air as their only other asset, had carved some of them a comfortable living in what might be called the social professions—promotion, marketing, advertising and business management. Certainly the British economy, and the Canadian for that matter, did not argue strongly for any objective measure of competence.

It was confidence and British stability that they sold to their Canadian colonial clients. A valuable commodity just after the war when Canada found itself emerging from a relatively backwoods nation into the complexities of the 20th Century. A valuable commodity during the booming 50's, 60's and early 70's. Somewhat less valuable now.

Peter and Dumas had met each other at exactly the right time. For Dumas, it had been a time of refugee bewilderment, too, but experienced a generation after Peter's. Dumas had decided not to fight in Viet Nam, had decided, instead, to fight on certain campuses since the enemy seemed closer. Eventually, he found himself in Canada. Eventually, he had met Peter Tompkins who began to give him freelance writing jobs. Advertisements. Newsletters. Fluff stories. A trickle of work at first, but Peter learned that he could depend upon Dumas to deliver. At some point it seemed easier to bring Dumas into the office than to have him continually running in and out. Still later, with the combination of Peter's client contact and Dumas' abilities in various directions, business increased to the point where they had worked out still another arrangement. Dumas billed Peter for the work he did on their accounts and vice versa, Dumas began tentatively to seek out clients on his own, and they shared overhead and Debbie.

Recently, the firm had begun to get a reputation for doing things, in a small and efficient way, and the realization began to dawn in an increasing number of corporate minds that Dumas must be the one doing it.

As Dumas' own bemusement wore off he'd learned that Peter's accent had been carefully learned, though not as painstakingly as Debbie's. They were peas in a pod, Peter and Debbie, and the royal blue carpeting, the walnut, the oiled fruitwood with its inlays and the Hogarth prints were both a daily reminder of, and talisman against, the shabby economic reality they had narrowly escaped. Though they differed by a good quarter century in age, Dumas had gradually learned that Peter and Debbie had been born almost the same distance and direction from Bow Bells. Just out of earshot, thankfully for their accents. It was a secret they shared together, making them closer to each other in some ways than Peter was to the Canadian girl he'd married twenty years ago and than Debbie was to her new husband.

For that matter, Dumas thought, damn near everyone in Canada had been a refugee from something and somewhere. Peter had taken him in, and Debbie, at about the same time ... Dumas slightly shell-shocked from the war and antiwar, Debbie vulnerable and deliciously gangly in her London micro-minis. Dumas remembered the years fondly. The three of them had grown, and pulled, together.

"Watson Mines?" Dumas paused to chew thoughtfully. "Peter, I mean no offense, but how did we ... ?" Watson Mines International was not one of the largest corporations in Canada, maybe, but it was certainly in the news a lot. Cyrus Watson, so the story went, had come to Canada right after the war from a refugee camp somewhere in Europe. Like many other young men he had gone to the north, prospecting, hoping to make his fortune. Where so many others experienced traditional disappointment, Watson had lucked out. Not in uranium first. Copper? Cobalt? Something. But it was the uranium that built the empire and opened up many other mines for other metals. It was no secret that Provincial Hydro desperately wanted to get its hands on Watson's uranium for yet more nuclear reactors. Watson played coy. Stayed away from long-term contracts.

"It's our size that got it. The marketing has ... er ... sensitive aspects," said Peter.

"I can imagine," said Dumas. "Peter? This wouldn't have anything to do with fuel for the Candu reactors, would it? You know, the ones we're selling for Argentina, Japan and ..."

75

"South Korea."

"Yeah. South Korea."

"Yes. It would."

Dumas chewed thoughtfully, vaguely overhearing the conversation of two good-humored businessmen at a neighboring table. Sam and Irving were quipping over their respective tastes in vodka. Sam, the fat one, insisted on Prince Igor in his Bloody Mary, while Irving, the skinny chap, was equally adamant about Alberta Ranchman in his screwdriver. They laughed and kidded. Old friends.

"Pete. You know that stuff can be used to make bombs. Like India did."

"The safeguards have been tightened up, Adrian. There's also the sale of fuel to the States to consider, too. We'll be in on that. There's a big push on by the Department of Trade and Commerce to stimulate as much export as possible, with the exchange rate so favorable."

"So, we're taking a lot of very technical sales literature, then."

"Correct. A lot of it."

"I'm going to need a lot of research material."

"Watson Mines will supply everything you need. Oh—they'll even take you on a tour of one of the mines, if you wish."

"Ah . . . No thanks, Peter."

"Now it makes sense, eh, Adrian? We're small. We can do everything within our shop and fewer people will be in the know. That's why we landed the account."

Dumas nodded. It made sense. The sale of uranium was a sore subject with a large segment of the public. India had managed to make a bomb with a reactor and fuel supplied by Canada. A peaceful bomb, the Indians had insisted. There had been an outrage of concerned public opinion that Canada had contributed to the spread of nuclear weapons in an already touchy world. The government had responded with tighter guidelines for the sale of reactors and fuel. The Canadian government now extracted a solemn promise from customers that they wouldn't make bombs. No doubt the Argentinians shook their heads solemnly, perhaps thinking of their territorial squabbles with neighboring Chile. No doubt the South Koreans were equally solemn, while keeping an eye cocked toward the 38th parallel and bearing in mind the strong American presence in places like Iran, Laos and Cambodia.

The truth of the matter, which no one could deny, was that weapons grade Plutonium 239 could be made with almost any reactor using natural unenriched Uranium 238. One of the advantages, of course, of fission energy, depending on one's point of view, is the fact that one can make more fuel than is used. High-energy Plutonium 239 is produced from low-grade Uranium 238 by the normal bombardment of neutrons from an operating pile.

"Peter? Did the . . . er . . . moral aspects of this ever occur to you?"

"Jesus H. Christ, Adrian! You're not one of those . . . ?"

"I don't know," said Dumas. "I think I'm becoming one of those. I'm beginning to think very carefully about the"—Dumas grimaced at the cliché—"well, the quality of life."

"So am I, Adrian. So am I. In fact, this account means a great deal to my quality of life. I'll tell you, Adrian, that I've been living a bit tighter than I like."

Dumas nodded. "Yeah. I know, Pete."

"Damn right." Peter looked at Dumas. Dumas saw a vulnerable look in the eyes. "I took on this account because I know you can do it, Adrian. And Adrian. I *need* it. Maybe I don't have to remind you of a few years ago . . ."

"No. You don't have to remind me."

"Then let's put it this way, Texas . . . 'Ahm callin' in my markers.' "

Dumas regarded Peter levelly. "I always pulled my weight, Pete. I don't think I owe you anything. This one . . . I'm going to have to think about."

"Adrian, please don't let me down on this. I can't do the job. You know that. Look, you're well off now, with your boat that you always wanted and all. Now let me get what I want. Help me. Like I helped you."

Dumas noticed the slight nervous twitch of Peter's mustache and for the first time realized that Peter's hair had thinned on top, gone a bit greyer over the temples, since they'd met. "What do you want, Peter?"

"I just don't want to start getting poor, again. Not at my age, Adrian."

6

Dumas glanced at the display of his watch. 10:30. He rubbed his eyes and regarded his handiwork. Mostly, he had to admit, the dominating feature was what appeared to be numerous strings of grey-blue spaghetti.

Dumas had decided to employ eight photocells. These were epoxied to ceramic magnets that could be moved at will over the surface of a square piece of sheet steel. A photocell could be positioned to represent some part of the test advertisement someone was looking at within the machine. A photocell could represent the brand name. The block of copy. The slice of cheese, outboard motor, lipstick . . . whatever. There were photocells enough for people, bottles, headlines or other major parts of the advertisement. As the person inside the machine stared at the advertisement, and as the pointer on the back of the helmet waggled, the flashing light travelled over the surface of the metal sheet. When the beam fell onto the photocell, a counter was triggered registering one focus on whatever that cell represented in the ad.

Eight photocells at sixteen wires each. Wires that led to the batteries. Wires that led to the electric counters. Wires that led to and fro from eight two-transistor circuit boards which amplified the signal from the photocells sufficiently to run something as power-hungry as an electric counter.

All of this wire was grey-blue because Dumas had decided that Radio Shack speaker wire, being flexible, was less apt to break with constant and amateur handling. This was, in some respects, a pity. The wire was not color-coded from the package and Dumas had had to spend tedious minutes coding with eight different colors of tape, tracing the appropriate wires from the correct cell to the corresponding circuitboards, batteries and counters.

But at last it was done. After a fashion. Superior Sheet Metal promised the console for tomorrow. Then the wires could be tucked away, the counters mounted and the numerous toggle-switches and lights fastened in their appointed places.

It had taken since two o'clock in the afternoon, but Dumas was pleased. It worked. Whenever the light flashed onto a counter, the counter glunked like a swallowing frog and invariably registered once for each flash that fell upon it. Over and over. Without fail. Dumas could swirl the light at random over the photocells and produce an electronic chorus not unlike a happy night-time swamp. The console would mute the sound somewhat, perhaps into a highly technological hum.

Dumas locked the warehouse door on Berkeley Street, took a short stroll through Cabbagetown and hailed a cab at the corner of Parliament and Queen.

The ten-minute cab ride up to Yonge and Bloor gave Dumas ample opportunity to enjoy the night-time city lights and strain to look through Warwick and Daddy's Folly windows in a vain attempt to glimpse the exotic dancers within. He ruminated also upon the photocells and the circuit boards he'd made. If they could activate counters, well, they could activate almost anything else. Fans, perhaps, lights, guns, bombs, alarm bells. Practically anything that required switching on. Dumas kept these uses in mind for a security system he had intended to install on *Radagast*. Then, there was a matter of the galvanic skin response unit he'd bought at Edmund Scientific and the still unresolved question regarding the sensitivity of Rachael's new philodendron. Very interesting possibilities there . . . if the damned thing could feel. Dumas had his doubts, in spite of what the book claimed. He would have to check that one out. Maybe he'd buy another galvanic skin response unit.

The cab pulled up in front of the Flyer Restaurant and Tavern on Cumberland. Dumas paid, got out and promptly twisted his ankle on cobbles fronting the lounge. Dumas knew that either he was more fatigued than he cared to admit, or he should reconsider the height of the heels on his Chelsea boots, a possibility he did not care to admit.

He had described himself carefully to the person who had taken the message for Mike. He'd been assured that Mike could find him. Describing himself was never one of Dumas' major problems. Above the probably too-tall Chelsea boots of oxblood, Dumas wore a coffee-colored whipcord suit. Always during the work week. He had four such suits, all identical, and several pairs of the boots. He had shirts for work, all wide-weave tan cotton. Fashion was not high on Dumas' list of priorities. A frustrating year of marriage had sufficed for Rachael to pry him out of the jeans and sweaters he had habitually worn and into a suit. Rachael soon admitted to her mistake. Dumas' powerful legs, combined with his inability or refusal to learn how to pull trousers up whenever he sat down, rendered the stylish flare baggy-kneed, bulged the fine summerweight weave. A flash of inspiration had whispered "Whipcord" to Rachael and she'd dragged Dumas into a tailor's. To her immense surprise, Dumas had been pleased with the result. He'd ordered two more exactly like it which had not surprised her at all. Rachael kept buying colorful ties and puffs for Dumas, and he wore them without seeming to notice.

If Dumas lacked imagination with his own clothing, he compensated for being so with great imagination reserved for Rachael's. Some he designed himself and a discreet couturier acquaintance transformed Dumas' sketches into reality. The black satin maid's apron with the white ruffles had been an enjoyable success. The leather and chain bikini another . . . although Rachael had thus far declined to wear it in public.

Dumas was wiping the foam of his second Labatt's Special Lite off his lips when it occurred to him that if Custer had really died for Dumas' sins then Dumas figured his demise had had compensations. The girl had been standing there for a few moments, he guessed, while he'd idly read the greatly distorted message on her tee-shirt. He looked up. She looked down, smiled, and extended a brown smooth arm.

"Hi, I'm Mike Red Sky," she said.

"Adrian Dumas," he said, shaking the hand and starting to rise.

Mike Red Sky plopped into the chair opposite Dumas, giving all the masculine associations of Custer's name a most definite feminine jiggle. Dumas cast his mind back and vaguely recalled the nut-brown face, bright black eyes and bust-length blue-black hair. The rest had been covered by a beadwork-decorated jacket. She'd been sitting at the back of the room with a smirk.

"Draft," said Red Sky to the waiter. "And salt."

"That your real name?"

"Uh, uh. Mirabila. But I don't like it."

"Wonder?"

"That's right. My mother didn't think she could have another baby. The priest suggested that Mirabila would be a good name."

"It is."

She shook her head. "Not good for nick-names. Mira? Bella?"

"What's wrong with Bella?"

"Oh, I used that when I was younger. Never Mira, though. Now I like Mike."

"Alright," said Dumas, watching her hang her satchel-strap over the chair back.

She squizzled her nose up, like a rabbit, a habitual mannerism, Dumas was to discover, whenever she smiled. Or was mildly displeased. She gave a little shrug to her shoulders and her bright almond eyes wrinkled humorously in the corner of their slant over high cheekbones. Her full lips pulled slowly into the curve of a Cymric bow as they drew into a smile. "Do you remember me, Adrian Dumas? From the meeting?"

"Yeah. Vaguely. You sat in the back in the beaded buckskin jacket and never made a peep. Sleepy-looking. Disgusted. Maybe spaced out."

Her nose squizzled again. "Ordinary suede."

Dumas was trying to place the color of her skin. When it stretched over the cheekbones as the bow of her lips was drawn it was ... what? ... golden-brown? ... with a hint of yellow-pink? That was it. Apricots.

"Buckskin isn't mandatory," said Red Sky.

"Alright." The odd Mongolian fold in the eyes on either side of her baby-like nose gave her face a timeless quality, Dumas decided, like something very new and very old at the same time. Becky's face the first time he'd seen it in the hospital had struck him the same way, as if the entire past and future of the human race resided in the face and, though unable to say it, Becky had somehow known it. As Becky had grown this quality had gradually disappeared, replaced by an open-faced here-and-nowness. Soon, she would go to school to start the long process of re-learning what Dumas suspected she'd known at birth and had lost somewhere over the past five years. What's the place all about? Where do I fit into it? What the hell am I supposed to extract from it? Give to it?

Red Sky's face above the nose retained Becky's sort of first-born knowingness, but the humorous eyes and dimpling double-curved somehow Celtic mouth seemed very attuned to a present that faintly amused. Dumas realized that Red Sky was saying something.

"Pardon?" he said.

She sighed slightly and squizzled her nose again. "I was saying that I think the animators aren't where it's at," said Red Sky. "But you weren't listening."

"No," said Dumas, "because I was thinking that you're one of the most beautiful wom-... er... persons... I've ever seen."

Red Sky's mouth dimpled and the black eyes twinkled. She shrugged casually and Custer jiggled. "It's the childishness," she said, "that you all want to protect and exploit at the same time. The usual."

"True," said Dumas.

The almond eyes crinkled. "I like you, Adrian Dumas," she said.

"What was that about the animators?"

"Nothing really, they're irrelevant."

Dumas nodded. "What can I do for you, Mike Red Sky?"

"Not for me, Adrian, for the Society."

"Right. The Mantouche Society. What the hell is that?"

"Mantouche?"

"Uh, huh."

"Mantouche is God," said Red Sky.

Dumas shook his head and held up his left hand for another bottle of Special Lite. "Mike... er... Miz Red Sky," he hesitated, "I don't know if even I can help God."

"Oh, you can," she said. "Mantouche isn't exactly God-God, if you know what I mean. God is all-powerful, all-knowing and doesn't need anyone's help. Mantouche is God, all right, but not exactly like that. Mantouche isn't a person, like God sort of is in the Bible, but Mantouche is an animal, sort of."

Dumas saw the waiter nod and add his third Labatt's to the tray of Mike's two drafts. "Maybe you'd better go a little slower, Mike."

She paused, thoughtful. "Okay, it's like this. Mantouche is the Indians' idea of God. That's different from the white man's idea," she said. "Because white people are such power freaks—well, it's only natural that their God is a power freak, too. All-powerful, all-knowing. Just like the white man," she dimpled.

"But this... Mantouche... he isn't all-powerful?"

"There're both she's and he's of Mantouches," said Red Sky. "Sure, Mantouche is all-powerful."

Dumas felt confused. He was thankful when the beer came.

"Mantouche, well, *regulates* everything," Mike continued. "Makes the seasons come at the right time. Have you ever wondered how a little seed knows how to make the right kind of tree?

83

How rabbits, wolves and bears know how to mate with each other and make little ones of the right kind?"

Dumas' mental excursion into what he knew of plant chromosome structure and animal pair-bonding behavior was interrupted . . .

"Mantouche tells them," she stated. "Not exactly *tells* them," she amended. "Mantouche *is* what makes the seed make the right kind of tree. Rabbits make rabbits and not, maybe, weasels."

"Sort of a generalized life force," said Dumas. He looked at Red Sky and they both laughed.

"Sort of," she nodded through her smile. "Not only that, but Mantouche regulates things that are not exactly, well, *alive* like we are. Like stars. Rocks. The wind. Mantouche really makes everything be what it is."

"You said it was an animal?"

"Well, yes, sort of," said Red Sky. She paused and sipped salted beer, gazing into the distance with a thoughtful pout. The bow of her lips drew and released the quickest of smiles. "Know about the Loch Ness Monster?"

"Er . . . something. Not much," said Dumas, taken aback.

"Mantouche," said Red Sky.

"Oh."

"That's why they see it sometimes, and can even get photographs, but have never caught one. It's a Mantouche."

"Alright," said Dumas. "What if they do catch it someday?"

Red Sky shrugged. "Mantouche is also just an animal. But different."

Something twigged Dumas' memory. "This Mantouche . . . ? Have something to do with Manitou?"

Red Sky's nose squizzled briefly. "Oh, yes," she said with a slight sigh. "When the first missionaries came to convert the Indians they asked our name for God. We said 'Mantouche' naturally. We told them about Mantouche in everything and also hiding in the lakes."

"And naturally, they assumed some primitive sort of animal worship and changed Mantouche into Manitou and into our idea of God," said Dumas.

Red Sky brightened. "That's it. These animals in the lakes, well they're Mantouche alright, but they're not all of Mantouche. Understand?"

"Just one thing. I've heard of this Loch Ness Monster like everybody else. There's similar things over here?"

"Of course. The Ogopogo in Lake Okanagan. And Ponik in

Lake Pohénégamook in Quebec. People go to look for them all the time. It's in the papers."

Dumas, now that he thought about it, did remember the stories that made humorous fillers in the papers from time to time. He'd mentally filed them under Sasquatches and Werewolves. "These things, all over—in Scotland and here—they're Mantouches . . . er . . . Mantouche?"

"Of course. Mantouche is everywhere. Ireland. Russia. South America. Everywhere."

Dumas nodded. "How can I help Mantouche, then?"

"Well," said Red Sky. "You can help Mantouche to regulate things."

"I thought that Mantouche already did that," Dumas reminded her.

"Oh, Mantouche *does*," affirmed Red Sky. "But the Mantouche always regulated . . . let's see . . . maybe 'gently' is the best way of saying it. Always. Before. Mantouche made sense and, well, everything made sense to Mantouche."

"Before?" Dumas cocked an eyebrow. "That would be before the white man came?"

Red Sky nodded emphatically. "Now very little makes sense. Mantouche is . . . well . . . *puzzled.*"

"Mantouche isn't the only one," Dumas said dryly.

"Mantouche always regulates gently, underneath all the movement, living and dying."

"And you're sort of saying that Mantouche's . . . ah . . . regulatory capabilities . . . are getting snowed under."

"Exactly!" said Red Sky with satisfaction.

"And, let's see, that people who are on Mantouche's side, so to speak, should start lending a regulatory hand."

"Hey, now you've got it!" she said eagerly. "Except, of course, that in the end everyone will return to Mantouche's way."

"But you'd rather have it sooner than later."

"Yes," said Red Sky. "That is important."

"Why not just let things go their natural course and return to Mantouche in the end?" Dumas asked.

He was surprised by the sudden tears welling in the corners of her eyes. She blinked and her lashes sparkled. "Because few will return if it keeps on going. Think of the people already gone. Almost no buffalo. Almost no cougars. The fish and bird people are dying too. Mantouche will be alone if it keeps going on."

Dumas could think of nothing to say.

Finally, "Where do you live, Mike?"

"Cape Croker Reserve. It's up on the Bruce," she said. She looked at Dumas brightly. "So that's how you can help, Adrian Dumas. . . ."

"What kind . . . what tribe, I mean?" asked Dumas.

"Ojibway. We call them nations," she added.

Dumas sipped thoughtfully. "Doesn't matter," he said vaguely. Dumas briefly considered that with the seeping radioactivity of the Douglas Point reactor and the inevitable contributions of others planned by Ontario Hydro, it was entirely possible that mutations might introduce Mantouche to completely new kinds of people in the near future. Two-headed rabbits, maybe. Giant rats. Funny-looking people-people. On the other hand, even mutations must have material to work from. Maybe sufficient roentgens would seep, eventually, so that the material would die before it mutated. Or, with over a hundred lakes already fishless from acid rain streaming downwind from Sudbury, Mantouche might never have the chance, even, of making the acquaintance of funny-looking fish-people.

"Last call!"

"Christ!" said Dumas, looking down at his watch. He'd missed the last ferry. Rachael would be worried. They'd counted on this eventuality, from time to time, living on the Island. "Mike, I have to phone my wife and tell her I'm staying over. Order us another round. I'll be right back."

The phone rang four times before being answered. He was lucky. She could have plugged in the answering machine.

"Sorry to wake you up," Dumas said, "but I've just missed the ferry."

Pause.

"No. Everything's fine. I finished the machine, more or less."

Pause.

"Late meeting, honey. Having a few beers at the Pilot."

Pause.

"It's possible, I guess. I don't know exactly what sh- . . . Mike . . . wants. Maybe there's a job."

Pause.

"Mike Red Sky. Ojibway. Represents a group on a reserve. It's interesting, but it'll probably turn out to be a freebie."

Pause.

"No, dear. I think I'll come over really early. To see you and Becky."

Pause.

"Right. Take care. See you in the morning."

Dumas walked pensively back to the table. Should he try to

scrounge the use of a couch from Ed and Pia? He hated hotels.

Dumas slouched down into the chair and poured beer down the side of his glass. "That's a tall order, Mike Red Sky."

She nodded, shaking salt and watching streamers of bubbles descending in her beer.

"There's so much. So little anyone can do except to look on and hope that people come to their senses." Dumas thought it was a forlorn hope.

"Some of the ideas you had at the meeting?"

"Sure. Sure. They'll work. Maybe—with luck. But even so, Mike, so much effort for maybe, just maybe, cleaning up one stream. Stopping one factory." The thought of it made Dumas weary. "Just a drop in the bucket. For all the effort."

Red Sky smiled and looked down. She nodded. "It seems so small." She looked up again at Dumas. "But, you see, Mantouche has always worked in small ways, too. Ever since the world began. And Mantouche works slowly. Any small thing really does help."

Dumas drained his beer. "This Society of yours, Mike, are you the only member?"

She seemed genuinely surprised. "Oh, no, there are plenty of members. In a lot of reserves. Let's see, there are five or six at Saugeen. Seven at Cape Croker. More at Shoal Lake. Mostly young people, but not always. There's some old people who just want to return to the old ways because of tradition. Then, the younger people mostly believe that the old ways at least didn't destroy the world. We have some educated members," said Red Sky proudly. "At Cape Croker one of us is a medical student. The Mantouche Society has members all over."

It figured and he nodded. If white youths were turning to fundamentalist Christianity and even older religions, it was only natural that the Indians would be reviving their old traditions, too. Especially among the young, as among whites. He remembered something about a West Coast medical official on the radio becoming concerned about the revival of Ghost Dancing in British Columbia. A health hazard to participants, the white medical officer had been maintaining. Compared to eating mercury? Compared to the despair of alcoholism? Compared to the decline of salmon because of white overfishing, diminishing the Indians' major food source? Dumas doubted it.

"Mike? How committed would you say these Mantouche members are?" He paused. "I mean, are they willing to give real active help on a project?"

"We are willing to fight for the future, Mister Dumas, if we have to. I don't wish to live in the world seeing Mantouche dying." She finished the last of her draft. Licked her lips. "Most of the others feel the same way. What's the use . . . ?"

Dumas nodded slowly. That, too, figured. And explained some. It helped explain Reverend Jim Jones' trek to the Redwood Valley in search of a haven from nuclear war and fallout and the later move to the remote jungles of Guyana. It helped explain the hoards of weapons for eventual use against the huge, vague enemy inadequately defined. And the final suicides. Dumas had long ago concluded that the increasing number of cults, and their potential for violence, came from this mixture of religious-environmental concern for a raped world, hatred for the despoilers and despair at their numbers and powers. Jonestown was no mystery. The Ayatollah's victory in Iran no inexplicable phenomenon.

The naïveté, the hatred and the despair, were terrible, vulnerable. In Iran to infiltration by agents of superpowers. In Jonestown to infiltration by money-seekers who hoped to become bestselling authors.

Elsewhere, psychologists, politicians and church functionaries joined in the banquet. All feeding off the newborn child of anti-progress and environmental concern and its throwback to ancient religious conceptions. Denouncing it, if it could not be adopted and dressed decently in familiar Christian, Jewish or Islamic ritual words. Explaining it, in the meaningless red herrings of psychological jargon. Patronizing it, as radio and television pundits and newspaper analysts earned their vacuous keep. But though bled for various purposes and profits, the child grew stronger daily, a natural result of appropriate response to stimulus. As inexorable as evolution. Somewhere under all the parasites was the urge for independent life. The tears for Mantouche of the Indians, Mantis of the surviving Bushmen. How odd that the names of God were so similar so far apart. Or, for that matter, what about the new regard for Alpha and Osta, nature-goddesses of European childhood moving like mist behind modern witchcraft and most of what people nowadays called "the occult"?

Perhaps the source of the child's strength would prove stronger and more enduring than the devouring complexity wrought by words of male saviors and works of male strivers and builders.

"You said that this Mantouche was both male and female," Dumas mused.

Red Sky regarded him curiously. "Of couse. Everything is

pretty well one or the other," said Red Sky. "Mantouche must be both at the same time to make the world run smoothly. Doesn't that make sense?"

"A great deal," said Dumas. "Just for laughs, Mike, tell me which one is our God? Male or female? The one in the Bible."

"That's easy. He's a man. The Bible always calls him a man ... he ... but it's not that."

"What is it?"

"Why I know?"

"Uh, huh."

"He's always getting angry. He's always jealous. And he's terribly afraid of women. Some of his priests can't marry and those who can think people should only fuck to have children, and then only with the man on top."

"Missionary position," said Dumas.

"What?"

"Never mind," he said, thankful that Rachael's very religious childhood had served merely to cause rebellions against the repression.

"Well," Red Sky insisted with a challenging twinkle in her eye, "doesn't that make sense?"

"I think that about sums it up, Red Sky."

Dumas saw the waiters stacking the chairs upside down on the table-tops, working in their direction and occasionally casting nasty glances their way. Dumas turned the tab over, reading the bill. He pulled a fold of bills from his pocket and counted out seven dollars.

"I can pay for my own," said Red Sky. "Four drafts." She stood up and deformed Custer as her right hand struggled down into the pocket of tight and faded jeans. With no hesitation her hand came up with a crumpled two-dollar bill. She tossed it on the plate. She paused and looked down at Dumas. "Will you help?"

Dumas rose, picked up the two-dollar bill and handed it back to her. "This one was on me," he said. "Sure, Mike. I'll help all I can. Where do we start? Got something in mind?"

She shook her head slowly. "Not really. I came to ask your advice. What do you think?" She hooked the strap of her leather satchel over her shoulder.

"I'll have to think about that," said Dumas. "C'mon, Mike, we better get out before they throw us out."

Dumas had had no chance to notice that Red Sky wore no shoes. Careful not to skitter on the cobbles himself, he envied the soft slapping and sure grip of her toes. She skipped over them, from mound to mound, playing hopscotch on the smooth cement sidewalk. She turned, grinning, as he came up to her.

"Let's go down to Yonge and Bloor where we have a better chance of getting a cab. Then I'll drop you wherever you live."

"Sure."

No, Dumas didn't mind dropping her at the corner of Keele and Bloor even though it was out of the way. He did mind, however, when she smiled in a warm way, shook his hand, closed the cab's door firmly and proceeded to walk off into the trees of High Park. Not a rambling gait had Red Sky, but a purposeful one.

Dumas stopped the moving cab. "Red Sky. Wait up!" he called through the open window.

In a brief conversation beneath High Park's elms Dumas discovered that Red Sky had hitched down Highway 6 from Cape Croker and then along the 41 from Guelph to Toronto. As soon as she'd figured he had the letter. The number in the letter had been a married girlfriend who was busy night and day with new twins in a very small apartment. Red Sky had waited for two days for Dumas to call, but after the first night, not wanting to put her friend to any additional trouble, Red Sky had moved nearby into the park. She came to the house in the morning to wash up and otherwise phoned from time to time to see if Dumas had called. No, she had no money for a hotel. Yes, now that she had spoken with Dumas and was certain of his sincerity, she would head back tomorrow. She was fine. She had two dollars.

Dumas sighed.

"It's not the babies," said Red Sky. "I'm used to baby noise. But they're her first and she's scared. They don't have much money. The husband is scared, too, and when he comes home they fight. He's looking for work. It's the fighting I don't like. The park is peaceful."

"It's also patrolled," Dumas pointed out. "And you're a vagrant. How the hell can you help Mantouche from inside a cell?"

Red Sky shrugged. "They let you out."

"C'mon, Red Sky." Dumas took her hand and pulled her along.

In the cab on the way back towards Edward's and Pia's house, Red Sky was persuaded to accept the twenty dollars that Dumas thrust into her hand. Somewhat later a yawning Pia, after giving Dumas a withering look, agreed to put Red Sky up for the night and said that Edward would see that she got on the right bus tomorrow. "And Adrian, you bashtard, Rachael will find out about your hanky-pankies. Shlumming with a poor Chinese girl who has no place to shtay." Pia cluck-clucked Red Sky up the stairs. Dumas rolled his eyes upward and returned wearily to the waiting taxi. At least Pia would feed her up good.

Later still, having paid off the cab at Harbour Castle, Dumas found that he lacked the money to pay in advance for the room. He was forced to use the green credit card that had never before been used, that Peter had insisted upon having Dumas acquire for prestige purposes. According to the ads, the card told people who one really was. Dumas had always hoped no one would find out.

7

As soon as the limousine came to a gently crunching stop in the pools of golden light thrown by matching carriage lamps, Watson stepped out onto the circular drive's surface of crushed stone and walked briskly toward the house. He arrived just as the butler was opening the high, arched doors and he squeezed through with no time for welcoming words. The butler and the steward exchanged glances and the steward walked out toward the long Lincoln to retrieve whatever possessions Watson might have left on the velour rear seat.

After that last evening meeting, Watson had stayed in Toronto to have dinner at the Le Provençal since it was right around the corner from the Colonnade on Bloor where his advertising agency was comfortably quartered. The meeting had dragged on and on and by the time it had ended well after seven, Watson had been able to convince himself that he was hungry. But he'd left the superb onion soup half filling its thick crock and barely nibbled the Veal Cacciatore, taking only a few sips of Barton & Gestier medoc. At length, he'd thrown down his checkered napkin and had rushed to the car.

The drive had seemed especially long.

Familiar scents at last came to him through the darkness, and the moon and stars showed him his way along the path. Far from the long shadow of the many-gabled house behind him, Watson at last rounded the corner.

Rose bushes?

It took Watson a few moments. He looked around wildly. Had he somehow lost his way? Taken a wrong turn onto another silvered path through the gardens? He glanced back toward the house to get his bearings and saw the lighted squares of windows in their familiar places. He closed his eyes and looked toward her. He opened them. Still, she was not there offering her solace with the widespread arms.

Watson rushed toward the rose bushes and swept their branches aside, heedless of the pricks of thorns. It must be here. Somewhere. She wasn't.

I'll fire whoever did this, Watson promised himself angrily. Someone's moved her. Then it came to him that none of his staff would have moved the Madonna. Further, there was absolutely no reason to have dug up the bleeding heart bushes.

Then it all clicked together in Watson's mind. They had him. Quite suddenly, Watson fell to his knees in front of the rose bushes. Hot tears burned under his eyelids and rolled down his cheek. Somewhere nearby they were waiting. Watson knew that it was too far from the house to run.

Presently, Watson heard the scuffle of a step on the path. Then another.

Watson waited. They had been following him for days, it seemed. Somehow, the gaunt man always knew where he was going. That took research and teamwork. So he was not alone, although Watson never saw anyone else. Only the thin face, with the infinitely sad eyes. The silent accusing stare. Coming out of church. Waiting at the elevators in the Royal York. Hailing a cab as he walked into the Colonnade.

"Watson . . ." It was a low, melodious voice.

Watson screwed his eyes tightly shut and worked his knees into the stone.

"Cyril Watçek . . ."

Watson heard the sound of sobbing and realized that it was himself. He wiped his mouth and nose with the back of his suit sleeve. He nodded. "Yes," he whispered.

"Look at me, Cyril Watçek."

"No," Watson whispered.

"You owe me that much, Watçek. She was my wife."

"Sarah . . . Bela . . ." Watson let the sobs come and sat back on his heels, hands clasped in his lap. Through watery eyes, he could see his own knees in their grey cloth covering. Raising his eyes, and blinking, Watson perceived the filmy and indistinct figure standing not far from him on the path. The figure stepped slightly closer. A light, it must be a penlight, suddenly illuminated the face in a reflected glow from his hand cupped beneath his chin.

"Look carefully at this face, Watçek. Peel away the years, the grief and the grey. Do you recognize it? That day at the camp. In the rain. The day you took my Sarah away?"

Watson squirmed in the pebbles. He nodded slowly. "I knew at the church last week. When you watched me."

"Tell me . . . do you feel cleaner in the church, Watçek? Does it help?"

"No, no, no." Watson snivelled and wiped his nose again. "Only sometimes, she helped . . ." Watson's hand waved helplessly toward the new rose bushes. Where the Madonna had been. ". . . but you have taken her away . . ."

"What makes you think that you deserve her grace and understanding, Watçek?"

"Nothing," Watson whimpered softly. "Nothing. Nothing."

"Yet, Watçek, you've enjoyed it for years, unearned. Just like you enjoyed my Sarah. I have had nothing, Watçek, through all these years."

"I know. I know, I know," Watson sobbed. What could the man want now, except revenge? "Y-you're going to kill me?" he stammered.

"Watçek, you'll never know how much I wanted that for years and years. I planned and I hated, Watçek. It kept me alive in the camp. After the war, when I found Ruzycky and Wilenczyk, then I hated even more. You didn't just rape her and kill her, Watçek. You played with her . . . with my Sarah . . . like a toy."

Watson sobbed and tears trickled down his cheeks to drip from the point of his chin into the slack folds of grey cloth on his lap. "Sarah . . . Bela . . . she was the first woman I had ever seen." He cupped his face in his hands. "And the last . . . " he whispered. "I . . . I couldn't help myself, God help me."

"Why should God help you, Watçek?"

Watson shook his head. "No reason, no reason . . . except that I need peace . . ."

Koffler spat on the crushed rocks of the path.

"P-please don't kill me. Not yet." Watson sobbed.

"Why not? Right here?"

Watson dropped his hands to his knees and looked up at the thin, dark man in the night. Koffler saw the moonlight glisten in the wet eyes.

"Because I would like to have a chance to atone, to find grace . . ."

The figure scuffled on the path and Watson thought that the man was gathering himself to rush upon him in rage. "No, no, please don't." It came out of Watson's throat hoarsely.

"Because I would like to have a chance to atone, to find grace . . ." Koffier mimicked acidly.

"Yes," Watson whispered.

"Watçek, Watçek," Koffler said tiredly. "I have dreamed of nothing but killing you all these years. Yet, now . . ."

Watson felt the pounding in his chest. He dared to breathe. Was it possible that the man would spare him? After what he'd done? "Listen, Mister . . . Sarah's husband . . . please, please . . . what can I do to make up—"

"To make up?" Koffler said bitterly. "You think you can make up my loss?" Koffler's shoes crunched softly and he loomed suddenly larger.

"No!" Watson shrieked and buried his head in his hands. But nothing happened. Watson dared to peek between his fingers. He did not raise his head and kept looking downward at the man's shoes in front of him. "I d-didn't mean it like that," he stammered. "But there must be something I can do . . . for her . . ."

Silence.

"For her . . ." Koffler said softly. "All these years, Watçek, I've thought only of my hatred. For her . . ."

"For her . . ." Watson repeated. Slowly, Watson dared to wipe his nose on the back of his sleeve again. "Anything . . ."

"She was so gentle, my Sarah. She cared nothing for wealth, Watçek, like you. She hated war and killing. She wanted to stay in the little village I longed to escape from. She loved children, Watçek."

Watson nodded slowly and waited.

"What would Sarah have asked of you Watçek, had she lived?"

"I will give my wealth away," Watson said simply.

"That's too easy, Watçek. If you are a sincere man, Watçek, if you truly yearn for God's grace, you may be able to do more good by controlling your wealth than by giving it over to someone else."

Watson, looking down at his shoes, waited. Finally he asked, "What do you want me to do?"

"I want nothing from you except your miserable life, Watçek. I am thinking about what Sarah would have wanted. Shut up."

Watson nodded silently.

Finally, the man spoke again. "I know something about you, Watçek. About your wealth. I am thinking about Sarah, as I remember her from so long ago, Watçek, and I think I know what she would have wanted, if she had lived." Koffler hesitated. "She would have hated this world, Watçek, even more than the war and suffering that you and others caused her. She would have hated you, Watçek, even if she'd never known you and you had never raped her. Do you know why?"

Watson shook his head.

"How you make your wealth, Watçek. You know that bombs are made, can be made, from the uranium you mine and sell. One has already been made, Watçek, in India. Sarah hated bombs. Now you will help make others by selling your fuel to other countries."

"I'm not responsible for the regulations . . ." Watçek began.

"Just like all the others. 'I was just following orders.' 'I'm not responsible.' I'll kill you now, Watçek, and have done with it."

Watson saw the shoes swivel as if the man were gathering his strength to strike or slash downward. "No, no, please," Watson sobbed. "I didn't mean that. I just meant that I have no control over how the fuel is used." He saw the legs locked, hesitating. "I can't control the government, and I can't control other nations once they have it," the words tumbled out. "But I could refuse to sell it," Watson finished.

"That would be just giving away your wealth. Like you wanted," said the deep voice above him.

"I have other mines," said Watson. "Other than uranium. The money would not be as much, but enough for many good works." Watson saw the legs and feet relaxing. He thought quickly. "There's one more possibility," he said, "that might have made Sarah happy."

"What is it, Watçek?"

Watson remembered that some Canadian provincial utilities had been anxious to obtain an ensured supply of fuel for planned reactor programs. He had never committed himself to long-term contracts because of the economic situation and because foreign sales were more lucrative. Nations abroad paid higher prices because they wanted the uranium. Sometimes for bombs. "There's something I could do," he began. "I could commit all of the uranium output for Canadian power companies—Provincial Hydro and Hydro Quebec—long-term contracts covering not much more than costs. That way, it will never be made into bombs. That way, there will be more money for good works."

The man remained silent. Then he said, "You could do that, Watçek?"

"Yes, yes," Watson said eagerly. "They've been after me for years, but I..."

"But you refused so that you could sell at higher prices to nations that might make bombs and war."

"Yes."

"Sarah hated bombs and war, Watçek."

Watson nodded.

"You'll do that, then, Watçek," the man said. "Then your fuel will be used only for peaceful things."

"Yes."

"How long will this take, Watçek?"

"Not long, I swear it. A couple of days to announce my intentions. Maybe a few weeks until the contracts can be finalized. There's bureaucracy. And government. But they want it."

"Make it easy for them."

"Yes. I will," Watson promised.

"Fail Sarah and I will kill you, Watçek. I promise you that you'll die with no chance for grace. No priest will ever find your grave."

Watson nodded. "But if . . . when . . . I do this. Then will you put her back?"

"Your woman of marble?"

"Yes. The Virgin."

Koffler laughed harshly. "Perhaps, Watçek, perhaps. You cannot face God, eh? But the Mother may be softer? Is that it? The women endure. And forgive . . . even something like you?"

Watson kept his head bowed. He heard the rustle of cloth and something fluttered down into his lap. A piece of paper.

"Perhaps I'll put her back. In the meantime, Watçek, there's another face for you to dwell on. Keep it in mind while you're making your deal with the governments."

Watson lifted his hand from his knee and turned the square of paper over. A small beam stabbed down from the man's penlight, swirled over his trousers and found the paper. Sarah's face looked up at him. And the Madonna's. A faded sepia print with scalloped edges, but Watson made out the soft brown hair and large eyes. The heart-shaped face and serene brow. The gentle suggestion of a smile. A smooth white throat. Uncrushed. They were very much alike, the Madonna and Sarah, as much as he could remember, allow himself to recall. Watson realized then that somehow his mind had chosen the statue because of its similarity to her. Tears trickled down his cheek.

"It's a copy, Watçek, of the only photograph I have of her. I wanted you to see it before you died. Now, perhaps, it will do some good. As she would have wanted. Look at it often, Watçek, and make it easy for them to buy your damned uranium."

"I will not fail."

"You'd better not, as you value your twisted soul in the next world. I don't think it can be redeemed in this one, Watçek."

Watson glimpsed a vision of a troubled priest seeking the unmarked grave where the man had hidden his body. In unconsecrated ground with no blessing to ease his going. As the priest searched ceaselessly, perhaps he could hear Watson's shrieks and screams, dimly, coming across the barrier of death from hell. He always writhed, gasping for air, by steel edges clamping his throat. A fire always burned between his legs. His scrotum sizzled and swelled from the cooking and became a hot, rubbery blister. The women popped it with the scratching of their long nails, and cackled in glee at the final long howl of agony they always produced. They did other things while he dangled there, gasping. Over and over. Forever.

Watson had never confessed it. He'd never been able to bring himself to, in the sight of God. Rather he hoped that Mary's understanding would soften the judgement. Mary might speak with God beforehand so that the inevitable confession would not sound so bad, the judgement not so eternal. If he could only edge closer to God while he lived, by praying for Mary's intercession, by going to church and by doing some good works, God's perspective might not be so brutally distant. It was his only chance to shorten the time of the blisters and the rending nails.

Sarah's eyes were open in the photograph. Looking at him with gentle reproach and seeing past his mind to the unconfessed burden on his soul. She knew, as his priests had not. Only the Madonna knew also. And she kept her eyes closed. Watson felt able to wriggle a bit closer when there were no knowing eyes upon him. He blinked his eyes and the tears thankfully blurred Sarah's stare.

"I cannot fail," he whispered.

The light suddenly was not there any more. "Whenever you come home, Watçek, I'll be waiting for you here. Late at night. You will tell me everything you're doing for Sarah and bring the proof."

"Yes, I will."

The shoes moved, and turned away. Watson heard the soft crunching as the man walked away down the path. When Watson found the courage to look up, the man had gone.

2

8

Dumas' legs were splayed comfortably apart in his faded Saturday jeans. Tanned arms bulged from tatty denim sleeves. Because he enjoyed the quank-quack-quanking of contentedly squabbling ducks, he tore a slice of toast in half and threw part of it through the open porthole. Dumas never heard the gentle plop of the toast hitting the water for all the splashing and honking.

Becky widened a jam-spread face into a smile. Strawberry. "Daddy, Daddy, isn't it nice they have breakfast with us?" she said. Then, more hopefully, "Maybe they like egg, too."

"You're going to eat all of that egg, young lady, every bit, before you leave the table," Rachael waggled a spoonful of fruit cocktail for emphasis.

Becky regarded the gooey yellow interior of her decapitated egg with disgust. She wrinkled up her nose. "All of it?"

"Right down to the bottom," said Rachael.

"Might as well buckle down to it," Dumas advised. He watched until Becky bravely dipped the small spoon purposefully inside. Dumas looked across the small table toward Rachael, "Could I get you more coffee, dear?" He thought that her smile was just a trifle too sweet.

"Thank you, sweetheart," she said, offering him the cup on its saucer.

Dumas took it and traversed the three small steps to the large pot. Poured. When he set it down in front of her, Rachael looked up brightly. "So kind of you, dear."

He slumped back into the booth behind his plate and went to work on the surviving sausage. "I'm sorry about the job, Rachael," he said. "Is that what's bothering you?"

Rachael had discovered that the library had already taken

steps to hire a replacement. The best that she'd been able to do was get a guarantee of part-time. In the autumn when things got busy. Right now, just the assurance that she'd get called if anyone were ill.

"Certainly not, Adrian. Well, maybe just a bit. On the other hand, darling, I *will* have more time for you and Becky." She dimpled.

"Or if it's the party, Rachael. Maybe we're trying to do too much today. We can leave the plants and the window boxes and just concentrate on the booze and party nosh," Dumas suggested.

"Well, honey-lamb, I mean, *you're* doing most of it. Plants for me, window boxes for me." She looked across the table with her head slightly cocked and her eyes wide. She pouted a kiss across the two feet of varnished plywood. "You do so much for me, Adrian. Too much, sometimes, really," she said.

"Finished!" Becky squealed it with obvious relief. Dumas peered suspiciously into the depths of the shell. "What do you know, it's all gone," he said.

"All?"

Dumas lifted the egg-cup and held it out toward Rachael, who squinted into it. "See, that wasn't so bad, was it?" Rachael patted Becky on the head.

"It was icky," Becky stated flatly. "Now can I go feed them?"

Dumas reached across and wiped some of the strawberry from Becky's cheeks. "Sure. Here." He reached into the waxed bag and withdrew two slices of bread. "But be careful. Don't lean over the rails too far. They might eat you too."

"You're silly. Ducks don't eat people. Just bread."

"Run along," said Dumas. "Walk, on deck," he amended.

"Yes, Daddy."

Dumas rose from the bench to let Becky out. She squeezed past and ran a couple of steps along the narrow aisle between the dining booth on one side and the stove, sink and small fridge on the other. Then she remembered, stopped and continued to the forecastle steps with studied slowness. Dumas watched until her blue and white Mickey Mouse sneakers had disappeared upwards behind a bulkhead.

He reached down for his cup and poured himself more coffee.

"And not only a devoted husband, concerned about philodendrons and window boxes for his wife, but a model father."

"Hmmm."

104

Dumas sat back down gingerly and watched Rachael pecking cubes of pear, wheels of banana and little balloons of cherries. She poked them daintily with her spoon, but did not seem disposed to devour them. "Oh, Pia called me yesterday," she said nonchalantly.

"You don't say?"

"At the library."

"Great. Suntan better?"

"Oh, much."

"Edward's feeling a bit more kindly disposed. I gave him a little job."

Rachael smiled warmly and longingly across the table, and her copper hair bobbed softly as she shook her head gently in delighted wonder. "And a loyal friend . . ." She sighed and returned to pushing pineapple triangles around with the spoon.

"Hell," said Dumas, "what else are friends for?"

"Let me see," Rachael mused, looking upward with pouted lips and tapping her spoon against them thoughtfully. She brightened. "They can take in homeless little Oriental waifs in the middle of the night. Poor, poor, fluffy little Siamese kittens. All cold and homeless."

Dumas searched hopefully on his plate for a scrap of sausage . . . or egg. Disappointed, he cleared his throat instead. "Ojibway," he declared bravely.

"Ojibway." Rachael finally brought a spoonful to her lips, pursed the fruit off with them, and chewed with a puzzled demeanor. "I suppose it could be," she said. "It's probably the exoticness. That long black hair. The golden skin. Slanted almond eyes, so downcast. I've heard that they're more . . . well . . . accommodating to a man. It's their tradition." Rachael took another bite.

"You forgot the magnificent jugs beneath the waif's thin tee-shirt," said Dumas.

Rachael's green eyes flashed, their grey diluted with anger, and Dumas almost ducked. "*Mike* Red Sky, indeed. So hardworking at that late, late meeting." Rachael's thin lips reminded Dumas of something dangerous and impatient, like a speculative cobra, for instance.

He sighed.

" 'It's interesting, but it'll probably turn out to be a freebie.' " Rachael duplicated Dumas' careful telephone manner. Her eyes sparkled emerald at him. "Was it, dear? A freebie?"

"Rachael, dear, you don't—"

"Oh, I do hope it was a freebie, darling. I know you wouldn't want to spend any money that could go to—to my window boxes. For our lovely dream home. For my plants. For Becky's ballet lessons. You are such a devoted man."

"You don't understand."

"I don't?" She cocked an eyebrow. *"You* don't understand. I knew what I married when I married you. I don't mind your having someone else every one in a while. I *do* mind your sneaking around about it. I *do* mind the girl you chose, a defenseless street waif. *Mike* Red Sky. Barefoot Indian hippie. Adrian, I'm sick."

Dumas shoved his plate aside and crossed his forearms on the table. He clenched his fist briefly and watched the muscles bunch in his arms. Idly. At length, he looked up. "You know me better than that, Rachael."

"I do?"

"Sure you do." He paused. "If I had wanted Red Sky and had had her, Rachael, I sure as hell wouldn't have taken her to Pia's, now would I?"

Rachael looked down.

"I went to the hotel anyway. As cheap for one as for two."

"Why did you lie, Adrian?"

"I didn't. That's her name." He hesitated. "Well, no, that's not her name. Her real name if Mirabila—'Wonder' in Latin—but Mike is what she calls herself."

"Pia said she was gorgeous."

"She is," said Dumas.

"You wanted her?"

Dumas considered this. "Yes . . . and no," he said. "I'm not sure that I could have had her—no, that's not right. I could have had her. I'm not sure it would have mattered to her . . . or to me."

"Oh my God," said Rachael. She looked at Dumas levelly. "You're infatuated."

"You're wrong," said Dumas.

"Am I?"

"Totally." Dumas sipped his coffee. "I love her."

Rachael looked at Dumas intently. "Adrian, is that true?"

"Yes, Rachael, It is." He grinned. "I think you will, too," he added. Dumas met the challenge in Rachael's eyes. "Have I ever cheated on you, Rachael?"

"Yes."

Dumas cocked an eyebrow.

"You haven't *ever* told the truth . . . About the Steinberg business."

Dumas nodded. "That's true."

"Why not?"

"Because it's better you never know," said Dumas. "For your sake. And Becky's."

"But how can I know if it's better?"

"Because you said you know what you married," said Dumas. "Think about it." Dumas waited. "Not about Mike Red Sky. I didn't have her. I'm telling you this. Not that it's any of your business. I was trying to tell you that by giving Mike over to Pia. I could have taken her to the Harbour Castle, Rachael. Would you have ever known?"

"No."

"And anyway," said Dumas, "I wasn't *that* cheap with Red Sky. I gave her twenty bucks." He paused. "Hey, that's something you could do, now that you're semi-retired."

"What's that?"

"Start keeping our accounts. That bookkeeper costs me a fortune."

"Starting with Mike Red Sky's twenty dollars?"

"Why not?" said Dumas.

"Charitable donation? I don't think it's deductible."

Dumas thought that he had a hunch. "No, honey. I think it'll turn out to be a legitimate business expense."

9

Peter pushed through the gate in the starboard rail. His cigarette dangled in his right hand and its glowing tip passed near the philodendron in the window box hanging on the rail.

Peter jumped as the electronic squeal crescendoed like a miniature siren. Across the deck, Dumas glanced away from Debbie to see Rachael shaking hands with Peter and offering a cheek for the inevitable kiss. "Excuse me, Deb," said Dumas.

"What in ruddy hell is that noise?"

"Oh, that's the philodendron, Peter. I think it was afraid of being burned by your cigarette," Rachael explained.

Dumas reached into the window box and turned down the volume of the galvanic skin response unit. The squeal subsided. "Let's try a little experiment, Peter. Butt your cigarette in that bucket there," said Dumas. Peter stooped to grind the cigarette out in the bucket of sand in the corner of the deck. Peter shrugged the shoulders of his Hardy Ames blazer back into place. He looked questioningly from Rachael to Dumas.

"Okay, Pete," Dumas motioned, "come back this way. Toward the plant."

Peter looked around and took a couple of awkward, foolish steps. Dumas turned the sensitivity of the unit up and the squeal rose in the air again, although not as loud as before. "What I was afraid of," said Dumas.

"What?" asked Peter suspiciously.

"It wasn't just the cigarette, Pete, old man," Dumas said sadly, "you're also putting out bad vibes. You're angry or tense. Where's Norma?"

"Oh. She sends her sincerest apologies, Rachael, Adrian, but she thinks she's coming down with hay fever or something, and she thought she'd better stay inside away from the pollen..."

"I'm sorry to hear that, Peter," said Rachael, "I haven't seen Norma for a while."

"Yeah. Too bad," said Dumas. He turned the volume down again.

Peter peered into the window box. "What do you mean, bad vibes?"

"That's what the plant says," Dumas shrugged. "Not my fault."

"What the plant says?"

"Oh, yes, Peter. They're very sensitive to people's emotions. They're also wary of getting burned." Rachael patted the leaves comfortingly. "There, there. No one's going to hurt you, Archi."

"I thought that only Adrian was bonkers, my dear," Peter smiled.

"This is interesting, Peter. I didn't believe it myself," said Dumas. "It was Rachael who told me about it." Dumas rummaged in the plant's foliage.

"About what?"

"Plant sensitivity," Rachael said.

"See. Look, Peter. This plant's leaves are hooked up to a GSR unit and ..."

"What's a GSR unit?"

"Oh. Galvanic skin response. Measures the electrical current on the surface of the skin. Like a ... well, a lie detector, close enough," Dumas explained. "Anyway, if you attach the electrodes to the philodendron's leaves, you get a reading."

"Just like a person?" Peter looked unbelieving at Dumas and Rachael.

"It is a person," said Rachael. "At least, it sort of acts like one."

"Utter bilge. Tommyrot. This is one of your jokes, Adrian."

Dumas raised his hands helplessly. "I'm as mystified as you are, Pete. I don't know why, but it works." Dumas parted the leaves and pointed to the small metal plates attached to two leaves with tape. Wires snaked away from the leaves and Dumas followed them with his finger. Peter stooped and saw the wires enter an aluminum box which had been shoved out of harm's way under the planter next to the rail. Dumas reached under and dragged the box out into the rose light of the Japanese lanterns glowing in the rigging.

"Okay, Peter, watch the needle on the gauge. I'm going to turn up the unit to get a constant reading." The needle climbed over the numbers and the electronic whine rose to a steady but subdued pitch. Dumas was conscious of others drawing closer and felt the slight heel of *Radagast's* deck. "See? We have a steady level now." He looked at Peter, who nodded.

"Maybe there's a short or something in the machine," Peter suggested.

Dumas grinned. "Okay, Pete. Just light another cigarette. Close to the plant."

"But not too close, Peter. Don't burn it," Rachael said.

At the first flick of Peter's Dunhill, the needle on the gauge began to arc slowly over the numbers and the whine increased until its shrillness dominated the deck. Dumas turned the volume down.

"That's simply amazing," said Debbie, taking her hands from her ears. "Just amazing."

"Personally," Marc drawled, "I wouldn't put it past Adrian to rig something like that for our entertainment." Marc smiled down.

"Marc!"

"No offense, meant, Deborah, or to you, Adrian, but we *do* know your sense of humor."

Dumas looked up the considerble length of Marc's white trousers and was reminded of two old-fashioned clay pipestems. He grinned and nodded at the handsome face surmounting the double-breasted navy blazer.

"I'm inclined to agree, old man," Peter said with a chuckle. He puffed contentedly.

"Alright," said Dumas. He shrugged. "Tell you what, Peter, if you'll sacrifice that cigarette by putting it in the bucket, we'll do something that can't be faked."

Peter grimaced, took a last deep draw, and twisted the cigarette in the sand. The needle on the gauge dropped back appreciably. Dumas turned a large knob slowly until the indicator pointed to a piece of tape he'd stuck to the aluminum. Dumas looked up. "I did this this afternoon and it really freaks me out. I've just jacked the unit up to another factor of sensitivity." Dumas smiled up at Marc. He rose from the deck and stepped away from the machine. He raised his hands. "See, ladies and gentlemen, as you can see, I am not touching the unit or the plant. And now, before your very eyes, ladies and gentlemen, you will see an amazing demonstration of the sensitivity of Archibald, the wonder philodendron." Dumas added mock-sincere apologies to a well-known Toronto columnist who had promoted a series of unlikely wonder Annabelle's and the group tittered in good humor.

"Do I have a volunteer?" Dumas looked around. He grabbed Marc by the elbow. "You, young man, with the expensive blazer, come right up on stage." He pulled Marc over beside him and held an imaginary microphone out toward him. "Your name, young fellow?"

Marc got into the act, looking around nervously like someone pulled unexpectedly out of an audience. He stretched his neck and straightened the impeccable Windsor knot of smooth paisley silk at his throat. "Ah . . . Marc McGuigan." Marc smiled nervously, looked, and waved into the equally imaginary camera.

"And where you're from, Marc?"

"Ah . . . Toronto."

"Right, Marc, a hometown boy. Marc, have you ever been aware of your extraordinary psychic power?"

"Ah . . . no."

"So few people are aware of their amazing capabilities, Marc, ladies and gentlemen," said Dumas. "We're gonna prove it to you, Marc. Willing to give it a try?"

Marc shuffled his feet. "Gee whiz, sure. I think so."

"Alright, Marc. Here's what I'd like you to do. Just walk a few steps away, say, over by that foremast there . . . the front one . . . and turn your back to us. That's right, Marc. Ready, Marc?"

Marc's coiffed black hair bobbed up and down. "What do I do?"

"Very simple, Marc. Without giving any indication of when you're going to do it . . . I'll turn my back so that I can't see you . . . I want you to wait as long as you like and then just begin to think hard. *Think* about lighting a match and burning one of poor Archi's leaves. Just imagine doing it. But wait a while before you start thinking so that none of us will know when. I'll turn my back so that I can't see you in case you move when you start concentrating."

Dumas turned and looked out over the high stern rail and saw the red globes of tomatoes drooping down obscuring the railing on either side of the center lantern. Beyond and between them, Dumas tried to sort out the confusion of shining aluminum and stainless steel masts and rigging of other boats. He enjoyed the continuous slapping of halyards on metal masts that sounded like the muted pealing of hidden bells as smaller craft responded to the wavelets. It took a considerable chop to make *Radagast's* halyards ring.

Dumas heard the whine rising over the ever-present tinkling

of distant rigging and the small constant slap of waves on fiberglass. The whine grew into a high-pitched whistle, then suddenly died down rapidly. Dumas turned to see Marc staring down at the aluminum box with unconcealed wonder.

"Well, I'll be damned," said Peter as Dumas walked to the box and stooped to turn the volume down again.

"Loving thoughts work just as well as threats . . . maybe better. For Archibald, but perhaps not for people. Why don't we give him a rest?" Dumas flipped the switch off.

"He wasn't near it?" Marc asked suspiciously.

"Adrian's back was turned all the time," Debbie said.

"Did it happen when you thought about it, Marc?" Dumas asked.

"I have to say yes."

Dumas rose slowly. "It's interesting, isn't it? Archi's not only aware on his own, but he can pick up human thought and intentions."

"But Adrian," Peter objected. "How? It doesn't have any eyes? No brain?"

Dumas shrugged. "I wish I knew," he said. "I'm as much in the dark as you are." Then he shook his head and looked around. "The bar's set up on top of the forecastle. I'll fix the first drink—after that, guests are on their own. House rule."

"Right. Scotch and water on the rocks."

"C'mon," Dumas said. "You asked for it. You got it."

"Oh, my Gawd," Dumas heard Debbie saying, "and I was thinking about becoming a vegetarian. When I think of all the flowers I've picked . . ."

"That's not the worst part," said Rachael. "If you had sensitive enough equipment you could hear tomatoes scream when you peel them. But it doesn't stop me," she added.

Marc sniffed. "I'm not sure it bothers me. I still maintain I'm a higher form of life than a salad."

Dumas wondered as he ignored the ice tongs Rachael had placed in the bucket and fished Peter's cubes out with his fingers. "Chivas Regal or J&B?"

"The Chivas, I think."

Dumas splashed a generous dollop of the amber liquid into the squat glass and added water. "Say when," he warned.

"When." Peter took the glass and sipped deeply. "Ah, Adrian. I needed that."

Dumas looked up, not heightened by the Chelsea boots, but more secure on the deck in sandals. "So what's with the bad vibes, Pete?"

"Can I smoke?" Peter cast a questioning glance at the plant.

Dumas shrugged. "Sure. I don't know if Archi minds at this distance, but anyway we won't hear him complaining. Use the bucket, though, Pete, if you don't mind. They are all around. There's one by your foot, there, at the base of the mast."

"Right." The Dunhill flicked and Peter hunched slightly, his mustache puckering. At last he stood back and blew two brief funnels of smoke from his nostrils, like a weary dragon. "Scared vibes, Adrian. And a bit of anger, I suppose. You haven't given me your answer yet."

"About Watson Mines. Yeah, I know." Dumas looked down to see his toes peeking out from beneath tattered jeans.

"I need it soon, Adrian. I need it to be yes."

"I know, Pete. I'm trying to sort it out."

"If we don't do it someone else will. It won't help, Adrian."

"That's always the way," Dumas nodded. "Someone else will do it. I know."

"So, the money may as well be ours, old chap. You can use your share to give to some anti-nuclear groups, if you wish. I'll increase that share." Peter puffed and looked out past *Radagast's* shrouds over the lighted marina and over the void of Toronto Harbor to the blazing city. Muted laughter and voices came to them across the water from nearby boats. "You could do more good with the money than without it. Good as you see it."

"I realize that, Peter," said Dumas.

Hadn't he said the same to Red Sky not long ago, more or less? How are you going to help Mantouche from a jail cell? "It's a question," said Dumas, "of when one decides, personally, to cop out. When one personally wants no part of it."

Peter chuckled. "Ah, Adrian, Adrian. Sometimes I don't know about you." Peter shook his head, sipped and poured another Chivas. He chuckled again as the bottle gurgled. "Look around, Adrian," he said. "Here you are parked in one of the most expensive yacht clubs in Canada and you talk about being copped out. Look at Rachael, there. Not my taste, not my generation, Adrian, but it's the same thing." Peter gestured with his glass. "Go on, Adrian. Have a look."

Dumas followed Peter's gaze and saw Rachael leaning against the poop deck rail with one arm resting on top of the companionway. The pareau flowed over her hips, dipping well below her navel, and fell to the deck in folds of glowing silk. The bright tropical flowers that rustled when her long legs moved as she crossed her ankles beneath the silk matched those woven into the sheen of her brief bolero top. It was as close as Rachael had dared to come to a lei. In public.

"Hey, Rachael! We found the address!" It was Marg's voice calling. Dumas looked down from the forecastle. Marg and Jim walked hurriedly, but carefully, along the floating pier. Marg obviously concentrated on keeping her heels from spiking down between the boards. Jim wore a dark suit uncomfortably as he helped Marg along. Rachael's head turned prettily and Dumas saw the lantern-glow ignite streaming coils of copper cascading over her shoulders.

Rachael turned back briefly to Marc and Debbie and then went quickly to the rail, leaning over and extending a golden welcoming arm downwards.

"Like I said, Adrian, the clothes, the generation are different. But the similarities are stronger. Your jeans. Rachael's skin. They don't fool me. Do they fool you?"

Dumas clapped Peter on the shoulder, smiling. "I don't think so . . . Peter, you'll have to excuse me for a moment. I have some hosting duties."

"I'd like the answer, Adrian. I can't carry the account without you."

"What about Monday morning, Pete?"

"I'll hold you to that." Peter lifted his glass in a toasting gesture. Dumas nodded and walked toward Rachael, Marg and Jim.

10

Koffler edged down the ravine bank carefully, from sapling to sapling with sure grips, snaking the penlight beam ahead to reveal lurking roots or sudden drops. He was thankful that he'd left the cloying scents of Watçek's garden above him. Koffler preferred the sharper smells of the woods.

Not far away now, he could make out the Bronco's parking lights between the leaves below. The paper in his hand was still damp from Watçek's sweat. Did the man habitually kneel? Must he always whimper?

Something rustled in the bushes off to the side. Koffler stopped, thinking about the Mississauga rattlers that Tchevsky had mentioned. Whatever it was skittered off, obviously on legs. Probably a startled rabbit. Koffler waited in silence to hear if anything else moved nearby. After a moment, he continued his careful progress down, making as little noise as possible. Not that it mattered much. Maybe the effect was a little more powerful if Koffler came and went silently, appearing suddenly to Watçek as a disembodied spirit or wraith. But in the end it didn't matter. A little thought would tell Watçek that he had to come and go somehow, just like any other human being. Watçek wasn't thinking either much or too well, and they would stay with the guilt and the ghosts as long as possible. But when Watçek began to think, and Koffler wondered if he ever would, he'd think also about the knowledge they had of him. The sham that could be made of his piety and integrity if the sad little story ever came out. That would probably be enough.

But for now Koffler moved as quietly as possible. It took several more minutes for him to reach the Bronco. Koffler climbed into the open door, but did not close it until Tchevsky had slowly driven a few hundred yards down the dirt road.

Beyond several turns among the tall trees, Tchevsky at last turned on the headlights and sped up.

"You have it? What does it say?"

Koffler read slowly aloud to Tchevsky, trying to concentrate on keeping the words within the small circle of the penlight as the Bronco bumped over the backroad.

For immediate release

Watson Mines International announces the imminent commencement of negotiations with the governments of the Provinces of Ontario and Quebec and with officials of both provinces' utilities corporations. The goal of the upcoming contractual negotiations will be to guarantee major Canadian utilities an assured supply of nuclear fuel for planned reactor expansion programs in both provinces.

Cyrus Watson, President and major shareholder of Watson Mines International, explains the new policy: "As a good corporate citizen of Canada, Watson International Mines believes that Canadian energy requirements must come first. We must have an assured source of relatively inexpensive energy for generations of future Canadians, even if that commitment will mean fewer corporate profits. I consider myself fortunate that the corporate structure of Watson Mines International allows me alone to make this decision. It is a personal commitment."

President Watson plans personal trips to all of the mines operated by the company in order to explain the new policy to workers. Although long-term agreements with Canadian energy utilities will result in greatly decreased profits and little increase in uranium production for the next decade at least, no layoffs are envisioned now or in the future.

Tchevsky chuckled. "Watçek dictated that himself."

Koffler gazed in admiration at Tchevsky. "He told me he had. How could you know?"

"Easy. It doesn't sound professional, Koffler. Also, he's so rattled that he got the name of his own company wrong. Read it over carefully."

Koffler mouthed the words as he read the letter slowly and silently. He smiled when he caught the mistake. "You're right."

Tchevsky grinned. "Did Watçek say when it would be released to the papers?"

"Monday morning."

"We'll read it that afternoon, then." Tchevsky stopped at the end of the dirt road and looked carefully in both directions before turning onto Highway 10. They were not too far from

Orangeville and could be asleep by a decent hour. "Watçek is certainly going to go through with this, Koffler."

"What gives such certainty, Igor?"

"Sam." Tchevsky paused. "And it would be better to say 'What makes you so sure, Sam?'"

"Idiomatic usage is always so difficult. Alright. What makes you so sure, Sam?"

"It's those trips he plans to reassure the workers. A good political move that means he's serious." Tchevsky chuckled. "The NDP would scream their heads off if Watson Mines looked ready to lay off workers. They'd push for a Parliamentary investigation and God knows what else. Watson's hands might get tied."

"The NDP? That's a political party here?"

"The most socialist one," Tchevsky said wryly.

"Oh." Koffler shook his head. Would he ever understand the complexity of North America?

Tchevsky, who was only moderately interested in chess, considered the combinations idly but carefully, happy that the analysis of it all had been left to more subtle brains. Still, he could ponder. He supposed that in addition to the definite strategic advantage of making Western-aligned countries scrabble that much harder for bomb materials, there was also a diplomatic advantage. Watçek wasn't the only uranium producer in the world, or even in Canada, but his output counted. Twist a few more Watçeks, with levers even now being fashioned, and the West's access to bomb material was severely crippled. The Soviets could then take another direction in the Strategic Arms Limitation Talks, could push for a SALT settlement, and the U.S. would have to waffle. What was that beautiful Watergate phrase? Twist slowly, slowly in the breeze? Well, that's what the Americans would do in the eyes of the world opinion. Waffle and twist, and back down desperately on SALT. True, there was uranium in other places. In Africa. Americans popular in Africa? Ha! Tchevsky loved to ponder ironies, and there were many in his business. He enjoyed the irony that the NDP would probably be most apprehensive about Watçek's move, but Watçek had countered that. Think of it. A party having many members who opposed nuclear power, yet forced to be concerned about layoffs in the nuclear fuel mining field because of the pressure of its supporting unions. Delicious. And what about the irony that made the entire plan feasible? That the capitalistic system itself and the psychotic guilt of but one industrialist could change the policy of a strategic industry. Delicious. For the good of the communist world and peace-loving socialists? Delicious.

What had been overlooked? Undoubtedly something. Tchevsky couldn't see what it could be, but he trusted that the drab little chess-playing analysts had long ago taken it into account. Tchevsky glanced over and saw that Koffler's chin was nodding on his chest. Koffler had done a good job.

Tchevsky reached over and gently poked Koffler's arm. "Koffler?"

"Yes?" Koffler shook himself awake. "Are we there?"

"No, but it won't be long. I was just wondering," said Tchevsky. "Would you like to learn how to play golf tomorrow? We have a free day."

11

"Okay, Jim, this is the last stop of the tour." Dumas flicked on a light and they walked into the stern cabin. Mahogany panelling gleamed richly, but bare steel beams crossed the ceiling very close to their heads, and there was no furniture in the empty room. "This is sort of a living room, I guess you'd call it," Dumas said. "I plan to cover those beams with phoney wooden ones and put carpeting down eventually. But that's probably a project for next year."

They walked the ten feet to the pair of windows that leaned outward. They looked down on the slim McVay daysailer that was moored astern of *Radagast.* "It's a good view, this cabin," said Dumas. "In the old days, this was the captain's cabin, but now it's better for sort of a rec room."

"It's a lot more civilized than Marg led me to expect. She said that you and Rachael were going to boil water on the stove for hot water."

"We were, Jim. But I got some unexpected money and things changed a bit. There's still a long way to go, though."

"Yeah, but a great way to live, Adrian."

"Like everything else, there's advantages and disadvantages."

"The disadvantages don't seem all that obvious."

"Oh, yeah? What about getting back and forth to work? Then, try, just try, to bring anything heavy or bulky over to the island. Like lumber. Or window boxes. It's a hassle. Then, just think what will happen when the water freezes in the winter . . ."

"I hadn't thought of that."

"Well, sometimes it makes me think. Twice," said Dumas. "No, hell, I'm only joking. It was the window boxes today." Dumas smiled wryly. "Well, enough of that. How's the job?"

"It's a change from going to school all these years, and a taste of what's in store for me, for good, next year."

"A change for the better, I hope," said Dumas.

"Oh, yeah, I suppose," Jim tugged at his bushy beard. "Marg's happy. They seem to like me and I'll have a permanent job next year after graduation."

"So this summer was sort of a trial period for you?"

"You can say that again."

Dumas laughed as required. Rachael and Marg worked together at the library and Dumas did not know Jim well. The couples had played a few evenings of bridge which Dumas and Jim had ceased to take seriously once they'd realized the game was merely an excuse for two nervous young mothers to exchange information and compare childrearing notes. "Forgive me, Jim, but you're in meteorology, right? I think Rachael mentioned that you're working with the government."

"That's right, Adrian." Then he grinned and pulled at his beard again. "Who doesn't, in this country?"

"Nothing wrong with that, Jim. Job security."

"Well, Adrian, I admit that after all the years as a student I was apprehensive about work. I decided to become a civil servant as quickly as possible. For all the obvious reasons that everyone laughs about. Boy, did I blow it." Jim shook his head.

"How's that?"

"I've had my ass worked off, that's how,"

"No little office, no feet up on the desk watching the clock?"

"Oh, I wish it was like that, but I can tell you a secret. Some of us do work." He pulled at his beard again. "Here's how it was, see. My first day on the job and I'm getting settled at the desk nice and easy. This guy comes up to me and tells me that I'm gonna head up a crash research project contracted by Provincial Hydro, see? Right. The next thing I know, Adrian, I'm up to my neck in mud, muck, leeches and black flies."

"Doing what, for God's sake?"

"Taking water samples out of the lakes. Lots and lots of lakes, I can tell you." He paused. "Got the bottle?"

"Oh," said Dumas. "Sorry." He handed the bottle of cheap sherry over to Jim, who took an eager swig, wiping the top with his sleeve when he finished. Dumas looked at the bottle and raised it to his lips. "Good stuff," he said appreciatively. He handed the bottle back to Jim.

"It's all I could afford for years. I sort of got hooked on it. Now I can't drink anything else. I carry a bottle with me to any party just to make sure I get it." Jim shook his head sadly. "Who else would buy it?"

Dumas grinned. He recalled the dead bottles he and Jim had killed more clearly. During the long waits between bids, leads and hands while they tried not to learn too much about colic, their daughters' masturbation—at three?—and resulting vaginal infections. The sherry had worked: Dumas remembered little.

"Anyway. That's what I did. Cap bottle after bottle of lake water. From lake after lake. Different depths. Different places around the shore. From boats. Standing in muck."

"But Jim, that's not meteorology . . . it's . . . it's . . ."

"Limnology," Jim supplied. "That's what I kept saying, believe me, to anyone who'd listen. 'Get a limnologist for this job,' I kept saying. But no one listened," he finished sadly.

"Yeah, but why were you doing it?"

"Well, it did turn out to be meterology in the end, after all. After getting all these water samples, then I had to do a study of all the lakes we worked in. Wind patterns over 'em. Surrounding hills and such. But especially rainfall. Then we sent the whole mess over to the Department of Defense atomic labs. Then they sent it over to Provincial Hydro."

"Oh, shit," said Dumas. "Radioactivity pollution?"

Jim raised the bottle, took a long drink and offered it to Dumas. "Nope. That'll be coming later."

"What, then?"

"Well, that's what I began to wonder. At first, like everyone else, I thought it was some sort of radioactivity. If so, Adrian, well, I had something of a stake in it because I was always standing up to my balls in this water, right? I got kinda curious. Be just like 'em to grab an eager student for something like that while the guy who was supposed to be doing the project farmed it out to someone more expendable. So, I started asking around to some of my buddies in physics, engineering and what not."

"Well, give, for God's sake. You've got me curious."

"I finally figured it out. And why Provincial Hydro was interested. It had to be the deuterium."

"Heavy water?"

"Right on. Heavy water."

"But you have to make that stuff, don't you? I mean it doesn't come naturally."

"Sure it does. About one molecule in every six thousand is heavy. Two neutrons. You don't *make* heavy water, Adrian.

You distill it. You take ordinary water and basically distill it over and over again until you collect only the heavy molecules and let the rest go. You get heavy water. After a lot of time and expense."

"I still don't get it," said Dumas.

"Neither did I, right away." Jim pulled his beard and took a short swig. "Then it came to me. Rain." He looked at Dumas as if he expected a reaction.

"Okay. Rain."

"Adrian, rain *is* a distillation process. I put two and two together. Some of these lakes were in a local weather pattern of wind and precipitation. Water got evaporated over and over from the lakes and the rain fell back into it. Over and over. Thousands of times a century for God knows how many centuries. What do you get?"

"Heavy water?"

"Correct."

Above them, on the poop deck, came the hesitant tuning of Rachael's guitar. Then a cautious strum. Another. Gradually, recognizable but amateurish chords. A ragged chorus of "Waltzing Matilda" wafted down to them through the stern windows. Dumas grinned at Pia's wailing rendition. It must have been Debbie's choice: she'd always been working her way to Sydney. Until she met Marc.

"Maybe we'd better go up," Jim suggested.

"Sure. In a minute, Jim, but I'd like to ask you a few more questions, if you don't mind?"

"Shoot."

"Is it enough to make an economic difference, this heavy water?"

"Yep. It's used as a moderator in the Canadian type of reactor and it has to be almost pure heavy water to work. Pure. Okay, it's those last few percentages of molecules that are expensive. Now, if you can start off with those percentages covered, sort of in advance, then you've got a big edge."

"I read somewhere that we had a surplus of heavy water."

"We do. Now. But a lot more will be needed for all the reactors Provincial Hydro plans for the next thirty years. What is it, twenty or thirty?"

Dumas nodded. "Something like that, I think."

"So that's why they're interested."

"You build the reactors on the lakes with heavy water?"

"More or less, only it isn't that easy. You still need a heavy water extraction plant. But the plant itself uses lots of electricity. Okay. So the trick is to build the reactor first beside one of these lakes with a lot of heavy water. Then, build an extraction plant on the lake. Right? Then, the extraction plant can use the reactor's electricity, some of it, to make heavy water so that the reactor can continue to run. It's a neat package and if you choose your lakes carefully, then the total cost is less and the efficiency much greater."

"Jim? Where are these lakes?"

"Prime cottage country, my friend."

"Can you tell me just one of these lakes?"

"Sure. Georgian Bay," he grinned. "That's one of the best ones."

"But there are others?"

"You bet. Some in the Muskokas. Some in the Kawarthas."

"You know what you've just said?"

"Sure I do, Adrian."

"You could figure out the probable locations of Provincial Hydro reactors over the next three decades. It would be a question of the heavy water in the lakes to begin with, access to population centers not far away, roads, and so forth. If one knew the lakes, it wouldn't be difficult to pinpoint prime locations."

"No trouble at all."

"You could do it?"

"Sure. So could you. You thinking the same thing I was thinking? How much environmental groups would pay for that kind of information? How much they need it?"

"That's just what I was thinking," said Dumas. "Prime cottage country, you say."

"That's right."

"The shit would hit the fan," said Dumas. "C'mon, let's go up. Just one more thing, Jim." Dumas paused at the doorway. "Would you be . . . er . . . interested?"

"We have Jeremy and little Mary, Adrian. I sure as hell would. I would go this far. I would tell you everything you need to know to pinpoint the locations. I'd check your work—on a twenty questions basis—that fair enough? If *you* do it. I can't afford to be on the government's blacklist. I'm still looking for that desk angled toward the clock, remember?"

Above them, Edward's voice rose in a doleful and only moderately successful "Red River Valley," sung with heart if not talent. Jim and Dumas listened where they stood even after Dumas had flicked off the light. Yes, Dumas thought, so many things pleaded for remembrance and second thoughts before bidding them farewell. And what wouldn't men do for women, and to them, to quell the loneliness all men seemed to have inside? Peter for Norma. Dumas for Rachael.

Dumas looked at Jim's fuzzy face in the light reflected off the water and through *Radagast's* stern windows. Dumas met the glint in the bright eyes and the set to the otherwise always humorous mouth. No, it wasn't the desk under the clock that Jim feared losing. It was Marg's chance for her house after all the years in apartments, the kids, and the loyal days at the library. The colic and the study. The brief repites of bridge and sherry . . .

"And the cowboy who loved you so true-oo-oo." Edward finished in a drawn-out tremolo that made Dumas cringe.

Jim smiled. "Have you read about it in the papers, Adrian? That Ph.D.'s are a dime a dozen? Plenty on welfare?" Jim offered the bottle. Dumas held it up in the meagre light. Two shots.

Dumas drank half. "I read that," he said. "Terrible. Shit, Jim, I'm a capitalist. Don't believe in swelling the welfare rolls."

Jim smiled and finished the bottle. "Deal?"

"Deal. Don't throw the bottle to seal it. A gentle roll will do fine."

Jim and Dumas climbed up the steps to the group on the poop. Edward was in the middle of *Four Strong Winds* and Rachael was concentrating on the chording, but she still managed to give Dumas a preoccupied welcoming smile. Marg patted a place beside her on the teak and Jim went over to sit beside her drawn-up knees. Dumas noted thankfully that her high heeled shoes lay on the deck in front of her wriggling nyloned toes.

Dumas waited for Rachael to finish her strumming before he slipped his hand beneath the silk of her bolero. She leaned back against his chest, giving him more access. "Here, Ed. You play," said Rachael, handing him the guitar.

"Yesh, Edvard. Ve have all had more than enough of your shinging."

"You can say that again." Marc's mutter was barely audible.

"Okay. Okay. I get the message. I was only trying to bring some joy into your drab, sordid lives. What does anybody want?"

Surprisingly, Dumas withdrew his hand from around the yielding large teardrop of Rachael's breast. "Edward, can you follow me in *Gunga Din*?"

"Oh, Lord," said Edward. "Must I?" Dumas only sang this when he was very, very drunk.

Rachael buried her face delicately in long fingers. The golden-copper coils shook helplessly. "But Adrian," she protested, "you don't *seem* that drunk."

"It must have been the sherry, down below," Dumas grinned.

"I'll vouch for that," said Jim.

"Yes, old chap, perhaps, but that doesn't make the accent any better. Or more bearable," Peter offered from beside the binnacle. "Why must you, old man, surrounded by bona fide Englishmen and women?"

"For the Empiah, Peter," Dumas paused. "Besides, the opening lines have some significance for me. Maybe for Jim." Dumas stood, struck a dramatic pose on his poop deck, and intoned the first lines, talking, while Edward strummed.

You may talk of gin and beer!
When you're quartered safe out 'ere!

"And some do more than talk," said Debbie until shushed to silence by Dumas' warning finger, waggling.

And you're sent to penny-fights at Aldershot-it.
But when it comes to slaughter, you'll do your work on water,
And you'll lick th' bloomin' boots of 'im wot's got't.

Rachael, head down and shaking with subdued laughter, heard only snatches.

An' 'e lifted up my 'ead . . .
And he plugged me where I bled . . .
An' 'e give me arf a pint of water green.
'Twas crawlin' and it stunk,
But of all the drinks I've drunk . . .
I'm gratefullest for the one from Gunga Din!

And later, but more slowly . . .

But I'll meet 'im later on,
In the place where we have gone!
Where it's always double-drill and no canteen . . .

"No canteen," said Edward deeply.

'E'll be squattin' on the coals,
Givin' drinks to poor damned souls ...
And I'll get my swig in 'ell from Gunga Din!

"Gun-ga Dinnn," said Edward.

When he had finished to the sound of tattered applause, Dumas sank down to the deck behind Rachael. He re-inserted his hand under the bolero top and squeezed the handful of softness gently. His thumb perked Rachael's nipple. "I don't know why I did that," he said.

"I don't know why, either," she answered softly, leaning back against him again. "I knew you weren't drunk. Did it mean something?"

"I doubt it," said Dumas.

After *The Wild Colonial Boy* sung wistfully by Debbie, *Danny Boy* sung by all equally badly and *Farewell to Nova Scotia* by Rachael's clear voice, someone noticed the glittering mansion of light gliding toward the island across the darkness of the harbor. The wide-beamed *Sam McBride* dispelled any illusions of breeding the night lights might have bequeathed her by blowing a vulgar raspberry. Soon, they could hear the eager throbbing of engines.

"Last ferry," Dumas said.

12

Dumas toiled beneath the silent urging of the flow chart on the wall and was deep into the trials and tribulations of late-Cretaceous dinosaurs. On the other hand, the script had to be kept simple. Intrigue must be written in, along with space-age speculation. Something that could be smiled, smirked and patronizingly presented by the seemingly omniscient television host. With illustrations that could be Chroma-keyed without too much difficulty by a prodution staff who didn't know an *Archeopteryx* from a *Morganucodon*.

How to transform a 60-million-year-old tragedy of dinosaurs into something of crucial importance to moon-walking humans?

For that matter, how to transform the geographic maunderings of an otherwise obscure medieval Arab cartographer into something equally interesting? Dumas had managed to do that for the last show. There had been lots of letters about the interesting implications of Hadji Ahmed's 1559 map of the world. If anything, dinosaurs should be easier. After all, they possessed inherently more drama than moldy maps.

With one part of his brain, Dumas registered the noises of Debbie coming into the office to open it for another five-day tilt in the business world. She would presently hear his typing and bring him coffee. He hoped that she'd turn on the air-conditioner soon because the almost-August heat wave was already dampening the back of his shirt against the chair.

By a little after 11:30 and two cups of coffee, Dumas had somehow written what he thought was an interesting programme for the television host. He turned from his window to the summons of a discreet knock on his door. "Come in." He expected Debbie, but accepted the Hardy Ames jacket and the trimmed mustache. "Ah. Peter. Good morning."

From the thin lips, Dumas knew that Peter expected the answer to be in the negative. Bearing in mind the view from the burrow's lip, Dumas had no choice. "Peter, I have some bad news for you," Dumas began wearily.

"Nothing compared to this." Peter tossed the newspaper on Dumas' desk. "Your morality was saved by the bell, Adrian."

Dumas sat down and unfolded the Star's first edition. He read about Cyrus Watson's personal commitment. The confirmation of negotiations by cautiously off-the-cuff statements of government and Provincial Hydro officials. The newspaper's own analysis of Watson's decision based upon known production. None for foreign sales. Dumas looked up.

"There's no reason for us, now. I can't get anyone important on the phone. They're in meetings," Peter smiled.

"But you have some sort of agreement, contract. Maybe they'll settle something on the retainer."

"Yes. The agreement. Well, Debbie was typing up the letter this morning, Adrian. She gave it to me to proof about five minutes ago." Peter looked down. "I think, Adrian, that's about it for me."

"Rubbish. There are other accounts, Pete. You used to get them before. You'll get 'em again."

"But it's gotten down to the point now, old man, where it's like starting all over from scratch. I'm too old to go out pounding the streets for business like I did fifteen, twenty years ago. Besides," he said tiredly, "it isn't the same anymore. The economy's not like it used to be. No one is confident. No one is expansive. Sort of pulling in their horns," Peter grinned, "as you Americans would say."

Dumas spread his hands helplessly and dropped them to the newspaper. He tapped the Watson story with his fingertips. "Hell, Pete. What can I do?"

Peter shrugged and his fingers wriggled searchingly in his pocket for the cigarette package. "Nothing. Now I have to explain it to Norma. Somehow." He hunched over to light his Rothman, looking out from under his brow at Dumas with an amused eye. "Wouldn't care to hire me, eh, Adrian?" he said as he snuffed the Dunhill and blew smoke. "I wasn't a bad account man. Once."

"How much was it worth, Pete? The Watson thing."

Peter mused. "Oh, I would estimate about fifty grand a year. Maybe a bit less."

Dumas winced.

"Exactly, Adrian. It would have bought a few holidays. Finished off the mortgage on the house. The car my son expects this year, now that he's doing well in university. Keep up my Registered Retirement Savings Plan."

"Now?"

"I don't like to think about it, Adrian."

"Surely you have something saved, Pete."

"Of course. But it's the overhead. Not just here, but at home." Peter waved at the world, vaguely. "Norma and I've gotten used to living high off the hog. I was hoping to keep it up. I dislike trotters."

"Can't be all that bad, Pete," Dumas laughed.

Peter cocked an eyebrow. "No?" He puffed thoughtfully. "I went over it in my mind, Adrian. Very quickly. With what I have in the bank, I can float about four months. Maybe five, the way it's going now. Then, I'm bottomed out. The accounts I have don't even break me even."

Dumas nodded. "I didn't know that, Pete. But I suspected it."

"The thing is, Adrian, I have to do some hard thinking. I think that I should get out of here—and hustle my backside to get a job, while the money lasts. Maybe I can find something before my bank balance bottoms out. I should be able to pull down twenty-five, maybe more, somewhere. As an account man with an agency. Take the accounts I have."

"I'm sure of it, Pete. No sweat. If you go, though, I'm going to wrap it up here, I think," said Dumas.

"What about our Deborah?" said Peter.

"It's not so bad now. Now that she's married."

Peter blew smoke and nodded in agreement. "I'm happy about that. What'll you do, Adrian?"

Dumas shrugged. "Same thing, whatever that is. But I can work from *Radagast's* stern cabin. Less overhead, if you're out."

"You'll do well."

"Well enough, I suppose," said Dumas. He paused. "I'm sorry, Peter. I wish there was something I could do."

"I was sort of hoping, Adrian, that you'd opt for continuing on with the business, the office and Debbie for a while, increase the number of accounts . . . I'd throw as much as I could your way from wherever I was working, what I could get away with. And then maybe sometime in the future there'd be enough business to warrant my coming back in. On a different basis," he added.

"It wouldn't really work, Pete. I was never as committed to the business as you were . . . are. I've never really wanted to own one." There was the other factor, too, Dumas didn't mention. He'd hire a better account man than Peter if it came to that. "There's something that I could do, though," said Dumas. "Even if I close up the office, I can take Debbie on for a little while until she can find something better. Or decide to get pregnant."

"I suppose that's better than nothing."

"Something else, too. I can take you to lunch. We can all go. Dick Turpin's?"

Peter smiled and nodded. "Alright. Thanks, Adrian."

"Okay. I need about five minutes more at the typewriter and I can leave with a clear conscience. You might tell our dear Debbie to repair her make-up and powder her nose." Dumas glanced at his watch. He'd make a bet with himself to finish before noon.

Peter closed the door and Dumas returned to furiously typing the wrap-up of the television show. In a few minutes, he tore the last sheet from the typewriter. 11:58. He'd made it. If Edward buckled down on taking those slides, the flow chart would be more than contented.

13

They walked out onto Yonge Street and immediately sagged with the weight of the heat. Peter and Dumas flanked Debbie to either side and they hurried as quickly as possible in the direction of the air-conditioning awaiting them in the Royal York. By the time they reached Front, Dumas' shirt was damp and Debbie boasted a mustache of tiny beads above her lips. Dumas thought enviously of Rachael on the water, cooled by Island breezes.

"Hey," said Dumas, "let's all pop into the bank and I'll get some money out for lunch. It's air-conditioned."

Debbie and Peter stood by the potted plants on the cool marble while Dumas waited his turn at the teller in a maze of plush velvet ropes. Dumas had noticed from the street that the jagged gold teeth against the sky had looked a bit more ravenous than usual, as always on a Monday. Well, why shouldn't it be pleased with its handiwork? One more soul had succumbed to the myth, propagated by the chartered banks, that one could have prosperity without either risk or very much competence. The Canadian way. The richly-gleaming tower of gold had taken one more victim. Soon, no doubt, Peter would come to it or another one like it for a personal loan to sustain his lifestyle just a bit longer. The loan would undoubtedly be granted. On a personal signature. With personal guarantees and against easily converted personal property.

No risk, thank you.

Had the chartered banks ever offered the risky business loans without personal guarantees? Not in Canada. Had they ever taken a flyer on a poor but competent someone who possessed only ideas and drive? Not in Canada.

Which explained why multi-nationals had such a foothold in

the country. There was little home-grown competition. Which explained why small business was dying a slow and agonizing death from Newfoundland to British Columbia. No risk capital to create new jobs.

Multi-nationals were not always the best corporate citizens, either. Especially on environmental matters. It wasn't *their* environment, after all. Canada's youthful thousands who would never find work were treated to the spectacle of their poverty being assured by the same system which condemned their future. By pandering to corporate giants and personal desperation like Peter's, the towers rose and the golden teeth of this one gleamed more richly. Did the ravisher really believe no reckoning would ever come? Apparently.

Thinking of the morality of corporate citizens, Dumas wondered about Watson's unexpected move. Folding the bills down into his pocket, Dumas walked pensively up to Peter and Debbie. They looked outside at the glittering pavement.

"Well. It's only a block to go," said Debbie. "Maybe we'll make it."

Dumas grabbed her elbow and encouraged her toward the doors. "I'll revive you with a gin and tonic," he said. "Peter, did this Watson thing come out of the blue? No hint?"

"Nothing. Last week they were talking expansion. This week it's a commitment that will stop expansion." Peter held the door.

Their heels clicked hurriedly along the sidewalk. "What I can't figure," said Dumas, "is why Watson Mines would do this at all. They've never showed such concern before. Provincial Hydro's been asking for this for years, right? Then suddenly, for no reason, it happens. It makes no sense."

"Not my worry, Adrian. I have enough of my own."

"But it's interesting."

"I'll re-type the agreement this afternoon, Peter."

"That's what we're talking about, Debbie," Peter smiled. "It won't be necessary. There's no account."

Debbie stopped on the pavement and looked from Dumas to Peter. "Oh, Peter. Tell me it isn't true?"

"I'm afraid it is, my dear."

"But that means you won't be able . . ." She stopped. "Oh. I guess that's why we're all going out to lunch together . . . ?"

"Something like that, I suppose," Peter admitted.

They walked the rest of the way in silence and by the time Dumas held the door open he saw that Debbie's mascara had begun to run from the tears on her cheeks. She slipped inside the restaurant quickly and disappeared in the direction of the women's room.

Peter and Dumas found a corner table and ordered drinks. By the time Debbie joined them with large dewy eyes and a forced smile, the ice cubes in her gin and tonic were measurably smaller. Dumas realized that she was no longer the scared and vivacious girl that he'd met years ago. Maybe it was just the fashions. Would Debbie still look the same in one of her old minis? Very much the same, he decided. She possessed the same superb legs, huge blue eyes, and the peaches and cream complexion hadn't faded. Sunshine still burst gold off her hair, more so now with the frizzy mass of tiny curls she wore than before, when locks had been long and parted in the center. Only someone who did not know her would fail to miss the hint of emptiness in her eyes. Did they lose some of their depth when she married Marc? Gave up the dream of working out to Australia? The flash of adventure was faded in the blue and it had been that sparkle that had made her legs in the minis seem so excitingly energetic, her nose so pert and her mouth mischievously petulant. The child and the girl had yielded to the woman and Dumas missed his young friend.

At first Debbie made suggestions. She could go out and help Peter scrounge up some new accounts. She would take a cut in salary. Adrian could take over the business and the office and hire Peter as an account man.

"Peter and I have already discussed that," Dumas explained. "Debbie, I just don't want to run a business the way Pete does. It's not me."

"What will you do, Adrian?"

Dumas shrugged. "Like I told Pete, if he wants to get out, I'll just transfer operations into the stern cabin of *Radagast*. Peter suggested that you should come with me for a while. It's a good idea. I could use your help."

"When—when are you planning to close it down, Peter?" she asked.

Peter patted her hand. "I haven't firmly decided to pack it in yet, old girl. I may give it a try for a couple of weeks, maybe months. But if something doesn't break soon, it's best that I go out and find a proper job." Peter smiled. "It'll do me good to have a boss again."

"Oh, Adrian. Couldn't you just carry on for a while?" Debbie turned to Dumas with a sincere smile and a rush of words. "Help Peter a bit until he gets some more accounts again. Keep it all together." She held his wrist. "Peter's helped us all . . ."

"Adrian and I have discussed that, too, Debbie. Last week." Peter turned to Dumas and smiled. "And I'd like to apologize for some of the things I said, Adrian. A bit of a cheap shot it was. I've been regretting some of my remarks last week, and on the weekend."

"Forget it, Pete."

"The point is, Deborah, I never floated Adrian. There's no reason for Adrian to float me now. None. We didn't start out that way, and I really don't want it to end that way."

Debbie looked down and nodded her head softly.

"Actually," Peter said, "as this realization slowly sinks in, I'm beginning to see how lucky I've been all these years. I just appeared at the right place at the right time. I know that now and I'm almost looking forward to discovering what I can do if I must."

The food came and while the waiter was sorting out the plates, Dumas reflected that maybe he had underestimated Peter after all.

Peter tucked into his roast beef with great good humor. He chewed and seemed to be thinking of something amusing. He encouraged Debbie to stop merely picking at her quiche, but to eat it. And drink the rosé.

"You know the irony of it all, Adrian?"

"What's that, Peter?"

"A year ago, I guess it was, I was thinking of getting out anyway."

"Why, Peter? You had some large accounts."

"Sure." Peter chewed with energy. "But I met some fellows in the real estate business. Now, I don't mean developing subdivisions or taking second mortgages, Adrian, I mean out-and-out speculation. Anyway, they sort of offered me a deal."

"What was that?"

"Well, they kind of liked my country gentleman manner, just like it rubs you the wrong way, Adrian, and they wanted me to travel all around the country—abroad, too—and scout around the edges of towns."

"Whatever for?" said Debbie.

"Interesting. They wanted me to scout out speculation opportunities at the edges of towns. You know, farm land that would be valuable someday because it was in the path of growth, but was worth not much now. Quite complicated, actually. Requires a knowledge of all sorts of things to pick the most likely direction of growth. Toronto's easy because the lake's in the way and there's only one real way to go. North. But a lot of towns could grow in almost any direction. But that's not what they wanted me for. They had experts for that. They wanted me to just travel around and talk to businessmen, town counsellors, farmers, developers. Collect the local gossip and ferret out the local power structure."

"Who had what investment in making sure the growth went in one direction and not in another?"

"Exactly, Adrian. You have no idea, apparently, how many towns start to spread, east, for instance, for no good reason except that one local developer happened to get hold of Aunt Sadie's old farm for peanuts. Maybe too many rocks. Rust in the orchard. Anyway, he gets it and subdivides, and somebody puts up little split-levels . . . okay . . . then somebody else buys some more land near Auntie Sadie's old farm for a higher price and he puts up a shopping center for the subdivision. Pretty soon, there's a suburb."

"I'm afraid I don't get it at all," said Debbie. Her face was no longer flushed and her eyes less moist.

"Look at it this way," said Dumas. "It would be nice to know who holds the various local versions of Aunt Sadie's farms . . . before the farm ever got close to being developed. Then, before anything's done with Sadie's one-sixty, you could buy just maybe ten strategic acres—before there's any reason for the price to go up—for that inevitable little plaza. Maybe a hunk of the old MacMillan farm which isn't doing too well, now that his son has decided to go off to Southern Cal to be a rock musician."

"Quite," said Peter.

"And if you already know the major roads, the rivers, streams and lakes that can't be developed or diverted without a lot of government hassle, then you have a chance of locating the best ten acres."

"Still," Debbie pointed out, "it sounds like a frightful amount of money."

"Yes, indeed," said Peter, "but these chaps had it."

"You were doing okay, Pete, but hardy in that kind of league. They were gonna cut you in?"

"In a veddy small way, Adrian. I think it was some fraction of a percentage. No, they wanted me on salary. To just travel around and talk. Actually, though, the way it worked out, the little fraction would have eventually amounted to a considerable sum. As the investments matured."

"You're not kidding," Dumas agreed. "When land starts to skyrocket for some reason, it keeps on going. Still, it takes a fair amount of money to play that game."

Peter named one of Canada's largest trust companies, which advertised its integrity continuously. He grinned.

"Come on!" Dumas crossed his knife and fork across his invariable chopped sirloin and regarded Peter with mild disbelief. "Them?" In all the advertisements about helping Canada grow, the firm had never mentioned its profiteering and contribution to urban sprawl upon badly needed farmland.

"It's good to surprise you, Adrian. Sure. Think about it. Who else would have the money to speculate on the scale required?"

Dumas thought. He easily named a few other trust companies and the major banks.

Peter took a bite of Yorkshire pudding and briefly closed his eyes in contentment. "Absolutely correct. And they're all into it. In fact, from what I understood, old chap, the competition's bloody grim."

"Land use laws!"

"What?" Debbie blinked. Her eyes shone bluer, and larger. It was the wine. On top of the gin.

"Land usage legislation," Peter repeated. "There's some concern about unplanned urban growth—"

"Eating up farmland that will be needed for food someday," Dumas interrupted.

"Correct. For instance, Debbie, land sales have to be approved in British Columbia now because the Fraser Valley is the only market garden area in the province," said Peter.

"And a lot of it was getting covered by concrete," Dumas supplied wryly. He turned to Peter. "So they're competing to see who can grab what's left that's speculable before there's any more legislation?"

Peter nodded emphatically while swallowing puffed potatoes. "That's it. Anyway, I told them I wasn't interested because I liked the business I was in. A year ago."

"Maybe there's still an opening," Dumas started eating again.

"Not with that company. I met the chap who got the job finally. I did it as a favor. They wanted my opinion of him."

"What about with a competitor?"

"I rather imagine that one learns about such things through personal contact. I could scout around, I suppose. But, Adrian, I really wouldn't like the work."

It dawned upon Dumas that his sirloin was not nearly so

warm as it had been and he resolved to pay more attention to it. He attacked it seriously for a few minutes and sat back with a sigh and a broad grin. He looked about and saw that Debbie's and Peter's plates were bare. Debbie appeared to be suffering a relapse of the glums.

"I guess we'd better go back to the office," she suggested.

"Why?" asked Dumas, "Nothing's really happening there." He looked around at Peter and Debbie. "Anyone for brandy and coffee?" He paused. "A fattening dessert?"

"You're going all out, Adrian. You don't have to," said Peter.

"Yes, Adrian. It's beginning to feel like the last supper. Besides," she added, "I think I have to start watching out for matronly spread."

"Make you a deal," Dumas leered at Debbie. "If we go back to the office, after we have brandy and coffee, and after you have a disgusting great dessert, if I talk with Peter alone for about an hour and he comes out with his mustache twitching with excitement like it used to . . . will you wear one of your old minis to work tomorrow?"

"Adrian! Minis are as dead as the dodo. And I'm too old."

"Bullshit. You just got into the habit of feeling that way recently. I don't care about fashion. What's in?"

"Handkerchief hems, sort of."

Dumas shrugged.

"I'm too fat," Debbie tried.

"You're actually a little thinner," Dumas insisted. "That's why I want you to have something fattening. Nice full thighs in minis turn me on."

"Adrian," said Peter, "you're onto something, aren't you?"

He ignored Peter. "Debbie, is it a deal?"

Debbie looked at Peter. "Far be it from me to even suggest that you trade your modesty, especially to the likes of Adrian here, on my behalf," said Peter. "On the other hand . . .."

She hesitated. "You're crass, Adrian," she said, picking up the menu card from the table.

"I know." Dumas pondered the selection seriously. "What about strawberry shortcake?"

Debbie's wide blue eyes fluttered briefly and Dumas was entranced by the shadows of the long lashes on her cheek. "I wonder if I can still get into the Courrèges boots . . ." She tugged her lower lip prettily. "Alright, Mister Dumas. Strawberry shortcake it is. And the mini. As long as I don't have to wear it *to* work. Just at work."

"Done!" Dumas shook her hand.

139

"Now that you've concluded your indecent contract, Adrian, perhaps you'll tell me what it's all in aid of."

"You, of course," said Dumas. "And me," he added. "Well, all of us. We'll all have to do our bit." Dumas looked at Peter. "Brandy and coffee, Pete?"

"Sure."

"Gee, you sure know how to impress a guy, taking him to lunch, Pete."

"That means I'm buying, eh?"

"Right. You're entertaining your consultant, see? And he's just made you not a fortune, exactly, but a tidy little sum."

"You don't say?"

"I certainly do."

14

Debbie was bending over slightly, feeding the kerchunking Xerox machine when Dumas entered. He closed the door softly, to minimize the clicking of the lock, and looked. Miss McGuigan was a girl who kept promises. Peter's mustache had twitched sufficiently to earn Dumas a micro-mini. The gaudiest one he remembered from happier years and an upbeat GNP, the silver shiny one. With the knee-length white plastic boots and matching ladder-hose. Where had she gotten those? Maybe she'd saved them.

Dumas whistled and Debbie straightened up immediately and turned quickly. A hand clasped a palpitating chest covered by a white silk blouse. Debbie wore a cameo on a black velvet ribbon around her neck. The cameo jiggled. "Damn, Adrian. You scared the life out of me. Stop drooling, Mister Dumas. I feel like an idiot."

"You're great," Dumas said simply. "When they have revivals, why can't they ever have 60's and 70's revivals? I don't see the attraction of grease."

"Truthfully, Adrian. You know, it's kinda nice. I can still get away with it."

"Still." Dumas shook his head sadly. "My God, girl, you're not even thirty."

Dumas walked to his door and unlocked it. Consider the intimate relationship between women's skirt length and the Gross National Product. When the GNP went up, so did the skirts. When the GNP percentages dropped, the hems plummeted. The amount of leg showing even tallied with the degree of economic health. The late 1960's had been euphoric on both counts, leg and growth. Rising oil prices and the embargo

141

had driven skirts down fast. Neither they, nor the GNP, had ever really bounced back.

Now the uncanny thing was the exactness of the correlation. What about a year when some Western economies were not badly off, but others were? What if France and Germany and Switzerland boomed, while North America sagged under the impact of devaluation? Simple. Handkerchief hems. Part up, part down. Problem. The designers had decreed this before the economic picture developed. They always did.

Dumas, sitting down behind his desk and rummaging around for the pad of paper that was there yesterday but had somehow disappeared when he needed it, decided that Ottawa was missing the obvious. Economics wasn't figures, trade balances and deficits and bank interest rates. All those were merely symptoms, for economics was, purely and simply, psychology. Ottawa was wasting a lot of money hiring economic experts to find a way out of Canada's fiscal morass.

Subsidize the clothing industry to make mini-skirts. Pay women to wear 'em. No problem. Men ran the economy. Men like feminine legs. Men feel inspired and confident viewing feminine legs. When men feel inspired and confident they take risks and spend money. *Quod Est Demonstratum.*

Pity that none of the government's experts could think of something so elegant and obvious. It was too simple. Maybe it would work for Peter.

Dumas found the pad—where he'd put it, naturally—and began on the list. It was a long one and detailed. Nonetheless, he was able to compose it quickly because he'd finalized it in his head last night.

It had been Dumas' rather preoccupied good-night kiss to Becky that had caused Rachael to give him a quizzical glance, for he had always maintained that good-night kisses and good-morning greetings were very important for children. Later, after Dumas had stalked up to the poop, Rachael had come up to join him. She'd lain down beside him on the deck. Deneb blazed out almost directly overhead.

"Look," she had pointed to another star, "doesn't it look red?"

"Altair." It was the month for birds, he had thought. Deneb in Cygnus, Altair in Aquila. Two differing personalities, swans and eagles.

"What's bothering you, Adrian?"

Dumas had crossed his arms behind his head. "I don't know." Then, he'd gone on to tell her about Peter's situation and what he'd determined to do about it. The plan that had come to him quite suddenly with the last bite of chopped sirloin.

Rachael had laughed and rolled over to peck him on the cheeks. "Adrian, my beloved husband, you are such a dévious man."

Dumas had grunted.

"What could be wrong? It's beautiful. I'm not sure it's . . . uh . . . the most moral plan in the world, but then again, neither are they."

"You don't mind?" Dumas was acutely aware that he'd done less moral things.

"Of course not," she'd laughed. "Do you?"

Dumas had squirmed uncomfortably on the teak. "Somehow it doesn't sit right. I'd like to think it was the morality."

"But you don't think it is?"

"Uh, uh."

"Neither do I. I've known you too long." Rachael had suddenly propped herself up on one elbow and looked down on him, smiling. "You know what I think it is?"

"Tell me, green eyes." Dumas had grinned.

"I think you'd rather just do it cleanly, but you're concerned about Peter and he and Debbie have applied just a little pressure, haven't they, Adrian, for old times sake? I think you're feeling a bit angry at yourself. And them."

"Maybe that's it, I don't know," Dumas had answered. "Something seems wrong with that bloody eagle up there, that's all."

Rachael had looked up to the vague triangle of stars which could be contrived into an eagle only by a stretch of the imagination. Altair, the brightest star in the constellation, was either the eagle's eye or a gleam on its beak, depending on which astronomy book one consulted. "It looks okay to me. Just like always."

"Then why do I keep getting the feeling it's swooping back and forth toward me?" Dumas had observed dryly.

"Maybe you've been typing too much, Adrian. Probably your eyes are tired." Rachael always had been a practical and down-to-earth person. She went below.

Dumas had continued lying there watching the stars wheel and the occasional streak of a meteor from the Aquarid shower. He had flicked his eyes down to see her go and had cherished the long legs and the delicate crease of derrière peeking from drastically cut-down jean shorts.

Dumas had stayed there until Taurus topped the horizon. By the time he'd gone below, great Aldeberan had barely struggled into view, hardly afloat above the waters of Lake Ontario.

His feelings of unease had shaken off only when Debbie's mini had distracted him, but it seemed that thin shadows darkened the room slightly from time to time, as if birds of prey passed before the sun, or more probably because scudding summer clouds played hide and seek with sunbeams that would have fallen onto his fire escape.

The telephone buzzed.

"Yes, Debbie," Dumas answered.

"I expected Mister Tompkins in early, after the way he left yesterday. There've been a couple of calls for him. Do you know when he'll be in?"

"Any time now," said Dumas, glancing at his watch. "He went to the library for me first thing this morning."

"Thanks, Mister Dumas."

On impulse, Dumas held the phone and dialed out. After assorted clicks and transfers, he succeeded in reaching Jim within the labyrinth of the Ontario government. It was a jovial conversation and Jim accepted the invitation, making a note of the address.

Dumas returned to his list about the time that Peter staggered into his office under the burden of books and pamphlets. "Just dump 'em on the floor," Dumas offered.

Dumas looked over the list, doublechecking it. He handed it to Peter. "We have to get everything, everything on this list, Pete. So, if you can't get it all at one office, you'll have to go to another one. You may have to go to Ottawa, even, tonight, and get some of 'em from the horse's mouth bright and early in the morning."

"Right," Peter nodded eagerly. He looked down the list of map numbers. "My God, Adrian, there must be a hundred here."

"Maybe. Remember, we have to work about one inch to the mile."

"Don't worry. I'll get every one by tomorrow afternoon."

"I've decided to send Debbie to Curry's for the art supplies," said Dumas. "So that's off you. She can go tomorrow when she's not compromised in the fashion world."

"Eh?" Peter looked at Dumas curiously.

"Nothing." Peter hadn't noticed. That meant, at least, that he was enthusiastic still. A night's sleep on it hadn't changed his excitement. Dumas smiled as Peter rushed out. Dumas tossed

144

his chart and map lists into the bottom drawer of the desk and buzzed Debbie to get her to bug Edward about the Lovable slides and the dinosaur slides. He wanted to see whether he could satisfy both the flow chart's schedule and Peter's cash priorities at the same time. He doubted that it would be possible.

Dumas lay full-length on the floor and chose at random from the collapsed pile of stuff Peter had dropped there. He happened to choose *Principles of Meterological Analysis* by Walter J. Saucier. Why not? Dumas sighed and began flipping pages at about ten-second intervals. He breathed regularly and his face was not particularly flattered by the blank stare on it.

He took a break for half an hour about mid-day when Debbie knocked, came in and reached down to hand him the Big Mac and the chocolate shake. It tasted more savory than Dumas thought usual, but perhaps it had only been the glimpse of white lace froth under Debbie's micro that had spiced it.

By five-thirty Dumas had flipped through the entire pile and was back aboard *Radagast* early enough to help Rachael pick a couple of tomatoes for salad.

15

Jim looked up, tugged his beard, and professed amazement. It was about time, Dumas thought. Jim had been going over the maps for an hour.

"There's one or two minor changes here and there," said Jim. "But really, Adrian, it's a fantastic job."

"Where are the changes?" Dumas bent over the desk. They worked together for about twenty minutes. Under Jim's direction, Dumas cut and removed some small pieces of red tape from the plastic. Sometimes, after reference to Jim's dog-eared map with its pencil shadings, Dumas would be forced to pull some more red tape from the roll, stick it down on the plastic, and trim.

They stood up and rubbed their eyes.

"Jim, your maps only took in the features like the heavy water itself, roads, powerlines, rainfall patterns and things like that. Look what happens when you add factors like government-owned land and land that for one reason or another hasn't been attractive for private owners."

Dumas unzipped the artist's portfolio leaning against the bookcase and took out another large plastic sheet. "Let's look at the master map of Ontario first," he said. He arranged the first plastic sheet with red blotches over the ordinary road map of southern Ontario. Then, he carefully arranged the sheet from the portfolio on top. "Okay, the black shaded areas here represent land that's heavily owned privately. The clear areas are Crown Land and land that is too rocky, too marshy or otherwise not suitable or attractive to the private buyer. What do you see?"

Black shading on the top plastic sheet obscured most of the red areas on the plastic sheet beneath. The names of towns, lakes and capes came through a bit blurred, but clearly enough, as did the veins of roads. Only a few red areas stood out brightly. These clustered around provincial parks, some Indian reservations on the Bruce Peninsula, wrapped around some of the more remote lakes of the Muskokas and Haliburton Highlands and scalloped the more rugged coastal areas of Georgian Bay's coastline.

"There's only twenty or thirty prime locations," Jim observed.

"And how many nuclear reactors planned in the next thirty years?"

"About twenty or thirty, they say." Dumas and Jim looked at each other.

"If I'm right. Maybe I'm not, but it more or less fits the pattern of the reactors that already exist. There's the Douglas Point thing and the planned one at Darlington, both next to provincial parks. The Pickering reactor is the odd one out, but even then I'm not sure because I think a lot of land around Frenchman's Bay is government-controlled because of a bird sanctuary or something."

"So, again, assuming you're right, Adrian, you've located all of the planned reactors. At least, it might be reasonable to say that you're fifty percent right and half of the reactors will be on these red blobs . . . But I still don't know where that leaves us."

"Land speculation," Dumas grinned. "What if someone had the money, right now, to buy up random acre parcels in these prime locations because of the probability that some day Provincial Hydro would like to buy that land, very quietly, to plunk a reactor on?"

"You're suggesting that environmental people should get together and buy up bits of this land?"

"That might be an idea," Dumas conceded. "But the costs would require public donations, publicity drives and the whole thing would come out. In a confrontation-type thing, Provincial Hydro and the government might very well simply cut their losses and come out into the open. Confiscate the land or appropriate it on a 'for the good of most citizens and Ontario's future' basis. Then what good have you done?"

"They would, too. There's too much power behind this nuclear drive. Look at that story this week about Watson Mines. They've got a cozy deal to supply all the uranium they'll need for the next thirty years if it's signed. They're going ahead with it."

"I'm not sure we can stop it, but it can be slowed down."

"How? No one has the power."

"Big business does," said Dumas. "Why not set up a conflict of interest situation between the power groups behind nuclear development and the power groups behind land speculation? That should take a while to sort out."

"They might just get together."

"Not if enough factions were involved, powerful factions. They could wrangle for years over the ownership of this remote and privately unowned land. If Provincial Hydro wanted to go ahead on schedule, they'd finally have to opt for building a few reactors in highly populated areas where they could purchase the acreage from just one or two owners. But that would make people think about the dangers of having a damned reactor in their hip pocket. It would bring the issue of nuclear safety home with a vengeance. If something's pretty far away from *your* house, well, you'll be willing to believe it's safe. But if it's next door you're going to be damned sure it's safe."

"Now I get it, Adrian. You want to give these maps to developers and let them speculate."

"Well, not exactly, Jim. I was rather thinking of selling the maps to several developers. At a fairly high price."

"Do you know how to make contact with speculators like that?"

Dumas looked at his watch. "I have a man doing that right now. It has to be done at a very high level. It has to be done very delicately. The source must be trustworthy . . . in the eyes of the speculator."

"How much?"

"I think, if we're lucky, Jim, that we can all make about fifty grand."

Jim whistled.

"That'll have to be split several ways, of course. Three ways, to be precise. But there's still a good bit there for everyone."

"What's my share?" asked Jim.

"I can't go higher than ten, Jim," said Dumas. "There's expenses and the contact with the speculators will take the biggest cut."

"Ten thousand or ten percent?"

"Oh," said Dumas. "Ten thousand, of course."

"That would pay off student loans and then some—and my job's finished?"

"Done."

"Mind telling me how you're going to work this?"

Dumas thought for a moment and then shrugged. "Why

not?" He and Peter had gone over it carefully. "Okay. First thing is that we sell a set of the detailed maps to one big speculator. There are four or five we have in mind, one in particular. My contact is meeting with 'em now. As soon as the maps are sold, the detailed maps, we give the master large-scale map of Ontario—minus the last overlay—to Environmental Insight. Along with a report, anonymous, talking in general terms of the heavy water-rainfall connection. Anyone could have stumbled on it. The main thing is that all of prime cottage country is speckled with red blobs of possible reactor sites. The press will jump on it. Hard. Then once it's on all the front pages then the other speculators will be wanting something more detailed. It won't be hard to sell them, then, because it's been pre-promoted. Also, the more detailed maps and report will make sense after the press garbles the Environmental Insight information just enough not to make complete sense. Then, there's the fact of Watson Mines' negotiations with the governments and utilities. It makes a pattern and they'll jump to buy in an effort to get in on the action."

"Sweet."

"The speculators will know, just like we do, that the powers that be will deny the authenticity of the Environmental Insight information. It'll be a one-day wonder on the front pages and then it'll die because no one will come forward to confirm the accuracy. However, you can sure as hell bet that the speculators will get hold of people who can say that it all makes sense."

"And the land starts getting bought up . . ."

"But very, very quietly," Dumas emphasized.

". . . by all the speculators competing with each other."

"The beautiful part is," Dumas grinned, "it's in everybody's interest to keep quiet. They will indulge in a lot of very silent in-fighting and back-stabbing. The leases will be more complicated than you can believe."

"That *is* sweet," said Jim.

"I was hoping that you'd see it that way, but I wasn't sure," said Dumas sincerely.

"A lot of us environmentalists types are holier-than-thou. But the greed of the devourers is their biggest weakness, if only it can be exploited. Trouble is," Dumas grinned, "you gotta dirty your hands. A lot of us are too lily-pure for that."

Jim cleared his throat. "I think, Adrian, that I won't mention it to Marg. And I'd appreciate it if you didn't either."

Dumas laughed. "Yeah, Jim. It's funny, isn't it?"

"What, exactly?"

"How we're so sure that sincere feelings, moral ones, shouldn't amount to any concrete personal advantage or enjoyment. We're certain that something must be wrong if they do. I know what you mean."

16

"Adrian, you're a bloody card," Peter said happily, writing out a cheque. "Who else could have thought of it?" Peter flipped the leaf of the chequebook and began writing again. "How do you spell his name, Adrian?"

"Peebles. P-e-e-b-l-e-s."

"Right." Peter filled out the stubs and tore out the two cheques. "Easy money." He handed them to Dumas. Dumas looked at the amounts. Three thousand and six thousand. He raised an eyebrow.

"Either you got more than we asked, Pete, or you're splitting fifty-fifty."

"Fifty-fifty, Adrian."

"But why? It was your contact that closed the deal. They'd never have bought it if they hadn't known you and trusted your opinion."

"But we would have had nothing to sell without you. Fifty-fifty."

"Thanks, Pete." He put away the cheque. It was absolutely true. "It went okay?"

"Obviously, Adrian. And it was good for my soul. I can tell you. Just like business was done in the old days. Nigel and I have known each other for what? Nigh on twenty years. Never all that close, you understand, but mutual respect. Found out once years ago that we'd been in the same outfit during the war. Different times. I mean, Adrian, he *did* offer me an important job, remember? No, Nigel had no doubt that I was onto something important. It went smoothly."

Yes, and Dumas had been exasperated with the dance. First, Peter and Nigel had gone to lunch to beat around the bush. According to Peter's enthusiastic report, Nigel had said that he might mention it to his people, and how was dear Norma? Then there had been Nigel's phone call to the office a couple of days later. Perhaps we should get together, Peter, to discuss it a bit further. What about a rubber of bridge and a spot of brandy at my place? Delighted. Peter took Dumas' sample map and sample report with him for the inevitable after-bridge natter. Peter explained it all, Dumas imagined, and sadly stated the price. Renegade professor, old chap, and a veritable bugger to deal with. I'm rather afraid it's likely to be take it or leave it. Of course, I can always try to make him more reasonable. Reliable? Why I should imagine so, Nigel. Brilliant chap. Erratic, of course.

Dumas could almost hear the billiard balls clicking. Almost smell the Tueros. Almost taste the Remy Martin. He bathed in the vicarious multi-colored glow of Tiffany lamps. He shuddered.

"I admit, Adrian, it did come as something of a shock to me when he called yesterday and asked me to prepare an invoice and come over after dinner."

"Didn't he tell you to make sure and bring the maps?"

"Of course not, Adrian. We understood each other. Still, I hadn't expected the decision so quickly."

What a pleasant surprise to see you again so soon, Nigel. Yes, Peter, what? Just drop whatever it is you're carrying anywhere, old man, lighten the load. The safety double-lockable case there will do nicely. Just toss it in, there's a good chap. Bother! What could I have done with it? Dumas imagined a flurry of pockets being patted. There! Fancy that, Nigel, why you've come up with a great bloody cheque. Damme! Where *is* that invoice? What'd'ye know, right here in my breast pocket. And how's dear Norma? Fine. And Millicent? Fancy, certified?

Dumas ruminated that they had, after all, gotten along for centuries as they were always reminding one. Dumas could never quite figure out how it had all gotten done. True, it had been undoing rather well recently, but there were still occasional sparks of the old muddling through. I say, what d'ye make of those ships? Spanish, I'd say, by the cut of their jibs. Shall we have a go? What, old man, and not finish my game? Marvellous bowl, I say! Absolute fluke, couldn't do it again if I tried. Ruddy distraction, what? Well, let's off. And somehow, with communication like that, they'd managed to beat the Armada.

"Er, Peter, did you manage to pump Nigel for names of his opposite numbers . . . elsewhere?"

"I couldn't be too obvious about it, now could I? I have a name or two, Adrian, but I'm sure I can just call the major trust companies and banks and eventually get through to the right people."

"How long will it take, Peter? They have to know about it before the Environmental Insight people break the story to the papers. If they know before, then they'll be more likely to believe our stuff is important and genuine."

"I'm sure that I can reach most of them before noon, certainly by five today. Of course a certain percentage will be on vacation, out of town—that sort of thing. But I'm sure that I can get through to five or so."

"Great," said Dumas, "because I've been thinking that I'd like to wrap this up as soon as possible. I've been thinking that maybe we should make another copy of the master map and give it to the papers ourselves. Then, we don't necessarily have to wait for Environmental Insight to get off its ass. It occurred to me, Peter, that the way those people work, they might not give the stuff to the press for weeks."

"Good point, Adrian."

"If the master map of Ontario were on the front page of the Star by say, tomorrow . . . what do you think Nigel's reaction might be?"

"I covered that, Adrian. I told Nigel that this professor chap was hot under the collar at someone and might release the general information to the papers. But not the detailed lake-by-lake maps."

"You have no qualms that the detailed maps won't be as exclusive as, er, Nigel might have wished?"

"My dear chap," said Peter, "once it's in the papers, can I help it if some smart grubby student can duplicate the information? In a more amateurish way, of course?"

"You're sure your conscience is clear, Peter? I don't mind making the calls to the others. Might be a better idea, anyway. You might slip up and use your real name. That might get back to Nigel."

"Adrian, really. Give me more credit than that. I'm fighting for my bloody survival."

"Okay. Maybe Debbie could make a few of the calls?"

"I've been thinking that might not be a bad idea," Peter agreed, "especially since these second-series maps are supposed to be a student effort. She sounds younger."

Dumas nodded. "Okay, then I'll be off," he said. "When I

get back from Environmental Insight, I'll make that other copy for the Sun or the Star, drop it off, and say that they can confirm it all through Environmental Insight. That should get things moving."

"It should indeed."

17

Dumas felt relatively pleased and walked jauntily in spite of the heat. He looked up into the pretentious gold expanse, grinned at the teeth of the serrated facade against the blue of the sky, and was a little more confident that at least a couple of human morsels might escape them in the end. Herded along through burgundy ropes, Dumas shuffled toward the teller and looked about. Six thousand dollars. What were Krugerrands going for these days? Shiny, heavy chewing gum sticks of gold? Six thousand would buy a measly twenty-four ounces of the yellow stuff where a decade before it would have purchased about a hundred and eighty. Inflation. Devaluation. Some wrong move by the government, or some twitch of gnome-like brains in Zurich, could easily rob Dumas of a hundred bucks before he reached the teller. What was today's exchange rate?

Dumas deposited the money and withdrew some for trinkgeld. He asked for his balance and was gratified that it seemed to warrant the girl's discreet whisper. On impulse, Dumas walked over to a side counter. He asked the smiling young man behind the Zapata moustaches about the price of gold. Dumas shuddered and the young man smiled condescendingly. Dumas walked out.

Someday, he reflected while exposing a damp armpit to public view as he hailed a cab, he would have to take the leap. With at least part of the money. A few little gold bars could snuggle in the steel box cemented into the concrete of *Radagast's* ballast, carefully wrapped so that they would not roam about in fresh winds and dent the only present occupant. As Dumas closed the cab's door he briefly recalled how Rachael had shrugged delicately a few years ago and had offered to pawn the bracelet. Not that it was worth all that much, but it had 1886 stamped on the back and the gold was so soft and heavy that Dumas continually expected it to ooze back over the numbers of the date. Rachael's only real piece of jewellery, handed down from a sea captain ancestor when Nova Scotians could still acquire a measure of prosperity doing such romantic things. Before the Tariff Act of 1879 had begun to destroy the Maritime economy in favor of Ontario's manufacturing interests. For the good of most Canadians. Now, of course, Canada possessed no merchant marine and the cost of shipping in foreign bottoms contributed toward the annual deficit in balance of payments.

The cab cruised rapidly along wide University Avenue. Dumas noted the flowers, the war monuments in the center boulevard and, up ahead where Avenue Road and University Avenue transmuted one into the other around the circular contention of Queen's Park, the red Victorian masonry of the Ontario Parliament buildings sat athwart streams of cars, purpose and activity. As it had done since Confederation, for the good of most Canadians.

Dumas imagined that somewhere within that tumble of red stone the Premier was even now trying to get at Alberta's oil at much less than world prices for the good of most Canadians. As with the brave Nova Scotian fleet, Alberta's Cretaceous legacy would dwindle to pump Toronto's vacuous gold towers yet higher for a few more years. For the good of most Canadians, who, of course, resided in Ontario.

The cab ground to a sharp stop on Queen's Park Crescent not far from Wellesley and Dumas handed the money to the cabbie quickly. Although he would not be long, Dumas knew the cabbie couldn't wait in the fast-moving river of traffic which circled continuously around the Parliament Buildings.

Naturally, the receptionist at Environmental Insight wore a peasant skirt and uncompromising little round-rimmed steel glasses. Wisps of black hair attempted to escape from her bun and some managed to struggle, curling, along a smooth, young neck. A lively bosom yearned to escape from calico as she turned quickly from her typewriter at the sound of bells.

"May I help you?" The granola that passed those lips remained uncontaminated by lipstick. Dumas figured that her sex was always natural and spontaneous.

"Maybe. But I think I can help you more." Dumas plucked the rolled map from beneath his arm and unfolded the sheaf of stapled pages he'd pulled from his inside pocket. He put the rolled map on the desk and spread the papers carefully beside her typewriter.

"What's this?"

"That," Dumas pointed to the rolled map, "is the probable locations of Provincial Hydro's planned nuclear power stations for the next thirty years or so. And that," he pointed to the papers, "is a report on why."

He was rewarded by the brown eyes growing even wider behind the distorting lenses. But the eyes immediately narrowed in suspicion.

"Who are you? We've been trying to get that information for years."

"A friend," Dumas smiled. Two flowers in the calico print did seem to perk from the otherwise shapeless bulges. He noticed that the considerable and continual struggle of tiny pioneer buttons was not quite concealed by the modest ruffles that ran down her front from her neck. She did not bother to acknowledge his gaze by any further mannerism of distaste. "Please wait, Mister . . . ?" Dumas did not offer any assistance. "I'll be right back," she said.

"Okay." Dumas walked over to the only window and peered out across the lanes of traffic to the shadows under the elms of Queen's Park. Black squirrels hopped and dipped hopefully, searching the ground for left-over peanuts and popcorn. Pigeons fluttered, sometimes, disputing the squirrels' right to kernels. Dumas could make out the glaring white cement of the library on the campus beyond the park. Maybe he would drop in to say hello to Rachael, or was she getting off at noon? He couldn't remember who she was standing in for, or why. He remembered something about a morning dental appointment. Maybe he should call first.

Dumas heard the sound of footsteps and then the heavy crackle of maps and plastic being unrolled. The shuffle of papers. He turned.

A tall and thin young man held up the report like a poker hand and Calico spread the map between ruffled wrists on the desk-top and drooped over it.

The young man lowered the report and revealed to Dumas a bony freckled face rimmed by an austere red-blond beard.

"I think," Dumas said, "that if you can take it all to some qualified people you'll find out that it makes sense."

"We'd like to know the source. Your name. We'll keep it confidential."

Dumas shook his head. With amateur, volunteer secretaries and clerks? Unlocked file cabinets? No, thank you. "None of that matters. All that matters is the accuracy and authenticity of what you have there. Check it out."

"But how did you get this?"

Dumas smiled. "Let's just say that there are some people, even in Provincial Hy—, even in the government, who are concerned about it."

"This was smuggled out of Provincial Hydro?"

"I didn't say that," said Dumas.

"If this is on the level, it'll be a bombshell," said the man.

"It does sort of make a mess out of Getaway Country, doesn't it?" Dumas left and walked out into the sun squinting. On impulse, he crossed the park and ambled to the library, but Rachael had left for the day.

18

Debbie buzzed at about four o'clock, just as Dumas was finishing the copy of the Ontario master map intended for some lucky newspaper. Debbie was telling him that Edward was waiting when there was a knock on the door and Edward rushed in. Dumas said, "Thanks, Debbie," and hung up.

"Adrian, the slides are great. Just great." Edward was at the window holding them up between thumb and forefinger. "I wish you had a projector here, but this'll give you an idea."

Dumas peered. Edward had managed to light the frieze of Hatshepset's ships so that the relief looked deeper and more definite than it was. "The Royal Ontario Museum didn't give you any hassle?"

Edward shook his head. "Now look at this one. Out of a book, but the lighting gives almost the same depth as the original." He handed the slide to Dumas.

Nefertiti's arched beautiful neck and clear brow. Quietly fearless eyes. Serene mouth. Dumas wondered if she'd been a blonde or brunette. Or even auburn. There was considerable variation among the Egyptians that came from a racial mixture, a mixture that produced people who sailed to the Zambesi to get antimony to make rouge for their women's cheeks and nipples, but who never made a warship.

"What about the dinosaur stuff?"

Dumas examined competent illustrations of therapsid reptiles, Welsh mice, would-be birds still languishing in a feathered lizard's guise. He nodded. "Good job, Ed. The dinosaur stuff is just so-so, but that's what's needed. The Lovable stuff is superb."

"I really got into that. It seems a shame to know that it's all in aid of cheap jewellery."

Dumas shrugged. Why? When Hatshepset and Nefertiti had worn their ivory it had had no sanctity of age. It was new and the two young women had doubtless clasped the trinkets eagerly. Their own craftsmen had fashioned lotuses no better than Lovable's busy workers carved roses. Maybe worse. It was the light in the eyes that counted and the caress of the bauble against girls' skin. That hadn't changed.

Dumas sat down and pulled out his chequebook. "Edward, I keep telling you that I need some sort of bill or invoice, not just the pictures."

"I'll send one in the mail," Edward promised.

Dumas snorted in disbelief and tore out the cheque. "Ed, you going anywhere near the Colonnade on your way home?"

"I can. Sure."

"Great. Mind dropping this off before five?" Dumas dumped the Egyptian slides into a large manila envelope with the Lovable copy, artwork and his invoice. He sealed the envelope and wrote the address in large letters. "The place is a den of advertising agencies, Ed. There are two on this floor. Make sure it goes to the right one. Just leave it at reception."

"Right."

Two hours later Dumas was smiling at the sight of Becky fishing for ducks with a string tied around a piece of bread. The big ones squawked and flapped, but Becky tried to flip the bread within reach of the still-downy brown-speckled babies. Dumas looked up and saw high in the stratosphere thin brush strokes of icy cirrus riding on the jet stream, warning of the future change of season. Another month and a little more and the equinoctial storms of September would howl in *Radagast's* rigging. Then, maybe, if everyone were lucky, a few enjoyable weeks of Indian Summer before winter closed in. Dumas wondered if the young ducks would be fully fledged by then. The miracle never seemed possible, but they always were.

He pushed against the gate in *Radagast's* rail and quickly withdrew his hand. The bumblebee floated menacingly in the air above the pansy that had camouflaged it, regarded Dumas balefully and finally whizzed off past his ear. Rachael had asked if next year she could train morning glories to twine up the standing rigging. Perhaps that was carrying it a bit far, Dumas decided.

"Hi, there!" Dumas glanced up unexpectedly into the front of Rachael's loose shirt where startling red nipples swayed on the tips of full, hanging cones of obviously malleable flesh. Rachael gave a little jerk and one cone rippled, while the other swung against a tomato which had succeeded in nuzzling against her shirt. Dumas was envious and was happy to see that brown hands picked it quickly for its insolence. The cones bounced.

Just as Dumas determined to look up further to acknowledge Rachael's welcoming smile, an electronic whine began and quickly grew into a screech. Dumas jumped and Rachael straightened up behind the greenery on the poop rail. Suddenly it came to him, and Dumas' face colored with a delicate flush of pink.

"Adrian," Rachael's voice tinkled with delighted laughter, "you're blushing! I didn't think you were capable of it," she added.

"Goddamned Peeping Tom," Dumas said with soft vehemence. He dropped his briefcase to the deck and walked over to hook the aluminum console out from under the window box on the rail and stooped to turn the volume down. On reflection, he switched the GSR off.

He stood up and turned just in time to see Rachael's café-au lait hips rocking down the steps from the poop. She was descending in a studied manner and the pucker of her navel pulled and waved with each deliberate step well above the faded blue beltline of her jean shorts.

"It's no good," Dumas grinned. "I turned him off."

Rachael stopped. "Adrian Dumas or Archibald?"

"Er, Archi."

"Oh . . . Well . . ." Rachael had two steps to go and she made the most of them.

Dumas stared at the tattered rough-cut hems of the shorts and almost could feel the smooth brown thighs sliding past each other. Faded little threads of white and pale blue writhed happily as they disappeared between Rachael's legs and quivered with excitement as they popped out again. Eager wrinkles converged toward the base of the zipper.

Rachael stretched down the last step to the deck. Her fingers squeezed the two ripe tomatoes she held in front of each breast, gently, and she kept her grey-green eyes wide and hazy. She pouted Dumas a slow kiss.

Dumas pecked the lips from a distance, arching carefully over the tomatoes. She opened her arms wide and he felt the lips part warmly. He explored them softly with the tip of his tongue, feeling her belly shoving firmly into his. Dumas felt the wrinkled zipper of the jeans rubbing up and down just below his belt like a cat licking.

He slid the palms of his hands down until they rested on the points of her hips and gently pushed away. Rachael cocked a hip and smiled. "How was that for a welcome?"

Dumas stepped back, glimpsing into the pulsing shadows where Rachael's belly still pumped demurely against the loose denim waistband, and looked up to consider the speculative dimples curving around the corners of her mouth. "What I've been hoping for all day," he said to the hazy green eyes.

Becky giggled.

"We'll do more about it later," Dumas promised. He bent to kiss Becky on the top of her head. "Now we have another peeping Tom," he said.

"Damn, I split the tomatoes." Rachael walked quickly to the forecastle with her arms outstretched. Dumas saw red juice and tiny seeds clinging to her fingers. Becky followed. "Mommy, I need some more bread," she pealed, dragging the string behind her.

Dumas picked up his briefcase and made his way below under the poop, ducking into the companionway beside the steps. Archibald, for all his prurient proclivities, was an amazing creature. He responded to anger and excitement within a range of about ten feet. Dumas had purchased a few more philodendrons and had scattered them about in the window boxes. They were, collectively, Archibalds. Dumas had wired them together so that they were all separately connected through the GSR unit. Something would have to be done about the unit, though—it would have to be mounted out of the rain down below. Maybe he should do that after dinner. Not a big job.

As Dumas changed into sandals, jeans and his tattered denim shirt, he wondered briefly if the system might possibly be patentable. Perhaps someone already had patented it. Some large corporations were experimenting with the phenomenon.

Over coffee after dinner Rachael reminded Dumas that the weather forecast for tomorrow was rain and possible thunderstorms.

"That means that you want me to rig the awnings, right?" Dumas had been trying to put this job off as long as possible. Besides, he'd been working late.

"It would be best, dear, if you can. I don't want to have to keep Becky below all day if it rains. And going from the cabins to the galley will be a hassle."

This had been one of Dumas' basic design conundrums. Since a galleon is a high forecastle in front and a longer, higher one in back with a lower deck between, Dumas had been hard pressed to figure out where to put various necessary things. Did one break up the sleeping arrangements and possibly sacrifice the stern cabin by putting the galley in the back of the boat and placing other bunks up in the forecastle? Or did all the cabins and bunks go to the back with the galley in the forecastle? Dumas had decided on the second arrangement although it meant that you had to walk from the living area across an open deck to get to the galley. Inconvenient for midnight snacks. In public view, at least, when moored in a marina, it meant that everyone had to get reasonably dressed before breakfast.

Nonetheless, Dumas had decided on this with visions of eventual lonely Caribbean anchorages in mind. Eternal sun and privacy. He had determined to rig an awning against the reality of rain, but had never gotten around to it.

"Alright," Dumas said with a sigh, "but I'll need your help. So I'll sit here and watch you wash up." He told Rachael about the successful sale of the maps and the front page stories she could expect tomorrow. He addressed most of his remarks to the slight swell of brown buttock that peeked from beneath the jean shorts and accepted the slight changes in the crease between it and Rachael's thigh as expressions and responses.

"I hope you don't have to get this down in a hurry," Dumas remarked wryly as he looked up into the peak of the gigantic tent that was the result of their combined labors. "What did the forecast say about wind?"

"Just thunderstorms," Rachael answered, wiping her brow with a forearm. Her shirt clung to her damply and the bunched wrinkles leading to the zipper of her shorts seemed darker. Beads of sweat shone on her belly and occasionally a tiny rivulet streaked down and disappeared behind the darkened waistband.

Dumas grunted. Winds could reach 60 miles and more per hour in your ordinary, garden variety thunderstorm. Regarding the rope that stretched like a clothesline between the masts, Dumas decided to put a few more lines from the edge of the sheet-like canopy that hung over it. It was not a proper awning because he had had no chance to have one made. But the mainsail stretched over the rope might be even better, Dumas thought. It was a hell of a lot stronger, after all, than something intended for an awning. He'd already tied the four corners outward with lines leading to *Radagast's* rail. The lines were belayed for quick release. Dumas looked at the arrangement with a jaundiced eye.

"You'll never be able to handle this in any wind," Dumas said. "I think I'll make it as strong as I can so that it might not come down on its own." He went below to fetch more rope.

After another quarter-hour Dumas could look about with satisfaction. The sail stretched tautly over the rope and was spread to the rail on either side by eight husky lashings. It was important to keep the thing from flapping as much as possible. The sail completely covered the area of the center deck and overlapped the castles at either end by a generous margin. Dumas strummed one of the lashings with a muscular pluck on the ropes. "Maybe that'll hold."

"Look at that, Adrian." Rachael was peeking out from under the awning into the West. Dumas crossed the deck and beheld a sullen phalanx of grey cloud advancing upon them. He'd felt something missing—the sunset.

"That's why it's so damned muggy. The rain's gonna be like a steam bath when it comes. Why don't you go change and have a swim to cool off?"

Rachael lifted her hair off the back of her neck. "Can't be bothered, dear. But I was considering sort of accidentally on purpose falling over the side."

Dumas looked down and considered the water. Not as clean as the club's pool, perhaps, but closer. No rainbow sheens of oil in sight. The occasional duck feather. Dumas went to the corner of the deck and lifted the ladder down from where it hooked over the top of the poop deck rail. He brought it back and slung it over the side next to Rachael. "Climb down," he said. "Oh, and feel around the hull while you're at it and see how thick the seaweed's gotten."

Dumas went below and returned with a couple of towels and a lantern. The deck was empty, but he heard the sounds of contented splashing, the occasional puff and sigh. He leaned on the rail and watched Rachael holding the ladder with one hand and feeling about down the side of *Radagast's* rounded hull. Rachael's shirt billowed all around, and, as the dock lights came on, her hair suddenly glowed like an impossibly intricate copper filigree; fine and delicate wires that the wavelets continually altered, spreading swirls upon the water.

"How is it?"

"More vegetables down here than up there."

Dumas found that difficult to believe. "Are you ever coming up?"

She smiled slowly up and pulled a sodden strand of hair from her cheek. Dumas saw a spark of dock light reflected from her teeth. "Why don't you come down? It's like sort of a luke-warm bath."

"I like hot and cold showers, remember?" Tepid lake water was not Dumas' idea of refreshment in muggy weather. Rachael flung her hair back with a small splash and climbed up the ladder, waiting at the top to let most of the water run off. "That's much better," she said. "I was wilting trying to wrestle that awning in place."

Her eyes sparkled again and the droplets on her face and lash-tips made her look cooler, even if the water had been as warm as she claimed. Dumas leaned over the rail and kissed her. He gripped her arm as she extended a long leg, shook it, flipped her foot energetically, and swung it over the rail, bending low to clear the rope edge of the awning. When she was back aboard, she turned to lean over the rail and wring her hair out.

Dumas waited until she was finished before he held her by the flare of her hips and pulled her backwards, gently, down onto the soft pile of the towel. She curled up. "I was wondering just how long I'd have to wait," she laughed. "I've been doing my best for the last two weeks. You've noticed, but haven't done a hell of a lot about it."

"Working too hard."

"Adrian, the Protestant Ethic doesn't sit well on you, somehow."

"C'mon, Rache. Be a sport. Turn over."

"O-ho, now that he's kept the lady on ice, when *he's* ready *she's* supposed to turn over. Just like a man." She curled tighter.

"Sorry about that," said Dumas.

"You've been such a *good* man, Adrian. So hardworking. *So good*. I've been looking for a little naughtiness. Lots of naughty boys at the clubhouse. Temptation. My bum's black and blue, dear, but so far I've managed to keep slapping them away."

Dumas peered. It didn't look black and blue. He grinned, and pinched.

"No thank you. Anyway, I don't like Pina Coladas," she said.

"Alright." A sudden thought struck him. "My God, Rachael, you don't really wear these shorts in the clubhouse, do you?"

Her shoulders made a deep parody of his own shrug. "Why not?" she croaked.

Dumas rested his hand on the backs of her thighs and let his fingers caress the rounded vee where her flesh clamped together. He let his fingers idly play upwards. "Because, dear, if you do, I know why you just lied to your beloved husband."

"Lied?"

"Your bum's not black and blue," he said. "I just looked."

"Well . . . it could have been."

"Probably. But in these it's much easier to do this." Dumas' hand had wandered far enough upward to be covering the very feminine indentation where the thighs dipped inward. His fingers went quickly under the narrow ribbon of denim that passed for the crotch of her shorts. He wiggled his fingertip across the smooth and hairless lips that barely touched, moistly. He pushed the lips gently aside.

"Adrian!"

He poked, slowly.

"Adrian." She arched her back away from him, but his finger followed. Finally, she moved back against his hand. Dumas felt her warmth and wetness. She contracted around his finger. Again and again. Dumas watched the tattered hem of denim pull high and deeply into the softness of her buttocks. Finally, she rolled over lazily on her back. Dumas squiggled down on the towel, keeping his hand in her warmth.

"Hello, beautiful," he said, his head propped on his hand.

"Hello, Adrian."

"I know I'm a lazy bugger," he said, "but please be so good as to unstick that wet shirt from your magnificent chest, sexpot."

Rachael glanced from side to side. The awning covered much of them and what view there might be from the sides was at least partly obscured by the window boxes hanging over *Radagast's* port and starboard rails. "Alright," she said deeply in imitation of him. "But don't light the lantern," she added in her own voice.

"Alright," he croaked.

She pulled the shirt-tails aside. Her breasts were slack from the heat, nipples unpuckered. An abrupt thumb-tip-like swelling was all that the nipple could show for itself, surrounded by mugginess as it was. Dumas remembered how it had popped, red and swollen from Becky's mouth, And from his own. Taller, and stiffer.

"Hello, beautiful," he repeated.

"I haven't worn these shorts and I haven't had to slap," she said softly, damp hair clinging against her squeezed cheek on the towel.

Dumas nodded. He withdrew his forefinger from her and began slipping the tips of all his fingers feather-like up and down the cleft of her lips beneath the denim. Her thighs opened. The released fabric allowed Dumas to lengthen his slow strokes.

He pushed a bit deeper between the lips and felt the slight resistance of the thick wetness she was making. Finally, his fingertips brushed, very lightly, the moist small tongue that licked up between the lips to meet them. His fingertips paused over it and he could feel it pulse distantly. Dumas backed his fintertips away and continued stroking, allowing the ripple of the lips themselves to give the tongue whatever caressing it required.

The shadows on Rachael's belly lengthened and shortened over the crinkled waistband of denim under the ghostly white glow coming through the expanse of stretched Dacron above. They began to contract too quickly and Dumas slowed his stroke and waited until the shadows lightened and deepened to the same rhythm as Rachael breathed in deep sleep.

"There, there, beautiful girl, just close your cat's eyes. Purr." Rachael's dampened long lashes closed slowly, extinguishing the misty green. Her pink lips curled at the edges and creases embraced their corners. Dumas remembered to stroke lightly and very slowly, for hers was about half of his own rhythm. Soon, Rachael's mouth sagged slightly open and each regular deep breath began to end in a little catch. And with each catch, the skin beneath her ribs sucked inwards and her stomach muscles quivered in the elongated shadows before the shadows dwindled again.

Very suddenly her hands reached down and pulled in opposite ways at the waistband of her shorts. Dumas heard a snick and a short whirr of metal. He helped her wriggle upward out of the cloth, unhooked it from around one awkward ankle and flung the wet denim aside. Rachael drew up her legs and he reached under one knee and found her cleft again. He resumed his long, slow and light stroking along the curving crevice. The sucking of skin underneath her ribs became deeper, her belly strained inward and fluttered more at the bottom of each breath and soon Rachael's hips curled back to ease the tension of the skin of her stomach when it pulled tightly down. "That feels so good," she said, stretching her arms down so that her hands could press against the muscles that strained and surged around her navel. "So good." Her arms squeezed her breasts together firmly.

After a few more slow, long strokes, Rachael gave a tiny gasp and a whimper and her belly sucked down and stayed there, fluttering, for a few seconds. Her fingers clutched. Her thighs came together and trembled as Dumas stopped caressing her and merely held the backs of her damp thighs gently. Presently, Rachael stretched her legs out flat and strained her arms well above her head and then relaxed. Contented eyelashes lifted from her cheeks slowly and Dumas could make out the barest hint of distant green looking at him, about the color of distant willows in a mild summer rain.

"That wasn't a big one," he said. "Not for you."

The corners of her mouth curved. "Not a big one, but a lovely little one. The big ones aren't always the best."

Dumas looked down Rachael's long and mostly-brown body. The tiny string-bikini triangle of white on the café-au-lait skin stood out surprisingly as a deeply clefted mound. Was it Nabokov's line? The cleft in the peach? In Rachael's case the fold was even smoother than in nymphet Lolita's, for Rachael kept herself shaved and pumiced in the ancient Arab and Egyptian manner. She claimed that it increased sensitivity.

Dumas gently covered the mound of white with his hand and let his fingers kiss the dimple where the fold began. He rearranged himself on the towel so that he could look down into her eyes.

"I don't see what you get out of it, sometimes," she said.

"I get to see a beautiful girl enjoying herself," said Dumas. "Sometimes you put on quite a show. When I'm . . . er . . . involved I'm too close to see your response as well. I know I can have you anytime. I will. But sometimes what I want isn't exactly what you want."

"What do you want . . . now?"

"I'm happy just to look at you, for right now."

"You like what you see?"

"Very much," said Dumas, "more even than when I first saw you."

"Really?"

Rachael strained her head up to look down her body. Her head fell back to the towel softly. "Not bad," she said. "I think, myself, that the boobs are just a little saggier. Maybe that's from not wearing a bra all the time, though."

"Maybe," Dumas said doubtfully, "I think it was Becky." He remembered how they had changed from rather pointed peaks of flesh into more rounded, fuller mounds when the milk began to come.

"Well, one thing changed because of Becky, that's for sure. My girlish flower bud nipples became ruddy teats. I sort of like the delicate little buds, myself."

"I don't. I sort of like the great ruddy teats better." Dumas bent down and kissed a nipple, mouthing it tenderly.

170

"Really?"

"Really." He paused. "That brings me to something I've been wanting to get around to for some time." Dumas looked around and waved about at *Radagast's* reality. "I pretty well have it all, Rachael, what I've always wanted. There's some money in the bank. There'll be a bit more pretty quickly. With the maps."

Rachael rolled over on her side, facing him, and leaned on her elbow, nuzzling her cheek into her hand. Dumas looked down her and smiled in amazement. The abrupt soaring of Rachael's hip from such a small waist had always entranced him. As he looked she drew one knee up to hide the white triangle. Unconsciously.

"You're saying that there's not much to keep us here."

"That's right," said Dumas. "I think I'd like to see some of the world. Now."

"Now?"

"How do you feel about that?"

"I've always known there would be a time for it. I've always wanted it, too, Adrian. Believe that. It's just that it will take some getting used to. When were you thinking about leaving?"

"Maybe a month or two. Before the winter sets in."

"That's why you worked so hard on these maps. The extra cash."

"Not entirely, Rache. I also wanted to leave Pete with more cushion than he had. So that I could leave while he was still doing his thing, keeping the office. And Debbie. Just like when I came."

"Where?"

Dumas shrugged. "South, that's for sure, where we can stay aboard for the winter without hassle. Maybe Florida to begin with. Later, the Caribbean. Maybe South America."

"Do we have enough money?"

Dumas grinned. "Not to do it forever. But I can work anywhere that speaks mostly English. That's quite a few places. Maybe I could get along in places where they speak Spanish and French, too . . . if I do a crash brush-up course."

"I know you've always wanted it, Adrian. Yes, let's go."

Dumas cupped a breast idly and raised the handful of soft fullness gently until it began to flow out of his hand. "There's no law that says we have to stay away forever," said Dumas. "We can come back here, or to Nova Scotia, anytime we want."

"That makes me feel better," Rachael smiled. "I know it, of course, but it reassures me to hear you say it. It's silly."

"No," said Dumas. "It's not silly. I promise you this, Rachael.

We'll keep enough in *Radagast* so that we can always get back. And we'll keep enough in your account here so that you and Becky can get back from anywhere, in a pinch, to your folks."

"If something happens to you . . . ?"

Dumas nodded. "Sure, that's always possible. So's anything."

Rachael leaned over and kissed him with closed eyes. Her breast squeezed all around his hand. "I don't like to think of that," she said.

Dumas shrugged. "Neither do I." He paused. "There's something else, Rachael, that it's time for."

"I know, Adrian."

Dumas grinned. "If Becky's ever going to have a brother or sister, well, her parents had better get busy. What about it?"

"Alright," she croaked. "We can start next month. I'll go off the pill."

"Hell," said Dumas, "there's nothing against practice, is there?" He flexed his fingers carefully on her breast and squeezed so that the nipple popped out. He kissed it.

"No, Adrian, absolutely nothing." Rachael let herself roll back and widened her legs.

Later, as Rachael sat on the bunched-up towel leaning her back against his chest, Dumas folded the shirt around her breasts. They sat out from under the awning high on the poop near the wheel and watched the cloud bank closing over the stars like a shade. The clouds rolled slowly toward the east. Just when Dumas was about to suggest that they go below, a rent opened in the cloud cover and it appeared to Dumas that Aquila would dive through.

As Rachael opened the companionway doors, Dumas turned aside to hook the aluminum box from under the planter with his foot. He stopped and switched Archi back on.

19

Igor Tchevsky's eyes meandered over the Sunshine Girl but his mind was elsewhere. While he idly took in the blonde ostensibly cavorting in the city fountain in order to cool off, he was thinking about the front-page story and not the third page photograph.

Tchevsky did not like coincidences.

Just a spot-check on one of the people on the list, and this fellow Dumas had gone to Environmental Insight. Now, the next morning, there was Environmental Insight confirming that they had a copy of the map. Dumas had gone in with a long rolled-up thing. Probably a map.

Watçek had supplied a list of all the people he'd dealt with recently—since the apparition of Koffler had appeared to him—and Tchevsky had gone about the methodical and dreary business of checking all these people out. Not that he expected anything to come of it. More as something to kill the time until Watçek's contracts were signed with the governments and utilities. A chance to give Koffler a little field training. Surveillance. Not that oblivious advertising men and drab accountants offered that much of a challenge. Still, it was better than nothing.

Tchevsky flipped back to the front page. Yes, he could not but agree that Ontario's vacation land might very well be threatened by Provincial Hydro's planned expansion of nuclear power stations. Tchevsky read again about the heavy water correlation. He didn't know very much about it, but it seemed to make sense. The threat was clearly there. Large areas of the Urals were uninhabitable because a Soviet nuclear generating station had gone critical in 1958 and had blown up.

But his own project was also clearly threatened.

The decision by Watson Mines to guarantee uranium supplies

to utilities had caused enough controversy. It was off the front pages, but still in the back ones. Almost daily there were NDP accusations of an under-the-table deal between big business and big government. This time it was thirty years of assured profit for Watson Mines at public expense—or so the NDP claimed—and the practical green light for questionable nuclear expansion.

These maps made it much worse. The allegations were probably flying now. Ontario's tourist industry and cottage country lay in the path of nuclear expansion and possible destruction. Provincial Hydro was going to look very bad. Perhaps bad enough to lay low for a while with the Watson deal.

Who was behind this? A coincidence? Watçek's own machination to undermine the blackmail?

Or worse.

Perhaps Tashkent had not been as secure as it had seemed. Was it possible that the RCMP and CIA had been waiting?

Tchevsky folded the paper and laid it on the seat of the Bronco. No, he decided, he would not tell Koffler yet. It might rattle him, inexperienced as he was.

One thing was clear to Tchevsky, however. Dumas needed watching.

20

Debbie looked at Dumas critically. "I'm not sure it really does all that much for you," she said.

"I can say for sure that it doesn't," Peter offered.

Dumas grunted. He peered into the mirror Debbie was holding. Rachael's cheap brunette fashion wig curled wildly down to his shoulders. It did not quite match the dark brown of Dumas' eyelashes. His one-day growth of beard was not quite shabby enough, he thought, but the ancient canvas windbreaker made up for it. The satchel-type briefcase was a recent morning's acquisition from the Salvation Army. The jeans and sandals were Dumas' own. He dreaded the thought of going out in the wind and rain and having the soaking wig drain down his neck while he waited.

"What surprised me," said Peter, "was the prompt response. He was calling before nine, apparently."

"I'm not surprised." Dumas frowned into the mirror. He shrugged. He checked in his satchel to see if he'd put everything in. "Pete, this guy is crystal clear that he's supposed to bring cash?"

"Oh, quite."

"Great. Well, I'm off," said Dumas. "By the time I get back, maybe someone else will have taken the bait."

"Let's hope so."

"Good luck, poor student," said Debbie.

Dumas went down the stairs to avoid any awkward questions from Gladys, who knew him sufficiently well to see through his disguise. He came down onto the street floor and saw his worse fears confirmed through the glass of the door. The rain made a steady patter of V's on the pavement. He sighed and pressed his cheek to the glass. Whenever he saw a cab coming, he dashed out waving. And dashed back inside again when he saw passengers in the rear, or when the cabbies contemptuously waved him off, swelled with the importance of being on a call. Dumas passed the brief times between sallies consoling himself that others shared his predicament. Across the street, glass doors grew foggy from those pressed within, staring hopefully. One stout gentleman in the lobby of the Victoria Hotel almost directly across the street seemed to disdain the struggle and engrossed himself in the tabloid Sun.

Dumas was lucky, all things considered. His sixth cabbie didn't give him the thumb, but swerved to the curb. He jumped quickly in but resigned himself to the fact that the wig was going to drain for a long while to come.

The taxi ride treated Dumas to multi-hued watercolor street scenes for the few minutes it took the cab to reach Yonge and Yorkville. Dumas paid and looked gloomily through the cascading windows to the shelter of the massive red brick building across the fifteen feet of sidewalk. He opened the door and bent his back to the rain, wrestling the satchel out. The librarian at the desk regarded his dripping person with distaste as he entered.

Dumas looked up to the high ceiling and around the curving balconies of the various floors. Somewhere, he could never quite figure out where, a few million books resided in the building. The shelves close to hand held no more than a few hundred thousand, but a requisition form magically gave access to all the other volumes. After standing long enough on the welcoming carpet for most of the standing water, at least, to run off him, Dumas smiled at the librarian on the security desk and let her rummage through the contents of his satchel. Papers and plastic sheet. Nothing that belonged to Toronto's reference library. The security check coming out would be more suspicious, but considerably shorter.

He pushed through the turnstile and headed for the semicircular glass tubes that led up the front of all the balconies, connecting them all from floor to ceiling. Little yellow capsules sped up and down the tubes, stopping at various levels, while people encased within looked out through curved plastic windows into the great void of the central court of the library. Dumas was reminded of busy small cells hustling along the veins of some huge, tall organism, stopping here and there to discharge or take on cargoes required by the metabolism.

He carried his own cargo up to the level dealing in anthropology, enjoying the panoramic view outwards as he was whisked up. Dumas felt the capsule float to a stop. He got out, peered over the top of the wall that curved around the perimeter of the mezzanine. He spotted the three-piece checked suit, salt-and-pepper ear-length coifed hair, yellow-tinted steel rims. Manicured finger-nails drummed silently upon the glowing blonde hardwood for a distant table-top. Dumas sighed sadly. The fellow did not look at all bookish.

He looked Dumas up and down when Dumas arrived at the table in squelching sandals.

"Ah . . . this table is . . . er . . . occupied." he said a bit patronizingly, Dumas thought.

"Fuck you, man," Dumas said softly. "This is a public place." He sat down and opened his satchel, fishing around as if looking for some study material. He looked and noticed that the fellow was trying to manage a threatening glitter with the aid of the yellow tint. Dumas smiled. The man rose slowly, still regarding him in the sort of way that Marshall Dillon might view a card cheat. He finally shrugged the lapels of his checked jacket and turned away.

"Don't forget your maps," Dumas said. It was nice to see the helpless snarl as his head swivelled. The man sat down slowly, apparently needing the support of his hands on the table-edge.

Dumas was inclined to think that the man was over-acting. "Here, you'll want to check them out." He shoved the case across the table.

"There're supposed to be fifteen little maps," the man said.

"Fifteen little maps, and two plastic overlays for each map, plus a typed 40-page report," Dumas amended. "Count 'em."

"Forty-six pieces?"

"Alright."

Dumas waited while the man slowly counted. The man nodded and transferred the maps and the overlays together with the report into his own black Samsonite briefcase. He took a thick envelope from his inside pocket and placed it on the table-top. He shoved it across to Dumas.

Fifty one-hundred dollar bills, Dumas counted carefully. He nodded and smiled. "Great, man." He folded the envelope into one of the outside breast pockets of the canvas jacket and snapped the flap down securely. When he looked up again, the man was already walking away.

After a while, Dumas got up and ambled over to the shelves and scanned along. Using forms and pencils provided by the library, he made notes of a few titles on the subject of North American Indians and their religious conceptions. Myths.

21

Tchevsky had decided to rent a room in the Victoria Hotel, not that he was impressed with their proud boast that they had rented rooms since 1907. He hardly noted the quality of the accommodation because he did not really intend to stay there. But the room made his presence in the area slightly more explicable.

Tchevsky had watched Dumas come and go. The more he watched, the more mystified he became. Why the ridiculous disguise? Exactly what was exchanged? Tchevsky could understand a meeting in the research library. The Royal Ontario Museum was fine, in front of the Egyptian bas reliefs. Perhaps even in the decadent shallowness of Daddy's Folly. But why had Adrian Dumas lingered in such a place? And why would anyone on some secret errand argue with the bouncer who was insistent about throwing him out?

Following Dumas home one night, he had discovered the ad man's unlikely abode. The next day, angry and frustrated at both Dumas' behavior and the talk it had taken him to get past the yacht club's polite but insistent gate-keeper, Tchevsky had jumped almost off the docks at the sound of the unbearable electronic screeching that had begun just as he had been about to haul himself up the boat's rail. What the hell kind of an alarm system was that?

He recalled ruefully that he hadn't even done anything except stand on the dock beside the boat, look carefully around, and swat at bees. What had made the buzzing? Some pressure sensitive device? Then when the stunning redhead had poked her head out the door and politely, but suspiciously, asked what he was doing, Tchevsky had undertaken the awkward task of moving his bulk along thirty yards of undulating dock. Nonchalantly.

Tchevsky wiped his face with his handkerchief and felt the runnels of sweat rolling down from his armpits under his tourist aloha shirt. He tried to look idle as he passed in front of Dumas' office building for the third time, with an ice cream cone bought jovially from a street vendor. Hating his sticky fingers and trying to sandwich sideways glances between desperate licks, Tchevsky found himself in the embarrassing position of suspiciously looking at windows of his own hotel. Not his floor, thankfully.

He'd first noticed it yesterday. Just a movement in the venetian blinds as Dumas had run off to Daddy's Folly. Tchevsky had seen the reflection in the window of the jewellery store on Dumas' side of Yonge Street. Dumas had pounded past Tchevsky's back on the sidewalk, but Tchevsky had seen the slit between the blinds widen and slide, apparently following Dumas' progress. Had he noticed the twin sparkles of sunshine on binocular lenses, or was that just his imagination?

Not long after, a well-dressed, tall man had come briskly out of the Victoria buttoning a scarlet-lined jacket impatiently and hurrying in Dumas' wake with intent eyes. Not that Tchevsky particularly liked to admit it, but was that an unnatural bump in the small of the back an instant before the man flicked the jacket stylishly down with a rapid shrug? Say, the handle of a Colt Cobra or a Smith & Wesson? An Airweight? Very possibly.

There it was again, the motion in the blinds. Tchevsky looked in the direction of motion and saw Dumas and the blonde girl walking toward him with white paper bags full of Big Mac's. They talked to each other with animation and Tchevsky noted Dumas' ill-concealed interest in the girl's jiggling bodice. Tchevsky turned and studied travel posters intently as they clicked by.

Admiring the cut-away model of the 747, Tchevsky came to the conclusion that Dumas was the best he'd ever seen. No studied naturalness. None of that blend-into-the-crowd drabness of your Everyman agent. Dumas stuck out like a sore thumb. He was too noticeable. Who would suspect him of doing anything secretive? That, no doubt, was why they'd put him out front. To get Tchevsky's notice. To make Tchevsky reveal himself.

Tchevsky no longer had any doubts about the opposition. It wasn't something that Watçek had cooked up.

Or was it?

22

Dumas leaned into the screwdriver and at the same time took the opportunity to glance at his watch. An hour, more or less.

He fastened two more screws and stepped back to look at the aluminum box mounted securely on the bulkhead of the stern cabin. "Okay. What I'll do eventually is to put the hollow beam here just like we planned and the box will be hidden in the beam, out of sight." Dumas' eyes travelled along the mass of wiring that ran to and from the box and coiled loosely up to the ceiling and through it, taped to the bulkhead at intervals with garish red electrical tape. "And I'll use the phoney beam as a conduit for this spaghetti."

"Yes, dear," said Rachael absently. "Hey, listen to this. 'A spokesman for Provincial Hydro today confirmed rumors that negotiations with Watson Mines International may be postponed for an indefinite period. The rumors came in the wake of last week's allegations by Environmental Insight that Provincial Hydro plans to locate nuclear power stations in the Georgian Bay, Muskoka and Haliburton tourist regions. The allegations, denied by Provincial Hydro, have spread concern among cottagers and residents of the area and among segments of the tourist industry. Kenneth R. Easton told Star reporters that the possible postponement of negotiations with Watson Mines International was not related to the controversy of last week in any way. "We're confident that an agreement will be reached," Easton told The Star, "but a period of reflection by both parties may be helpful in coming to an agreement about the duration of the contracts." The negotiations began when Watson Mines International recently offered to guarantee uranium fuel for Provincial Hydro's reactor expansion program, something the public utility has stated is of prime importance to the future supplies of energy in the province.' Blah, blah, blah . . ."

Dumas snorted.

"Hey, you don't think the deal is off, do you? That might make Peter happy . . . or would it?"

"That deal's not off, Rachael. Or Watson would never have offered it. Hydro needs the stuff, Watson wants to sell it, and I'm sure the government will make sure it comes together. They're just backing off because of our maps."

"You're sure?"

"Pretty sure." It doesn't matter anyway, Dumas thought. "Anyway, Peter and I have made enough to satisfy me. Just this last exchange."

"Hey, here's something else, down here at the bottom."

Dumas turned to see two brown knees poking out from under the outspread Star, incongruous unattached fingers curling around opposite edges of the paper and the copper-gold oval of the top of Rachael's head. She was leaning back against the transom, reading from the soft light still coming through the stern windows.

" 'Cyrus Watson, President of Watson Mines International, was reached for comment in McKerrow, Ontario, about seventy miles west of Sudbury where he was speaking to McKerrow Mine workers as part of his program to inform mineworkers about the effect of long-term uranium contracts with utilities. "The only issue is the length of the contract," Watson explained. "Provincial Hydro has been asking for a duration of twenty years guaranteed supply, but I would prefer a longer period in order to make absolutely sure that the reactor program can be fully implemented at reasonable cost." Bruce R. MacDougall, a public information officer with Watson Mines International's head office in Toronto, emphasized that Watson will continue his program of meeting personally with mineworkers. "There's no doubt this deal is going to be finalized," MacDougall told reporters, "because it is very much in the public interest." Watson is next scheduled to speak with the Point McNicoll mineworkers on the Labor Day weekend. MacDougall said that while in Point McNicoll, Watson would take the opportunity of visiting the Martyr's Shrine near Ste-Marie-Among-the Hurons outside of Midland.' "

"Such a religious man, our dear Cyrus," said Dumas wryly.

"A bloody hypocrite," Rachael said with unusual vehemence.

The *Sam McBride's* horn reverberated like some monstrous Victorian breach of etiquette. "I guess I better get a move on," Dumas said. He walked over to lean down and peck Rachael on the top of the head. As he left the stern cabin, he flicked on the alarm system. The amazing thing about the Archis was their ability to sense whatever it was they sensed through almost anything. Wood, stone, steel. Dumas had experimented and, if placed inside, the plants would react just as well to someone's feelings outside *Radagast's* hull. Dumas had been given to much wonder and some speculation as to how the Archis did it and had discovered that researchers at Duke University were just as baffled as he was. "I kept *telling* you about it, but you wouldn't listen," Rachael had said as he had expressed his considerable awe. "See, you should have read *The Secret Life of Plants* and *Experiments in Parapsychology* when I was bugging you about it," she had said, sniffing with somewhat patronizing satisfaction. Dumas wished he had, too, but he'd been making bombs at the time.

He came out on deck and nodded affably to Archi and watched the *Sam McBride* maneuver slowly offshore of the island, lining itself up to come into the dock. He heard the soft padding of Rachael's bare feet coming along the linoleum corridor to the companionway. She brushed up deck behind him. He glanced around the railings and at the moldings over the companionways to both castles. He could see the tiny reflections of the 2N5777 photocells embedded in the wood because he knew just where to look, but he doubted that anyone else would notice them. He'd placed them where he thought a stranger on deck, at night, would be most likely to shine a flashlight. For now, only the alarm would go off, but Dumas had been thinking that, later and with ingenuity, other interesting things could be made to happen. Aquila had gotten under his skin.

"What are you thinking, dear?" Rachael, in bare feet, did not have to lower her lips a trifle to kiss him, but had to stretch up a bit because of the heels.

"Hmmm? Just that I'd rather you stay below while I'm gone tonight. I feel jumpy, maybe because this seems to be the last exchange."

"Sure. If it'll make you feel better."

"Yeah. It would."

"Guilty conscience?"

Dumas grinned. "Maybe." He kissed her. "Just humor me. If you want something from the galley, get it now and please get below before it's dark. It occurs to me that there's been a lot of money paid out for what we have and someone might get it into his head that the maps could be gotten for free. That they might be aboard *Radagast*."

"But you've been disguised," said Rachael.

"A pretty dumb one, if you ask me," said Dumas, "and one that's not hard to see through. I haven't really taken precautions. It didn't seem necessary in the beginning."

"I'll promise, no matter what, to stay below until you're back . . . but, Adrian, if you know anything for sure, shouldn't you tell me?"

"Of course I should. And I would. But I don't. Just a feeling. Something in the back of my mind."

"Alright. I promise. Absolutely. But you be careful."

"Don't worry about me." Dumas watched while Rachael went below through the companionway. He heard the lock click into place. On impulse, he checked to see if the forecastle companionway was locked, too.

The *Sam McBride* was taking on passengers. Dumas opened the gate in *Radagast's* rail and jumped lightly down onto the dock. By running, Dumas managed to squeeze aboard the ferry just before the linesmen cast off the hawsers.

Watching Toronto's skyline growing slowly even taller through the ferry's windows, Dumas reflected that there were few places safer than *Radagast*. Its steel construction extended even to the doors, for the ports of a ship must be at least as strong as other parts of her. Although wood molding camouflaged the plate, or at least softened it, *Radagast* battened down would admit only the smallest runnels of water from even pounding waves and would admit no unwanted intruder unless he came equipped with a blow torch and plenty of time.

Dumas caught a cab hovering at the ferry terminal and sped to the office building. After a hurried change on the fourth floor, he returned to the dusk-lit street and managed to hail another cab. This one took him to a little restaurant at the corner of Bathurst and Bloor. Dumas could never remember the name, but it served the best Hungarian goulash in town.

He ate his goulash while glancing through the large front window of the restaurant from time to time, keeping on the look-out for the man who was supposed to come, and enjoying the constantly changing patterns of light produced by the whirling reflective balls and flashing neon of Honest Ed's across the street.

Eventually, the man wandered in and looked hesitantly around. Dumas had been hoping that the man would be able to find the restaurant from his careful description of its appearance and location. He raised his head and nodded in a friendly fashion over the bowl of goulash.

It went much the same way as the others had gone. The hostility, suspicion, careful counting and payment. Dumas' turn to do some careful counting. Not everyone appreciated that this restaurant with the dark central European interior hardwood partitions between tables gave ample privacy. After a cup of coffee and a chat with Dumas, the man left with his maps as the others had done. And Dumas folded the envelope in one of the pockets of the canvas jacket, and snapped it shut, as had become a habit.

The last one, apparently.

Only four had called back after the newspaper coverage of the maps and Dumas had been mildly disappointed in the lack of the go-gettiveness in Canadian big business. Still, a total of five large real estate speculators zeroed in on a few parcels of land should make some difference. It had certainly made a difference in Peter's world view, and in Dumas' bank account.

It was just as Dumas was ambling along reading some of Honest Ed's blandishments like "Come this Way, You Lucky People!" and idly looking at the displays of Back To School clothing bargains that he saw from the corner of his eye in the reflection from the display window a stout passer-by suddenly turn and come up behind him. The man's image superimposed itself over his own in the glass.

"That's good advice," the man said.

"What is?"

"Come this way, you lucky people."

The man pressed something hard and blunt into the small of his back and Dumas decided to accept the unspoken inference that the something was potentially lethal.

"Alright," said Dumas. "Where to?"

"Down the alley there to the parking lot behind this building. And walk naturally. And smile, like I'm an old friend who's surprised you."

Dumas turned slowly and smiled broadly. "Why George, you old rascal, I haven't seen you in a dog's age." He began walking beside the man the few steps down Bloor to the alley beside Honest Ed's.

"Ain't it the truth, Adrian? What are you up to these days?" asked Tchevsky jovially.

Dumas shrugged. "Hell, George, you know how it is. A hustle here, a hustle there." The man nudged Dumas gently but firmly into the alley and they continued walking.

"Into the parking lot. See that red and white Bronco in the corner over there?"

Dumas headed for it. He had remotely considered the possibility that some customer, albeit in a somewhat farfetched scenario, might decide to take the maps and a bit later try to retrieve the money. And Dumas had a plan worked out for this extreme possibility. He put it into operation.

"Ah, George? Sore about the money, eh? Consider the maps a gift. Here, I'll give you back the money." Dumas started to snap open the pocket of the jacket.

"I'm not interested in your money, Adrian."

Dumas was surprised and not altogether pleased. He stood beside the red and white Bronco which was not parked safely under a watchful light.

"Open the door. It's unlocked."

Dumas swung it wide. He was nudged again with the hard and blunt something. He got in. Tchevsky closed the door and locked it with his key. As the man walked around to the driver's side, Dumas considered the possibility, but rejected it, that he'd be able to get out and far enough away in the small amount of time that would be required if the something were a revolver, for instance.

Tchevsky climbed into the driver's seat and as his right hand came into view Dumas realized that he'd been wrong. It was an automatic and held below the level of the dash.

"Why didn't you run, or try to run?" the man asked.

Dumas shrugged. "Because, if you were serious, I wouldn't have made it. If you're not serious, it doesn't matter." He paused. "Besides, I'm curious. If it's not your money, I'd like to know what the hell is going on."

The man sighed. "You're not the only one, I'm afraid, Mister Adrian Dumas. Unfortunately, I must know what is going on."

Perhaps, Dumas reflected, some third party yearned to muscle in on the map-selling business, not knowing that the market had bottomed out. But how had anyone found out? "George, I don't know what it is you want, but I'd be willing to cut you in, since you're so insistent."

"Cut me in on what, Mister Dumas?"

"The maps, of course," said Dumas tiredly.

"Mister Dumas, I wouldn't have this highly illegal weapon, nor would I be prepared to use it—and I am—if I didn't fully appreciate one fact."

"What's that?"

"That I'm expendable, Mister Dumas." He paused. "I don't want to get stopped by any routine spot checks. Please be so good as to put your seat belt on. It's down on the floor to your right."

Dumas shrugged. He turned to fish around for the seat belt down by the door sill. It felt as if a pillow hit him, and he went to sleep.

23

It was the pins and needles in his hands and feet that he felt first. Then, in the distance, he heard the sound of a raucous party, laughter and loud music. The occasional tinkling of glasses and beer bottles.

His eyes fluttered open and he shook his head. Dumas looked up to deal with the pins and needles in his hands and found that his wrists were tightly wired to the brown enamel tubular bedframe. He managed to pull himself up on his feet, but he couldn't move them far because they were wired to the legs of the bedframe at floor level. The pins and needles were easily explainable. His hands and feet were a becoming shade of blue. Dumas shook his head and was able to gather that he was tied at the foot of the bed. The man sat on the mattress edge about three feet away and his weight made a considerable dent in the cut-rate Hudson Bay type blanket. The air felt chilly and Dumas could not explain the distant party.

"Where am . . . ?" he began. Dumas' dulled senses didn't make much sense of the movements of the man. They were too fast. The pillows again. First on one side of his face and then the other. Dumas heard a distant cracking sound. Then, cold water on his face and the pain began as a tiny sting and then a heavy sick pounding in his nose. Dumas managed to focus down onto the striped brown wool of the blanket. Red blots were appearing there beneath his head. Dumas realized that his nose was bleeding. The wool seemed capable of absorbing much more.

"Can you hear me, Adrian?"

Dumas nodded. As his head bobbed, Dumas idly noticed that he was naked.

"Good. I did that to show you that I don't really have much

time. You know that. You look to be a strong man, Adrian, and I may not be able to break you in the time I suspect is available to me." The man sighed. "But I have to do my best."

"What do you want to know?" Dumas snuffled up blood and spat.

"First things first, Adrian. I want to tell you the rules of this game. I'm going to ask questions. If I'm not pleased with the answers, Adrian, I'm going to gag you tightly and hurt you. Feel at liberty to scream behind the gag. Nothing but a hum or bearable growl will come out. Now, when I think you can talk without screaming, Adrian, I'll remove the gag and you can tell me what I want to hear. If you try to call out instead of talk, Adrian, I'll knock you unconscious, gag you, revive you. And hurt you so much, so long. Understand?"

Dumas' eyes pounded pinkly and he imagined yellow blobs floating in front of his eyes. Still, he could make out, as the man stood up, the assortment of objects on the bed. Coat hanger. Corkscrew. Paring knife. The man chose the coat hanger.

"Now, Adrian, where do you work?"

Dumas spat. "With Pete Tompkins on Yonge Street not far from Wellington."

"That's right, Adrian. I know that. What kind of work do you and Peter do?"

"We're a PR outfit, I guess. We do a little of everything in communications."

"You worked for Watson Mines International?"

"We were going to, but we never really did—the account sort of faded away with that Provincial Hydro fuel business. Nothing for us to do."

"Why did you compile those maps and sell them, Adrian?"

"To make Pete some money, mostly. He'd been counting on the Watson Mining thing and when it fizzled out he was in a bad way."

"Let's talk about these maps of yours, Adrian. Remember, I haven't seen them. I just saw you taking some long rolled-up things into Environmental Insight. They looked like maps to me. So they are maps. What kind of maps, Adrian?"

"Just like in the papers. Maps showing likely locations for future Provincial Hydro reactors."

"But how did you get the information, Adrian?"

"By putting two and two together, mostly. A friend of mine stumbled onto the heavy water connection during a summer job with Provincial Hydro. After that it was easy to make maps."

"Alright. So you gave some maps to Environmental Insight.

But you've been selling them too. I've seen one exchange. Tell me about it."

"Money. I'm selling the maps to land speculators. And I'm hoping that if the speculators compete with each other in buying the land then Provincial Hydro's plans will be complicated."

"And you and Peter will make some money at the same time."

"Yes."

"This friend of yours, Adrian. The one with the summer job. What's his name?"

Dumas looked down at the scarlet blanket. He spat redly onto it. He looked at Tchevsky. "That's something that I won't tell. He's only a student and it was just a summer job. He just stumbled onto the heavy water correlation by accident. He isn't important to you."

Tchevsky studied Dumas' eyes. "We'll come back to that. Adrian, who are those men across the street in the Victoria Hotel? I know about them. They watch you. Why?

Dumas looked up with such a genuine expression of amazement that Tchevsky almost became willing to accept the possibility that Dumas didn't know about them. "Men?"

"Yes, Adrian, the men in the hotel. They watch you with binoculars. Here's my question, Adrian. Listen carefully, now. Who do you really work for? Who are those men? What are those maps really intended to accomplish besides making money for you and Peter and slowing up Provincial Hydro's nuclear expansion? What's your friend's name?"

"That's four questions."

The man shrugged. "Just answer them. In any order you like."

"I don't know about the men. I made the maps to make some money we lost by the Watson thing falling through. I work for Peter and myself in communications."

The man took the cloth out of his pocket and tied it tightly around Dumas' head, through the corners of his mouth. "The tragedy is, Adrian, I almost believe you. But you're too odd a fellow. Unfortunately, I simply have to know the truth. Even if it kills you. Even if you've already told me the truth. Hold on, Adrian, I'm afraid this is going to be bad."

Tchevsky eyed the broad back sadly. He shrugged and lifted his arm and brought it down and across the back with all of his strength. The coat hanger whirred in the air, but made not much of a sound on impact. The welt came up immediately, long and red and raised. Dumas leaped and jiggled the bed.

Tchevsky nodded to himself and concentrated upon making a criss-cross pattern of red ridges. Dumas leaped and writhed. Tchevsky heard the rasping gargle fill the room of tightly closed windows and pitied the bulging neck cords. Some of the welts, when crossed by another, split and blood began to trickle along the groove of the spine. One impossibly long gargle came as Dumas strained up so that the wire cut into the wrists.

Then he sagged down, hanging from his bleeding wrists.

Tchevsky tossed the coat hanger on the bed and took the empty glass from the cheap night table beside the bed and walked slowly into the kitchen to fill it with water. When he returned, Dumas was moving faintly. Dumas' jaw muscles clenched spasmodically and his chest heaved. The blood from his nose made his breathing an audible gurgle and snuffle. Tchevsky grabbed the brown hair and looked into the upturned face. Tears streamed from the eyes and there was still a bit of a gargle coming from behind the gag at intervals. Still, Tchevsky didn't think that Dumas would scream now. He poured the water down into the face. The eyes opened. They looked tired, Tchevsky decided.

"Adrian, Adrian. You're stronger than I thought. I don't think that with you I can afford to waste time taking the gag on and off. Just answer my questions with nods and shakes of the head. They're simple enough, after all. Ready?"

Tchevsky paused and shook his head. He patted Dumas' wet cheek tenderly.

"Okay. Adrian. Do you know who those men are, the ones who watch you from across the street in the Victoria Hotel?"

Dumas shook his head.

"Adrian, I'm afraid it has to be the corkscrew this time. Tell you what, Adrian, we'll try it in the deep flesh of each buttock first. Then, if you don't answer. Well, I'm afraid I'll have to go around front and try the corkscrew another place. I think you can guess. I'll leave it to your imagination."

Tchevsky walked slowly over to the bed and picked up the corkscrew. He saw Dumas' wide eyes following him. Tchevsky walked around in back and smashed his thick forearm across Dumas' shoulders. Dumas doubled up over the bedframe. Tchevsky jabbed the corkscrew in and held Dumas down with his weight. As Tchevsky slowly rotated his wrist, he heard the gargling begin again and saw the hollows in the neck pound. The blood was running up into Dumas' nose and soon the gargles changed into deep croaks.

When the corkscrew was buried deeply, Tchevsky took his

weight off Dumas and pulled the corkscrew out. He stood aside.

Dumas' body shot back, spine arched and head straining toward the ceiling. The gargle lasted a long time and the eyes bulged.

Dumas' mind was red and his eyes pounded out of focus. He could not concentrate, but he knew that he had managed to concentrate while the man was twisting it into him. He had forced his silent screams to come in a rhythm. Between the screams he'd clamped his jaws to blind out the pain and had ground his teeth into the cloth of the gag. The blood had moistened and stretched it. He had been able to get in a few good shears with his molars. Dumas, as soon as he could make out the knots in the pine-planked ceiling, remembered to collapse as before.

"Adrian, tell me, do you know who those men are?"

Dumas did not want to shake his head. But he knew that he could not allow the man to remove the gag. He stalled as long as possible.

"Come on, Adrian. I'll start again, anyway. Just once more back here and then we move around to the front."

Dumas concentrated on letting his body be as slack as he could make it. Tchevsky lifted him up by the hair and flung him over the bedframe.

"Yes, Adrian, it does take a lot of energy to scream and to hurt, doesn't it? You can't last much longer, Adrian. Why not just tell me?"

Dumas shook his head.

Again he felt the weight falling upon him, pushing the brown enamelled tube deep into his stomach so that he could hardly breathe to scream. Just as well—he could use the agony for chewing.

Tchevsky waited and waited with the corkscrew poised in the air. Until there was a slight relaxing of the body under him. One could only sustain even terror and hideous anticipation so long. Then he jabbed.

The body jerked beneath him, but without as much energy as before. Tchevsky twisted and heard the croaks and gargles come rhythmically, but too quietly this time. Would Dumas pass out? Did he know anything? Tchevsky twisted. Then he got off and was gratified to see the body writhe across the bed frame, hump and gurgle, but without enough strength to rise. Tchevsky watched the handle of the corkscrew jiggle and wave above the blood oozing out. He pulled. Dumas staggered back again, but it was not the same arrow swiftness of response. He's almost done it, Tchevsky thought, hearing the mixture of gargle, sobs, croaks that came out of the taut neck together with the wheezing breaths and bloody bubbles spewing over the lips. Tchevsky thought that because of the angle on the front seat of the Bronco it was possible that he'd overdone it and hit Dumas too hard with the pistol butt. There had been no room for the calculated swing, and Tchevsky had had to put all his force behind the blow. He decided that Dumas was fading quickly because the concussion was taking over. He doubted that anyone could fake that kind of slackness in the face of so much pain. Besides, why? Dumas would not escape the agony anyway.

Dumas sank slowly to hang by his wrists, gasping and sobbing.

"Alright, Adrian. We have to move around to the front. I haven't much time."

Tchevsky knelt on the end of the bed by the frame. He reached over and pulled Dumas up by the hair until his left hand found Dumas' crotch. Tchevsky grasped the scrotum and cracked the testicles together. Dumas arched high on his toes, his legs rigid and trembling. Tchevsky eased the pressure until Dumas stood slumped in front of him.

Dumas had been waiting, hoarding his strength in the red pain, chewing on the gag. He'd been trying to work some life back into his fingers. Only one thumb seemed to work reasonably well—his right one. Dumas could barely make it into a hook. He swallowed his blood, held it in his throat to wet his vocal cords, and let it go down to his stomach.

"I'm afraid that this is going to ruin you, Adrian. You might as well tell me. Do you know who those men are?"

Tears rolled down Dumas' cheeks. He felt the hand squeezing. He'd managed to slump enough so that his knees were flexed. The hand squeezed and he felt sick to his stomach. Tchevsky's other hand held the corkscrew. Dumas saw the arm tense back.

Dumas gathered what strength remained to him. He pulled up his arms and drove up with his knees at the same instant. He did not even feel the wire cutting into his wrists. At the same time, he leaned with all his weight to the right.

Dumas had hoped to be able to lift the narrow bed with the man's weight on it high enough to turn it over. Instead, something else happened that Dumas had not expected. He lifted the bedframe and twisted, but before it could go over, the twisted frame allowed the wooden slats supporting the springs to slip out of the angle-iron beams. Tchevsky and the mattress slid toward the head of the bed where the slats had given way. Dumas felt pain shaft up from his groin as Tchevsky's fingers were flung unexpectedly away. He felt the tears spurt from his eyes. He gargled. He wanted to howl toward the ceiling, but he forced himself to bend his head down. His slow thumb hooked behind the cloth and his molars chewed desperately. He jerked his head and felt the fabric start to tear. He jerked again, seeing the man struggling to his feet on the soft mattress and slanting springs. Dumas jerked again and the fabric parted over his tongue and remained clamped under his thumb as he raised his head. Tchevsky stomped drunkenly up the mattress. Dumas stooped and jumped up and backwards again. The bedframe moved perhaps a foot, but the mattress slid further under the frames and Tchevsky staggered and fell against the cheap brown enamel tube of the headboard. It popped out of the grooves in the angle-iron frames that supported it. It and Tchevsky fell to the floor.

Dumas began screaming the moment the bloody gag had slid from his mouth. He screamed wildly now, seeing Tchevsky fighting off the headboard, desperately because he had a chance he had not expected. He gathered his strength and humped sideways, carrying the mattress and springs until they fell clear of the sprung angle-iron frames. Dumas bucked to the window across the small room, screaming, and smashed the glass behind the cheap shade with his elbow. The shade pulled into the hole in the glass his elbow had made, released, and slatted up the window, rolling over and over at the top. Dumas smashed into the glass with his elbows and the back of his head and he felt it cut him and shatter all around him. He never stopped screaming. Tchevsky was up on his feet and coming toward him. Dumas howled until his neck might burst.

Tchevsky stopped in the middle of the floor. He glanced quickly at Dumas and the open window. Dumas never noticed. His eyes were closed and he was conscious only of his own last shriek.

Tchevsky hurried to the front door of the cottage. Dumas did not hear the sound of the Bronco starting, but quickly being shut down again. Finally, his breath gave out and he sagged again by the window, hanging from his bloody wrists.

3

24

He recalled his tongue being dry and bloated, filling his mouth. He choked. A dusky face with slanted eyes looked down upon him in a kindly way and held wetness to his lips. Doubtless Gunga Din.

Then he began hearing the bells. They tinkled and clanged. Sometimes they were loud. Sometimes there was nothing. But always the bells came back, sooner or later.

Then it came to him that his eyes were open. He heard the bells plainly and they were real. He smiled and closed his eyes again and there was nothing.

Quite suddenly he was looking at steel beams shining above him in bright sunlight. And he heard the bells. All sizes. Dumas turned his head to the right. *Radagast's* stern windows. The windows seemed to rock and the mast of the *McVay* tracked across them like a pointer. Dumas noticed the *McVay's* halyards slapping against the aluminum mast. The bells.

He turned his head to the other side. Not far away beside him, a mass of long black hair trailed off the mattress and onto the wooden floor. He looked down from the hair and accepted the humps under the sheet. Dumas felt around with his hands and decided he was lying on something with a frame of tubular metal. But his hands could move very little. He remembered the brown tubular bed. Dumas whimpered. The fat man had him again, on *Radagast* . . .

Oh, God, Rachael.

"Rachael!" It was a scream. The tears streamed from Dumas' eyes and he sobbed.

"Mister Dumas, Mister Dumas," the voice called, far away. He heard feet padding.

"He's awake," the first voice said.

"Adrian? Adrian. It's me, Rachael." Dumas felt hair on his face, stroking his cheek. Something warm and moist touched his mouth. A kiss. "Did he get you?" Dumas' words came thickly.

"No, no, darling. I'm alright. Becky is alright. We're together. We're on *Radagast* . . . I love you."

Dumas sobbed and he remembered nothing.

It was not so bright when his eyes opened the next time. But the halyards still slapped the mast of the *McVay*. He ached. He turned to look toward the other mattress, but no one was on it.

"Rachael." He managed to keep his voice calm. It was a call. He heard a child laughing. Becky. "Rachael." Again the padding of feet along the short corridor linking *Radagast's* cabins. The girl came toward him and knelt beside him. Long black hair. Dumas looked at the tee-shirt without comprehension. "Mike? Mike Red Sky?"

"Yes, Mister Dumas."

"Where is everybody?"

"Having dinner in the front of the boat."

"Oh."

"I'd better tell them you're awake. How do you feel, Mister Dumas?"

"Bad," said Dumas.

Dumas turned his head and watched ragged grey clouds streak across the windows and the mast arc. He listened to the ropes slapping all about the marina. Presently, he heard hurried footsteps. He turned to see Rachael stooping down beside him. She looked haggard.

"How are you, dear?" she said, smiling warmly. She bent to kiss him awkwardly and Dumas realized that there was something white covering his nose because he could see, cross-eyed, the mesh of cloth. He wanted to reach up and hold her, but his arms wouldn't raise.

"What's wrong," said Dumas, "that my arms don't work?"

"Oh, it's just the straps to keep you from moving your wrists, darling."

Dumas began to remember specifics. "How bad is it, Rache?"

He saw her turn away, sniff and wipe her eyes. She tried to choke back a sob.

"Hell," said Dumas, "I hope it isn't that bad."

She turned back with a forced grin and shook her head. Her tears sprinkled onto his face. "You're going to be all right, Adrian. Thank God. I . . . I . . . just don't like to think about what was done to you." She cried, sobbing and knuckling her eyes. "I shouldn't be crying," she sniffled. "I'm supposed to be chipper and encouraging."

"I don't like thinking about it much, myself," said Dumas. "If you'd take the straps off my hands, Rache, I could touch you."

"I'm not sure I'm supposed to yet, Adrian. I have to ask the nurse."

"Nurse?"

"Oh, yes, Mister Steinberg's nurse. She's very good." Rachael paused. "I'll go tell them."

A most unpleasant pounding began in Dumas' nose. It spread to his eyes. Thinking about it, and wondering about it, made little pains begin to develop everywhere. Now that he thought about it, his wrists and ankles throbbed. It slowly occurred to him that his back was merely one large throb. Dumas gritted his teeth. By the time the nurse knelt beside him, he was allowing himself tiny gasps with each breath. Why had he bothered to come awake?

"Well, how are we today?" the grey-haired lady smiled brightly and her face crinkled around the eyes and mouth. The eyes looked into his intently. She slipped back an eyelid. She took his pulse.

"Can you give me a run-down?" asked Dumas.

"What, on you?" she said impatiently. "I've seen worse football injuries. Concussion and a broken nose. Aside from that, only superficial cuts, abrasions and contusions."

"It doesn't feel all that superficial," Dumas winced.

"That's because you're on the mend. Mending pains."

Dumas looked beyond the nurse and saw Rachael hovering at the door. The nurse rose and spoke to her too softly for Dumas to hear. Rachael nodded, nodded and smiled. The nurse left and Rachael came over to kneel beside him. "She says that you're doing well. She's going to give you something to let you sleep, now. Tomorrow you can talk more. The doctor's coming soon." She kissed him.

25

The following late afternoon Dumas was leaning gingerly against the poop deck steps, not quite sitting, and trying to enjoy the warm rays of a gentle sun. He was prepared to exchange nasty glances with everybody. With the thin mustachioed doctor who shook his head sadly and pursed his lips. With Rachael, who worried a small piece of her own full lower lip between her eye teeth. With the nurse, should she raise her head, although Dumas suspected that she might be ostensibly examining his teak deck to hide a smile. With Steinberg.

"Right," said Dumas. "Now that that's established, we'll tackle the matter of food. I want something solid and I want it now." He smiled with self-satisfaction, the effect of which was only slightly marred by the fact that the smile pulled his nose and he winced. "Hop to it, Rachael," said Dumas. "Food."

"Yes, dear," said Rachael. "What about a grilled cheese sandwich and a bowl of sou—"

"No more soup."

"Yes, dear."

"Mister Dumas, you really shouldn't be up for a few more days," the doctor intoned gravely.

"Why?" asked Dumas. "Will I die?"

"I doubt it. But you've had a concussion and your body's taken a beating. You should rest."

"And starve to death," said Dumas.

The doctor spread his arms helplessly. "There's still a chance of a blood clot on the brain. Haematoma. And floaters."

"Floaters?"

"Yellow blobs that float around in front of your eyes and obscure your vision. That could be serious."

"I'll watch for 'em," Dumas promised. "You'll be the first to know if I see any."

"You will need to take the medication, Mister Dumas. All of it. On time." The doctor looked at Rachael.

"I'll see to it, Doctor. And thank you," Rachael smiled a little apologetically.

"Don't worry, I'll take it all. Especially the pain pills." Dumas said fervently.

The doctor looked questioningly at Steinberg, shrugged, and began to help the nurse down from *Radagast's* deck to the dock. "Watch out for that bee," Dumas called. He watched them trundle down the dock with satisfaction. Presently, he turned his head slowly back and his gaze fell upon Rachael. She fled to the galley. Dumas nodded in satisfaction. Next, his eyes traversed a small arc of railing, blue water and sky, until Steinberg's tall figure came into view. Dumas looked him up and down. With his arms crossed, Steinberg's long and flaring Italian-cut jacket flared even more. Dumas glimpsed the scarlet silk lining. A discreet grey and tan check today. Ankle crossed nonchalantly, the expensive fabric only slightly confused by the freedom of modest flare at the cuffs. Steinberg's black pebble-grain loafers molded to the contours of his feet comfortably. Above the colorful splash of the wide Paisley tie, Steinerg smiled. His brown curly hair seemed friendly and although the coils seemed randomly roaming over a high forehead and tucked carelessly around the ears, Dumas noted that not a hair was out of place. With three women, including young Becky—and that was one more question—and only one rather spartan head aboard *Radagast*, Dumas doubted even Steinberg's ability to maintain his usual level of sartorial splendor. "You're not staying aboard, are you?" Dumas asked.

"Harbour Castle."

"Ah." Dumas nodded. "We have to talk, Steinberg."

"Yes, Adrian, we do. But I think you're pushing yourself a bit to do it now. Besides," Steinberg smiled wide and slowly, "I have several advantages. I've talked with Tchevsky, in a manner of speaking."

"That's nice," said Dumas. "What's with the 'Adrian'? You're damned right I'm pushing it. I feel like hell. But doctors and nurses make me nervous. I wanted them off my ship. Who the hell is Tchevsky?"

"That's a long story, Mister Dumas . . . as you prefer . . . but we're getting toward the last chapters. Colonel Igor Tchevsky. KGB. Your hospitable host of a few evenings back."

Dumas looked at Steinberg wearily. "A few evenings back. How many?"

"Four. And four days, counting last night. We brought you home night before last. You spent almost two days in, well, a private clinic."

Dumas grinned and immediately winced. His nose pounded in reproof and soreness spread to the backs of his eyes. Floaters? Dumas blinked. It was gone. The waving masts seemed to wave more than usual. "Steinberg, can you help me below? I feel queasy."

"Okay, easy does it, Ad— Mister Dumas. Watch your head." Steinberg helped Dumas down the companionway steps and along the short corridors of louvered doors. Dumas saw the tube frame of the stretcher glowing in the light of the stern windows. He lay down carefully and thankfully. Steinberg flicked the blanket on the mattress nearby and sat down, pulling his trousers up by the crease and elegantly crossing his legs. "What do you want to deal with first?"

Dumas considered this carefully. First things first. "Rachael."

Steinberg nodded. He paused, looking upwards. "This is the story. As soon as we got you out of the Whispering Larch Cozy Guest Cottages not far from Lindsay, and got you into the clinic on Wynford Drive in Don Mills—that would have been about four ayem—and as soon as we knew you'd live, about four-fifteen, I called Rachael here."

"How'd she take it?"

"She was worried and suspicious. She'd heard my name and said that you had told her to stay on board while it was dark. She was worried sick because you hadn't come home or called, but she wouldn't even consider taking the police launch I had offered to send."

"Good girl."

Steinberg nodded. "So, all things considered, I figured it was best for her to stay put. She couldn't do anything anyway. I told her that you would be okay and that you were under a doctor's care. Police drove her up to the clinic the next day."

"What does she know?"

"The truth. That someone worked on you somewhat harshly."

"Does she know why?"

"No," said Steinberg. "Do you?"

"No." Dumas paused. "Does she know about this Tchevsky fellow?"

"Ah, no."

Dumas nodded carefully. "Did you . . . er . . . broach the subject of our previous . . ."

Steinberg smiled. "Involvement? Would that be the word? No. Adrian, I figured that would insult your intelligence. And mine. You wouldn't have told her."

Dumas snorted gingerly. "There goes the Adrian, again. You remind me of my friend Ivan."

"Igor."

"Igor. But with you turning up, I guess she suspects something."

"One thing about Rachael, now that I've gotten acquainted with her," Steinberg mused, "is her ability to shut up. No questions. No statements. She kept her concerns confined to your immediate problems. I admire that."

Their heads turned to the door at the sound of padding bare feet. Mike Red Sky hesitated before Dumas waved her in. Custer jiggled above the tray. Being a progressive and a liberal, Dumas recalled that Rachael had never cared much for Custer. Possibly less now. Mike set the tray down in front of Dumas' stretcher, smiled, squiggled her nose slightly at him, and left. Dumas looked down at the grilled cheese sandwich and the chicken noodle soup. He sighed and picked up the spoon.

"Er . . ." Dumas slurped. "That's another little thing I don't quite get. Not that I mind it one bit, but how the hell did Red Sky get on board?" He paused and slurped. "More to the point, why is Red Sky on board?"

Steinberg shrugged. "You mumbled and sobbed quite a bit at the clinic, Adrian. Mostly Rachael and Becky. A few Peters and Debbies. Then, some references to Mike Red Sky, Mantouche . . . that came out quite often interspersed with some Oh God's. You asked if she'd gotten the bus to Cape Croker okay. That was about the time we had matched Tchevsky's photograph. Oh, about noon. It all became exceedingly interesting to me. I sent someone to Cape Croker for this Mike Red Sky."

Dumas hunted around in the noodles for a chunk of chicken. "You talk with her?"

Steinberg sighed. "Yes."

Dumas grinned cautiously. "I'll bet that was interesting."

Steinberg's face became serious. "Actually, Adrian, it was very interesting—by then Tchevsky was mumbling from time to time as well. It was then that I began to figure out what had happened, after talking to Red Sky and to Peter."

"That's nice," said Dumas. "Mind telling me?"

"All in good time, Mister Dumas. Maybe tomorrow. Anyway, since Red Sky seemed to be a friend of yours—oh, she was very emotional when she saw you—and after Red Sky and Rachael had had their little chat down in the coffee shop, well, Rachael invited Red Sky aboard. It didn't bother me. Besides, Red Sky turned out to have not a cent. Saved on my expenses."

"Alright." Dumas put the spoon down. He lay back on the stretcher. Steinberg suddenly disappeared.

Steinberg looked at Dumas breathing. There was still a bit of sniffle, but the breath was deep and regular. Steinberg lifted one bandaged wrist from the floor and placed it on the stretcher. He picked up the tray and walked to the door. The sandwich, he noted, had not been touched.

26

Steinberg looked down the dock wistfully and splashed another dollop of Chivas Regal into his glass. Dumas leaned against the forecastle, making sure that the edge of the deck and bulkhead met no lower than the small of his back. This entailed much leaning and the use of his elbow. His eyes followed Steinberg's gaze. Peter helped Debbie balance carefully as they walked along the dock. Both of them carried large papier mâché vases of flowers. "Just what I need on this boat," said Dumas. "More flowers."

Debbie had gone all out. Her micro-mini, ladder stockings and Courrèges boots earned an admiring whistle from the young and tousled crew of the *McVay* who were otherwise absorbed in making harbor furls in the mainsail. Debbie pretended not to notice, but Dumas perceived a slight turtling-in of her long neck for the few steps that brought them next to *Radagast's* rail. Climbing aboard would be a problem for her, with the boys in the slim, low *McVay* attentive. Debbie whispered in Peter's ear and, against all his training, he manfully moved around her to her left side. Debbie grimaced and reached one long booted leg onto the deck while the boys in the daysailer voiced audible disappointment at Peter's slim body in the way.

"I'll do it, Adrian. Just stay here," said Steinberg. He walked quickly to the rail and extended one subdued and small-blue-checked sleeve down toward Debbie's extended cream arm. Dumas saw her fingers curl around Steinberg's French cuffs. Steinberg hauled her aboard easily and proved too much of a gentleman to look anywhere but for her face. He took the vases from Peter, placed them on the deck, and then offered a manly hand-clasp to help Peter make the short jump aboard.

Debbie started to stoop carefully to retrieve her flowers.

"Just leave 'em there, Debbie, we'll take care of them later," Dumas said. "Thanks for the legs," he added. "It perks me up." Debbie grimaced.

"It was my idea, old man," said Peter. "Said it would do you a world of good."

"My Gawd, you look 'orrible, Adrian," She peered into the eye-holes of the bandage over his nose. "All red and blue and puffy."

"Where were you mugged, exactly, Adrian?"

"Er, somewhere near Honest Ed's, up on Bathurst."

"Should stay out of those areas, Adrian, late at night. I've been reading in the papers about more violence in street crime. Senseless beatings. Toronto's getting just like any other city." Peter rubbed his jaw. "I was just wondering, Adrian. The money was recovered, wasn't it?"

"I only started wondering about that today, Pete. Other things on my mind. I'll check it out. You know how these things are, though. Maybe it'll be held for evidence or something," Dumas said doubtfully.

Steinberg chuckled. "Adrian, that knock on the head has scrambled you just a bit. Don't you remember?"

"Gee," said Dumas, "I'm afraid I don't, Mister Steinberg."

"They never got anything, Adrian. And the police don't have any suspects at all. Some good citizens heard some noise, that's all, and the muggers ran."

"The money?" Dumas queried.

"Rachael. She got it with the rest of your things at the hospital—well, the clinic. She asked me to deposit it a couple of days ago. I did."

"What a client, Adrian," Peter said admiringly.

"Oh, I like to think I'm more than just a client, Peter," Steinberg waved the hand with the Chivas Regal deprecatingly. He chuckled and smiled. "Adrian and I have developed a close relationship over a time. Similar interests."

"That's right," said Dumas. "Who but a friend would do that sort of thing?"

"I'm glad to hear that the money's safe," said Peter.

"Right. I'll be in the office in a couple of days and give you a cheque, Pete."

"It's a little difficult for Adrian to get about, with all the climbing up and down, so, Debbie, Pete? Can I get you a tall, cool drink? I know Adrian has gin and tonic."

"Well, maybe a short one, Mister Steinberg. Don't want to tire Adrian."

"Yes, thank you, Mister Steinberg. Adrian, where's Rachael?"

"Rache? Oh, she's below, Debbie. Catching up on her sleep. She's been sitting up with me a few nights. I hear. Especially the first couple."

"New baby-sitter?" Peter gestured toward the poop. Dumas looked back. Red Sky was sitting cross-legged by the binnacle teaching Becky to play cat's cradle.

"Red Sky's a friend. She came down to help out."

"*That's* Mike Red Sky?" Peter rubbed his jaw. "Your Mister Steinberg called, from the clinic, I think, and said you wanted her address. Asked me to look in your files for it. Hope you don't mind, Adrian. Just Cape Croker."

"Not at all, Pete."

"I rather imagined a fellow, with a name like that," said Peter.

"She's been a big help. Spelled Rachael off a bit with Becky and the bedside watch."

"Trust you," said Debbie. Dumas grinned.

"Lovely child, isn't she?" They turned at the sound of Steinberg's voice. He unfolded himself out of the forecastle companionway and handed the glasses to Debbie and Peter. Steinberg gazed briefly up toward the poop, thinking about the tattered, faded jeans and bare feet. They reminded him of Marryanne. Steinberg could almost hear the soft brush of denim bell-bottoms on the pavement and the small little slaps of bare feet on Augusta Street sidewalks. Almost hear the halting rock beat and Maryanne singing the chorus . . .

Rollin', rollin',
Rollin' on the ri-ver.

And that was yet another time, and not long ago, when he'd wondered about Dumas. And had guessed wrong. This time he definitely had the upper hand.

"If you like that sort," Peter chuckled. "Had my fill during the war."

Dumas marvelled at the way Steinberg's usually genial brown-grey eyes went icy. It reminded him of the way Rachael's could change. Only Rachael's flashed in brief anger. Steinberg's just went cold and Dumas figured they'd always stay that way. For Peter.

"Peter was stationed in Palestine, and Egypt, during the war," Dumas remarked helpfully.

"You don't say," said Steinberg.

Peter's mustache twitched and he finished his drink in one last hasty gulp. "I really think we should be going, Adrian. Don't want to tire you," he said again.

"Give Rachael my love," said Debbie, looking uncertainly between the men. "And try not to look so 'orrible, Adrian, when you come into the office."

"I'll do my very best," Dumas promised. "And don't worry about the cheque, Pete."

"Forget it, old chap, I just want you to get better," he said sincerely.

Steinberg made a point of walking Debbie to the rail and helping her golden head to bob down without mishap from the level of *Radagast's* deck to the dock. Peter had to jump without assistance. Steinberg waved curtly to him. He watched Debbie's long legs stride along the dock, giving her an unseen slight smile. He came back to Dumas slowly. "How does it feeling knowing that Red Sky is just a bloody Wog?" Steinberg asked.

Dumas shrugged. "He doesn't know what he's saying."

"Maybe you're right."

"He was programmed more than forty years years ago, Steinberg. Mind trekking below and getting me a Labatt's?"

When Steinberg thrust the beaded bottle into Dumas' hand, Dumas looked up and saw that warmth had returned to the brown-grey eyes. "Maybe it's time I knew your first name," Dumas said.

"Mendel, Adrian. But my friends call me Sam."

Dumas thought carefully. "Ah . . . Sam . . . first things first. Thanks for hauling me out of the Whispering Larch Cozy Guest Cottages. Thanks for dealing with Rachael like you did. Thanks for thinking. Thanks for Red Sky. Thanks for depositing the money. That about covers it."

"What about thanks for the doctor and the nurse?"

"I doubt that your doctor is within medicare, Sam. A lot have opted out of the Ontario Hospital Insurance Program," Dumas said. "A lot. Think of the concern it's causing in Ottawa. Destroying the universality of the whole medicare scheme. When do I get the bill? I can hardly wait."

"On the other hand, Adrian, the relationship between doctor and patient is very special. All sorts of things to do with confidentiality. Me? I'm undecided on the issue. You won't get a bill."

"I was afraid of that."

"Why? I checked. Your cable-code is still 'Hardradha'."

Dumas took a long swig from the bottle of Special Lite.

"You're sure that stuff mixes with Demerol?" Steinberg asked.

Dumas shrugged. "So it is, Sam. So it is."

As a young and not particularly welcome Prince in the Danish court, Harold Hardradha had been encouraged to roam abroad. The Viking eyes were perhaps too speculative. The right arm too strong, the blade too burnished. 'Son,' the old king had suggested, 'I heard they can use men like you . . . well, almost anywhere else. Byzantium, for instance.' It was a long, hard way away. This suited the old king fine. Hardradha had wandered. At length, he'd become captain of the Varangian Guard for the Emperor of the East in Byzantium. At length, Hardradha had returned home and had become king in the usual way. A certain edge with the reflexes. In the meantime, Hardradha had seen much in the world and some historians were disposed to think that his travel tales had formed much of the basis for *The King's Mirror*, a little-known book subsequently employed as a teaching aid for future kings of the Norse. It contained surprisingly accurate information about the nature of the world. During the campus unrest of the late sixties and early seventies, Dumas had chosen Hardradha's name as a code for his contributory work to violent strategy against an unresponsive government. To their loss, the kids in Chicago in 1968 had not listened. Nor at Kent State. Dumas continued to use the name as his cable-code when he began to flourish in his communications business. Steinberg had been the only one, so far, who'd twigged to the name's significance. To Steinberg's embarrassment. In Niagara Falls.

"I'm pretty sure that Hardradha has another job," Steinberg said.

"Hmmm." Dumas ruminated gloomily upon Hardradha's end. As an old king, Hardradha had joined fortunes with one Earl Tostig who had lost his Earldom in Danelaw to Harold Godwinson, of future Hastings fame. Tostig with Hardradha had met Harold Godwinson in the center of Stamford Bridge. The future King Harold of the English was willing to fight, but not predisposed to.

'Tell you what,' quoth Harold to Tostig. 'I'll give you back your Earldom. Okay?'

Tostig, perhaps thinking wistfully of London, said, 'Gee, Harold, that's nice. Unfortunately, I have this guy Hardradha with me, you see? You know what a heller he is. What are you going to give him?'

Godwinson, eyeing Hardradha speculatively: 'Six feet of English earth.'

'Shucks,' said Earl Tostig, 'that ain't very generous.' With the implication that Hardradha, who was busy polishing his sword, might take more

Godwinson was not deaf to the inference. He eyed Hardradha more carefully. 'You're right, Tostig,' said the future King Harold sadly, 'Hardradha is a big man. I'll give him six and a half feet.'

Withal, they had at it. Hardradha got the six and a half feet promised upon Stamford Bridge. It had always seemed to Dumas that history laughed when Harold so easily vanquished such a one as Hardradha, yet lost in 1066 to an erstwhile tanner from Brittany who called himself William. Had it not been for the rain at Hastings that day, which slackened English bowstrings, the story might have been very different. The thought of William the Tanner, and tanned hides generally, made Dumas wince and his back throb.

Steinberg smiled. "The Stamford Bridge Complex, we call it in the trade," he said.

"Something like that," Dumas admitted, "although I was thinking more of William and tanned skin. That made me think of Tchevsky."

"The problem is, Adrian, I'm afraid you bought the whole bundle."

"Apparently, but I'm not sure how." Dumas had been giving this serious thought. What with the maps and Tchevsky's impatient questions there was perhaps the glimmering of an answer. And with Steinberg's admission of surveillance. Not that Dumas was altogether resentful of it. After all, without it, Tchevsky might have been able to offer extended hospitality in the Whispering Larch Cozy Guest Cottages. Dumas did not like to think about that. "If you had me under surveillance, I'm sure it must have been because of our previous involvement. Then, I must consider that I spent some time in your private clinic. Not long, perhaps, but perhaps long enough. I hear that sodium pen can work wonders."

Dumas noticed that Steinberg was examining the fleecy puffs of clouds. They sometimes blinked over the sun and made the day cooler than it would have been. To judge from his delighted smile, Steinberg seemed to derive great pleasure from them.

"Adrian, Adrian. There's a vast difference between knowledge and proof. And don't get me wrong, I'm not maintaining that I know anything. The doctor emphasized that temporary amnesia, all sorts of meaningless garble, can result from a concussion. Not to mention the assorted shocks you suffered. Hard to make much of it."

"Alright." Dumas considered this. "Don't take any offense, Sam, but lack of absolute knowledge never proved much of a deterrent with you chaps in the past. Recall the Bay of Pigs, for instance. The Shah vis à vis the Ayatullah in Iran. Any number of hasty actions taken without absolute knowledge."

"You're in a tough spot, Adrian. I wouldn't like to be on the outs with the KGB and, well, our side at the same time." Steinberg grinned. "You got your tail in a crack."

"True," said Dumas. "When are you going to tell me how it got there? Don't I get to know that much, at least?"

Steinberg sighed. "So few people understand and appreciate the value of knowledge. The cost of it. I expected better of you, Adrian. After all, you perceived the value of your little maps. It's so difficult to take upon ourselves the qualities we expect in others."

"What do you want, Sam?"

"You're a resourceful man, Mister Dumas. I have budgetary limitations. You know, government re-appraisals of priorities? Lower appropriations every year, when compared to the effects of inflation and devaluation. It makes life tough, when you're trying to do an efficient job."

Dumas looked down at Steinberg's pebble-grain loafers and up at his Pucci tie. Life didn't look tough.

"I could use some help from time to time. Like now, for instance. Especially from someone as competent as you."

Dumas grunted. "From time to time, Sam?"

"Little favors, Adrian, from time to time."

Dumas reflected ruefully upon the tribulations of Doctor Faustus and the only limited success of Daniel Webster in having one butterfly-soul unpinned from the devil's colorful collection. "Er . . . is there an end to this time-to-time business, Sam?"

"People are always so concerned with eternity, don't you find, Adrian? Maybe we could all take a lesson from Mike Red Sky there." Steinberg mused philosophically. "Perhaps there'd be less tension, ulcers and what-not in modern life if only we'd accept what each day brings." Steinberg turned brightly and looked at Dumas earnestly. "Why, Adrian, even the Good Book instructs us all. Take no thought for the morrow, for the morrow will take care of itself," he intoned piously.

"I get the point, Sam." Dumas raised the bottle and let the final, flat drops run onto his tongue. "There's only one thing, Steinberg. I'll have to draw the line if Rachael and Becky are endangered." Dumas thought that Steinberg's laughter came unforced, genuine and good-natured. Dumas watched idly while he hooted, held his tummy and turned away to give distant boats the benefit of his humor. At length, Steinberg coughed delicately. His eyes were merry, with little laughter-tears in the corners.

"You continually amaze me, Adrian. Here I've been thinking all this time that you're a straightforward man. With no capacity for subtle humor, no appreciation of cynicism, but you just proved me wrong. Think of it. Here's a guy who can't lean his butt against his own boat while he's swilling beer because of the attentions of the KGB a few evenings back, talking to his good friend in the CI—well never mind—who's had him under surveillance because of a small explosion. He says, says he, and perfectly seriously . . . 'I'll have to draw the line if Rachael and Becky are endangered.' Meanwhile, please note that Rachael and Becky can't move safely off his boat within the immediate future because he made the boat damn near impregnable and it's wired for sound and God knows what else." Steinberg paused. "And by the way, Adrian, I'd like you to explain the alarm system to me someday when you have the time."

"Right."

"Seriously, Adrian. I don't mind walking away. Now. Maybe you can deal with what's going on. Maybe you're willing to take the chance that Tchevsky was merely one lonely KGB agent putting in some practice while on a Canadian vacation." Steinberg moved toward the rail, framed by Toronto's distant skyline. "It's a big world out there," Steinberg waved expansively. "Too bad that Rachael and Becky won't be able to see much of it for a long, long time."

"You've made your point, Sam. Mind getting me another beer?"

Steinberg walked back from the rail, grinned as he passed Dumas, and entered the forecastle companionway. He popped up presently with another bottle. "You win," Dumas said. "I'm yours."

"There, that wasn't so hard, was it?" Steinberg beamed. "Now. Spill."

Steinberg shook his head sadly. "It's the same old story, Adrian. Greed. Yours. Let it be a lesson to you. You and Peter got the Watson Mines account, to help merchandise foreign uranium sales. Then, Watson changed his mind. Gonna give all his uranium to Canadian public utilities. Your account falls through. Greed, Adrian. You invent a brilliant little speculation—I admire it—to recoup some of the money Watson Mines would have made you . . ."

"I did it mostly for Peter."

"That so? See where generosity can get you. Anyway, it worked. You made a front-page controversy and you sold your maps. Very embarrassing for Watson and for Provincial Hydro. They had to start laying low on the fuel contracts. You made lots of money. Only one problem . . ."

"What's that?"

"You never really wondered why Watson Mines International changed its tune so quickly. Why you and Peter had the account jerked out from under you."

"Hell, Sam, I figured that Watson had been playing coy with Provincial Hydro for years in order to drive up the price. When Hydro became desperate, Watson'd sign a long-term contract to assure easy profits for a generation."

Steinberg looked up at the clouds, eyes wide and innocent. "Why beholdest thou the mote in thy brother's eye, but considerest not the beam that is in thine own." He paused. "Or, for that matter, Adrian, with what judgement ye judge, ye shall be judged."

"Meaning what, exactly?" Dumas was impressed by Steinberg's biblical knowledge, and somewhat surprised by his study of the New Testament.

"Meaning that Watson's decision was not made for the reasons you think. Not made for the reasons that you, for example, might make it."

"Oh."

"Quite. Watson was twisted by the KGB to make that decision. It was important to them. It was a matter of conscience, Adrian, I've come to learn. More or less." Steinberg spat over the port rail. It was symbolic rather than wet, Dumas was happy to observe.

"So my little . . . er . . ."

"Greed."

"Okay. It got in the way of something important to the KGB." Dumas pensively sipped Labatt's. "Tchevsky connected me with the maps. Noticed your surveillance of me across the street.

Scratched his head about my ridiculous disguise, *Radagast's* alarm system and probably much else. Put two and two together and came up with about thirteen."

"By Jove, I think he's got it."

"Did you know about Tchevsky's little plan . . . before?"

"I would like to say yes, Adrian."

"So I put you onto something very, very big. By accident."

"You may rest assured that Washington and Ottawa are extremely grateful, Mister Dumas."

"That's nice." Dumas thought about uranium and its various uses. "Sam? Is Watson's output so great that having it tied up domestically would make a strategic difference?"

"Yes. By itself, not crucial. But a few more diversions of a similar nature among other producers would make a big difference. Remember, Canada and Katanga are the world's largest producers. Maybe you're aware of the difficulties in Katanga?"

"Hmmm."

"Yes. It would make a difference. Especially to some Western allies who could otherwise accidentally on purpose come up with bombs. Like, I'm looking across the 38th parallel; into Jordan; maybe gazing with interest from Bangladesh over into Sinkiang."

"While we look holy as hell at SALT."

"Right. Now I know he's got it."

Dumas stared up at Red Sky on the poop. A movement up there had caught his eye and he noticed that Red Sky was standing up and holding her hand down for Becky. They came down the steps and across the deck toward Steinberg and himself.

"What's happening?" Dumas asked.

"Now we're going to feed the ducks, Daddy. They're coming."

Dumas raised himself up as well as possible on his toes, bracing himself with his hand on the edge of the forecastle. Sure enough, a line of them was swimming along between the docks, gabbling along the waterlines of moored vessels. There's plenty of duckweed on *Radagast's* bottom, thought Dumas. Come on over, guys, and peck away. But Dumas knew that the ducks would get bread from *Radagast*. Becky and Red Sky climbed back out of the companionway armed with several slices. Red Sky said nothing as she passed by Dumas, but she smiled and squiggled her nose again. They climbed up onto the poop and began flinging crumbs overboard. Dumas heard the gabbling become excited. Mantouche, I'm afraid you're outgunned.

They're gonna get you. One way or the other. Seeping radiation from vacationland reactors or fallout from eventual mushroom clouds.

Dumas flung his hand harshly at Red Sky and Becky. "Ever strike you, Steinberg, that the world has grown awful shitty?"

"Very frequently."

"It wasn't just greed, Sam. I wanted to throw a monkey wrench into the reactor program. In fact, I'd've done it without the money."

"I know."

"Now, the way you lay it out, there doesn't seem to be a way clear."

"I'm not sure, Adrian. Not that I think it's all that great, you understand, but I think the primary danger is from a disruption of the balance of power. Don't think that the Russians wouldn't press an advantage if they had one. Or us. Then, remember something else. If the Russians get the upper hand, Adrian, even if there's no war and they get just a freer hand in the world, bear in mind that they use nuclear blasts for mining and making reservoirs. Their idea of safe levels of radiation differs from ours. And there's no dissent. Even lip-service dissent. How'd you like to see bomb-made mines and reservoirs all over the world?"

"I wouldn't."

"Then remember that there's still a chance that the bombs won't be used. A small one, but a chance. If there's a balance of power. If it has to go somewhere, Adrian, and it apparently must, then there's a case for saying that bombs are safer than peaceful reactors."

Dumas nodded. "I've already agreed to help, Steinberg. I have no choice. I'm just thinking about a troubled and puzzled Mantouche," he said absently. Then, "What do you want me to do?"

"I want you to read something, Adrian, and give me your opinion on it. I don't know what can be done. But I've been told to come up with something. Quick."

A red-gold blob materialized in the gloom of the poop companionway. Slowly it resolved itself into Rachael's head which came, yawning out of the doorway. Rachael looked over to the matching setting sun. She smiled sleepily in their direction and then crooked her head to look up at Red Sky and Becky leaning over the tomatoes on the stern rail.

"What's anyone want for dinner?" she asked. "Is Sam staying?"

"Tell you what," said Steinberg. "Why don't we order over a

bucket or two of chicken? Adrian and I have some work to discuss, so I have to stay. Adrian, can you manage chicken?"

"Sure."

"Rachael?"

"It's better than trying to cook something. Adrian, we have to do some shopping." She looked from Dumas to Steinberg. "Wouldn't it be safe just to take the ferry over to Harbour Square?"

"We'll manage something tomorrow," Steinberg promised.

Hurry up and get stronger, Dumas. Like this you can't protect a damn thing. "Flip you for the chicken, Sam."

27

It was good, and Dumas licked his fingers before flipping the last page over. He had not been able to manage many of the french fries and only a little of the cole slaw. "Thanks, Sam, for bringing me such a nice little bed-time story," he said. Dumas handed the papers back to Steinberg when he'd wiped his fingers carefully with the serviettes provided.

"Sweet dreams." Steinberg put the papers into the slim black briefcase that was open beside him on the mattress. He closed the case and twirled the combination wheels. "Got any ideas?"

"Sure. Why don't you just go to Watçek-Watson . . . and tell him that you know the whole sordid little story? Tell him that the real Koffler died a dog's death in Tashkent after Tchevsky wrung him dry. Tell him that Koffler is a KGB plant to make him do his thing for Provincial Hydro and the balance of world power. It'll make sense." Dumas bit daintily into a french fry. "By the way, where is Koffler?"

"Good question. He'll have gone to earth somewhere after Tchevsky didn't come back."

"For that matter," said Dumas, "where is Tchevsky? Your private clinic?"

"What you don't know won't hurt you."

"Oh, yeah?"

"Perhaps that was an unfortunate expression. No, he's no longer at the clinic."

"Anyway, why can't you do that? With the description of Koffler, you'll pick him up eventually. Wrap up the loose ends. Send Tchevsky back dabbling his lips with his finger and a vacant stare. The Russians will dispose of them."

Dumas noticed that Steinberg looked disappointed. Steinberg shook his head slowly and sadly. "Adrian, I must confess that I

221

expected more from you. More subtlety. And don't tell me you can't muster it. I was on the other end of it not long ago."

"How come you can never please clients? First you say I'm straightforward, now you expect subtlety."

"Think. One," Steinberg ticked fingers, "we don't want to pick Koffler up. We want him to keep working on Watçek-Watson because Koffler is a junior agent. With Tchevsky out of the way, if it can look like an accident, Koffler will have to establish contact with someone else. Get a new senior partner, as it were. Moscow will send someone out here to poke around. Check out Tchevsky's demise. If Watçek-Watson looks clean, then they'll just resume operations. Only we'll know. By watching Koffler, maybe we can be led to bigger fish."

"It's been five days already, Sam. They know Tchevsky's disappeared. They'll suspect the worst."

"Sure they will, but they won't *know*. We haven't even bothered to look for Koffler at all. Being inexperienced, Koffler may imagine all sorts of things, and tell Moscow so, but anyone experienced will go very cautiously and discover that no one has Koffler under surveillance for the simple reason that he *isn't* under surveillance."

"Tchevsky?"

"I have a guy out now looking for a reasonable place near an embankment and deep water where there was either a *bona fide* accident five days ago, or else where the safety railing was not there for some reason or other. You know? In a day or two we'll find the red and white Bronco down there. Snagged by a frustrated fisherman, glimpsed by a scuba diver. Tchevsky will be in it." That icy glint in his eyes again, for a moment.

Dumas snorted.

"The operation's so important that they'll have to assume it's genuine." Steinberg looked down at his fingers. "Two. Who says Watçek-Watson would believe us? He's no fool after all, to come as a penniless immigrant and build a mining empire. He's ruthless, too, in his own way. Knowing the importance of his product as he does. Watçek-Watson might figure that the Koffler was real, that we bumped him off and are feeding him a load of manure. If that happens, then we'll be worse off than ever because Watçek-Watson's guilt will have to satisfy both Sarah and poor Irving. He'll go ahead."

Dumas nodded.

"You've read Watson's bio, Adrian. The guy's a religious freak. Tchevsky's story makes a lot of sense. The beautiful part of the plan is that once he's programmed by the phoney Koffler, the KGB *could* just walk away as soon as they know Watçek-Watson *believes* . . . and we're powerless to stop it. Just beautiful."

"But they haven't just walked away. I guess Koffler is still on the job. Tchevsky was."

"That's because they're Russians. They're methodical. They also want to know if we've gotten any hint of the operation. So they stay on Watçek-Watson to see if anything unusual turns up. If it doesn't, and it won't because we won't surveil, they'll go ahead."

"But I already turned up, Sam. I'm the joker who tells the Russians that something is fishy."

"No, you're not."

"I'm not?"

"No, because Tchevsky never let Koffler know. Tchevsky himself didn't know what to make of you. Koffler is inexperienced. Tchevsky didn't want to panic him without good reason. That's why he took the risk of shaking you down. If you were CIA or RCMP, Tchevsky had lost nothing because his cover was already blown. If you weren't CIA or RCMP, then Tchevsky might have a body to hide, but the operation was safe."

"But he knew I was being watched, Steinberg. He kept asking me about the men in the Victoria Hotel."

"Sure. It looked bad, which was why Tchevsky took a risk at all. But he could be sure of nothing because you're such a strange fellow. Your dumb disguise. The map-selling. It looked bad, but Tchevsky also had to consider the possibility that you were being watched on suspicion of say, petty larceny. Or drug trafficking. Or blackmail. Any number of possibilities. Your strengths, Adrian, your very predictable unpredictableness—well, it paid off for you once. This time it got you into hot water."

"So, you've been handed the perfect set-up . . . if you can dispose of Tchevsky half-way convincingly. If you can find a way to bend Watçek-Watson."

"Yes. And three," Steinberg flipped the ring-finger triumphantly, "if we can do all that, then the Russians might not know how it was done, or if it was done at all. Since we know their targets—and there aren't many of them, let's face it—in the uranium business, we're fore-armed. We know what they will do, and whom they're going to do it to."

"If."

"If." Steinberg's eyes twinkled. "That's why I'm looking to you for subtlety, Adrian. After the last episode, well, my career could use a boost. You wouldn't want to lose a friend in such a unique position, would you?"

"Gee, Sam, I'm not sure."

"That wasn't smart-assed, Adrian, my last question. Think about it. Think very hard." Steinberg's eyes were friendly, but they no longer twinkled. "I've learned recently that the world is a strange place," said Steinberg. "One needs to have an idea of why one bothers to put up with all the horror. Maybe it's because of Red Sky's and Becky's feeding ducks."

"You didn't . . .?"

"No, Adrian, I didn't. You outsmarted me, pure and simple."

"Good. I thought you were going to spoil my day," said Dumas.

Steinberg grinned. "And in the process, you made me think."

Dumas grunted. Yes, it was more than possible. And yes, it might do wonders to have a friend in Steinberg's position. But Steinberg was right. He had to have a limited victory at least. With Dumas as the patsy, it would be all the better. It didn't have to be a total victory. Better if it was. Bend Watçek-Watson, keep the operation going until then so that the Russians would suspect nothing. Make 'em try again. "I was just going over your requirements in my mind," said Dumas. "They collectively amount to a tall order, Earl Tostig."

Steinberg grinned. "I know."

"God help us." Dumas began the slow and painful process of turning over so that he could stare through the stern windows. He winced and puffed.

"Do I take that to mean that the audience is over?"

"Not at all, Sam. It's just that I can't seem to lie comfortably any way. Been too long on that side. Need to flip . . . Wow," said Dumas. "What a moon." It rose low and red just over the full elms. It floated the *McVay* in a crucible of molten bronze. "Times like this when I figure it was all worth it."

"It is a tall order, isn't it? To keep the Russians doing their thing with no suspicion up until the instant we can change Watçek-Watson's mind. To do it so that they don't even know that it's been done. To encourage 'em to try again so that we can be onto them in advance."

"Like I said," Dumas repeated, drinking in the moon, "God help us."

Steinberg leaned over on the mattress so that he, too, could see the moon hanging full in the stern window. They were silent for some minutes.

Dumas yelped.

Steinberg's head snapped up from contemplation of the pattern of the blanket. Snakes and tortoises, it looked like. He saw Dumas sitting up in the stretcher, silhouetted by the moon. It looked incongruous around his head. Like a halo. "You all right?"

Dumas moved quickly to take his weight off his buttocks and swung his legs off the stretcher, gasping. "C'mon, Sam, we got work to do." Dumas hobbled toward the door.

"Where are you off to, Adrian."

"The galley. I work best on coffee. By the way, can you make it?"

"Passably." Steinberg heaved himself up from the mattress.

"You got pencil and paper in that case of yours? You better bring it anyway." Dumas managed to climb up the companionway steps. Rachael, Red Sky and Becky were just about to enter. They'd enjoyed their chicken in the galley.

"Good evening, girls," said Dumas. "Steinberg's following. Please let us get out first." They stood aside as Dumas walked out on deck. It was still warm, but the breeze had a whisper of chill in it.

"Adrian, you should get some sleep," said Rachael.

"I feel fine. Been sleeping too much recently. You're the one who needs the sleep." He paused. "And Red Sky? I think we're going to help Mantouche. Just a little, though. A holding action."

"Mantouche doesn't need big pieces of help, Mister Dumas. Just little things. Then Mantouche can start to get it back together right." In the half-light Dumas saw the almond eyes bend over her cheekbones and the flash of her teeth. "I knew you wouldn't forget," she said. "I'm glad I came."

"I hope so." Dumas turned back to Rachael. "Double-check the alarm, dear. We'll be down in the galley. You may as well lock the companionway."

Steinberg ducked out onto the deck. Dumas pecked Rachael and Becky and pulled back from Red Sky just in time. "Nighty-night," he said.

"There's only one fairly important question to what I'm about to propose," Dumas remarked cautiously, bracing himself in the forecastle companionway before negotiating himself down into the galley.

"What's that?"

"How good is your working relationship with the RCMP? How much clout can you manage with local police forces?"

"Passable." Steinberg paused. "The questions are, ah, interrelated."

About three-thirty, Dumas and Steinberg came up on deck to rest their eyes from the dim study under *Radagast's* shipboard bulbs. Steinberg was rubbing his eyes with his fingertips. Across the deck Dumas saw the poop companionway open and a pleasant apparition emerge. Custer floated white above a swath of brown as Red Sky stretched, raising elbows to heaven. Below the swath of nut-colored belly, a strained and shallow triangle of white proclaimed panties. Below that, again, apricot legs locked, muscling downward to mahogany toes on the teak deck. Red Sky yawned. "Lovely child," said Steinberg. Red Sky recovered quickly, smiled and walked across the deck. She complained of the mugginess and a clinging Custer proved her point.

"There's coke in the galley, and crackers and cheese if you're hungry. But don't get crumbs into the Paisley," Dumas cautioned.

"Lovely child," he agreed.

28

They'd come and gone all morning. Steinberg had brought Lance along to help out.

"You remember Lance," Steinberg had said. "Lance, meet Adrian Dumas."

"We've met, but never formally," Dumas had remarked wryly. They had shaken hands. Thereafter, Lance had commenced to come and go with Steinberg. They left empty-handed, save for lists Dumas or Rachael had prepared. They came back somewhat later with boxes and full plastic bags. They had borrowed the yacht club's dolly. They had sweated. The piles of stuff on the deck had grown larger. Dumas revelled in the smiles and frowns of concentration that played upon the faces of Red Sky and Rachael. They scurried and organized. And some times re-organized. Rachael did not appear haggard.

Lance leaned his elbows on top of the deck tiredly. Red Sky handed him another cardboard box of canned goods. Lance disappeared into the black rectangle of the open deck hatch. That was something he'd have to do one of these days. Have some strong plywood chests made up, and given a coat of polyester resin.

Dumas noticed movement down the dock and recognized Steinberg's creases and pebble-grain shoes beneath the huge box. Well, it wasn't heavy, at least. Occasionally, Steinberg peered around the edge of the box to get his bearings. Wouldn't do to fall in the drink with that load. As Steinberg approached *Radagast*, Dumas thought it politic to bestir himself. He walked over to the rail and took the box easily from Steinberg's upstretched arms and lifted it over and onto the deck, making sure not to offend Archi in the window box.

Steinberg hopped nimbly aboard and wiped his brow. "Is that the last of it, Adrian?"

Dumas peered into the box. The circuit boards were wrapped in lots of paper towelling, as he had directed. Also, they had been put in last and were on top. Beneath the loose rolls of soft white paper Dumas catalogued reels of wire. Lots of wire, tape and the plastic-covered terminals of many heavy-duty 6-volt batteries. "You're sure you got everything on the list? Everything?"

"I swear." Steinberg sank wearily onto the poop deck steps, but was shooed off temporarily when Rachael came down with a potted Archi from the stern-rail planters. Steinberg sat again. "The more I think about it, the more I like it."

"Good."

Steinberg stared at the pile of canned goods still on the deck. Lance popped up out of the hatch. Red Sky handed Lance another box. Steinberg looked up at Dumas, who was looking toward the fuel dock and wondering just how *Radagast* was going to maneuver around all the angles required.

"Dumas . . .?" Steinberg's voice sounded suspicious. "Adrian, you've put enough food aboard this tub to last for months. More than enough to get to Sturgeon Bay. There *are* stores up there, you know. Food. Booze. Everything. Sunglasses."

"Seamanship, Steinberg. One must be prepared for calms, storms, being thrown off course." Dumas waved an expansive hand across the southern horizon. "Besides, Sam, when I come back from Georgian Bay I might just keep on going. I intend to."

"That's your business. After."

"Quite right. Lance . . . are you tying all those boxes down as tight as possible?"

"Yes, Sir."

Dumas nodded affably. He looked at Red Sky. He'd been contemplating hopefully exactly what would happen when the time came to wash Custer. And there he was fluttering in the port shrouds. And there Red Sky was wearing another Custer. There seemed to be an endless supply of him in Red Sky's leather satchel. Dumas had been mildly disappointed, although he had little doubt that Rachael would have leaped into the breach to clothe the poor child. Pounced.

Steinberg got shooed off the steps again. Rachael hurried after the last Archi up on the poop. "Sam, why don't you escape from the mainstream of traffic flow by going down into the galley. It's cooler there. There's cold coke in the fridge."

Dumas dragged the box of electrical supplies over to the poop companionway. He was able to get it below with less trouble than he had expected. Must be mending, as the nurse would have put it. Dumas carried the box back to the stern cabin and allowed his mouth to twist in the tiniest expression of distaste at all the confusion. Mess was more like it. He found a place for the box. On impulse, he left the stern cabin and went back partway along the corridor that led eventually to the companionway steps and the deck. He unlocked one of the louvered doors and switched on the light. He went a couple of steps down the narrow curving steel stairway and closed the door behind him. No good having Becky exploring and breaking her neck. Dumas went on down, ducking slightly. At the bottom he could not quite stand upright.

He checked the level in the oil tank. Maybe enough to get to Ajax. He glanced along the stainless steel rods that led up through the low ceiling and ultimately made Becky's closet shallower than the others in their metal casing leading up beneath the binnacle. The joints of all the rods looked greasy. Good. The water tank was full and just for the sake of completeness, Dumas followed the stainless steel pipes out from the tank to where they disappeared into hollow concrete wells in the cement ballast. No water in the wells. Good. He saw the ring of welding in the rib where the pipes passed through *Radagast's* hull. They coiled, outside, several times the length of the keel and came back aboard, returning to the water tank. In the center of the sharply veed floor the Coppus turbine was a large white disk on edge fed by a tangle of pipes.

The disadvantage was, of course, the time necessary to get steam up. None of that turning the key and roaring off. The advantage was that Dumas could, if necessary, feed the boiler with wood, coal or any number of things. Also Coppus turbines had been known to run flawlessly for thirty years without a major overhaul in their normal job of running electrical generators for auxiliary power from building heating systems. Another advantage was that by keeping the boiler barely ticking over, and by shutting and opening a few valves, the hot water could be diverted to small radiators, brass and salvaged from an old apartment building suffering under the wrecker's ball, located in the cabins. For now, the Coppus feasted upon fuel oil. If there was enough fuel to reach Ajax, Dumas reasoned, *Radagast* should be able to make it across the harbor. Why twist through the docks and risk crushing the fibreglass toys like so many eggshells? Expensive eggshells.

Dumas climbed out of *Radagast's* bowels and locked the louvered door behind him against Becky's curiosity. Before going back on deck he turned in the narrow passage to look through the porthole opposite the door. The water appeared to be quite a bit closer. Dumas looked eye-to-eye with the owner of a cruiser across the way who was polishing his tinted glass. They exchanged smiles. The cruiser's glass opened.

"Fitting out?"

"Hell of a chore."

"Where you bound?"

"Georgian Bay."

The man looked surprised. "So late? The summer's almost over."

"Then south," said Dumas. "The Caribbean."

"Hurricane season."

"I'll hole up in Lake George," Dumas answered.

The man nodded agreement. "Good voyage," he called.

"Thanks."

Dumas left the glass open and went up on deck. Lance was out of the hold and was fitting the hatch-cover into place. Red Sky and Rachael were sliding a box of canned goods across to the forecastle companionway. Dumas noticed plastic bags of powdered milk. Rice? Steinberg was about to get shooed off again.

Dumas went up beside the binnacle on the poop and played with the brass levers. They seemed to move easily and he heard the clunking of the stainless steel rods below. Well and good. Now the awning. And lowering the yards to bend the sails. "Steinberg," he called. "I think you better take off your jacket." This was no way to fit out for a voyage. It should be done as he'd planned, once. With pleasure taken at storing and preparing every item so that you could think about the water and the wind . . . palm trees . . . as you put each thing in place. Take time to smell the hemp of extra cordage. Not that people used much hemp nowadays. Dumas kept some for the smell.

"What now?" Steinberg looked up. He still appeared eager. The same could not be said for Lance, who shuffled up beside Steinberg. On the other hand, Lance had brought the loads of canned goods.

From the poop, Dumas pointed at the various articles. The awning. The yards, explaining what had to be done. A sea gull, hovering at the masthead, made his spirits buoyant and Dumas came quickly down the poop deck steps to lend a hand. He was glad to note that the red scars of his wrists and back did not hurt with all the pulling on ropes, but just felt as if the skin had drawn tighter. Especially his back, under his shirt. He'd wear it for a while, perhaps until the scars turned a decent white, or at least until the red faded a bit. Enjoying his first night without bandages, Dumas had crept into their cozy double-bunk last night as was his wont without pyjamas. Rooting around in his small closet this morning searching for something suitably ragged to wear for the day's work, he'd heard a little gasp from behind him and had whirled to see Rachael's hand over her mouth. How strange they could change bandages without much emotion as long as one was decently and obviously sick. Like lying on a stretcher.

By heaving hard on the halyard with Steinberg, Dumas managed to set up a small pounding in the bridge of his nose. The ache did not spread behind his eyes and no floaters wobbled across the up-jerking aluminum yard. Dumas decided that he'd leave the bandage on for a while. He'd wear pyjamas for a while.

"That about does it," he said.

"Fuel," said Steinberg. "You better gas up."

Dumas explained the culinary preferences of the Coppus, why he'd chosen the cumbersome propulsion of steam. Steinberg raised an eyebrow and acknowledged that *Radagast* could be taken just about anywhere.

"Where there's at least seven feet of water," Dumas commented, "and hopefully a hell of a lot more." He pointed across the harbor to the peaked warehouses, all either pastel or trendy waterfront-red, to the concrete jetty where the distant brass of a few yachts glinted richly in the sun. "I think I'll just drive straight out, hang a gentle right and park over there. I'll call Zappy Flame Home Heating and have my five hundred gallons delivered. The truck can drive straight out to me."

Thinking of parking brought to Dumas' mind the vision of the sad Abarth squatting on fat tires in the Harbour Square garage. He would have to come back and tie up in Toronto for at least a week to take care of loose ends. "Steinberg . . . ? How'd you like to buy an Abarth? Twin cam. One owner. Low mileage. A bit difficult to start in the winter, maybe, but high performance once it warms up. No heater to speak of. Laughable defroster."

"Ah, no thanks." Lance had almost regained the deck from his climb up the mainmast to check the yard shackles. His face was red with exertion and with the heat. He ambled across the deck to Steinberg, not enthusiastically.

"Lance," said Dumas, "I have a great idea. Why don't you escort all the girls to the yacht club pool? Sit at a table, order a tall whatever and one of the club's delicious steaks if you like. Put it on my tab. Don't take your eyes off their bikinis for one second. Hover outside their dressing rooms, even, and flash your phoney RCMP card when necessary."

"Maybe you better get into harness, as it were, Lance," Steinberg added. "And wear your windbreaker. Sit under an umbrella."

Lance smiled. He looked cooler already.

Dumas went below to tell Rachael and to phone over to the clubhouse to explain the aspect of Lance's protective instructions to the steward. Dumas was apologetic about being so touchy because of an unexplained little mugging. The steward understood perfectly.

"See, Lance? There are compensations to this job," Steinberg said. Lance nodded and jumped down to the dock, turning to make absolutely sure that neither Rachael nor Red Sky experienced any difficulties whatever. Rachael dimpled. Red Sky squiggled her nose. Becky quacked a yellow plastic duck in his face. They walked off down the dock with Lance's head questing from side to side.

"It's nice to see a professional at work," said Dumas, impressed with Lance's keen-eyed scanning. "But if Koffler wasn't told by dear old Tchev, I don't see the danger any more. I wish I'd known about all that before I sold my soul," he added.

"On the other hand," Steinberg rubbed a pensive finger alongside of a shining nose, "is there a law about having Tchevsky under covert surveillance by yet another KGB type? Sometimes they do that, you know."

"Hemnph."

"You say this will take you about two weeks?" Steinberg cast his brown-grey eyes doubtfully over *Radagast*, especially the burgee fluttering in the steady west wind.

Dumas looked up at the burgee also. He shrugged. "It's about six hundred and fifty miles, more or less. Two weeks should be ample, Sam. I expect to be in Sturgeon Bay by the twenty-first of the month, give or take a day or two. That gives us almost two weeks of margin."

"If you say so."

This had been the only part of Dumas' plan that Steinberg had questioned. Dumas had learned that Steinberg possessed small faith in anything that could not run to a schedule. On the other hand, the advantages were too great. Steinberg was freed from security duties at the price of losing Lance for two weeks, for there was no place safer than Dumas' boat under sail. Unless the KGB felt willing to lay on a helicopter or a launch, which Steinberg thought unlikely. Causes talk. It got Dumas and family out of the way on a perfectly understandable pretext. It gave Steinberg a worry-free two weeks to enter into somewhat delicate negotiations between Ottawa and Washington, not to mention the Ontario Provincial Police and Midland's and Port McNicoll's finest. It cut down on expenses. He could get out of the Harbour Castle and out of the Victoria.

"By the way," Dumas commented. "Don't forget that radio equipment. We might need it at a pinch."

Steinberg nodded, viewing the burgee suspiciously.

"Stop worrying. It'll all come together. There's only one thing that worries me."

"What's that?"

"I hope that the cigarette commercials got tested," Dumas said dryly, "cause the machine won't be worth much for a few weeks."

"Mind explaining to me exactly how it works. And how? Someday when this is over."

"Sure." That was yet another loose end that had to be tied. He'd have to put the machine back together before heading south. Maybe the acquaintance would buy it? Dumas briefly considered the likelihood of receiving on-going royalties from the tests and decided that a straight buy-out was probably best. The problem with the world was definitely honesty. He sighed. "Steinberg, I'm going below for a shower and a change. There's binoculars in the case on the binnacle . . . that thick brass pipe thing up there sticking out of the deck. Please be so good as to watch the pool. I'm interested to know exactly how Red Sky fits into Rachael's old mauve two-piece. It was a knit and it stretched."

"Oh."

29

More loose ends. A shelf-full. Not to mention the files. Maybe he could just burn the files. But not the books. One doesn't burn old friends.

"If you're intent upon it, Adrian, I'd be happy to store the ones you can't take."

Dumas considered that Peter's house seemed safe enough for the time being. "Okay, I'd appreciate it. I'm not leaving immediately. I'll be back in a month or so. Maybe I'll change my mind." The office suddenly seemed homey, the walnut familiar, the air-conditioner a personal triumph. Dumas had stopped running and had slowed to a walk on the blue carpeting. Its deep pile had given him a firm footing to turn and meet his enemies and pursuers. He'd gained enough room on the unlikely battleground to accommodate Rachael and Becky within the compass of his sword-tip. He smiled.

"Okay, Pete, I'll make the cheque out for three. Please see that Peebles gets his share as soon as possible."

"I've already put it in the mail, Adrian."

"Thanks for that." Dumas wrote the cheque and tore it out. "Oh, and I may as well give you two months' overhead while I'm thinking of it. Just lock my office and pretend I'm on vacation. It may be just that anyway." Dumas wrote out a second cheque. Peter folded this one, too, without looking at it and shoved it carelessly in his side pocket.

"I think you'll probably reconsider, Adrian. I, for one, hope so and I'm sure that Debbie feels the same way."

"Maybe I will."

"So I won't shake hands, old chap. See you in a month or so. Have a good rest." Peter waved cheerily and left.

Steinberg was waiting, but probably not impatiently, chatting with Debbie. Dumas' hand burrowed into the inevitable old-fashioned walnut in-tray. Lovable's cheque. The television show's. Dumas noted the amounts with satisfaction. Damn. Edward. Dumas wrote out a thi..d cheque. Should have given it when they brought the flowers. But he'd been hearing bells still.

Dumas turned out his light and locked his office. Cablecode: 'Hardradha'. "Debbie. Please get this to Edward as quickly as possible," he said, handing her the cheque. "Maybe you should call Pia now. If she's in, have a cab take it up today."

"Yes, Adrian." She looked up at Dumas and then uncertainly over to Steinberg.

"I'll wait at the elevator," Steinberg said.

Dumas was touched to see the little tears sliding down Debbie's peach cheeks. She rose from her chair and kissed him. Her lips lingered an instant, warm and full. "Thank you, Adrian Dumas. For Peter. And me. I feel so badly about what happened to you. Gawd, you're my only brother."

"What's all this? I'll be back, Deb, and I'm none the worse for wear." He smiled. "Do that again, Sis."

Dumas' heels clicked rapidly in step with Steinberg's long strides. They hurried toward the gold tower. Dumas mentally considered what had gone into it recently, what had gone out, what he must leave in to keep covenants with Peter, Edward, Rachael. He could take out enough, say, for a comfortable year in Curaçao. Very comfortable. Not quite so comfortable other places. A homestead for a lifetime on the tracts just being opened by the Brazilian government along the Xingu in Mato Grosso province. Or maybe six cautiously comfortable months in the vicinity of Monaco. Peter would be able to navigate the icebergs of the coming winter. Spring might become bitter.

Dumas walked out with his black and aluminum briefcase heavier by somewhat less than three pounds of the soft, heavy metal. He reflected sadly that the paper money, in smallish bills, weighed a considerable fraction of the gold's own heft. Luckily, his briefcase was not nearly so slim as Steinberg's, or it would never have closed over the few books Dumas had hastily snatched from the shelves, some selected files, the money and the gold.

"Shouldn't you lock that thing?" asked Steinberg.

"Don't dare," said Dumas. "One of the combination wheels sticks." After a few weeks, the wheels had not made their initial businesslike snicks. The middle wheels had started to scrape. Nor was the lining of the case so thickly padded as Steinberg's, and the silk of the interior was a middle executive's hopeful silver, not Steinberg's carefree Paisley. Still, crammed between paper books, money and files, Dumas did not think that the meagre little bars would scratch on the *McBride's* gentle ride across the harbor. The case had been a gift from Rachael, a few years ago, and came not long after she'd pushed a clumsy, swelling belly from tailor to tailor in search of whipcord.

"I always lock mine," Steinberg said.

Not always, Dumas thought. "Why? Is there always treasure in it?"

"No," Steinberg grinned, "but there's always pirates."

"You got it wrong. I'm the pirate. Don't I have the galleon?"

Steinberg unlocked the cream Mercedes and Dumas climbed onto the perforated leather upholstery. Dumas observed that when Steinberg turned the key there was no sound at all, but that didn't deter Steinberg from craning to look out the back window, nor did it prevent the car from sliding backwards out of the parking space. "Gee, Sam, it kinda makes me nervous, a car that doesn't appear to have a motor. Too long with used cars, in my youth. Now, the Abarth, Sam—when you turn the key there's this sort of terminal cough, see, and then an almighty roar. A few beastly shudders and—"

"No, thanks."

Dumas shrugged. "Suit yourself." You could lead a horse to water, after all, but you couldn't make him drink. "To each his own."

"And different strokes for different folks."

The Mercedes glided up the entrance to the ferry terminal a few minutes later. Steinberg did not seem to mind stopping at the curb in a no parking zone and switching the car off. Or, at least, Dumas thought so. Steinberg twisted toward him and laid an arm along the back of the seat.

"Be careful, Adrian."

"What? On the *McBride*?"

"Lance isn't all that experienced. Willing."

"I know," Dumas smiled.

"Just be a bit careful."

"I'll write, or phone, if I need money."

"Don't do that, Adrian. Please. Expenses. I have something for you instead . . . of money," Steinberg reached over and unlocked the glove compartment of the Mercedes. He handed Dumas a more or less triangular leather case. It had a zipper running along much of its perimeter. Dumas unzipped the case and peeled back the leather lips an inch or two. He felt lascivious. The padded silk lining didn't help matters, but he poked until his finger felt the cold butt.

"Hell," said Dumas, "I could get arrested for this. I need a fire arms acquisition permit." Dumas hunted for room in his briefcase, but found none. He looked around in the Mercedes and plucked the dainty plastic bag from Steinberg's plastic bin under the passenger dash. "Ever think of getting one of those perfumed girls standing by the palm tree?" asked Dumas. "They sort of hang and hula from the rear-view mirror. Exotic, antiseptic aroma." He dropped the gun into the bag.

"Good luck, Adrian."

"You're doing the work."

30

"It is sacred to my people," Red Sky proclaimed. Somewhat dramatically, considering she was Ojibway, Dumas thought. She pointed toward the smudge of land on the horizon and hopped up onto the forecastle deck to get a better view. The land was mostly grey, but still somewhat green. Dark dusty-black pines waved away at angles dictated by the prevailing winds. The trees showed as tiny crooked hands, at intervals, above the smudge.

Dumas consulted the chart of Cape Croker's environs. Carefully. Waving his right arm toward the land he felt *Radagast* heel and he glanced up at the sails and the burgee. When *Radagast's* bowsprit pointed to a distant beckoning pine, Dumas held his hand rigid. The sails did not exactly correlate with the fluttering burgee and wind was spilling inefficiently from the leeches. Dumas was not about to warp the yards around for the short distance remaining. The north wind would serve for this new course. Who was he, anyway? Eric Tabarly?

"We'll come up under the lee of the cape," Dumas shouted back to Lance, and was somewhat disconcerted to discover that Lance, all bronzed, weathered and legs apart stalwartly behind the wheel, just nodded curtly and kept his eyes fixed upon the pine. Give 'em an inch and they took a mile. "What I mean," said Dumas, "is that as soon as we see land over to the right, we'll park."

"Aye-aye. Abeam to starboard," Lance sung out.

Dumas sighed. He glanced over towards Rachael, whose gaze was tearfully upon Red Sky astride the forecastle. Red Sky stared wistfully into the west and the sunset, her long black hair whipped to the south, her jeans chattering to a nervous Custer on the new course.

"Adrian," Rachael sniffed, "just look at her. The modern daughter of a lost people. Facing the future resolutely. Drawing from the wellspring of her ancient traditions."

Dumas recalled that Rachael had, indeed, studied sociology at York University and that she was also, on occasion, inclined to emotionalism. It came, probably, from reading poetry at the library during coffee breaks. Dumas cupped his hands. "Red Sky!" he called. She turned slowly on the forecastle, smiled, and jumped down to the deck. On the new course, Dumas was gratified that Custer had begun to perk a little on the tee-shirt. He jiggled more pointedly. Rachael reached out and took Red Sky's hand as Red Sky came up and dropped, cross-legged, near the binnacle.

"I guess the sight of it kinda thrills you," said Dumas.

"It is sacred to my people," Red Sky said simply. She looked down, and Rachael squeezed Red Sky's long brown fingers.

"I'm glad to see that the ecumenical movement as we know it has spread among our Native Peoples," Dumas remarked dryly. "I thought the Bruce Peninsula was sacred to the Hurons?" Anticipating, Dumas squiggled his own nose.

"It is all one, Mister Dumas. Wherever Mantouche lives. The land must live."

"Okay, I'll buy that," Dumas grinned.

"You don't understand, Adrian," Rachael said sincerely, "the deep reverence with which the Native Peoples regard the land. It's not just property to them. It's . . . it's . . ."

"The mother," Red Sky supplied.

"Yes, the mother," Rachael said.

"With Mantouche. Well, Mantouche *is* sort of a mother," Red Sky gazed off into the sunset. "The land is a mother that never dies."

"Oh, Mike. That's beautiful." Rachael squeezed the fingers again.

"And none the worse for being a Pathan saying from the northwest frontier of India," Dumas pointed out.

Red Sky shrugged. "We all live in the Family of Man," she said.

"You can say that again," said Dumas.

"Pathan, Ojibway, Huron . . . who cares?" said Rachael. "What matters is the sentiment, Adrian. Can't you understand that?"

"Hmmm. Red Sky? Do me a favor? When we're through up here, can you have another heart-to-heart chat with Rachael there? Fill her in on the wars, slave trade and such-like things inspired by that land yonder. It might save me some alimony."

"Adrian is a good man . . . deep down," Red Sky said sincerely to Rachael. "I know why you love him." Rachael's eyes flashed soft green compassion up at him and she squeezed Red Sky's hand again, nodding.

Dumas snorted.

Fifteen hours later, after Lance and Dumas had spent much of the night firing the boiler, taking in the sails tightly to the yards with lengths of rope, and edging very cautiously deep into the lee of Cape Croker, Red Sky was impelled to remark: "Can the wolf howl?"

This was in response to Dumas' serious query as to whether she could handle the very broad-beamed twelve-foot canoe that Lance was lowering from *Radagast's* starboard quarter. Everybody's a comic, thought Dumas. He tiredly hooked the swimming ladder over the starboard rail and Red Sky began climbing down. As soon as the canoe was afloat, Lance passed Dumas the end of the long painter. Dumas drew the canoe along the waterline to the ladder. Its bow cleaved full, gurgling ripples in the limpid water. Heavy water. Red Sky climbed in and knelt on the bottom. The canoe barely rocked.

"You sure you don't want the Seagull?" Dumas asked. Red Sky looked up. "Mike, keep doing that and you'll be all wrinkled," he said. Red Sky pushed away from *Radagast's* side and dipped her paddle. The bright yellow canoe glided across the flat water toward the weathered wooden houses, snowmobiles parked on trailers and glinting in the early sun, and dead cars lurking among the bushes. Dumas could make out some children running between the houses and dogs snoozing on distant grey front steps. He could also see skiffs drawn up on shore and all seemed to boast outboards. Why should Red Sky be so stiff-necked about the little Seagull?

"How long will it take?" Rachael asked.

"Maybe all day. She'll want to explain everything to her buddies." Not to mention consulting with the band's lawyer, Dumas thought. He turned to look up at Lance, who was cranking the davit back up. "Hey, up there! Why not lower the other one, Lance? We can tether it to the rail and you and Rachael can paddle about if you like."

Lance nodded and walked across the poop to the other quarter and began lowering the other canoe.

"Maybe Lance would like to try some fishing," Dumas said to Rachael. "You can show him where the stuff is?"

241

Rachael nodded. She looked over the rail down into the water. "Look, Adrian, you can see all the way to the bottom. It's so clear. It doesn't look deep."

"Well, it is, luv," Dumas said. "Fifteen feet."

Dumas started for the poop companionway, hesitated and made his way over the forecastle deck. He dropped into the beak and looked under the edge. The chains curved away out under water. Dumas tugged on them and they seemed a sluggish weight. He looked up at the sky. High above, streamers of cirrus headed east, but lower down puffy white clouds scudded southward. At water level there was hardly a breath. Yet. The wind from the north skipped over Cape Croker and blew above the height of *Radagast's* masts. Which was not to say that conditions could not change. A veer to the east and the wind could drive him the length of Colpoy Bay damn near to Wiarton before he could get steam up. How to dodge Hay Island? White Cloud Island? Dumas tugged on the chains and was reassured by their stubbornness.

Dumas went below for a nap, thinking as he entered the companionway that Lake Erie had made him unduly edgy, and the thunderstorm in Main Channel. But Lake Erie had been bad. It was the shallowness, of course, and the fetch for the west wind. Almost three hundred and fifty miles of water for waves to get built up under a steady blow. The worst had come at night, which hadn't helped matters much. Dumas had been theoretically prepared for the beak to take on water— why else the perforated floor?—but the reality had come as something of a shock. And the howl from the rigging. The pounding. Dumas sincerely hoped that Lake Erie could be as bad as the Atlantic, as some sailors claimed. *Radagast* had plowed through without damage.

Dumas opened one of the louvered doors—someday they'd be solid mahogany and not just stained softwood—and fell into the double bunk that took up the entire width of their cabin. He rolled his legs under the overhanging plywood bookcase—someday he'd put the stain over the sealer—and fell asleep.

The chattering of feminine voices. The creak of the davit. "Oh, isn't that beautiful, Mike?" It was Rachael's voice. Dumas stirred.

"Adrian, just look at this!" Rachael twirled on deck, holding the dress to her shoulders. Dumas could see that the dress was long and white, with long and full sleeves. It was decorated on the front, but with Rachael flapping it he could not make out the design.

"It's a ghost shirt . . . for a girl," said Red Sky. "Sort of a ghost dress, I guess."

Red Sky leaned a golden elbow on the rail and was smiling at an enthralled Rachael. Red Sky's bare toes played in the crack between teak planks. Rachael came to a stop, like a winding-down dervish, and Dumas picked up the hem of the dress. He rubbed the material softly with his thumb.

"Doeskin," Red Sky said. "White doeskin. Mandatory." Her almond eyes were wide.

Dumas saw that the design was a beadwork cross on the chest and broken zig-zags bordering the hem and the cuffs of the sleeves. "A cross?"

"That was an ancient symbol long before the priests came," said Red Sky. "The zig-zags are Mantouche swimming. See?" She cocked one arm up with the hand bent over, something like a Balinesian dancer. "See? Mantouche swimming. Mantouche just swims with his neck out of the water, that's all."

"Weren't ghost shirts worn by the Sioux, at Wounded Knee?"

"Sure." Red Sky smiled enthusiastically. "You can put it on, Rachael. If you want."

"Oh, no, dear. I don't think I'd better. It's special." She handed it carefully back to Red Sky.

Red Sky held it up to her own shoulders and kicked one foot out so that she could look down. "It is a pretty dress," she said and tossed her hair back. "Can I hang it in the back cabin? Becky's closet is a little small."

"Of course, you can, Mike. I'll go get a wooden hanger for it. One of Adrian's." Rachael took the dress back again and went below.

Becky pirouetted on the hatch cover. "I want a dress like that, Daddy," she demanded shrilly. Red Sky walked over and knelt to hug Becky. "I'll send your Daddy some doeskins. I promise. Maybe just one, for you."

"How'd it go, Mike?"

Red Sky stood up. "The members all agreed. They'll be there. They'll drive down."

"How many?"

"Four or five, Adrian. That enough?"

"Plenty. If they all show up. What about the lawyer?"

"Oh, they'll show up all right. The lawyer? He told me that nobody in their right mind would sign such a thing."

"That's probably true," said Dumas. "But he did draw all the papers up?"

"Yes, Adrian. But since he said it was so stupid, he wouldn't do it for free. I had to give him the money."

Dumas shrugged.

"But not all of it. I managed to get him down to fifty dollars." Red Sky's hands pushed down into her jeans and came out with a fistful of crumpled bills. Dumas removed them from the crooked fingers carefully because of the breeze. "I could have gotten it for free," said Red Sky, "but you didn't want me to do it."

"You're worth a good deal more than fifty bucks, Red Sky." Dumas recalled how, recently, out in Alberta, money owed to the Indians had been diverted to pay for a running water system to Indian Affairs officials' homes. White homes, naturally, not red ones. There were other little scams, as the number of half-breed babies born each year testified. Shocking morality, those girls. Want your teeth fixed, honey? Your Daddy need another bottle? Baby brother needs a special formula and bottles, because Mummy's gone all dry from tension, eh? It's the winter's food is it, dear, with the salmon so scarce from the trawlers? Well, maybe we can do something about it all. Come over here. That's right, just sit on my legs. No, no, honey. *Astride* them, like on a horse, you know. Still in cotton panties. My, my. Damn these tiny buttons.

And the whites weren't necessarily the worst. Dumas knew of a band-owned outdoor drive-in theater in northern British Columbia where, for a small fee paid to the chief, little brown girls would snuggle in town boys' Z-28's and Mustangs. They were so light, these girls, that the springs hardly rocked. One didn't need the serviettes because their cotton panties absorbed most of the popcorn butter. Dumas had been tempted, but had refrained.

He looked at Red Sky. Custer boasted no buttons. Just rolled up.

"Well . . ." said Red Sky. "It saved you fifty bucks and it wasn't much. Just a feel."

Dumas sighed. He handed the bills back to her. "Put it on account, Red Sky," he said. "Maybe, someday, when I've had a few drinks, I'll hell it up to Cape Croker and collect."

"You already have that much, Adrian. Help Mantouche and you have everything, for all time. I swear."

"That's one hell of an incentive," Dumas grinned. "Anyway,

keep it. I may not be able to help Mantouche that much. Meanwhile, I'd rather buy. Cleaner."

She shrugged the money back down into the depths of her jeans and then patted Becky, who clutched at the bumping side seam of the denim. "I don't quite understand, but it always seems to make you folks feel better," she said.

"I do." Custer died for our sins, maybe, but if one continued to be tempted to play, one should at least have the decency to pay.

Rachael came back out of the poop companionway. "All hung up, dear. It won't wrinkle."

Steinberg was waiting. Not apprehensive, yet. Just waiting. Dumas waved an arm and started for the beak. "C'mon, Lance. Let's get those anchors up. Rachael, go below and get up some more steam, and feed what's there to the Coppus. Red Sky, open some tuna-fish cans down in the galley. Take Becky. Open a couple of beers and put the bottles on deck. This is gonna hurt my back."

Rachael paused by the poop rail before going below and reached up to pick a couple of tomatoes. She tossed them to Red Sky across the hatch cover and the length of the center deck.

31

Radagast's mooring lines creaked and Dumas twitched the end of his rod hopefully, although he was many miles from Gloucester Pool. Who could tell? Perhaps a lunker pike or muskie had swum up the river to taste Port Severn's attractions? It was always possible.

He could still hear the shower hissing in the cottage forty yards away. Before that, it had been the steady tinkle of water. The shower and the tub . . . hot water. Unlimited supplies of it. Dumas considered the vision of them all piled into the water at once. Becky's plastic duck quacking. Water slopping into Rachael's deep navel over brown tummy. Red Sky's long black hair plastered over yet another all but transparent Custer. Snuffing and puffing in the steam like so many obscenely happy hippos. Was Becky already learning? At her age? Obviously—no. It was ridiculous. They couldn't all get into the hot water at once. Either Rachael or Red Sky was lying spread on a bed, with clouds of fog drifting toward the ceiling, while the others splashed, like morning mist rising moist from a field of mushrooms. Dumas' rod-tip twitched. Women. Was *Radagast* so bad that three pairs of feminine eyes had bulged at the sight of Rawley Lodge? Surely there was sufficient hot water for their needs?

In the back of his mind Dumas heard the tires crunch into the parking lot of the Lodge. Presently, he heard chattering and looked over his shoulder to see Steinberg and a chipmunk dodging each other around a spruce not far from the Mercedes' front fender. Dumas twitched his rod once more, waited hopefully, and reeled in the line. What could he expect on canned bacon? Still, nothing. It was better than the bony sunfish Lance insisted that Red Sky cook. In the Indian way. Slit and spread

247

to planks of pine in front of the fire. Dumas had followed Red Sky's lead and had chosen the tuna-fish. Lance seemed happy enough.

"Any luck?"

"Not for the past few days. What about you?"

Dumas laid the rod on the deck. Anytime, now, a fish would jump. He twisted around on his haunches and was pleased that there was no twinge. "How'd it go?"

"Where is everybody?"

"Lance is in the Lodge eating stacks of pancakes. He's been doing that, since the sunfish. The women are in that cottage there. The one with the steam coming out the windows."

"The Mantouche people?"

"They're driving down. Be here any time."

"Then it looks good," said Steinberg. "You'll never know what hassles I had in Ottawa. Washington."

"Really? Great. Let's keep it that way. By the way, Sam, you didn't forget the projectors, did you?"

"Not a chance. What are you using for bait?"

Dumas raised his hook and flapped the bacon at Steinberg.

"Hell, man. No wonder. Wait a minute." Dumas watched Steinberg walk briskly away. A few minutes later, after Dumas had watched Rachael, Red Sky and Becky gaggle together out of the cottage and toward the Lodge's dining room, Steinberg hopped aboard with a bucket. Steinberg peeled off his jacket and draped it over the rail.

"Got another rod?" he said.

Dumas went down into the galley and untangled another rod from the corner of the locker. When he came on deck, Steinberg was baiting a minnow.

"Just run the hook right through the head," said Steinberg. "Just here, behind the eyes. They don't feel a thing."

32

Dumas and Steinberg paid scant attention to the historic log buildings in the distance. The fact that pious Brébeuf had walked among these woods, and had loved them, some 330-odd years ago did not prevent Dumas from trampling hurriedly through the underbrush stringing wire and planting potted Archis in holes that Steinberg had dug. Meanwhile, Lance was busy digging yet another hole behind a large bush and cursing when he encountered roots, which was often. From time to time, either Steinberg, Lance or Dumas would glance up toward the picnic table not far away where Rachael, Becky, Red Sky and her fellow Mantouche members from Cape Croker exhibited an apparently inexhaustible appetite for hot dogs.

"Adrian, is this deep enough?" Lance called from behind the bush.

"Be there in a sec. Coming." Dumas patted a thin layer of earth over the already full pot containing Archi, pushed up from his crouch and walked over to where Lance was standing hip-deep and sweating in his pit.

"Oh, yes, Lance. That's fine. Fine."

"Good." Lance climbed wearily out and brushed off his regulation Parks and Recreation cover-alls. The pit was just right, Dumas hoped. Mostly behind the bush, but also extending out to one side a couple of feet. The dry ice could go in the part of the hole that was behind the bush. The bush might camouflage a too-definite source of mist. A little fan would blow the mist from behind the bush to the clear ground beside it, where the mist would be useful.

"Take five, Lance. Have yourself some lemonade."

Dumas walked over to where Steinberg was lifting out the last spadeful of earth from a neat hole the size of an Archi pot.

Dumas was amazed to see that Steinberg could actually sweat like other people. His shirt even had semi-circular stains in the armpits. The Parks and Recreation cover-all lacked sufficient style.

"You should have worn the cover-alls like the rest of us. Trying to look like management or something?"

"Somebody has to, Dumas. Do you think this will work?"

"Gee, Sam, it's a little late to be asking that type of question."

"You're right, there. When you described it all back on *Radagast* it seemed clever. Now, when it comes down to some holes and wires, Adrian, it seems ridiculous."

"Ah, that's because the major ingredient is intangible. Imagination. But it's here, all around you."

"I'm beginning to think that the major ingredient was the Chivas Regal the night you laid it on me."

Dumas clapped Steinberg on the shoulder. "C'mon. Let's have some nice, cold lemonade. Think of it this way, Steinberg. Even if it doesn't work, well, you're no worse off than you were before. Believe me, the KGB won't be able to make anything out of this. Mike and her friends cover that."

"That's true enough," Steinberg acknowledged hopefully. "We'll have the time, maybe, to do something more sensible when—if—this flops."

"Before we go over there, Sam, there's a couple of things I want you to reassure me about. Like, you're sure that *all* the local cops are in on this? I mean some guy who wasn't briefed and just comes on duty, say, could be somewhat upset."

"No, Adrian. That's all set up. The place will be crawling with cops . . . for his safety. There's also a paramedic unit nearby, although his heart is supposed to be in good condition. But if the bugger croaks we're all into it up to our necks."

"Let's hope he doesn't." Dumas looked up at the sky. "Now, Steinberg, if you're very smart you'll pray it doesn't rain. We're going to have to run through this tonight to make very sure that everything works. Everything. Then, we'll have to take the more short-circuitable stuff aboard afterwards and re-connect it up tomorrow. I'm worried about the dew." And also the possibility of an early frost, which might depress the Archis. "That means that this area will have to be cleared—we went over that—and that might not be easy on a Saturday night."

"The cops and the Parks people will start roping it off as soon as I give the word. The explanation is that the plants we're planting here, and the grass seeds, need a night or two of rest from trampling feet until they bed in."

"Any time?"

"When you say so."

"Watson?"

"No change in plan so far. He's speaking at the Legion Hall to the mineworkers in Port McNicoll tonight. He's supposed to come to Midland late tomorrow afternoon, visit the shrine. He goes back to Toronto, Caledon, on Monday morning."

"Let's hope that he doesn't get an attack of the seculars and decide to leave the shrine until next year."

Steinberg grimaced at the thought. "If that happened, Dumas, I'm desperate enough to arrange car trouble. Ottawa and Washington are concerned enough, too."

"Let's get some lemonade."

When they came up to the picnic table, Dumas was pleased to see that although Red Sky seemed to be enjoying the hot dogs, she was also studying her script. "It's just sort of an outline, Mike," Dumas cautioned, "you'll have to play it by ear."

"Oh, I'm prepared to do quite a bit of ad-libbing, Adrian," Red Sky assured him.

It's up to you, Dumas thought.

33

"You must be living right, Adrian," Steinberg muttered doubtfully. They stood on *Radagast's* high poop and watched the fog bank roll landward from the leaden water of Sturgeon Bay. Wisps were already curling to explore the wharfs and boats of Midland's modest waterfront. If it kept coming, it would blot out any view of the town completely.

"It is the season for it, Sam. I did expect some haze. Nothing like this. But we have our own fog if we need it. This is nice, but it's too much of a good thing. It's not warm, either. I hope Watson doesn't catch pneumonia."

Steinberg pressed a button on his watch. The display lit. He showed his wrist to Dumas, who nodded.

Dumas walked down from the poop and stuck his head into the companionway. "Okay, gang," he called loudly enough to be heard in the back cabin, "time for the real thing."

Presently, Mike and the other Ojibways trooped on deck. The boys did look rather fearsome under the paint, but their conversation was innocent enough. Cars and girls. Dumas hoped they'd keep their solemn promises to keep their mouths shut. Red Sky looked divine with her long tresses falling starkly on the virginal white.

"Why is Red Sky in costume?" asked Steinberg. "She doesn't have to be seen."

"I think she's just getting into the spirit of the thing," Dumas said. "You have to agree that she looks the part. Stanislavsky Method."

"Oh."

Dumas raised his hands for silence. "Okay, gang. Now, the cars are on the waterfront about a block away. What do we say if anyone should see us before we reach the cars?"

"LaSalle and the *Griffon* pageant," came the chorus.

"Right." Dumas beamed.

That had been another reason for bringing *Radagast*. In 1680 the intrepid LaSalle and his faithful companion De Tonty had built the first real ship on the Great Lakes, the tiny galleon *Griffon*. After taking on a valuable load of furs, the *Griffon* had been lost on her maiden voyage. Some claimed to have found her remains, but there was no proof. Much speculation, however, as to *Griffon's* final watery grave. The most educated guesses placed the site of the tragedy somewhere between Manitoulin Island and the Bruce Peninsula. With Ontario trying to boost tourist trade in the face of mercury-polluted streams and lakes, tiny fish and acid rain, well, it might make sense to create pageants. In fact, Dumas had been seriously considering such a pageant as a commercial venture. So what if the *Griffon* had been lost in August and this was Labor Day? Historical reality must move over for economic necessity. Keep the tourists up in vacationland for one more weekend with galleons and redskins. The townsfolk could dress like Hurons or Frenchmen, at their pleasure. Tourists could gawk, take guided tours aboard *Radagast-Griffon* . . . at a price. Tiny cannons could be fired, perhaps. Snapshots taken. Cash registers rung. Maybe there was a Huron Maize festival this time of year. Bound to be. Galleon rides and corn roasts. Might sell.

"Dumas."

"Sorry, Sam. Just thinking. We're off. Lance, please button up the boat until we get back. Tight. Maybe you'll need some heat. Rachael knows how to fire up the boiler and turn the knobs."

34

Sentio me vehementer impelli ad moriendum pro Christo.

Watson writhed in the clammy sheets. Brébeuf had known of his coming martyrdom and had embraced it, not shirked it. The huge cross had flown high in the heavens, coming from the southeast, from Iroquois country. Brébeuf had seen, had knelt, had smiled as the apparition passed over.

"How big was the cross, brother?" Brébeuf's colleagues had asked at the Madonna's mission deep in the wilderness.

"Large enough to crucify us all," Brébeuf had answered without fear.

Brébeuf and his companions were tortured to death at St. Mary's church in Huron country. Long ago. It is said that his tormentors were able to extract no sound from Brébeuf's lips. They smiled, even when beginning to blacken and blister. Watson writhed. Was some sort of martyrdom necessary for him, too? To set him free? Was that the price of grace?

Watson had come to the shrine to find the answer. Surely, ground consecrated doubly, to the Madonna and by a martyr's blood, would be the proper place to give a sign, a message. But while he had prayed, nothing had been given. No indication that his life was even noted. Watson had prayed at the shrine of the martyrs, pleading for instruction . . . but fearing it.

Let me be as Brébeuf, one part of him said. But fear clutched his belly. And another part of him screamed silently. "But please don't ask that of me, for I am not Brébeuf. You know that." The thought had been growing all day that, perhaps, martyrdom was to be the price of grace. The Madonna in the Church had been disappointed in him. It seemed that way. Martyrdom must be realized and accepted, not imposed on someone kicking and screaming. Whimpering.

Watson had come here on purpose. He had planned it long before. But, while praying, he had begun to suspect that a larger Will than his had been at work, to bring him to the shrine of Brébeuf and a Church dedicated to the Madonna. For had he not always spoken with the Madonna these long years? Was his life not uncannily like Brébeuf's? We both came from Europe, after all, and spent lonely years in the wilderness. The same wilderness. Within miles of each other, though centuries apart. We both looked for a sign. Brébeuf had received both his celestial cross and his crucifixion.

Watson wiped the cold sweat from his forehead. Yes, it must be. No sign had been given so far. That must mean that he needed time to prepare himself for the price of grace. It would be terrible—it always was. Brébeuf had endured the red-hot hatchet heads searing into his flesh, the ripping fingernails. The gunpowder rubbed into wounds and ignited. The scrotum broiled . . .

"Oh, My God! Mother of God!"

It was the hell Watson had always imagined. Brébeuf had suffered the agony at the hands of the Iroquois women. Watson had not realized the similarity before.

"Oh, God! Mother of God!" It could not be coincidence. The Will had worked to bring him here, while he, in his mortal arrogance, had believed it was his own purpose. The Will confronted him with his own hell by Brébeuf's example. It had to be. Watson's eyes stared wildly. He flung himself off the clammy bed and onto his knees on the floor. Oh, God. Mother of God. Not that. Not that. I am no Brébeuf that I can withstand it . . .

But Cyril? Would you rather endure martyrdom for a few hours here on earth or everlastingly? A few hours for eternity?

Watson closed his eyes. He whimpered. "Eternity," he whispered. "I . . . I'm sorry. Forgive me. I am weak."

Get a grip on yourself, Watson. There are no more martyrs. Not in Canada. There are no Iroquois to whoop in derision at the shrieks of the weak . . .

There was a knock at his door.

Watson's eyes flew wide. *The call?*

Nonsense. This was a motel. It was the Twentieth Century. But . . . a coincidence?

The knock again.

"Who is it? I . . . I . . . won't open until I know who it is?"

"Room service, Mister Watson. Your hot chocolate."

Had he ordered any? He couldn't remember. Yes, he had it quite often, late. He must have. "C-coming," Watson said.

He opened the door while belting his robe and saw the bare feet first. He looked up. His mouth opened to scream, but it never came. The ether blacked him out.

35

Watson clutched the grass, trying to hear only the crickets. But he could not help but hear the screams, although they seemed far away. When he dared to crack his eyelids, he saw the flickering of the flames. Arms roughly lifted him up. Tears streamed from his eyes. It was time. It was time. "No! No! Please!" He sobbed, but the arms led him toward the stake.

Watson could not help but look at the other stake still flickering. A glowing pillar in the night and the mist. Something black and shapeless, now, hung from the burning ropes. Was it his imagination, or did the thing twist? No, nothing could look that black and shrivelled and still live. Could it? The ropes burned through and the thing fell into the branches that glowed around the base of the stake. Watson shrieked. He pulled back, bucking, but his feet slipped on the dewy ground. Brown hands bruised him. He felt the rough ropes on his bare ankles and on his chest. Mother of God. No, no, no. Don't let them.

They danced around him silently. Their faces twisted with hate and pagan cruelty. One of them danced up and swung at Watson with a hatchet. Watson lunged out of the way as far as he could in the ropes. They danced closer and began grabbing at his clothes. Oh, God. They were beginning. Watson whirled his head and saw one of them tending a fire. The hatchet heads glowed cherry red.

He threw back his head and opened his mouth desperately to the heavens. The shrill, lonely sound reverberated from the trees all around and then sank away into the uncaring mist.

The Indian by the fire took up one of the hatchet heads with long tongs and came toward him slowly. Watson screwed his eyes shut and raised his head, shrieking, waiting.

Waiting.
Waiting.

He dared to open his eyes. The hatchet-head smoldered on the grass a few feet away. The Indians seemed to be frightened. They cringed. Then Watson noticed a faint beam of pearly light shafting down from behind him into the mist ahead. Was there a slight hint of a figure in the mist?

"You must pray for me to be made manifest, Cyril. Pray hard. Only my presence can save you." A bell-clear female voice. The Madonna?

"Pray, Cyril. Pray for me to come. As you have never prayed before."

Watson closed his eyes and his mouth moved rapidly. He raised his head to heaven. He tried to temple his hands, but the ropes prevented him. He tried to kneel and succeeded in sliding down the stake.

"No, Cyril. Do not close your eyes. You have done that too long. Let them be opened unto me, Cyril. Behold me. Believe."

Watson opened his eyes. The image had grown stronger in the mist. He looked around at the Indians. They were slinking away from the Virgin. Watson knew that he might yet be saved.

The image dimmed.

Oh, God. He'd not been praying for her. He'd been thinking of his own safety, not adoring her. She was leaving . . . *Forgive me, Madonna. Forgive me. I am beholding only you.* Watson looked and incredibly the image grew stronger as he thought fervently of her. Only her. If his mind wandered to the crouched, painted figures in the flickering light, the miracle dimmed. When he filled his mind with love of her, it grew strong. Strong. Watson saw her in the curling mist. He had prayed hard enough to let her come to him. It all depended on him, he realized. The purity of his heart and mind, the fullest beholding of her in adoration, made the Virgin glow brightly. And any waver of thought and she dimmed.

Watson filled his eyes with her. Her arms appeared to reach out to him. He forgot about the Indians and his fear because they no longer existed. Watson smiled for the first time in years. Tears streamed down his face, but they were tears of joy.

"Believe, Cyril Watçek. You may attain grace. It was foolish of you to keep yourself from the Father all these years. You cannot hide. You know that, for the Holy Spirit is everywhere. Behold! It moves in the trees for you, but only if you believe and pray and think and feel only for God, for me, and for my Son."

Dumas ruminated upon the unnerving thought that this was, in fact, true. Behind all the sham. True, the image of the Madonna brightened and darkened in response to the dictates of a rheostat. And true, at a certain brightness of the Kodak Carousel up there in the trees behind Watson's stake, the 2N5777 photocells clicked on under the increased pressure of photons and tripped switches, which turned the fans on. Presto. The rustling of the Holy Spirit in the trees. Dumas would have preferred to leave it at that, but nagging honesty forced him to admit that it was the Archis who were the keystone of the entire circuit. When Watson believed and loved, they tripped switches of their own. And everything else worked. And only then. There was some connection in the circuit that boasted no wires, rheostats or photo-sensitive transistors. Some conductor that Dumas had contrived. A conductor so sensitive that it could span the abyss of communication between a philodendron and a man . . . and only God knew what else. Perhaps anything and everything. As well as he could in his prone position under the rose bush, Dumas shrugged. He was immediately pricked by a thorn.

Watson's eyes filled with her light and he saw nothing else. He had never before felt such an outpouring of love and prayer from his heart. The Madonna grew impossibly bright and the bushes nearby began to whisper. A small part of his mind doubted the miracle and he sought to check it. But before he could consciously decide to stop thinking of the Madonna, he realized that her image had already begun to dim. There could be no doubt and Watson regretted his own. It was a miracle of himself and God united. The image shone and the Spirit moved when he adored. And only then. Watson gave himself up to God. His joy was made manifest, witnessed, by the testament of the Madonna's blinding image and the joyful dancing of leaves.

"Cyril Watçek, do you not understand that you have not worshipped God all these years, but have worshipped Sarah and Koffler instead? Did they not fill your thoughts?"

"Yes, Madonna," Watson whispered.

"Your thoughts were not upon God, Cyril, but upon your own sins. That is why you have had no peace. You can have peace, Cyril. Every day. Every hour. Every second of your life you may know peace and the grace of God."

"How, Madonna?"

"By merely living in love, Cyril. By beholding me in your mind always. By adoring God always . . . But you have not lived in love, have you, Cyril?"

"No, Madonna. I have not."

"You have assisted in making war and danger, have you not?"

"Yes. I have known that."

Dumas felt Steinberg's elbow in his ribs. "That's not in her script, Dumas. What the hell is going on?" Steinberg whispered urgently.

"Damned if I know, Sam. Shss. Not too loud."

As far as their space under the rose bush would allow, Steinberg whirled to face Dumas. "Is this some sort of double-cross?"

"Maybe she's just over-acting," Dumas suggested. "Red Sky is something of a ham. Look at her."

Steinberg turned his head to see Red Sky coming slowly through the mist, arms outstretched and materializing in the image of the Madonna from the Kodak's slide. Steinberg's eyes widened. Dumas took the opportunity to loosen the glass stopper on their back-up supply of ether with his thumb and forefinger. Dumas concealed the bottle as best he could in his fist while propping himself over his switches on his elbows. Steinberg turned to him angrily. "She wasn't supposed to be seen. Only her voice," he whispered.

"I told you she could be something of an upstager."

"I've got to put a stop to this. God knows what she could make Watson do." Steinberg began to lurch to his hands and knees. Dumas' fist tilted under Steinberg's nose.

"Keep down, Sam." Dumas shoved Steinberg's head into the ground. "Now you've done it, Sam. You've gone and spilled our emergency ether supply."

Red Sky came slowly through the mist in her Ghost dress, the red cross splashed on her breast like a stigmata, her heavy-lidded eyes closed. "Now, Cyril, is the time to close your own eyes to the world and know peace. You know what you must do. What you want to do. All has been prepared for you. Turn from the world, Cyril. Turn to God."

Red Sky placed her palm under Watson's brow. Watson's body sagged in his bonds. Dumas had not seen her use the ether she was supposed to be carrying. Red Sky smiled down at Watson and motioned for the Ojibways. Dumas saw the med student check Watson's pulse. Red Sky handed the student her

bottle of ether and shook her long hair back as her friends carried Watson back to the car.

"Quick, Red Sky," Dumas called out softly, "help me with Sam. He knocked the ether bottle over and we're so tightly packed under here that he couldn't move in time. There. Grab his feet. Pull. C'mon, Mike, harder." Once Steinberg began sliding out, Dumas had room to wriggle from under the rose bush himself, but gasping from thorns.

Red Sky was cradling Steinberg's head in her lap by the time Dumas stood up. "Don't just look at him, Mike. Fan him!" Dumas said, picking thorns from his palms. Approaching crouched shadows told Dumas that some of the support personnel were creeping from their hiding place. Presently Dumas heard a whooshing of fire-extinguisher foam being directed at the still-glowing embers around the other stake and sizzling of smouldering tomahawk-heads being quenched.

"He's coming around, now," said Red Sky. Steinberg commenced to mumble and moan. Red Sky laid a comforting hand on his brow, too.

Epilogue

Green fans spread ghostly down from the north and wavered above *Radagast*. The rays pulsed and glowed in the dark sky.

Dumas returned his attention to the lighted card within the binnacle and gathered at the white froth that stretched behind the stern into the blackness. Straight. He noticed that Rachael still looked up toward the heavens, bundled in a thick sweater with her arms crossed. She smiled up from the center deck to Dumas at the wheel. "First aurora this year," she called. "It looks like a hand."

Steinberg came up out of the forecastle companionway and balanced the length of the deck with a mug in either hand. He climbed the steps slowly. At length, he extended a mug to Dumas. Dumas sipped the rich, warm chocolate gratefully. Over the rim of the mug, Dumas noticed that Rachael was going below. The light from inside the stern companionway disappeared as the doors closed.

"I'm glad you accepted the invitation," Dumas said to Steinberg. "I really had nothing to do with it, Sam."

"I'm not sure that I believe that, Adrian. But what you said does make sense."

"Well, Sam, I thought about it for a couple of weeks, going over it all in my mind. Every detail I could remember. It must have been then, after we'd worked almost all night." Dumas shrugged. "You were tired. Slipped up. She had time to read everything down there 'cause we sat up on deck until nearly dawn."

"I remember now, Adrian. When you wrote me, I remembered. It's just that she seemed so childlike. I never really thought she was involved."

"She certainly had an agenda of her own, didn't she? Determined girl."

"Maybe that's not all."

"What do you mean?"

"I've been thinking that it was a dangerous thing from the beginning. Not that either of us could have known. I mean, we wanted to push Watson just enough to stop feeling guilty. He wanted to go further, probably, all the time. Maybe Red Sky had nothing to do with it anyway. Maybe Watson would have done it anyway. Who knows?"

"I didn't want to spoil your day, Sam, but I've had that in the back of my mind, too."

Steinberg sipped his chocolate in silence.

"But it didn't turn out all that badly for you, Sam. Not in the end. The Russians must be as much in the dark as we are. They'll try again and you know who to watch."

"True enough. We've already come to that conclusion. The Russians certainly can't consider this a victory—it didn't go according to their plan."

Dumas thought about Mantouche. He . . . she . . . it. Mantouche had a bit of a breather. Not long, maybe, but a bit. "Do you think he's happy?" Dumas said on impulse.

"Unfortunately, yes, the damn hypocrite," Steinberg said. "Feels holier than hell now."

Dumas chuckled. "His Board of Directors can't be too happy. We know Provincial Hydro isn't."

"I guess not. How'd you like to be handed a healthy mining empire, minus the biggest money-maker?" Steinberg thought for a few moments. "They're gonna try like hell to open those mines up again, somehow. They will, too, eventually. Maybe some sort of government nationalization."

Dumas nodded. "But probably no one could get away with it until Watson dies. Could be years." Dumas turned to Steinberg and smiled. "Sure you want to be dropped off in Montreal, Sam? You could stay aboard when we hang a right at Sorel. Pretty soon you'd be in the Caribbean."

"Can't. Got to work. Think I'll turn in, Adrian." Steinberg glanced up at the aurora. The hand had seemingly shrunk back into the north. It might be large, still, for Red Sky up at Cape Croker. "I was just thinking of Red Sky," said Steinberg. "She's the kind of girl I'd sort of like to marry, in a way." Steinberg paused and shook his head. "But I couldn't. I've never been able to abide crumbs. I knew she'd get 'em on the Paisley."

Technical Note

Although most Algonkian-speaking American Indian nations utilize the Mantouche-Manitou-Mantou root to indicate what white men call "God", the word used in this book—Mantouche—comes from the Cree of James Bay in Quebec and not from the Ojibway. It is also true that these northern tribes consider Mantouche to be an ordinary animal in addition to being a creature with divine properties. Those "lake monsters" which periodically make news in Canada and elsewhere are, according to American Indian tradition, Mantouche. I am indebted to James Red Sky of the Shoal Lake Reserve for patient correspondence wherein he attempted to explain the difference between Mantouche's powers and the omnipotent God of the white man. I hope that I have portrayed Mantouche correctly and trust that James Red Sky will not mind my giving the fictional Mike Red Sky the loan of his name.

The relevance of naturally-occurring deuterium in dictating the placement of future nuclear generating stations is accurately presented in the book. This information was given to me by a former consultant with the provincial hydro utility who wanted the fact exposed, but who feared for his job if he himself exposed it.

The sensitivity of plants to "psychic" stimulus has been proved in numerous experiments. I have relied to some extent on the research of Peter Tompkins, co-author of *The Secret Life of Plants*, but have also conducted some experiments with philodendrons and galvanic skin response. For those with a technical bent, the perception-testing apparatus described in the book does exist (see *Marketing*, July 18, 1977 and September 19, 1977) and was the subject of television presentations by Global's "Science International" and by Radio Quebec. The components mentioned specifically in the book, when incorporated with a philodendron/GSR sensor and sufficiently sensitive micro-amp relay switches, should produce the effects presented. A security system based upon plant sensitivity is, in fact, under development.

As for the major plot of the book, I think we would all prefer to believe it fiction.

PROVOCATIVE READING FROM WARNER BOOKS

THE DICK GIBSON SHOW
by Stanley Elkin (95-540, $2.75)

Like *The Great Gatsby*, he wants life to live up to myth. An itinerant early media man, he travels across the country working for dozens of small-town radio stations. He is the perpetual apprentice, whetting his skills and adopting names and accents to suit geography. Stanley Elkin captures the essence of the man and the time. His "prose is alive, with its wealth of detail and specifically American metaphors," says *The Library Journal*, "and the surreal elements are tightly controlled," with "brilliant sequences . . . compulsively readable and exhilarating."

THE LIVING END
by Stanley Elkin (92-537, $2.25)

Whoever thought the holdup of a liquor store in Minnesota would lead to all this? Not Ellerbee, good sport and wine and spirits merchant. Not Jay Ladlehaus, who robbed and helped kill him. Not Quiz, the dieting groundskeeper who hates dead people. Not Flanoy, the little boy who plays Suzuki violin for the Queen of Heaven. Maybe not even God the Father—who, here, is called upon to explain his ways.

CRIERS AND KIBITZERS, KIBITZERS AND CRIERS
by Stanley Elkin (91-543, $2.50)

"An air of mysterious joy hangs over these stories," says *Life* magazine. Yet the *New York Times Review of Books* reports that, "Bedeviling with his witchcraft the poor souls he has conjured and set into action, Stanley Elkin involves his spirits sometimes in the dread machineries of allegory and fantasy." Stanley Elkin deals in contradictions. He is a master limner of "joy" and "dread." CRIERS AND KIBITZERS, KIBITZERS AND CRIERS proves the inadequacy of a simplistic response to life. "This book," *The New York Herald-Tribune* had said, "reveals Mr. Elkin as a writer of conspicuous intellect, talent and imagination."

THE BEST OF THE BESTSELLERS FROM WARNER BOOKS

REELING
by Pauline Kael (83-420, $2.95)
Rich, varied, 720 pages containing 74 brilliant pieces covering the period between 1972-75, this is the fifth collection of movie criticism by the film critic Newsday calls "the most accomplished practitioner of film criticism in America today, and possibly the most important film critic this country has ever produced.

P.S. YOUR CAT IS DEAD
by James Kirkwood (95-948, $2.75)
It's New Year's Eve. Your best friend died in September. You've been robbed twice. Your girlfriend is leaving you. You've just lost your job. And the only one left to talk to is a gay burglar you've got tied up in the kitchen.

AUDREY ROSE
by Frank De Felitta (95-473, $2.75)
The Templetons have a near-perfect life and a lovely daughter, until a stranger enters their lives and claims that their daughter, Ivy, possesses the soul of his own daughter, Audrey Rose, who had been killed at the exact moment that Ivy was born. And suddenly their lives are shattered by event after terrifying event.

A STRANGER IN THE MIRROR
by Sidney Sheldon (93-814, $2.95)
Toby Temple is a lonely, desperate superstar. Jill Castle is a disillusioned girl, still dreaming of stardom and carrying a terrible secret. This is their love story. A brilliant, compulsive tale of emotions, ambitions, and machinations in that vast underworld called Hollywood.

COAL MINER'S DAUGHTER
by Loretta Lynn with George Veesey (91-477, $2.50)
America's Queen of Country Music tells her own story in her own words. "How a coal miner's daughter made it from Butcher Holler to Nashville . . . it's funny, sad, intense, but what makes it is Loretta Lynne herself . . . a remarkable combination of innocence, strength, and country shrewdness." —Publishers Weekly

OUTSTANDING READING FROM WARNER BOOKS

THE EXECUTIONER'S SONG
by Norman Mailer (80-558, $3.95)

The execution is what the public remembers: on January 17, 1977, a firing squad at Utah State Prison put an end to the life of convicted murderer Gary Gilmore. But by then the real story was over—the true tale of violence and fear, jealousy and loss, of a love that was defiant even in death. Winner of the Pulitzer Prize. "The big book no one but Mailer could have dared . . . an absolutely astonishing book."—Joan Didion, *New York Times Book Review*.

ACT OF VENGEANCE
by Trevor Armbrister (85-707, $2.75)

This is the true story behind one of the most frightening assassination plots of our time: the terrible corruption of a powerful labor union, the twisted lives of the men and women willing to kill for pay, the eventual triumph of justice—and the vision and spirit of a great man.

HANTA YO
by Ruth Beebe Hill (96-298, $3.50)

You become a member of the Mahto band in their seasonal migrations at the turn of the eighteenth century. You gallop with the warriors triumphantly journeying home with scalps, horses and captive women. You join in ceremonies of grief and joy where women trill, men dance, and the kill-tales are told. "Reading *Hanto Yo* is like entering a trance."—*New York Times*

WARNER BOOKS
P.O. BOX 690
New York, N.Y. 10019

Please send me the books I have selected.
Enclose check or money order only, no cash please. Plus 50¢ per order and 20¢ per copy to cover postage and handling. N.Y. State and California residents add applicable sales tax.

Please allow 4 weeks for delivery.

_____ Please send me your free mail order catalog

_____ Please send me your free Romance books catalog

Name_____

Address_____

City_____

State_____Zip_____

MS READ-a-thon— a simple way to start youngsters reading

Boys and girls between 6 and 14 can join the MS READ-a-thon and help find a cure for Multiple Sclerosis by reading books. And they get two rewards — the enjoyment of reading, and the great feeling that comes from helping others.

Parents and educators: For complete information call your local MS chapter. Or mail the coupon below.

Kids can help, too!

Mail to:
National Multiple Sclerosis Society
205 East 42nd Street
New York, N.Y. 10017

I would like more information about the MS READ-a-thon and how it can work in my area.

Name_____
(please print)
Address_____
City_____ State_____ Zip_____
Organization_____

1—80